February 1984
To Bob & Jane
with great admiration
and affection.
Kue & Madge

BY ROBERT CRICHTON
The Secret of Santa Vittoria
The Rascal and the Road
The Great Impostor

The Secret

a novel by
ROBERT CRICHTON

of Santa Vittoria

SIMON AND SCHUSTER • NEW YORK

The Santa Vittoria of this novel is a real place,
but none of the characters described or mentioned
in the novel are real, and any resemblance to living
persons is purely coincidental.

Published by Simon and Schuster
A Division of Gulf & Western Corporation
Simon & Schuster Building
Rockefeller Center
1230 Avenue of the Americas
New York, New York 10020

Manufactured in the United States of America

DISTRIBUTED BY FUNK & WAGNALLS, INC.

For Judy, who for four years led
two lives and sometimes three lives, so that
I might write these lives.

In the long run, one life means nothing.

CAPTAIN SEPP VON PRUM

In the end, nothing is more important than one life.

ITALO BOMBOLINI

THE BEGINNING OF THE
BEGINNING

THE ORIGINAL MANUSCRIPT of this book was left outside the door of my hotel room in Montefalcone, in Italy, in May 1962. It arrived in the manner of the classic foundling. Wrapped in coarse brown paper and held together by cheap twine, the bundle literally fell into my life when I opened the door one morning. A note pinned to it read: "In the name of God, do something with this."

As with most foundlings, this one was a bastard. The note was not signed, the title page was missing, the manuscript had no professed father. It was not a manuscript at all, but a collection of disorganized notes. I let it lie in a corner of the room for several days, since I resented it as an intruder in my life, but as it also is with most foundlings this one cried out to live, and one night I untied the twine and began to read the notes. They were written in a bad hand in English and Italian and in the dialect of this region, and sometime in the night I realized that it might prove to be my burden to raise another man's child.

What to label this book has been the subject of argument. The collector of the notes, whom I now know to be Roberto Abruzzi, calls it a history. One note, perhaps intended to be the title page, reads:

THE SECRET OF SANTA VITTORIA
THE DIARY OF A TRUE EVENT

Some important things have been found to be true. There is a town of Santa Vittoria, and the great central incident around which this story revolves, the secret, is history.

Some of the people named in the book are alive and still tend vines on the side of the mountain Santa Vittoria clings to. But others have never existed, including some who are pictured in a good light. Much is made about a green light that burns in the Piazza of the People in memory of the martyr Babbaluche, but there is no such flame. And just when one is tempted to doubt there ever was a cobbler named Babbaluche his name is found carved on a wall in the rock quarry where he is said to have given his life.

The difficulty in finding the truth lies with Santa Vittoria itself. The city, as they call it, is an Italian hill town, one of those clusters of houses which can be seen from any main highway, a huddle of gray and white shapes pressed up against the side of a mountain as if they were sheep fearful of falling off it, which they sometimes do. Some are unreachable except by mule or on foot or by military vehicles, and the towns are as isolated on their mountains as any island in the sea.

The people have no tradition of outsiders and no procedures for handling them. They are not hostile, but they are suspicious and afraid of them. History has proved that to talk to strangers sooner or later leads to trouble or ends up costing money, and so history has rendered them incapable of telling truths to outsiders. They don't lie, but they never of their own will provide the truth. There are people in Santa Vittoria who are capable of denying knowledge of the town fountain when it can be heard bubbling behind their backs.

And if one hopes to reach the people, Italian is the wrong language to use. Italian is the language of Rome and, as such, the tongue for taxes and trouble and misunderstanding. For the native of a hill town, Italy is somewhere beyond him, and Milan can be less understood and more mysterious than America. The walls of his town and the fields around them are his Italy and the main piazza is his Rome. His loyalty is to himself and to his family, and if there is any left over it might extend to his street and even to his section of town. In times of crisis such as Santa Vittoria knew, when everyone's safety and money are at stake, loyalty might extend itself to take in the entire town. But beyond that there is nothing more. What is Sardinia to Santa Vittoria? Loyalty ends with the last grapevines at the foot of the mountain.

And Santa Vittoria is grapevines; it is wine. That is all there is. Without the wine, as they say here, even God Himself could not invent a reason for Santa Vittoria. My failure in Santa Vittoria is that I was seen thinning their fat black wine with mineral water, and by that one act I had adulterated the meaning of their lives and diluted the result of their sweat. They never even lied to me after that.

As for Roberto Abruzzi, I have never seen him, but I have talked with him. He would telephone me at my hotel and then ask me to call him back so as to save money, and we would talk for long periods of time. Abruzzi is an American who cannot go back to the United States, or thinks that he can't go back, because of something that he did. I am not certain that he is an American. It is possible that he is an Italian who feels that by posing as an American he might find a better market for his notes. The intricacies of the Italian mind, the strategies employed by the poor in hill towns to see themselves through just one day, are not known in this country. But when you read what he writes I think that, like myself, you will believe him.

In return for food and the use of a house he was asked by the people of Santa Vittoria to tell their story and record for them the great thing the people of that city did there in the summer and the fall of 1943. They asked Abruzzi to write the book because, as an American, he was supposed to know how to do such things.

It wasn't easy for Roberto Abruzzi to begin. No one in Santa Vittoria had written a book and not too many people there had read one, but everyone knew how this book should be written.

"Put down anything, put down a lot. Long books are better than short ones," Vittorini, the old soldier and the most cultured man in Santa Vittoria, told him. "Say anything just so you say it beautifully."

The priest, Padre Polenta, handed him this note one morning:

Remember this, Roberto. One's words must glide across the page like a swan moving across the waters. One must be conscious of the movement without a thought of what is causing it to move.

It was enough to stop him for a month. His pen, as he told me, was like the ugly orange feet. The people had contracted for a swan and he was going to deliver a swine. But in the end Roberto wrote what he did because he had a stronger reason for doing it than to satisfy the vanity of Santa Vittoria. As he is willing to admit, he has been a thief about it. In order to tell his own story, which he feels is a shameful one but which he knew had to come out of him before it consumed him, he has stolen the far greater story of Santa Vittoria. Roberto Abruzzi was a deserter during the war, but it is his hope that if he can tell about it, some people might be able to understand him and he might some day be allowed to return to the United States, where he was born, and build a new life again. This is the price that he asks the reader to pay in return for the story of Santa Vittoria. It is not a high price to pay.

Here, then, is the foundling that I agreed to adopt. From that bastard, the ragged bundle of notes of Roberto Abruzzi, has grown this book.

Montefalcone, 1962
New York, 1965

14

1 THE BEGINNING

THE HOUR this story begins is known. The minute is known; the exact moment is recorded. Even the state of the weather is known. To some this might not appear to be remarkable, but when it is considered that there are entire generations in the history of Santa Vittoria about which nothing at all is known, the statement becomes remarkable.

It was Padre Polenta who recorded the moment. He had been working in his wood-lined room at the top of the bell tower when he first saw the light coming down the River Road from Montefalcone. At times the beam of light would be sharp and clear, and then the bicycle would enter a patch of fog clinging low to the Mad River and the light would become a round wet globe, like a lantern dropped in a lake, or the moon before a snow. The light

17

annoyed the priest. Like many people who don't sleep at night he felt the night belonged to him. He left the window of the tower and made an entry in his daily record.

> 1:21 A.M. The goat Cavalcanti on the prowl again. Tell his mother to keep him home before her boy is found dead.

Beneath this he added, in purple ink and underlined three times:

> The winter fogs have come again. Ha! A new record.

The priest hated the fogs. He lived in the top of the bell tower because of them. He felt that his lungs were lined with a kind of fungus that absorbed water and he had given up a rich parish in the north of Italy and taken this poor place to escape the wetness of the northern winter.

"What about fogs?" he had asked. "Do you have fogs? Some of these mountain towns endure fogs."

The parish committee had all looked at one another as if the word *fog* was one they had never heard before.

"Oh, there are the winter fogs," one of the committee members finally said. "A few days or a week. I suppose you could go away for a week."

"I have a dread of sopping lungs," Polenta had said.

The first year was good, but in the second year the winter fogs came up from the valleys and slid down from the high mountains in October and lasted through the winter until April. With the fogs a bitterness had come to the priest, and it grew deeper with the years. With his last money he repaired the ancient campanile in the Piazza of the People and with good dry wood he paneled the room at the top where the lookouts had once stayed. The top of the tower floats above the fog line, and one day years ago the shepherd moved up into the tower and left his flock below.

After that he came down once a week to say Mass (to celebrate the death of Christ, Babbaluche the cobbler always said) and to give the last rites and to bury the dead, the two sacraments the people claimed Polenta enjoyed dispensing. They forgot his name and he was content to leave it that way. Polenta is a crude corn meal eaten by the peasants in the north. Here it is considered food fit for swine.

* * *

When the priest went back to the window for a second time he was surprised to see that the rider had already turned off the River Road and was coming across the cart track that leads to the foot of the mountain and the climb up. There was a moon then, and streamers of moonlit fog shifted in the streets below like bright banners, but they only disgusted the priest. When the rider dipped into the shadow of the mountain, where the road can no longer be seen even from the bell tower, Polenta went back to his work.

It was strange work for the priest to be doing. No one knew about it here until after he died, and then the people were amazed and felt ashamed of themselves for having despised him all along, which was, after all, how he must have wanted them to feel. He was occupied with restoring the Great Ledger of the Parish of Santa Vittoria, in an effort to re-create some kind of history for the people and the city. There are people who feel Polenta did this out of a love that he was unable to show, but others think that it was only an exercise to keep him from slipping back into peasant ways, the lot of many who move to these mountains. The Ledger itself shows it. The young priests arrive here and for a while the Ledger is filled with entries of births and deaths, and each year the entries become fewer and less informative until finally there are none at all for years on end, and the writing in the book, if there is any, becomes unreadable—the young priest has become an old peasant.

There is no passion to the work. Fabio della Romagna, who is the only person from Santa Vittoria to have gone to the university, believes that because the priest was such a stubborn and bitter man, that once he began it he refused to leave it until it was done. This may be true, but on this one night Polenta had made a discovery that amused him and even excited him. He found that if he took a page from the Ledger, one filled with births and deaths and baptisms and marriages, from one century, and then took a page from a hundred years before or a hundred years later, it was impossible to tell which page belonged to which century. This night he had three pages on his work table, one from 1634, one from 1834 and one from 1934.

The same names were on all the pages. The same first names and the same middle names and the same last names. The same people were getting born and getting married and getting buried, and the same children were having their First Communion and receiving their Confirmation, and the same children were dying in the same old trusted ways. The rest of the world might have been changing over those centuries, but it would be impossible to prove it by Santa Vittoria.

The priest was counting the family of Pietrosanto. In 1634 there were listed in the Ledger the names of forty-six members of the Pietrosanto family. Three hundred years later there were thirty-eight Pietrosantos, but this did not include the three who had gone off to war some place and were listed as missing. After all the plagues and the wars and the disease, the fires and landslides and the fights and feuds of three centuries, after the wide-spread honey-coated arms of America, there were five fewer Pietrosantos in the city (Thank God for that much at least, Babbaluche the cobbler would have said), and almost all of them were living in the same houses on the same lanes, finding shade under the same trees that stood then, all of them, the Pietrosantos, as solid and as sturdy, as stubborn and as bullheaded as ever before.

In 1634 this city could count 1,168 souls. Three hundred years later there were thirty-nine fewer. This year the Ledger could show the same number of births but two fewer deaths, a tribute to the miracles of modern science and to the skills of Lorenzo Bara, the town doctor. The motto of Santa Vittoria: "See Doctor Bara and die." Only nine people had died without his aid in the preceeding ten years.

Facts are facts and they are usually lifeless things, but one fact was beginning to depress the priest. The more he went through those similar names the more it became clear to him that with the exception of the Sicilian boob, Italo Bombolini, he himself was the only person who had come to Santa Vittoria by choice.

One arrives here through the natural passage of the womb. One leaves in a box of wood through the Fat Gate out to the cemetery beyond the walls of the town just above the vineyards on the terraces. In between those times you tend the vines and grow the grapes and make the wine and live the best way you can.

* * *

Padre Polenta would insist he didn't sleep. For men who claim not to sleep it is important for them not to be caught asleep, as if it were some kind of honor for them to go around with bags under their eyes. But the truth is that Polenta never heard the rattle of the bicycle being pushed across the cobblestones of the piazza and that the young man who was pushing it had to shout four or five times before the priest heard him and went to the window.

"If it's someone dying," the priest shouted down, "he can die just as well in the morning."

"No one is dying, Padre. It's me, Fabio, Fabio della Romagna."

He didn't go away from the window because the Romagna family was one of the few in which the priest had ever been able to find any merit. They donated a fat wheel of cheese each year to the parish and some years a keg of wine.

"What do you want?"

"I want to ring the bell, Padre. I want to wake up the town."

"It will be morning in two hours."

"It's Mussolini, Padre."

"Who?"

"The Duce." Fabio shouted very loudly.

"What about the Duce? Do you want me to come down into that fog for the Duce?"

"He's dead, Padre," Fabio called up. "The Duce is dead."

The priest went away from the window and looked around the wooden walls of the room. It was strange to him. He lit a tallow candle and wrote in the daily log.

2:25 A.M. Cavalcanti turns out to be F. della Romagna. I learn that the Duce is dead.

He took the candle and started down the dark steep stone steps that wound down inside the walls of the tower. Fabio met him at the door. He was tired and wet with sweat, but he was happy.

"You should see them in Montefalcone," the young man said. He described how the people were dancing in the streets and setting fire to portraits of Mussolini and burning Fascist symbols and how the soldiers had deserted their barracks, and the police headquarters had been burned and how even the *carabinieri* had gone to the hills.

"I suppose they'll go after the churches next," Polenta said. "They usually do."

Fabio was shocked. "They're going into the churches to pray, Padre," he said.

"I'm sure."

"To give thanks for their deliverance, Padre."

"I'm sure. Go on, go ring your bells." He allowed Fabio to come into the bell tower, but he wouldn't help him find the bell ropes in the darkness.

"Find them yourself. I'm not going to help you," the priest said. He wasn't sure how he felt about Mussolini. There was the Lateran Treaty; the Duce had signed it and by that act had done more for the Church than any one other leader of Italy, but the Duce had been a fool and a clown, two traits that the priest despised above all others. Had he been born God, the priest had said, it was the clowns who would occupy the lowest rungs of hell.

Despite the fog he started across the Piazza of the People to his church, Santa Maria of the Burning Oven, to be there in the event of any trouble. He was near the fountain when he heard Fabio call to him.

"Oh, what a morning this is going to be for Italy, Padre."

The bell began to peal and then thunder over Santa Vittoria, swinging free and out of control, the entire tower trembling and then the windows of the houses around the piazza. No one came into the piazza. Fabio ran to Santa Maria.

"The people," he called to the priest. "What's the matter with the people?"

"You've been away at the school too long," Polenta said. "They don't believe the bell any longer."

The summer before, all the people had run to the Piazza of the People—to help fight the fire, when the bells had begun to ring.

22

When most of the town had collected, torches were lit and they found themselves surrounded by a company of Blackshirts from the barracks at Montefalcone.

"We shall now proceed to pay our back taxes," the officer announced. And they went through every pocket and every house in Santa Vittoria until every unburied lira in the city was taken.

"This is no city to catch fire in," the priest told Fabio. "Now when the bell rings, everyone gets up and bolts the door. That's the kind of Christians you have in this town."

There is something about the truth that makes itself understood. When the bells ceased ringing, Fabio ran up and down the piazza in front of the houses, telling everyone to come out, that he had good news for them, and gradually lights were lit and finally some of the Pietrosantos, most of whom live along the lanes leading into the piazza, opened their doors; and when they saw it was Fabio running about in the fog they came out.

There is a thing about Santa Vittoria that must be understood in order to understand this place. Whatever is known in Santa Vittoria is known by everyone in Santa Vittoria as soon as it happens. Some say it is because the walls of the houses are so thin that what is said in the first house is heard in the second and passed through the walls to the third, down through Old Town and up through High Town. Others say it happens because everyone is related to everyone else, that everyone shares the same blood and the same hearts and nerves and so what is experienced by one is felt by the next. Whatever it is, after the Pietrosantos went into the Piazza of the People it was soon thick with the others.

They put Fabio up on the steps of Santa Maria. Pietro the Bull, the oldest and still the strongest of the Pietrosantos, hung Fabio's bicycle from the statue of the turtle on the fountain so the beam of his bicycle lamp would shine on the young man. It threw Fabio's shadow back onto the church façade and when he held up his hand before speaking the hand was twenty feet high on the stones.

"A great thing has happened today," Fabio called out. His voice is as thin as his body, but it is clear and it can be heard.

"A great thing for us. A great thing for Italy." The people

leaned forward to hear Fabio, because good news is not a common commodity in this place.

"Benito Mussolini, the tyrant, is dead," he cried.

There was no sound at all from the people. The face of Fabio showed that he was puzzled. He asked if they heard him and no one answered, but Fabio knew that they had heard.

"The Duce has been put to death this day," he called.

Still the silence, the only sound the water pouring from the fountain.

"What is that to us?" someone shouted. "What are you trying to tell us?"

"Why did you get us out of bed?" they called. "Why did you ring the bell?"

His face was anguished. It is a fine face, long and clean and narrow like the blade of a new ax, the eyes deep and dark like ripe olives, and his hair so dark that it seems blue at times. Fabio's skin is white and fine, not the color of copper pots like most of the faces here.

"What does it mean to *us*?" the first man shouted again. He wanted an answer.

"It means freedom," Fabio said, and he looked down.

The people respect Fabio, but they were annoyed by what he had done. He went down the steps of the church and they cleared a path for him so that he could get his bicycle down from the Fountain of the Pissing Turtle.

"You've been away too long, Fabio," a man said. "We don't go to school here, Fabio. We work. We grow grapes, Fabio. You shouldn't have waked up the people."

"Excuse me," he said. "I'm sorry. I'm sorry."

"It's the books," a woman told him. "You've strained your mind." Everyone nodded, because it is a known fact here that a few books are all right, like wine, but too much can be bad. Books break down brains.

It was the cobbler Babbaluche who saved things, although it is usually his role to ruin them.

"Leave the light there," he ordered. He has a voice which sounds as if his throat was plated with brass; it is always irritating and it is always heard. He limped, because he is a cripple, to the steps of the church.

"I'll tell you what it means to you, you socks filled with shit," Babbaluche began.

There is no point in keeping it a secret. The cobbler is a man who is fascinated with excrement. Under the laws of Italy it is not allowed to put down on paper, even on paper that is not to be published, the things Babbaluche calls the people of Santa Vittoria. He compares our nastiness to that of a man who rises in the morning and finds that the shoe he has just put his foot in has been used the night before as a chamber pot. He can say these things because of something that happened to him years ago in front of all the people and which they allowed to happen. Babbaluche was a penance we had to bear.

"How many of you would like to sink your boot in Copa's ass?" Babbaluche shouted.

There was a cheer then. It was an ambition of everyone in the piazza.

"As of this morning you have that right."

He went through the rest of the city leaders, the members in good standing of the local Fascist party who were known as The Band.

"Who wants Mazzola?"

There was a cheer for the ruination of Mazzola. There was nothing political any longer about The Band. They had long ago ceased contributing to the national party or to Rome. They kept Santa Vittoria for themselves and stole from it, not too much at a time, but all of the time.

The loudest cheer of all was reserved for Francucci. When Copa had taken over the city twenty years before, he had made his one speech.

"Bread is the staff of life," he told the people. "Bread is holy. Bread is too sacred to be left in the hands of greedy individuals. No penny of profit shall ever be made by any individual from the exploitation of the people's bread so long as I am mayor, so help me God."

He closed all of the bakeries in Santa Vittoria and opened the

Citizen's Nonprofit Good Bread Association and put his brother-in-law, the mule drover Francucci, in charge. Francucci's first act was to reduce the amount of wheat that went into a loaf and his second was to raise the price. Within a year after that the families of Copa, Mazzola and Francucci moved out of the wet dark caves they had lived in for one thousand years in Old Town up into the sunlight of High Town, where the gentry, what there is of gentry here, live.

"I offer you the ass of Francucci," Babbaluche said. There was a terrible roar from the crowd.

They would turn the irrigation water for the terraces back on. The Band had turned it off years before, when the people refused to pay for their own water. They would fix the Funny Scale on which all of the grape growers had to weigh their grapes before selling them to Citizen's Wine Cooperative.

The people began to get angry. There is a saying here that if you can't do anything about something, pretend it doesn't exist. But now that the people could do something about them, the old hurts that had healed began to hurt again. It is impossible to guess what the crowd might have gone on to do had not Francucci chosen that moment to come down from High Town into the piazza.

"Why were the bells ringing?" he asked. It is asking a great deal to expect anyone to believe that the baker would have come down then; one would have to know Cosimo Francucci to understand how it could happen.

"Why are you looking at me like that?" he cried. "Take your hands off me."

They used the baker like a soccer ball. He went from one end of the piazza to the other, and every player along the way had a penalty shot at him. When he could move no more they called his family to come down and take him away, and when they couldn't carry him Fabio had to help them carry him back up the steep lane to High Town, more dead than alive. That is the way Fabio is. When he got back down to the piazza the people were starting back to their houses. The bloodletting had had a soothing effect. As the baker's blood had flowed, the blood pressure of the people had dropped.

"They shouldn't do that," Fabio said.

"The people are entitled to their blood," Babbaluche said. "The people have a need for blood. They have a taste for it. Now give them big blood, important blood," the cobbler said. "Tell them how the Duce died."

"They don't want to hear that," Fabio said. "They want to go home."

"The people always want to hear when the mighty stag is brought to the ground by a pack of common dogs," Babbaluche said.

The cobbler was right. Fabio told them how the Fascist Grand Council had gathered in a palace in Rome the night before and how one man, the Count Dino Grandi, rose to his feet and in the face of Mussolini, before the eyes of the Duce, began to read a resolution.

Resolved: The members of the Grand Council and the people of the glorious nation of Italy, having lost all confidence in the ability of the leader to lead any longer, convinced that he has destroyed the will of the army to fight any longer and the people to resist any longer. . . .

The people sat on the wet stones of the piazza and listened to Fabio.

"Die," one of them shouted. "How does he die?"

Fabio told them how at the end the Duce turned to his son-in-law, husband of his own flesh and blood, and said to him, "And you, Ciano. Flesh of my flesh. Even you."

"Yes, even me. You have done all that you can do."

And how the next afternoon, on the burning hot empty Sunday afternoon in Rome the king had summoned the Duce to the royal palace and met him in the garden and behind the hedges so no one could see them, sang the Duce a song that the soldiers were singing.

"What have you done to us, Mussolini?
What have you done with our Alpini?

I'll tell you what you've done, Mussolini.
You have murdered our Alpini.

That's what you have done, Mussolini!"

"And you? Do you believe it?" the Duce says.

"All the soldiers are singing it," the king says.

"Then there is nothing more to say."

"No, there is nothing more to say."

He told them how they put the Duce in a long black ambulance and took him through the streets of Rome. The Duce tells the guard that he isn't sick and the guard says, "But the people of Rome are fickle."

And how they took him through the ancient burning city, past all the monuments to the past Caesars, through the arches built for the great men, until they come to the walls of Rome and the Appian Way, the route that all the conquerors have taken to come to Rome. At a crossroads the ambulance stops and the people of the village look inside.

"An old man is dying," one of them says.

Mussolini says one sentence: "The people of Rome have always destroyed their greatest sons."

And how after that they drove past the country towns and then into the upland villages, the hills and the mountains growing higher, into the Abruzzi and then up into the snow fields into those mountains where the snow never ends. In the valleys it is night, but the snow fields are still touched by sun, and here he is met by four members of the Alpini who tell him to undress and when he is naked two of them take his arms and two of them take his legs and they lower him into a hole they have cut into the hard ice and they begin shoveling snow into the upright grave until only the great head is not buried.

"You dishonor Italy," the Duce says. They are simple men but one of them was equal to the job.

"No, we honor the dead of twenty years by doing what we do."

So in the manner of the Alpini, Fabio tells them, the Duce has died, frozen to death in foreign snow.

When he was through with the story some of the women were crying, not for the Duce, but for the men of Santa Vittoria who were sent to the Alpini. They left one morning in May 1941, twenty-three young men, marching down the mountain, singing and shouting all the way to the Montefalcone road, the feathers on those silly hats bending with the breeze, the people standing on the Fat Wall waving and waving until the last of them could be seen no more. Not one of them was ever seen or heard from again.

We know now that this isn't the way the Duce died, but we always tell it this way because we like his death this way and it is more fitting to us.

T HERE WAS no way to keep the people in the piazza after that, because the sun had come up. It had not yet reached down into the piazza itself, but the people could see it touching the tiles on the roofs of the houses and nothing could hold them after that.

"No one works today," Babbaluche shouted. "A day of holiday."

"A day of celebration," Bombolini called. But the people didn't listen to either of them.

The sun drives the people here. It is an instinct that has been bred into them. Even when they can't see the sun or it can't be seen, in the darkest lanes in Old Town, when the sun comes up the people get up. It drives them out of the houses and it drives them down to the terraces to tend the vines.

"Tell them, Fabio," the cobbler said.

"This is a great day for Italy," Fabio said. "No one should work today."

They poured out of the piazza and down the streets to get their tools, deaf to anything now but the needs of the grapes, and in a few minutes there were only five or six of them left in the Piazza of the People. These men went across the piazza from the church and sat around the edge of the Fountain of the Pissing Turtle, while Fabio climbed up and took down his bicycle.

"For twenty years I dreamed of this day," Babbaluche said, "and now look at it." He swept his hand around the empty piazza. "This is the kind of people you have in this place, Fabio. Don't ever allow yourself to forget it."

They sat and listened to the water until the priest passed in front of them on his way to the bell tower.

"There will be a Low Mass for the dead," he said to Fabio.

"For one of the heroes of the Church," Babbaluche said.

"The dead will be respected," the priest said.

"And when do you think the Vatican will get around to the living?" the cobbler said.

It was an old game that the two of them played, and neither of them heard the other any longer. But it bothered Fabio.

"To think that I, Ugo Babbaluche, outlived that bastard Mussolini," the cobbler said. "It's something. I'm alive and that bastard's dead."

"It calls for a drink," Bombolini said, and all of them, at once, as if someone had set off a silent alarm, stood up and began to follow the wine seller across the piazza to his wineshop. He was unlocking the folding iron gate over the front door, when his wife looked out of the window above the door.

"See that they pay," she said to him. "See that you make them pay." He was embarrassed.

"She lacks a sense of history," he said.

It was damp and chilly in the shop, but the warm air from the piazza and the warmth from the wine soon warmed them.

"What do you think is going to happen?" one of them asked.

"Nothing," Pietrosanto said. "Why should anything happen?"

It is the feeling here. No matter what takes place in Rome or happens in the world, for a few days or a few weeks things might be a little different, but they always return to the way they were before.

"The Germans will come," Fabio said.

He had put his head down on one of the tables because he was tired. He was suddenly embarrassed to be the center of the men's group. He had never spoken much with the men before, and now he was one of them.

"No they won't," one of them said. "Why would they want to come here?"

"If Italy gets out of the war," Fabio said, "the Germans aren't going to leave Italy for the Americans and the English."

"No," Pietrosanto said. "There's nothing here for them."

"There's nothing here for *us*," Bombolini said.

Fabio could only shrug his shoulders. He couldn't push too far, but still he told them about the tanks and armored cars he had seen coming into Montefalcone.

"Montefalcone is Montefalcone and Santa Vittoria is Santa Vittoria," the cobbler said. "One is a jewel and one is a shit house."

They drank to this.

"Only a man born in Santa Vittoria can ever learn how to make a living out of it," one said. "What would the Germans do here?"

They drank to this as well.

The wife of Bombolini came down the back stairs and into the wineshop and she looked at their glasses of vermouth and anisette and she stared at their eyes.

"Did they pay?"

"They paid," Bombolini said.

"Let's see the money." She went to the drawer in the table by the big wine barrel. There was nothing in it.

"This is a historic day," Bombolini said. "You don't ask for money on a day like this and you don't accept it."

They nodded their heads at Rosa Bombolini. They were afraid of her. She has the toughest tongue in the city and no shyness about putting it to use. She studied them.

"What a bunch of patriots." She began taking the glasses from them moving them toward the door. "Take your patriotism out into the piazza where it belongs." When they were in the sunlight at the door she said, "That's the trouble with this country. The whole place is filled with penniless patriots."

They could hear the sound of a drum coming down from one of the lanes in High Town that lead down into the piazza. Capoferro the town crier was announcing the Duce's death.

"You should put your fist in her mouth," one of the men told Bombolini, and all of them nodded; but each one knew that if he were married to Rosa Bombolini he would keep his fists to himself.

"Women and asses and nuts require strong hands," Pietrosanto said. They all nodded. "It's a sad house where the cock is silent and the hen crows."

They nodded at this too, including Bombolini. There was a blast from the automobile horn that Capoferro carried and then a roll on his goatskin drum. He was coming down into the piazza.

Only people born here can understand Capoferro. He has some kind of trouble with his speech and sometimes it takes two and three people to understand him, but at least what he says is remembered. There must be some kind of law of the world, Fabio thinks, a law of compensation he calls it, that makes crippled men carry messages and unhappy people run happy places and people like Capoferro become town criers. He had come across the piazza now and was beating the goatskin drum.

"Nido Muzzlini dead."

Barrrrombarrrummmbarrrum. A squeeze on the automobile horn.

"Tyrant dead. All Idly weeps."

Barrrrombarrrummmmbarrrum. Horn.

"Benidolini is no more. Idly moans."

"No, no," Fabio said. "Italy is happy."

"Oh," Capoferro said. He struck himself on the head with his drumsticks. He looked at the men.

"You want to celebrate?" the crier said. "For some wine I'll drum you a dance."

"Wait," Bombolini said. He went back across the piazza and around to the back entrance of the wineshop on the Street of

33

D'Annunzio the Poet and he came back with two bottles of wine.

"Keep your back to the shop," he said. It was good vermouth. They passed the bottles around.

"I'll drum the tiles down from the roofs," Capoferro said. He took a very long drink, it is said that he is over one hundred years old and it is probably true, and he began to drum. At first none of them did anything, but then Babbaluche began to dance. He is crippled because of something they did to him here, but Capoferro slowed the drum beat and the cobbler began to drag himself across the stones of the piazza in a slow dance.

"I never thought I'd dance at his funeral," he shouted.

The sun was hot now and they had had nothing to eat since the night before, and the wine began to go to their heads. After a while Bombolini began to dance with the cobbler and they went around and around the Fountain of the Pissing Turtle while Capoferro beat the goatskin drum and some of the men clapped their hands. Babbaluche's daughter had come up from Old Town into the piazza, and when she saw her father she seized his arm and brought it up behind his back the way the *carabinieri* do it, and she began to pull him across the piazza with her to the Corso Mussolini that leads down into Old Town. He gave the bottle to one of the men and that was a mistake, because Rosa Bombolini saw it and came out of the wineshop and across the piazza to them.

"You thieving sons of bitches," she said, and she took the bottle.

"Do something with her," Capoferro shouted above the drum. "Control your woman."

"You had better leave," Bombolini said. "She's going to break your drum."

Since the wine was gone and the drum was no longer playing and it was hot, they began to leave and soon only Fabio and the wine merchant were left in the piazza besides the children and the oxen and the old women getting water from the fountain. They had nothing to say to each other.

"The best thing I can do right now," Bombolini said, "is to go back to bed. Goodbye, Fabio."

It was the end of the celebration. Fabio was alone. He decided to go down into Old Town and sleep on a mat in his cousin Ernesto's house and he crossed the piazza and started down the steep Corso. It was very hot now. The door to the furnace of Africa, as we say around here, was open. An old woman was sitting in the darkness of the doorway next to Ernesto's door.

"What was all the noise about?" she shouted at him. She was hard of hearing.

"A death," Fabio shouted at her. "Someone died."

"Who?"

"Mussolini. Benito Mussolini."

She looked at him and shook her head. "No, no," she mumbled, "no, I don't know him."

"It's nobody from here," Fabio told her.

"Oh." Her face became as dark and blank as the doorway.

The house smelled. In truth, it stank. Ernesto was no house-keeper. There was a pot of hard cold beans over the fireplace and although they were hard to swallow Fabio ate them with enjoyment.

"So this is my feast. This is the reward," he said aloud.

He found a mat and cleared it off and stretched out on it and looked up at the smoke-darkened ceiling. There was no sound at all in the city, not a cock or a child or an ox, and Fabio fell asleep. It was now nine o'clock in the morning.

This then was the extent of the celebration of the death of the dictator. Thus did the twentieth year of the glorious reign of the Everlasting Imperial Fascist Empire come to a close in the city of Santa Vittoria.

FABIO WOKE in the early afternoon. He was still tired, but he woke because he was hungry. He looked around the small house, but there was nothing in it to eat, not a piece of stale bread or hard cheese. He was sorry he had eaten all the cold beans. He left a note for Ernesto, "Ants would starve to death in your house if ants would come into it," and he went out into the Corso Mussolini and started up it toward the Piazza of the People to try to buy some bread and cheese and wine. The midday sun blinded him and he was forced to hold onto the walls of the houses until his eyes could adjust to the glare. When he reached the piazza he was conscious of groups of people standing about in it looking back down toward Old Town, but he was too blinded to see what it was they were looking at.

The Piazza of the People is the center of Santa Vittoria. It is a flat plateau of cobblestones that divides the city in two parts. Above the piazza is High Town where the houses sit on a saddle of land in the sun. No one knows why the city wasn't built there in the first place. The people who live in High Town are called Goats. The people who live around the piazza are called Turtles because of the fountain. Below the piazza is Low Town, or Old Town, where the Frogs live, because in the spring, after a rain, little green frogs hop in the dank, moss-green streets until the rats and the cats and the children get to them. On a tourist map, although tourists don't come here, Old Town is listed as the Medieval Section which makes it sound better. Frogs almost never marry Turtles and Turtles don't speak to Goats. That's the way they are here.

The city is steep. The Corso Mussolini, which runs through Old Town up to the Piazza of the People, is so steep in places that the street becomes flights of stone stairs. The Corso runs down to the Fat Gate which is the main passage through the Fat Wall which the Romans began and which someone else finished and which runs all of the way around Santa Vittoria. There is another way out, the Thin Gate, but this is used mainly by small boys and goats since the track that leads down the mountain from it is so steep.

If you stand in the center of the Piazza of the People, where Fabio was standing, you are almost at eye level with the second pride of Santa Vittoria, the one achievement of the Fascist movement here, the tall soaring cement-skinned water tower which rests on three great long thin steel legs like the head on the top of an enormous spider. Written on the cement tank in black block letters were these words.

MUSSOLINI IS ALWAYS RIGHT

On the other side, although little of it could be seen from the piazza, was

DUCE DUCE DUCE DUCE
DUCE DUCE DUCE DU

Below the tower in Old Town, near the Thin Gate, was the first pride of the city, the Citizen's Cooperative Wine Celler, and on the roof of the celler was a large blue and red sign which read "Cinzano" since most of the wine made here is sold in the end to the Cinzano family.

Fabio could see none of it. In the wineshop his problem was reversed. In the shop it was dark and he was blinded again. He had passed Rosa Bombolini, standing in the doorway with her arms crossed and staring toward Old Town, but she had not followed him when he entered the shop and he was forced to feel in the darkness for a chair. He waited for his sight to return and as he sat he heard someone crying.

"Can I help you?" Fabio said. The girl didn't answer him. "Do I bother you?" He waited. "Is it you, Angela?"

"Yes, it's me."

He tried to say something that would sound helpful or sensible, but he could think of nothing to say to her. Nothing at all. Not any single word would come to him. He closed his eyes and tried to force one single word to come and nothing came, only her name, and he knew that wouldn't do.

There was this about Fabio then. Although he had never actually spoken to this girl alone or said her name aloud before or heard her say his name, he was in love with Angela Bombolini. This kind of thing happens here more often than in other places. There is a kind of love here that is called "thunderbolt love."

A girl looks out of the window and she sees a boy she has seen ten thousand times before and all at once a thunderbolt hits her and she realizes that she is madly in love with him. From that moment she dedicates her life to him and is even ready to submit for the Final Proof, the Final Truth, if he were to demand it of her, even though he might not know her name or that she exists. When it happens they say, "Fabio sees Angela in his soup."

She is everywhere.

The great torture and fear of the thunderbolt lover is that the one he loves will not return the love. Life is impossible then and unbearable. So great is the fear of being rejected, of being left with the empty horribleness of a life deprived of love, that many thunderbolt lovers never admit to their love and suffer their love in silence. Every once in a while they kill themselves and people always are amazed because they have no idea of the hell the dead person was fleeing from.

Most people, girls and boys, when struck by the thunderbolt, show the effects as clearly as if they had been struck with a true bolt. But Fabio is more clever than most people. All that he did was blush. When Angela's name was mentioned he turned scarlet or if he passed her in the piazza he turned a deep red, but no one so far was conscious of what was taking place. He was still trying to think of the proper thing to say when he realized that Angela's mother was standing over him.

"Did she get what you want?"

"Oh. Oh, no. She didn't. I want some bread and cheese and wine."

"Why didn't you get him what he wants?" Rosa Bombolini shouted at Angela. "He sits here dry while you wet the floor."

He saw Angela get up and go into the back room, and his heart flew out to her. It was the only word. The heart flew to her. He had now managed to say six or eight words and get her in trouble. When she came back she put a plate of cheese in front of him and a glass of wine.

"No bread," she said.

"Why not?" It wasn't what he had wanted to say.

"Francucci," she said.

"Oh, yes. The baker. Of course." She must think that I am an idiot, Fabio thought. "I didn't mean to get you in trouble."

"She doesn't like my crying."

"You have a perfect right to cry," Fabio said. "Cry all you want." He felt his face turning red. He sat at the table and ate the cheese, listening to her cry.

"Why are you crying?" he said at last.

"You know why," Angela said. "Why are you torturing me?"

He found himself turning red once more and wondering what it was he did that caused him to harm the person he least in the world wished to harm.

"I don't know why," Fabio said.

"Him," she said. "You saw him."

She nodded her head in the direction of the door and the piazza beyond. He went across to the window and cleaned a section of it and looked out. The groups of people were still in the piazza. He could see across the piazza and down toward Old Town, toward which all the people were looking, even though he was forced to look over Rosa Bombolini's broad shoulder. He could see nothing at first, but finally his eyes were able to pick out the movement and he felt his heart jump. He could feel his heart at that moment actually rise in his chest and touch something in his throat, as if he had a live fish in his chest.

"Oh, Mother of God," Fabio said. He made the sign of the cross. "What is your father doing up there?"

Two thirds of the way up the water tower, still at least one hundred feet below the concrete tank and the safety of the little iron railing that runs around it, not moving at all now, silhouetted against the sky and the mountains beyond Santa Vittoria, gripping the little thin, narrow, rusty ladder that climbs up to the tank itself, clung Italo Bombolini.

"What is your father doing up there?"

As soon as he said this for a second time Fabio knew two things: that someone was going to have to help Italo Bombolini and that it was going to be himself.

"Why does it have to be me?" Fabio said aloud.

He was astonished and ashamed that he had said it aloud. He turned away from Angela then. The figure was moving once more, moving with a terrible slowness upward.

"He's going to be all right. I've climbed mountains. I know how people climb. He knows his way around up there."

She began to cry again.

Fabio went outside and tapped Rosa Bombolini on the shoulder.

"Do you have a length of rope? A good strong one?"

"Oh, no," Rosa Bombolini said. "You don't risk your life to save his fat pride. He's going to fall. Let him fall."

"He's still going up."

"Because the son of a bitch can't come down," she said, and Fabio turned red again. He had never heard a woman talk about her husband or a man in this fashion before. "He's going to come down in that piazza like an ox falling off a roof."

"I'm going whether you get me the rope or not," Fabio said.

In the end she got him a rope. She got him two good lengths of rope and she also came back with a basket containing cheese and some olives and two bottles of wine and a *fiasco* of *grappa*, the strong raw brandy the peasants distill here.

"I can't carry all of this," Fabio said.

"Angela will meet you in the Corso with a knapsack," Signora Bombolini said. Angela passed them then, still crying, and because she was running she was forced to lift up her skirts, and despite the fact that it was a matter of life and death, all that Fabio could seem to keep his mind on was the quality and condition of her legs, that they were so strong and well-shaped and so brown and clean-looking.

"Why are you so red?" Rosa Bombolini asked him. "Are you sure you are all right?"

I am very much all right, Fabio thought. I am about to save the father of the woman I love, and she will be grateful to me for the rest of my life. He broke into a trot, although he knew he should save his energy. He met Angela Bombolini at the curve in the Corso Mussolini down below Babbaluche's house.

"Let him fall off," the cobbler told him. "It would be a public service to the city."

Angela handed him a black knapsack made of imitation leather that had once been the property of the Young Fascist Scouts, and the outer flap of which read: "This sack belongs to Bruno. Don't touch or *death*." On the other side, burned into the leather, was: "Believe   Obey   Fight —Your Duce."

It caused both of them to laugh.

"I'll pray for you, Fabio," she said. It was the first time he had ever heard her use his name.

The ladder shocked Fabio. He had not looked at it in many years, and he was frightened to see how narrow and inadequate it was. It was not a ladder at all, but long lengths of pipe, five or six inches around, which were joined together and into which small round iron spikes had been fixed, at intervals of six or eight inches, to serve as foot and hand holds.

"Don't look up, Fabio. Just go up," someone said to him.

"Don't go up. You can't help him."

He tightened his belt so his shirt would stay in and slung the ropes around his shoulders and tied the bottoms of his pants around his ankles with rough twine so they wouldn't flap.

"You're a fool to go, Fabio. Why should you get killed for him?"

Fabio pulled himself up onto the pipe and for one moment he was forced to look up, and he was astonished to see how far up the fat wine seller had managed to pull himself. The metal was hot to the touch but not hot enough to burn and he took a deep breath then and began to climb. It was not hard for him at first, but he was surprised how narrow the little spikes were; they felt even smaller than they looked. Something wet touched his hair and he realized it was paint from the buckets Bombolini had yoked about his neck. He tried to look neither up nor down, but out across the mountain slope, the green terraces down below, across the valley; he fixed his eye on Montefalcone. All at once there was a tremendous shout from the people in the piazza below. He pulled himself in against the pipe and waited for the body of Bombolini to rush by him.

When nothing happened he looked up and he could see Angela's father hanging out away from the pipe like a door that the wind has blown open. Bombolini had missed his footing; but somehow, instead of falling, he had managed to hang on with one foot and one hand and now he hung there, swaying back and forth, trying to pull himself back to the pipe. Fabio could feel the pipe trembling from the effort and it frightened him, and then he heard a second cheer from the piazza and he looked up and Bombolini was climbing upward again.

* * *

Across the piazza from the wineshop, in the cellar of the Leaders' Mansion where The Band had barricaded themselves, they heard the shout.

"It won't be much longer now," Dr. Bara said. "They're getting the feel of it. The mob is feeling its muscle. It's only a matter of time now."

All of them were there, Copa and Mazzola, Dr. Bara, Vittorini the mail clerk, their families, their children and even Francucci, his eyes sealed, his teeth broken, his lips split.

"Maybe they won't come," Mazzola said. "Maybe they're cheering something else."

"They won't hurt *us*," the wife of Francucci said. "We've already paid the price."

"What, for twenty years of rotten bread?" the doctor said. "You have only paid the first installment."

"If we knew who was leading them we might be able to figure out something," Copa, the mayor, said.

"Every man has his price," Mazzola said.

"Where the hell is Pelo?" Copa asked. "I'll break that bastard's neck."

They had sent Romano Pelo, the least offensive of men, a shadow of a human being, to go into the town and find out what the noise from the Piazza Mussolini was about. He had not come back. Now they sat in the darkness of the cellar of the Mansion, the government house of Santa Vittoria, behind barricaded doors, and waited and listened.

"If we can only last into the night," Mazzola said. "They'll forget us. The people's memory is short."

Mazzola was always hoping for the best. There was another shout from the piazza, this time loud enough to seem to come right through the stones of the house and it made the baker begin to weep.

"All I ever did for them was to bake their bread and now they want to come and harm me," Francucci said. He was becoming obsessed with the idea that the people wanted to put him in his own bread ovens and bake him alive.

"We must find a way to surrender to them before they can come to us," Vittorini said. "In that way we can surrender on our own terms."

Little by little, as the day wore on, the mail clerk was assuming command in the cellar. He was not a Fascist, but he was a paid employee of the state, a "functionary" as he preferred to call himself, and since Vittorini is above all things a man of form he felt it his duty to be counted with the recognized legal machinery of government.

If the Communists ever take over Italy or Santa Vittoria, Vittorini will hang a picture of Marx in the post office.

"The thing we must do now is seize the initiative," Vittorini said.

"Very beautiful words," Dr. Bara said. "Well stated."

The most impressive fact about Vittorini, more impressive even than his character, is the uniform he is entitled to wear, and which he wears on all state and religious holidays, and which he had the wisdom to put on this morning.

It is from one of the fine regiments although no one remembers the name of it now or the number. It was made from a white whipcord twill that had been cleaned and bleached so many times that it was impossible to look directly at Vittorini in the sunlight. Across his chest he wore a red-and-white-and-green silken sash, and on the sash was a gold medal that swam in the silk like a sun rising from the sea. There were black patent-leather boots that flared out at the knee and a sword in a golden scabbard that clinked against the cobblestones when he crossed the piazza to enter the church. The green epaulets are trimmed with gold braid, but most of all it is Vittorini's hat. The hat is made of shiny black patent leather with a little stubby visor and from the top, which is high, cascades a fall of cock's plumes, a shiny black-and-green shower of them so that when Vittorini walks Vittorini ripples.

"We must discover the nature of the enemy," Vittorini told them, "and capitulate to it. They must not come and take; we must *give*. It is the only way."

He shook his head to emphasize his point, and the dark river of feathers began to run again.

"These are very beautiful words," the doctor said.

"Where in Christ is Pelo?" Copa said.

THE IRON GRILLWORK of the catwalk that circles the top of the water tower had been burning for half the day and it was hot to the touch, but Bombolini never felt the burning when he crawled up onto the walk. He sank onto the iron and almost at once he slept. He had no intention of ever getting off the tower. He had prepared himself to die. He even yearned for the release of dropping softly down through the softness of the afternoon sky. He knew the people in the piazza were waiting for his last performance and he wouldn't disappoint them, but at the moment he was too tired even to contemplate dying. That would have to wait until he woke again, unless he rolled off the walk while he slept. Until then he lay stretched on the iron slats and burned.

When he did wake he was conscious of three things. His eyes were pressed against the open slots of the grillwork and he could see from the shadows of things far below him that time, a good deal of time, had passed. Part of his body was in shadow. He watched an ox plod along a track through the terraces. The road was ankle-deep in dust, and white and bone dry, and it looked as if it had been drawn through the green terraces by a piece of white chalk. At each step a plume of dust spiraled up behind the cart and hung in the still air of late afternoon like a white banner.

I am thirsty, Bombolini thought. I am dying of thirst.

He could see the people working on the terraces in the vineyards, deep among the vines, working in the shaded tunnels of fat, green grape leaves, resting in the cool of the wine-green shade. And he could hear the sound of water bubbling by his ear, just on the other side of the thin concrete skin of the water tank.

I am being driven crazy, Bombolini thought.

And finally he became conscious that someone else was on the tower with him. From the other side of the tank came a rhythmic sound, a soft and steady lapping like waves on the side of an anchored boat.

Before I roll off I will find out who is on the tower, he told himself. He tried to say something, but there was no sound. He tried to move and found that it was impossible. I can't even kill myself, he said to himself, and he sighed, and then his eyes saw the wine bottle, the cork out of the neck, standing at attention like a little soldier a few inches away from his hand.

I will drink a little of this wine and then roll off, he told himself. The wine was hot from the sun, but the heat didn't bother Bombolini. He could feel the wine run down his throat and enter his stomach and then begin to course through the bulk of his body as if it were the sun itself. The second swallow was easier and each one after that became easier, every mouthful exploding inside him like a small hot sun, the source of life itself running inside him. He could feel it go *poom* in his stomach. The wine was working for Italo Bombolini the way a transfusion works for a man who has lost too much blood. When he was through with the bottle he found he could sit up, and he leaned against the concrete and all at once allowed his legs to drop over the side of the catwalk, which caused a great shout from the piazza.

"Who's on the tower?" he said.

"Fabio."

The sound stopped but then it resumed, the *slap, slap* of the paintbrush against the concrete.

"I knew it would be Fabio," Bombolini said. It was an effort for him to talk. "If anyone would come for me I knew it would be Fabio. Fabio?"

"Yes?"

"God shower His blessings on you, Fabio."

Fabio was unable to answer. Things like this embarrass the people here. It might be all right for Sicilians, but not here. They are very emotional and vulgar and sentimental, much too emotional for us.

"Let me see you, Fabio."

"No. When we both are on the same side the catwalk starts to fall off."

"Fascist bastards," Bombolini said. "They cheated on the specifications. They were supposed to put up a ladder and they put up that pipe and pocketed the difference. They were supposed to put a platform up here and they put up this thing. How far are you now?"

Fabio had already painted out MUSSOLINI IS ALWAYS RIGHT and was halfway through the eight DUCE's.

"Four more to go, eh?"

"Yes. Whoever did it, overdid it," Fabio said.

"I did it," Bombolini said.

Fabio was silent. It embarrassed him to think of a man risking his life to climb a tower and write DUCE DUCE DUCE all over the side of it. And he could not imagine this man as ever having been young.

"I was young once, you know. I was tall and lean. I used to look like Garibaldi. I had long shiny-black hair. I wonder what made it curl? Ah, well. When I was through I wasn't even tired."

Fabio went on with the painting.

"I know what you're thinking, Fabio. You don't have to tell me," Bombolini said. "But you have to try and understand how it was then. It wasn't like this now at first, Fabio. He was beautiful at first, Fabio. He was promises for us."

They felt the tower tremble and they gripped the iron railing, but then it passed. The mountain rises and falls here, a little bit each day, like a giant shifting in his sleep.

"And what promises, Fabio. I don't mean the stupid ones like building the army and making Italy fierce again. They were going to help us build a school and pay for teachers. Everybody was going to join in. They were going to help us build a road, and we were going to plant the hillsides with grass and trees so the land would stay on the hills and the water would stay on the land and there would be no more landslides. We *believed* that, Fabio. Oh, there was excitement then, Fabio. Everything seemed possible. And we believed."

"How could you?" Fabio said. "You believed because you wanted to believe."

"Yes. And because he believed, too. I really think Mussolini believed."

"And then none of it happened."

"Some of it happened. This thing, this tower, happened. Oh, we were going to be like America here, Fabio. Look." The wine seller pointed although Fabio could not see him. "Can you see Scarafaggio from where you are?" Fabio said that he could. "When the tower was built they fell down in the streets with envy from looking at us. 'Our turn next,' they said. 'It's happening. The miracle is happening.'"

He told Fabio of the famous morning when the tower was to be dedicated. The dignitaries had come from Montefalcone in cars and been taken up the mountain in oxcarts decorated with flags and flowers. A great flag had covered the top of the tower and when the string was pulled and the tank was revealed, there, shining fresh and black in the morning sun, was MUSSOLINI IS ALWAYS RIGHT and all the DUCE's, and on the catwalk was Italo Bombolini.

"I was a hero once, for a few days, and then they turned the water off," Bombolini said. "After that I was a fool."

When the leaders from Montefalcone had gone The Band assumed control of the water tower and began to charge for the water. When the grape growers refused to pay, the water was turned off, and soon the cement spillways began to fill with leaves and dirt and the people went back to the old way, praying to God to send rain, and He was, as always, not quite generous enough. But the people forgot about the tower.

While he talked Bombolini threw the bottle off the tower, and there was a shout from the people as it arched out over the town and finally crashed in a tinkle of glass on the roof of the Cooperative Wine Cellar. A minute or two afterward an old man with white hair and a face as red as wine came out onto the roof and shook his fist at them. It was Old Vines, the keeper of the wine.

"I've upset the sleep of the wine," Bombolini said. "If he had a rifle he would shoot us off this tower. Are you almost done?"

"Yes. Two more DUCE's and one DU."

"I ran out of paint. No," he said, "it wasn't Mussolini himself at first. We didn't blame him. It was the water. The country might have been falling apart, but we couldn't see it. You know what The Master says. 'Men are apt to deceive themselves in big things, but they rarely do so in particulars.'"

"I don't know who The Master is."

"Niccolò Machiavelli," Bombolini said. "He's my master. Have you studied him?" Fabio said that he had.

"Well I read him. I memorize him," the wine seller said. "I have read *The Prince* forty-three times."

The young man was astonished by this information, and he didn't believe it. His father had once told him that beneath Bombolini's clownish exterior there was a better mind than anyone could expect, but Fabio had never been able to see any sign of it.

"I don't suppose there is any more wine?"

Fabio thought about it. If Bombolini got drunk it might be the end of them both, and yet the wine had made the journey down seem possible. He opened the knapsack and uncorked the second bottle of wine and slid it along the catwalk.

"God shower blessings on you, Fabio. Rain them down on you. Flood you with them, Fabio. God drown you in blessings." And he began to drink the hot red wine. They were silent while he drank.

"When I'm through with this bottle," Bombolini said, "I'm going off this tower, Fabio."

"Oh no," Fabio said.

49

"I can't disappoint my audience. Look at them down there. They've been waiting for me all day."

"I didn't come up here for nothing."

"Can you imagine what they would say? The poor son of a bitch can't even *fall* off the tower."

The young man began to paint more swiftly. The paint was running short, and he was becoming tired. If he was ever to get Angela's father down, it would have to be done soon, before he got too tired, before darkness fell on them, before the effect of the wine began to wear off.

The men and the women were on their way up from the terraces by then. Wherever Fabio looked he could see people coming out from the shadows of the vines onto the track that comes up the mountain from the terraces. A great number of them were already up the mountain, so when Bombolini let fly the second bottle the noise from the lower piazza, and now from the Piazza of the People as well, was the loudest of the day. Fabio by then had reached the bottom of the bucket and was on the last letter. It was strange, but there was exactly enough paint left to paint out the last letter, a *U*, and not a brushful more.

"Now throw the bucket," Bombolini said. Fabio threw the first bucket far out over the town, away from the piazza, out over the Fat Wall so that no one could get hurt.

"Now the brush." He threw the brush. There was a shout from the crowd. He threw the cheese, the olives, the second bucket, and each time the crowd roared and the noise grew louder and by the time Fabio threw the knapsack the piazza was in an uproar.

"All right, let's go now," Fabio shouted. He had counted on the excitement to stir the wine seller. He came around to the side of the catwalk where Bombolini sat, and as he did the rusted iron bolts that had been drilled into the concrete years before suddenly cried out, *screamed*, in protest. He ran along the narrow walk and past Bombolini and on to the spiked pipe so that his weight was no longer on the catwalk. Now the people in the piazza were silent. There was no sound from the city at all.

"They don't want you to fall, do you see?" Fabio said. "If they wanted you to fall they would be shouting for you."

While he talked he reached up and began to work the lengths

of rope under the arms and across the back and around the waist of Bombolini. His plan was crude, but Fabio felt it might work. He would tie the wine seller to the pipe, literally lash him to it, and then bring him down it spike by spike. He would place Bombolini's foot on the next rung, or spike, below and then work the ropes down around him and the pipe and when he was secured there he would lift the next foot down. He would bring him down, all bound with ropes, like a bear being brought down from the high mountains. He made Bombolini slide along the narrow catwalk until he was at the pipe and then dip down until his feet could find the spikes to stand on. Even from where they were, so high above the piazza, they could hear the people suck in their breaths. When he was tied to the pipe they didn't start at once, because both of them were tired even then.

"Why are you doing this for me, Fabio?" Bombolini asked. Fabio didn't answer him. How could he mention Angela? He wondered if he would have been on this pipe now for anyone else's father, but then he realized that only Angela's father would be doing such a thing.

"Why?"

"Because you were a man in trouble. It is people's responsibility to help others in trouble."

"Oh, Fabio," Bombolini said. "I don't know where you get ideas like that. It is people's responsibility to look after themselves and nothing more. Let us try a step."

Fabio lifted Bombolini's right foot and brought it down to the next spike below, and then he climbed up so that his head was level with Bombolini's waist and he worked the ropes down a foot or more. They did it several times and rested.

"Fabio?"

"Yes."

"I want you to know one thing, Fabio. If I ever get off this tower and I am alive, if there is ever one thing in the world that you want and I can give it to you, I want you to ask me for it and I will give it to you."

Why couldn't he say it right then? Why couldn't he be honest with himself and with this man he had lashed to a spiny pipe and whose life he was saving at the risk of his own? One word. A few words—Yes, there is one thing: Angela; I want your daughter Angela in marriage. Instead, all he could do was murmur, "Come on, come on," and feel himself turning red.

Just before they began again, Bombolini began to point to the north. "Oh, my God," he said. "Can you see that? Can you see there?"

"Yes. Something is burning," Fabio said. "Some city is on fire."

They could see a cloud of gray, which the late afternoon sun turned gold at the top. It rose from a city which sat on the top of a mountain like a crown, and the crown was in flames.

"The whole mountain is burning," Bombolini said, and it was true.

I<small>N THE</small> Leaders' Mansion they could hear the shouts from the piazza, and the cheering. The noise was now steady and they knew the crowd was growing, but none of them was ready to believe that the cheering was for Italo Bombolini.

"Why would Pelo tell a thing like that?" Mazzola asked.

"Because Pelo is a bastard, that's why," Copa said.

Pelo had come back from the Piazza Mussolini and when no one in the Piazza of the People was looking he had knocked twice on the door as directed.

"Who are they cheering?" Vittorini had called.

"Bombolini." Vittorini could not believe his ears.

"Italo Bombolini," Pelo said. "The wine seller. The wine merchant. The Sicilian boob."

"I don't believe you," Vittorini said.

"But it is the truth," Pelo said, and then he had run.

And ever since then the noise had grown louder and with it had grown the need for The Band to know who was the leader so they could plan some kind of counteraction.

"But suppose it *is* true," Dr. Bara said.

"Then we will have to deal with Bombolini," Vittorini said. "In a war one doesn't choose one's enemies. If an insane mob has chosen Bombolini then we have no choice but to deal with the man the mob has chosen."

"Ah, well," the doctor said, "we will soon find out who the leader is, whether we want to or not." And Francucci began to weep again.

"I want the priest. I want my priest. I want to make my last confession," the baker said, and then some of the women began to weep as well.

"Shut up and start acting like a man," Copa shouted at him.

"I don't know how," Francucci said.

"He's right though," Vittorini said. "We need the priest. Every member of the *fiancheggiatori* must be united for the common defense."

The *fiancheggiatori* is the alliance of the Crown and the Vatican with the bureaucracy and big business which forms the traditional combination of power in this country. The man who can keep the *fiancheggiatori* satisfied and in balance with one another is said to hold the key to the kingdom. It was one of the postmaster's favorite words, but as Babbaluche pointed out one day the only thing missing from the combination was the people. They sent a young boy into the piazza to go to the bell tower and summon the priest.

"Tell him someone is dying," Mazzola said. "That will be sure to bring him."

They put Francucci in a far corner of the cellar, in the deepest part of the darkness, but even from there he could be heard, saying it over and over like a litany in the church.

"They are going to roll me in flour and sprinkle me with water. They are going to put me in an oven and bake me like my bread.

"They are going to roll me in flour and sprinkle me with water. . . ."

54

* * *

"No, I don't believe it," Mazzola was saying when the boy came back with the priest. "I refuse to believe it. No mob, even a mob from this city, would be insane enough to choose Bombolini for a leader."

But Padre Polenta told them the same thing, and they were forced to believe it.

"Yes, it's true," the priest said. "The people are cheering Bombolini."

"But why? Why Bombolini?"

"It is in the nature of mobs to cheer fools," the priest said. "Now where is the dying man?"

Doctor Bara waved his hand around the room.

"Everywhere," he said. "All of us. It is only a matter of time."

There was a great shout from the piazza then. The force of it was so strong they could feel its weight on the door. And each shout was followed by one after it and then another, like soldiers on the march. The shouts grew so loud and so steady that Francucci himself could no longer hear his own litany.

* * *

The shouts were the counting. Fabio had gotten Bombolini three quarters of the way down the pipe when the counting began. Someone in the piazza had counted the number of rungs that still remained and when there were fifty of them the people began to shout the number left.

"Forty-nine."

"Forty-eight."

Great explosions of sound. The progress would come in flurries, four or five rungs, and when the two men got tired and held on, the people held the number and repeated it, over and over, until the men went on.

"Forty-seven, forty-seven, forty-seven . . ." Like a steam engine waiting in the station.

They had come to see Bombolini fall off the tower, but now the mood had changed. Now they were cheering him down. When there were only thirty-four or thirty-five spikes still to go, however, with the end of the ordeal so near and yet with the distance still great enough so that if he slipped and fell he would die, Bombolini found he could go no further. His leg muscles had become like strands of wet pasta. They trembled and quivered, the strength had gone, he hung from the ropes on the pipe like a quarter of beef in the market place.

What happened to Fabio then must be seen at least as having the hand of God behind it. He was coming back up the pipe to put Bombolini's feet back on the spikes to keep him from being squeezed to death by the ropes when the *grappa* flask that he was carrying clinked against the pipe. He had forgotten about it, since Fabio doesn't think in terms of alcohol; but at the moment when he needed it, at a time truly of desperation, something caused the bottle to strike the metal.

The *grappa* they distill here is strong. It can be used in a cigarette lighter or in a blowtorch. On a cold day it is like carrying around a bottle of live coals or putting a stove in your pocket. Fabio took the flask from his shirt and reached up, and because Bombolini was now too tired even to drink, Fabio began pouring little surprises of *grappa* down his throat.

The effect of the brandy was immediate. From the piazza they could see Bombolini's vacant glazed stare pass from his face. His color, which had passed through purple into a whiteness like the whiteness of the dead, began to return to him. When Fabio got his feet back onto the spikes Bombolini was able to keep them there and the boy could feel muscles in the legs once more.

"Give me the bottle," Bombolini said.

He began to pour the *grappa* down his own throat, steady strong swallows now, perhaps one a minute, an ounce or more each swallow and in five or six minutes the flask of *grappa* was emptied and he hurled it down into the piazza. He had drunk ten ounces of grappa in less than ten minutes.

"We're going down," Bombolini shouted to Fabio. There was a great cheer from the people in the piazza.

"Take off the ropes."

Fabio shook his head. Then Bombolini began to work the ropes off himself, and when they were loose he threw them to the people and began to start down. He was slow, but he also was steady and careful, the foot feeling for the next spike, finding it, the whole body balanced correctly before the step and then the step itself.

"Thirty-four, thirty-four, thirty-four."

Another step.

"Thirty-three, thirty-three, thirty-three."

They could hear it all the way up the Corso Mussolini, they could hear it through the barred doors and the stones of the Leaders' Mansion. They could hear it from every corner of the Piazza of the People, although they didn't know what it meant then.

"It's starting again," Dr. Bara said in the cellar. "They're getting ready to come again. It's stronger now."

Dr. Bara had no fear for himself. It was his belief that the people would be too selfish to harm their only doctor. "You had better have a plan," he said.

"I have a plan," Vittorini said. He said it so vigorously that the feathers rustled and it was reassuring. "I will make him take our surrender. It is now a matter of timing," the old soldier said. "Timing is all."

"And don't allow ourselves to forget one thing," Dr. Bara said. "The Italian soldier is a master at the art of surrender."

It made them feel better, all of them, and the feeling lasted until they heard a noise, the noise, one so strong that they felt it, the loudest noise almost certainly ever heard until then in Santa Vittoria.

* * *

He had gotten down, by himself, to the last spike on the pipe and then his feet had touched the stones of the Piazza Mussolini. At that moment there was a great cheer and he had fallen forward and they caught him before he hit the stones and began to carry him, to shove him actually, through the mass of the people in the piazza toward his cart. They put him up on a great solid two-wheeled Sicilian cart, made of iron oak with oak wheels rimmed with iron, painted pink and blue and covered with sweet religious sayings, and when the hands released him he fell off and had to be caught once more and put back up onto the seat, where they

57

propped him up so that he wouldn't fall again. It was at this time that he said the eight words that were the occasion for the greatest single sound in the history of the city.

Before telling you the words, it is necessary to tell one thing about this place and the people who live in it. Life here is hard, harder than outsiders can ever see. No one gets anything here without working for it, and many work hard and get nothing. It sometimes seems in truth that the harder the people work the less they have to show for it, as if work creates loss. Who knows where the fault begins or where it lies? The only truth is that there is never quite enough of anything here. Why do they stay? For the same reason that all peasants stay. They hold on to hunger, which they are accustomed to, because they are fearful of starvation.

Because of this, the greatest fear of any peasant is that someone will take something from him that he has worked for. The pain of it is too unbearable.

It is one reason all peasants are ungrateful. If someone gives a peasant something, he can only assume that it is a trick, or that the person doesn't want the thing he has given, or that the person is crazy.

All of this, then, is why the greatest joy of Italian peasants, and maybe peasants all over the world as well, is to get something they didn't work for: to get something for nothing. And the best things to get are the things that are sweated for each day. A pearl is good to get for nothing, but its value isn't known in terms of sweat. Pearls are good, but bread is better.

* * *

So the shout, then; this noise—now it can be understood. They put Fabio in the back of the cart and Bombolini was propped up in the high front seat and they began to push on the heavy wheels, back and forth at first to gain momentum to start the cart back up the Corso Mussolini, when he motioned to them. They didn't hear him clearly at first.

"Say it once more," a man shouted at him. "Clearly."

He made a last effort. He swallowed and cleared his throat and called out.

"Free wine for the people of Santa Vittoria."

He slumped down in the seat, face forward, and it is doubtful if either he or Fabio ever heard the sound itself that greeted the words, although it soared up the Corso and it cascaded into the Piazza of the People and it thundered against the door of the Leader's Mansion and it caused the stained-glass windows of Santa Maria of the Burning Oven to tremble.

The Corso is steep and narrow, and it was hard to get the cart moving, because not enough people could get behind it. But a crowd also has a will that makes itself felt, and just the sheer pressure of people, the desire of the crowd, seemed to be enough to start the cart moving upward. At the stone steps the men were forced to stop and rock the big iron-rimmed wheels back and forth to get up over the stones, and as they did they began shouting—*"Bom"* as they went forward, *"bo"* as they rolled back, *"li-i-i-i"* as they strained up over the stone, and a short, explosive *"ni"* when they made it over the lip to the next step. The people behind the men pushing the cart took up the shout, and soon the Corso and then the whole of Santa Vittoria was vibrating with it. They could hear it in the highest part of High Town—*"Bom bo li-i-i-i ni! Bom bo li-i-i-i ni!"*—and over the walls and in the high pastures. One old woman who was watching oxen said it sounded like the start of a great storm and made her afraid, and Luigi Longo, who was coming back from another town after fixing a pump there, said it sounded like a trombone announcing the angel of death.

* * *

Vittorini had not been idle. In the Leaders' Mansion they were ready for Bombolini. They stood behind the heavy oak door and listened to the shouts of the people and waited for the proper moment. The barricades had been pulled aside and the door was opened a crack to allow Vittorini to see into the Piazza of the People, and behind him were The Band. Copa stood just behind the old soldier with a medallion of the office of mayor held in his hand. Mazzola, behind Copa, held the great brass key to the city, which unlocks nothing here. Dr. Bara had put on a white coat and hung a stethoscope around his neck. Polenta, unfortunately, was dressed only in a soup-stained cassock, and on his head was the little skull cap which was ragged and stained with oil, but because he thought he had been coming to offer the last rites he had his tall silver crucifix and this would be important. The women had been sent through the Mansion and they had stripped it of every religious statue and holy picture the house possessed. Those who had no picture or soapstone saint were given a baby or young child to hold in their arms.

Vittorini himself had taken the Italian flag from a hallway and had worked the flag down the edge of his sword so that it hung like a banner when the blade was extended.

"Open it just a little wider," Vittorini said. The sound coming up into the piazza from the Corso was deafening. The soldier was at military attention.

"The timing is everything now," he called to the doctor, but Dr. Bara was unable to hear him.

* * *

Before anything else, they saw Bombolini's head rise from the Corso Mussolini, up toward the piazza, and then they saw his neck and his shoulders and then they saw the top of the Sicilian cart and finally as the cart came up into the Piazza of the People, they saw the bodies of the people pushing him.

"My God," Dr. Bara said. "He comes like a king from the East."

He was above them all, riding along above them, swaying back and forth above them, as if he were floating on a restless sea. The people were still shouting his name, and they came flooding out of the confines of the Corso, spilling out into the vastness of the piazza and around Bombolini and the cart, like the first wave of a tide.

Someone in the Leaders' Mansion moved toward the door then, but Vittorini held him back.

"Not yet, not yet," he shouted.

The cart had no direction. Once out of the Corso, it had gotten out of the control of the men who had been pushing it. It rolled out into the center of the piazza, propelled there by the pressure of the people behind it. It wanted to turn to the left in the direction of the wineshop and away from the Mansion of the Leaders, but the men pushing the wheels were unable to make the turn, because of the press behind them, and the cart continued out toward the Fountain of the Pissing Turtle.

"*Now!*" Vittorini commanded.

The door of the Leaders' Mansion was thrown wide open. The old soldier was the first to go through it, his sword pointed directly out in front of him with the flag fluttering in the wind that blows every evening in this city.

Copa came behind him, the imitaton gold of the mayor's medallion glinting in what still remained of the sun. Mazzola held up the key to the city of Santa Vittoria. After him came Dr. Bara, and with Bara was Padre Polenta with the silver crucifix held aloft for everyone in the piazza to see, and then came the women holding up the statues and the holy pictures and the old and young women with the babies held up or at their breast.

"*Now!*" Vittorini shouted again.

He lifted up his sword so that the flag was overhead, the priest lifted up his crucifix and began to wave it up and down. Mazzola waved the key, and Copa flung the medallion up and down, and all the pictures and all the statues and all the babies waved up and down.

Nothing happened. The cart continued out into the piazza. Allow this much for Copa. He is a man of action, and action was required.

"The sons of bitches," he shouted to Vittorini. "They try to ignore our surrender."

He ran back into the Mansion and when he came outside again with the gun, the cart was no more than ten feet away from the fountain. He unloaded his first shot from the double-barreled shotgun over the crowd in the piazza and the second was even lower, so low that several people were cut and stung by the bird shot. The movement in the piazza stopped, the pushing ceased, the pressure on the cart stopped.

Copa put two more shells in the gun. One went over the heads of the people in the back of the crowd and in the silence the explosion sounded much louder. The other he fired into the bell tower and the pellets caused the bell to go *pling* and *ping* and *cling* and then the bell itself to rock lightly back and forth with the clapper just touching the brass and sounding a mournful *blung, blung* that we use on the days of death.

"Once more," Vittorini said, and all of the pictures and the medallions and the sacred cross and the babes started to rise and fall again.

And allow this much for Bombolini. Although he was drunk and exhaustion had stolen much of his sensibility, it was he—of all the people in the piazza standing there with their mouths agape looking at the smoke curling from the end of Copa's gun and watching the wind ripple the feathers of Vittorini's hat and Vittorini's flag—who knew at once what was taking place.

There is a line by Machiavelli which Bombolini has written on a card and carries with him.

> Fortune is a woman. It is necessary, if you wish to master her, to take her by force before she has a chance to resist.

Give this much for Bombolini, then. He saw his fortune and he raped her on the spot.

"To the Leaders' Mansion," he called.

There was a moment when it seemed that the marriage might never be consummated. The will of the crowd was for wine. But the people had a decency about them, they were willing to wait for their wine and with a great effort, with an agonizing slowness, the cart was turned and the people in its path were pushed aside, and Bombolini and the Sicilian cart began to bounce along the cobblestones of the piazza in the direction of the Leaders' Mansion. It was his determination to say something memorable to seize the occasion, but he never had the chance to open his mouth.

"By the powers vested in me by the legitimate government of the city of Santa Vittoria," Vittorini began. His voice, like that of all good soldiers, was loud and carried command.

What Dr. Bara had said about the Italian soldiers and surrender was correct. Vittorini and the rest of them were impressive in defeat. The old soldier talked for almost one half hour without, as anyone could notice, taking a breath. Since they didn't understand the purpose of the talk, the people in the piazza didn't understand the words, but they liked to hear them because they were beautiful and Vittorini was full of eloquence and his sentences flowed like rivers and his words glided like swans on still waters.

It is not necessary to put down all the details. It is enough to know this: that in exchange for a sacred and a solemn vow by Bombolini that the persons and the property of those who had gone before—which meant The Band—would be respected, he, Italo Bombolini, would be handed the key to the city and the medallion of the mayor would be placed around his neck.

"Do I so have your sacred and solemn vow?" Vittorini said. "Remember, it is witnessed by the priest and thus by God Himself."

Someone prodded Bombolini.

"You so have my solemn pledge," Bombolini said. Vittorini turned directly toward the people in the piazza then. While Polenta sanctified the pledge by making the sign of the cross, Vittorini lifted his sword and the flag.

"Citizens of Santa Vittoria," he cried out to them. "I give you your new leader."

There was almost no response from the people. They had not understood, and it still was not clear to them. What response there was—a few cheers and a few groans, a shout of laughter from Babbaluche, the sound of snoring from Fabio in the back of the cart—soon died away in the rush of the late afternoon wind and finally the only sound at all was that of Vittorini's flag fluttering. It was beginning to grow dark in the piazza, although the sun was still bright on the roof tops of the surrounding houses. Vittorini made a small sign with his hand; he turned it upward as if to say to Bombolini, "I have done my job, the rest is up to you," and Dr. Bara pushed up behind the soldier.

"Get the medallion," he said. "They don't want him. Get the medallion back. We have made a terrible mistake."

But at that moment Bara was proven wrong. Bombolini had turned around on the cart and back to his people and had said something to them, and this was followed by an enormous cheer and a great surge of movement. Vittorini turned to Bara.

"And what would you call that?"

Men seized the great cart wheels. They almost lifted that iron oak cart into the air in their eagerness to turn it around and drive it back across the piazza.

"And what would you call that if he isn't the leader?" Vittorini said. "They would have torn us apart."

The women lowered the holy pictures and the statues, and Padre Polenta began to walk back across the clearing piazza to the bell tower. The others turned around and started back inside the Leaders' Mansion, because one of the promises Vittorini had made was that they would be out of the Mansion by sundown that evening.

The wine seller had said four words: "And now your wine."

* * *

When Rosa Bombolini heard the sounds coming up the Corso Mussolini she had shut the shutters of her windows and run downstairs and closed and locked the iron gate that guards the front of the wineshop and then gone back upstairs and stood behind the shutters, where she could see into the Piazza of the People without being seen.

Her husband's cart came to a stop twenty feet from the wineshop.

"Open the gates," Bombolini shouted. When there was no answer, someone handed Bombolini a cobblestone that had been pried out of the piazza. Bombolini gave the stone to one of the younger Pietrosantos and made a sign, and the young man sent the stone crashing against an upstairs shutter.

"Open the gates," he shouted again. The shutter opened this time and his wife looked down from the window into the cart.

"I open no gates to no mob," Rosa Bombolini shouted to them.

"This is no mob. These are the citizens of Santa Vittoria," Bombolini called back. She made a gesture with the fingers of her right hand that only men ever make here and then only when they are among men.

"I *order* you to open these gates," Bombolini called.

"Order?" She made that laugh that all Santa Vittoria is familiar with, the one they are afraid of. "Whose order?" The words were spit on her lips.

"The order of the mayor of the city of Santa Vittoria."

He held up the key to the city and then the medallion of the

64

office of mayor, and the people cheered. She opened the shutters wide then.

"Up the fat you-know-what of the indescribable mayor of this indescribable city," she shouted.

The new mayor looked very tired then and sad. He pointed to the gates.

"Down," he said. He described the action with his hands. "Pull them down."

She was at the window again. "You son of a bitch. I own this house. I own this wineshop. You listen to me. You touch those gates and you never walk into this house again."

It would be his first decision as mayor. He didn't look up at her when he made it, but the decision was made.

"Down," he ordered. "Take them down."

It was the Sicilian cart that did the job. They lifted Bombolini down from the cart and then they ran it back and forth to build up the proper rage, like a bull preparing to make his charge, and all at once they released it. The gate was no match for the cart. The iron was old and the hinges and bolts that held it were rusted. It gave almost a once, and after that the front door gave, and then the entire front of the wineshop. The plate-glass window came all apart and it shattered into the shop and into the piazza. The reign of Italo Bombolini had begun.

I T WOULD BE gratifying to be able to write that the people of Santa Vittoria acted in some other way than they did that
night. But the people acted like proper Santa Vittorians and like
people getting something for nothing. Because the wine was free,
everyone drank too much, and drunkenness and greed are never
gratifying.

Someone set fire to a goat and it went blazing down the Corso
Mussolini and nearly set fire to a stall. Someone threw a bottle
from a roof and cut someone. It was not all bad. Some of the
young people had accordions and a shepherd came down from
the high pastures with pipes, and although they don't dance here
often the men danced and then the women and finally even the
men with the women.

There was an omen for Santa Vittoria that evening, the one thing that for a time calmed the people. While the first barrel of wine was being drunk, just after the sun had gone down, a strange early evening star was seen glittering to the north and east of the city. It hung up above the mountains there, shining in the gold of the late sun before dipping down into the shadows of the mountains. Everyone agreed it was a good sign.

"That bastard Bombolini's in luck," someone said. "Someone is looking out for him."

If the harvest was good this year, for years to come people would look into the sky on this day to see the good omen again and announce that there would be another good harvest. If someone died, his family would look for the star on this day in fear that they would see it and someone else would die that year.

But the star was forgotten, that night at least, when the second barrel was opened. No one at the end was sure how much wine was drunk. Bombolini says that three hundred gallons were drunk. It is a lot of wine for one thousand people, when many of them are very old and very young and over half of them are women.

Long before midnight the dancing stopped. No matter how much wine was drunk the people would be down on the terraces in the morning when the sun rose. Only the young men were still up. A team of Turtles was playing a kind of soccer game with a team of Goats in the piazza, but even that was quiet and slow. One of the players found Fabio sleeping on the wet stones by the Fountain of the Pissing Turtle.

"You'd better get up," he told him, "or you'll die in the night air."

"I have no place to go," Fabio said. He was more tired than drunk.

The soccer player pointed him in the direction of the Leaders' Mansion.

"There's room for you in there. Bombolini is living there now. His wife has thrown him out."

Fabio crossed the piazza and stood outside the door. There was a light inside the house. He knocked, very lightly, and when no one answered he tried the door and it opened and he went inside.

He was surprised to see Bombolini sitting on a box, with a tallow candle by his side, and reading a book. He wanted to say something but could not think of the right thing, and he continued across the room until he was behind the mayor.

The book was old and grimy. It had been abused by use and time. Lines of the text were underlined, and some of them were underlined two and three times, and some of these were in different colors, with all kinds of notes written in the margin.

One read: "No, not true in Santa Vittoria."

Others Fabio could see said, "How very true" and "Try and tell that to the Fascists."

"Oh," Bombolini said. He closed the book.

"I didn't mean to scare you."

"Well you succeeded."

Fabio came around in front of the new mayor.

"You were reading your Machiavelli."

"I'm going to need him now. He's going to have to tell me what to do."

Fabio sat down on a large wooden bench, one of the pieces the Band had left behind.

"I want to stay here for the night if I may."

"Fabio. You may stay here for the rest of your life," Bombolini said.

"No. Just for the night. I am very tired."

Bombolini picked up the light and took Fabio upstairs to a room where several blankets and an old coat were stretched out on the floor.

"I want you to take my bed," he said, and when Fabio refused he forced him to lie down on it and went away with the light. Fabio has no idea how long he was there before the mayor returned.

"Fabio? Are you awake? Listen to this." He thumbed through the book he held and held up a hand with one finger extended, a gesture Fabio was to recognize later as the sign that Bombolini was about to quote from Machiavelli.

" 'The wise ruler ought never to keep faith when by doing so it would be against his interests!' "

Fabio sat up. "Who says that?"

"The Master," Bombolini said. "The wise fox, Niccolò Machiavelli."

"Why are you asking me?"

"Do I have to keep those promises I made?"

"You gave your word," Fabio said. "Your *sacred* word." Bombolini closed the book with a loud noise.

"I knew I should have asked Babbaluche," he said.

There was darkness, and Fabio slept. But when he woke again there was a light in the room once more.

"Just one other sentence, Fabio. An interpretation." The mayor held up his hand. " 'Men must be either caressed or annihilated. They will revenge themselves for small injuries, but they can't do so for great ones. The harm the leader does must be such that he need not fear revenge.' What do you make of that?"

Fabio did not want to be part of any bloodletting, but he was tired and the words seemed to have only one meaning. "I think it means you're supposed to kill them." Bombolini thought about that for a while, and before he said anything else Fabio was asleep.

"I think you are right," he said sadly, because he had little stomach for blood and at the same time a respect for the words of The Master. The next time Fabio awoke, the room was light again, but this time the light came from the piazza. He had been able to sleep for several hours, and he felt better because of it.

"Fabio della Romagna, I want you to join my cabinet," Bombolini said to him. "I want you to be a minister in the Grand Council of the Free City of Santa Vittoria."

"I am flattered," Fabio said, and it was the truth. "I am proud you ask me, but my place is in Montefalcone. I have to finish my studies at the academy. It would not be good to quit now."

"Just for the emergency," Bombolini said. "For the duration. I need you. I need educated men. That's what you will be, Minister of Education. No. Minister for Advanced Education. You can live right here. We'll get a bed for you and a desk, and Angela will bring us something in the morning and make us supper at night. It won't be bad."

It was the thunderbolt again. It was all at once the most amazing idea that Fabio had ever heard—Angela carrying his breakfast;

Angela meeting in doorways, saying good morning and saying good night; Angela preparing food for him with her own hands; Angela meeting him by error and design and chance in all those personal and private ways that can only occur when two people are alone in a house.

"I don't know," Fabio said. He could barely bring himself to talk.

"Everything will be upset in Montefalcone. You said the Germans were taking over the town."

"Yes."

"Then I can put you down," Bombolini said. He took out a soiled card from his pocket and at the bottom added Fabio's name to the list of names. The card was old and the names on it were old and only Fabio's looked freshly placed on the card, and he realized with a start almost as strong as the one he had felt before that this man, whom they called the Sicilian boob, the least likely man in all of Santa Vittoria to ever become a leader, had for months and perhaps years been walking about with a fully formed government in his pocket.

Bombolini closed the shutters and it was dark in the room once more.

"You should sleep," he said. "But before you do I want you to think about this so you can think about it while you sleep. The Master says it is necessary to rule by fear or rule by love. One way or the other. I want you to think about the course I should follow."

When Fabio awoke the sun was fully up and the old blankets were hot against his skin. He thought about the night, the wine, the dancing—which he hadn't done, although he had looked at others dance with her—the strange star in the sky, an omen for good or evil, and about the new thing, Angela and himself in this house and about something Bombolini had asked him to think about and which he had forgotten.

He lay on the floor and became conscious of a strange sound coming from the piazza, a tinkling of glass, as if a river of glass were running across the piazza stones. When he looked out of the window he could see a group of old men and women with long-handled brush brooms sweeping the streets and the piazzas, sweeping up the broken glass of the night before. Such a thing had never happened before in Santa Vittoria; God's winds swept and God's rare rains washed. He was still watching the work with admiration when Bombolini came into the room, clean now and refreshed, although he could not have slept.

"The Public Works Corps," he said. "I stole the idea from the Fascists."

"But how do you pay them?"

Bombolini smiled broadly and handed Fabio a square piece of paper.

3   THREE   3

SANTA VITTORIA LIRE
This paper redeemable for
legal currency at the
end of the emergency

Italo Bombolini
Mayor
The Free City of Santa Vittoria

"Do you really intend to honor it?" Fabio asked. Bombolini was shocked by the suggestion.

"You can fool the people about many things, but only a fool would be foolish enough to fool the people about money."

"The Master," Fabio said. "I'm getting to recognize him."

It was clear that the mayor was very flattered. "In truth, Fabio, it was myself," he said.

Fabio was impressed. "You should write those down," he said.

"In truth, Fabio, I don't write that well. If someone else could write them down . . ."

It was in this manner that *The Discourses* of Italo Bombolini came into being. There are still several copies in Fabio's hand somewhere in the city.

"The people are saying we were born under a lucky star. A good omen, a good sign. I hope they are right."

"I hope they are right," Fabio said. But all he could think about was when Angela would come with some broth or pasta. Bombolini leaned down toward him.

"Do you remember I asked you to think about whether I should rule by fear or rule by love?"

Fabio told him that he did, but that he had had no thoughts.

"Well rest your brain then, Fabio," Bombolini said, "because I have made my decision. I have decided to be lovably fearful."

2 BOMBOLINI

THE STAR they saw was me. The omen sent to Santa Vittoria was myself.

This is the place where I enter the story. It is the price I ask you to pay in return for hearing the story of Santa Vittoria, which is admittedly a better story than my own. It is something that I have wanted to say to my own countrymen, *my* people, for twenty years; an apology written in the hope that some will understand and even that if enough understand I might some day be able to go back to my home and rebuild what is left of my life. I will try to make it short and make the price as inexpensive as possible.

On the morning that Fabio told the story of the death of Mussolini, after it, while he slept, I was flying in the *Odessa Darling*, a B-24 Liberator bomber, somewhere over Italy. I have figured since that we might have crossed almost directly over Santa Vittoria at eight o'clock that morning, although no one here recalls a plane passing over that morning.

I already knew the fate of Mussolini. The pilot of the *Odessa Darling*, Captain Buster Rampey, had told me about it before we took off that morning.

"They kicked out that Muzzlini, you know that? What do you think about it?"

I shrugged my shoulders. I thought nothing about it.

"I just thought you might want to know," Captain Rampey said. "I thought you might want to be the *first* to know, you know? You bein' Eyetalian and all like that."

"No, sir."

"I just *thought* you would."

"No, sir."

It was our fourth mission, and the first over the mainland of Italy. We had bombed Pantelleria and Lampedusa and some other island I have forgotten, but this was to be the first flight over Italy.

I recall the beginning of the flight very well, because every once in a while, when I feel trapped here on this mountain like a sailor in a small boat at sea, I feel like flying again, to get out of here, up above all these people I have come to know so well and who think they know me so well.

We crossed the sea, the Tyrrhenian Sea, early that morning. We flew with the sun, flying low over the blue-green water and the shadow ran along the top of the water like some great dark fish coursing just beneath the surface. I never saw Italy until it came upon us, a surprise from the water, all green, so different from Africa, darkly green like the underside of grape leaves. We followed the coast, what I now know is called the Divine Coast, rushing along over the cliffs and the white houses clinging to the cliffs and the little towns strung along their steep sides and somewhere we suddenly turned in over the mainland. After that I didn't look at the land much, because my aim was to see and to shoot an Italian plane. The reason for this was that the other members of the *Odessa Darling* didn't trust me. One night after he had been drinking in the Officer's Club Captain Rampey came and found me in my barracks.

"Tell me one thing true, Abrussi. If you was to see an Eyetalian plane in the air you wouldn't fire on it, would you?"

I told him that I would. He pronounced the word "fire" as *far* and although I have forgotten many English words now I can still recall every word the captain said to me and the way that he said them.

"You don't have to lie about it, Abrussi. I won't hold that against you. You think if my people left Texas and some war came up that I would go back and shoot at Texas people?"

I said that I thought he would if he were ordered to do it. He gripped me by the front of my shirt.

"Shoot *my* brothers? Shoot at *my* flesh and blood?" He let go of my shirt in disgust. "I just wish you would be honest about it. Then I might be able to respect you."

After that I was accepted by the rest of the crew as a built-in handicap, like an engine that never functioned right. They even had a plan for me called Plan Paisan, in case of an attack by Italian planes. Lieutenant Marvell was to leave his post as navigator and to man my machine gun. There was nothing personal about it.

* * *

I was looking then to prove them wrong. If planes were sighted I wanted to fire at them and hit them before Marvell could relieve me of my weapon. Then some time that morning, while passing over a patch of dark pine woods, the *Odessa Darling* flew into a grove of budding flak—puffs of black smoke and little flowerings of metal. The sky bloomed with them. I had thought we were through this dangerous garden and all of the bursts were behind us, when the plane leaped in the air as if it were suffering a convulsion. The plane shuddered and we started down all at once, in one great sudden dip, as if someone had pulled a plug in the sky.

"Please Jesus, don't let there be fire," someone said.

At the end of the drop the plane began to skid through the sky, slipping across it as if we were being towed on a wire cable, going down but across the sky at the same moment, and then there was a thudding sensation, a series of bumps when I thought we were brushing the tops of trees or mountains and then we held, the plane had gotten a hold of the sky again.

He was a good pilot. It is strange now to think that I owe my life to Captain Rampey.

For a long time we flew in silence, trying only to hold the plane in the sky, fearful of trying to turn or to even lift the plane. We flew on, low, and the mountain towns came floating up at us and then faded away like islands in a high green sea. After a period of time—how long it was I couldn't say or even guess—we began to edge up in the sky again and much later Captain Rampey began to make the turn back again, to wheel the *Odessa Darling* around in a huge slow arc in the sky.

There was no talking. We listened to the strange sounds we were making, they frightened us, and then Rampey called to Marvell.

"I want you to pick me out a nice little town on the way back. One directly on the line to home."

I could see Lieutenant Marvell checking his maps from where I stood at my post. He was a careful worker.

"I got you one," he said after a while. "We won't even have to bank for it. Name of . . . name of . . ."

"I don't *want* to know the name," the captain said. "Just tell me before we get there."

"Yes, sir."

"We didn't come this far for nothing."

"No, sir."

"Got to ditch these bombs *some* place."

"Yes, sir."

"Don't want to waste the *whole* Goddamn day."

"Wouldn't do, sir."

"Wouldn't do at all."

We could see people along the roads, and I could even see the dust rising behind the carts when the oxen put their feet down. Some of the people waved to us. I don't think, even if I met some, I would ever tell the people the way their town had been chosen.

78

They probably think it was an act of God or an act of War; it wouldn't do them any good to know.

When we were five minutes from the target area Lieutenant Marvell announced that it was time to begin to ease the *Odessa Darling* down.

"I don't see anything," Captain Rampey said.

"It's just on the other side of that mountain," Marvell said.

"You wouldn't trick me," Rampey said.

"Sir!"

The *Odessa Darling* started down.

"Going to get us some *paisans* today."

It was a good-sized town, a city really, about three or four times the size of Santa Vittoria. It was on the other side of the mountain, but on a smaller mountain of its own, below the taller mountain, and it covered the crest of it, all white and orange tiles, ringed by a wall, so that in the sunlight it seemed to be a crown on the crest of the mountain. Going down on all sides of the mountain were the dark-green fields that I later came to know as terraced vineyards from my experience here. In the center of all this greenness, circled by its wall, from the air the city looked like the bull's-eye on an enormous dart board.

"Marvell?"

"Sir?"

"You picked us a *jewel*, hear?"

There was trouble with the doors of the bomb bay; some of the flak had damaged the mechanism that controlled them. The bombardier tried to work them open, but before he succeeded we were already over the city.

"I can get you a target further down the line," Marvell said.

"No, I want this one," Rampey said.

They unscrewed the barrel of my machine gun and began to use it as a lever to pry the doors open. We were low then, and I could see the city clearly. The piazza was crowded with people and stalls and carts and animals. It must have been market day. At one end of the piazza was a large building, much like here, that I took to be the town hall. At the other end stood the tower of the cathedral of the city.

"There's your aiming stake," Captain Rampey said.

The shadow of the *Odessa Darling* slid over the town, across the wall and over the piazza and the church façade, over the orange roofs, turning them for a moment a dark red, and then over the other wall, like a dark messenger. We have a saying in Santa Vittoria: "Good is recognized only when it goes away, evil when it comes." But, in this case at least, it wasn't true. When the shadow crossed over them the people looked up; some just went back to their work and some of them waved to us.

When the bomb bay doors opened the *Odessa Darling* swung around and came back for the town. Captain Rampey didn't wait for the cathedral after all. When the plane passed over the city walls he said, "Kick 'em on out," and all of us became bombardiers. We rolled the bombs through the door and pushed them through and kicked them out with our feet, and they began to follow each other down upon the city, wig-wagging back and forth the way the bombs do, swimming along after each other like fish in a school.

You try to follow the bomb that you personally sent on its way, one that felt the touch of your hand or your foot, and you think that you do; but when the explosions begin and the stones and the roofs and then the fire and the smoke begin to erupt you realize that you will never be able to tell exactly what you have done.

We were low enough to see the confused game the people in the piazza were playing. At each explosion—the explosions seemed to walk across the town with giant strides toward the piazza—the people would run in one direction, and at the next they would turn back and begin to run toward the place they had just left.

Eventually they must have found their heads, because the second time we turned and came back over the city the people in the piazza were gone. In all of the piazza there was just one man and he was kneeling in the center of it working the bolt of a hand operated rifle and aiming it at the *Odessa Darling*.

"*That* son of a bitch could hurt someone," Marvell said.

This was the run on which the 500-pound delayed-action demolition bomb would be used. This is the heart and even the very soul of the *Odessa Darling*.

"You have it ready and I'll tell you when," Captain Rampey told the bombardier. He was an expert at this, a genius at it perhaps, the owner of a very special talent that God had given him and which could be used only once or twice in a lifetime. If it hadn't been for war Rampey might never had known he possessed it.

"Now," he said; and on that word the bomb was pushed out. For a moment it seemed to fly along with the *Odessa Darling* before arching over the town and suddenly dipping down, and as it did, every one of us, even the ones without the fine instinct of Captain Rampey, could see that it was going to be a success.

It appeared when it reached it to just touch the gray slate roof of the cathedral and then to go through it so swiftly that the hole it made in the roof seemed to close behind it the way water does over a rock. It was a delayed-action bomb and with a bomb such as this there is always the fear that it might not explode, but then this one did, somewhere down among the dark cellars and in the foundation where a great many people from the piazza must have been hiding. The first sign of success was not the noise of the explosion or the sensation of pressure from it that can at times lift a plane into the air and drop it down like a boat when a wave runs beneath it, but the sight of the front of the cathedral, the entire façade, the great circular stained-glass window that had once been the front of the cathedral, coming apart all at once, every piece seeming to come apart at the same instant and flowering out onto the stones of the piazza. After that, the fire began, a spurt of flame from the bowels of the church that took a great part of the slate roof with it, and then the sound, so that when we began to pull up only the far walls of the cathedral still stood. The man with the rifle was gone.

"There's only the small bombs left," Marvell said.

"Let's not waste them," the captain said.

The center of the city was flaming and hidden in smoke when we made our turn, but the far ends of the town were still not touched; so it was decided to begin to drop the small bombs on the terraces down below the city wall so that we would be sure this way to hit the far ends. People were running along both sides of the wall and some of them were even running along the top, and when the first of the bombs began landing down in the vineyards some of the people jumped down from the walls and began running in the direction of the bombs. They didn't seem to know what to do with themselves. An ox pulling a cart went mad with fear and began running down over the terraced walls until it must have broken its legs and the cart it was pulling landed on top of it.

"Someone ought to put that thing out of its misery," Lieutenant Marvell said.

In one part of the city, out along the north walls, was an open rectangular patch of green, a different green from any that we had seen, a lighter green, more even and much brighter than the darker green of the grapevines, and as we came up on it I could see that it was a playing field and that the large red-tiled building next to the field was almost certainly the city school.

In the field I could see a man and a woman standing far apart from one another; in between them, at regular intervals, were little dark stripes stretched out on the grass. There were white lines on the field, I suppose for soccer, and at first I thought the dark lines were some kind of markers for the game, but as we came on them I could see that they were children. The bombs were beginning to come up the terraces by then and the first of them were even reaching the walls, but the man and the woman still stood in the field and none of the children moved. I suppose the man and the woman thought it would frighten the children if they were to get down on the grass with them. When the bombs came nearer the children began to curl up, and in their black school uniforms they looked like little balls of soot rolled up on the bright-green grass.

The sticks of bombs, the ones that might reach them, were already in the air, but I began to wish that I could hold them back in some manner. The children in the playing field must have trusted their teachers, because although the noise must have been getting terribly loud and frightening none of them moved; they stayed exactly where they had been placed, out on the grass; and it was right, because it is much safer to be out in the open than crouched under a school desk where one might be buried under the old beams and stones of the school and trapped there in fire.

But I still have this feeling, about the bravery of their teachers and the bravery of the children. If only they had looked up they might have seen the line of black things dropping and been able to get up and run to one side of the field away from them. But they stayed where they had been told to stay, face down on the playground, never moving at all until the first of the bombs landed among them, and even after the second and the third, when the bright-green grass began to fling up into the air along with pieces of the earth and the flame of the bomb and the dark little balls of soot.

A soldier does his duty, and this was my duty. And I think now that I might have been spared some of the pain, had it not been for the boy. When the bombs had stopped, I could see him running across the grass to what still remained of the school gate and I could see that his clothes were on fire and that the boy was burning. Even from where we were I could see that he held something white in his arms and I knew at once that it was important to know what it was. What can be so important for a boy to refuse to drop when he is burning. It is this that makes me wake up some nights and find that I am crying out to drop it and I find my arms are striking out and I am trying to put out the flames with my hands.

The street outside the school was wide and there was no one in it, and so it was easy to follow the boy. It was impossible not to follow the boy. The street was steep, but instead of running down it he began to run up the street, and so I know that he must have been trying to reach his home and whoever took care of him there. He didn't run far. After a few steps he went down to his knees and he seemed to stay that way for a long time, although it was probably a very short time, I hope only a moment, before he fell, face forward, onto the stones of the street; and as he did, the white thing that he was holding was freed and it began to roll and then to bounce its way back down the steepness of the street. It was his soccer ball, and it continued to bounce and roll away from him long after the boy had stopped burning and we had begun to pull up from the city to avoid the pillar of fire and smoke that was rising from it. But I could still see that white ball burning in my own eye, the way the sun will burn there for minutes after you have looked at it, and then even that ceased and we had banked up and away from there and were headed back for Africa.

83

"That concludes the program for the afternoon," Captain Rampey said.

The shadow of the plane was leaping over the green fields, and behind us the city was burning like a crown set afire.

"I will tell you one thing," Marvell said. "We did us a job of work."

Those were the last words that I remember hearing on the *Odessa Darling*. I have no recollection beyond that, but I must have done all the things that must be done to cut oneself loose from an airplane, as complicated as cutting the umbilical cord that ties the baby to its mother. I have no recollection at all of stepping out through the bomb bay doors or of pulling the rip cord on my parachute because at that moment I had no desire to do it. My first recollection is of dropping down onto Italy, the rays of the late afternoon sun glowing in the white nylon of my canopy as if I were hung to a silken lantern, and it must have been this that caused me to glitter in Santa Vittoria, far to the south of me then, like a star or an omen in the evening.

I was happy at that time, sometimes it seems to me like the happiest moment of my life and I don't know why. At other times I see it as the saddest, because it cut me loose from myself, perhaps forever. I dropped out of the sun into the shadow of the mountains to the north of me, and it was cold, and the gold of the canopy turned to a whitish blue, and then I struck the terraced side of a mountain that was no longer farmed. The earth was hard, the earth was clay and rocks, and when I hit it I heard a bone snap in my leg and a little later I felt it. The cooling air of the late afternoon caught in my canopy and I began to be dragged down and across the old terraces until I finally became caught in some old vines and was held there by them. I pulled the parachute around me and made a nest for myself as a wounded animal would do.

Later, in the night, I was wakened by some small dark men who smelled of manure and wine. They said nothing to me. They lifted me up and put me in a large basket that stank of earth and manure and grape mold and they put the basket on the back of a mule and took me back up the mountain I had landed on. I thought they were going to kill me, and I didn't care then. I was in great pain. I was now a deserter. I was alone. Of all the Americans I knew I had for some reason declared my personal end to the war and I was ashamed of myself. Who was I, to have attempted such a thing? The arrogance of my act overwhelmed me and I would close my eyes and soon as I did I would see the burning boy. As I look back on it now, there was very little reason to wonder why I wanted to die.

They kept me in a little hut made of branches and twigs and straw, out in the middle of a field. I have no idea for how long. They fed me some kind of white runny goat cheese and hard bread and bitter olives and wine, and if it hadn't been for the wine I think I would have starved to death. One night they came and got me and put me in the basket again and toward morning, when I could stand it no longer, I heard the clop of the mule's hoofs on stone, and looking up from the basket I could see the roofs of houses and I knew I was in some sort of town. They dumped me here then, in the shredded old grape basket, in the Piazza of the People at the door of the Leaders' Mansion. Italo Bombolini was mayor of the city, as I was to learn, and he had already been mayor for several weeks by then and perhaps for longer.

From *The Discourses* of Italo Bombolini.

> The duty of the people is to tend to their own affairs.
> The duty of government is to help them do it.
> This is the pasta of politics
>
> The inspired leader, the true prince, no matter
> how great, can only be sauce upon the pasta.
>
> —Bombolini

Two weeks after Italo Bombolini had taken over as mayor of Santa Vittoria, everyone—with the exception of the priest Polenta, who despised him, and the cobbler Babbaluche, who wasn't prepared to see him as he was—recognized one thing about him. Bombolini was a leader; he was a born leader, he was a natural leader. He was, at times, an inspired leader. He was, in his own words, "sauce upon the pasta."

His leadership was so natural and he seized power with such grace that people who only several weeks before could not say his name without first prefacing it with "boob" or "fool" began to realize they had seen these traits of leadership in Bombolini all along.

"Do you remember the time he kept Giovanetti from killing his wife by talking to him and getting the pick out of his hand? I said to myself right then 'He may *look* like a clown, but here is the soul of the leader,' I said. I can say this much: I was one of the first to recognize it."

Everyone had his own way of discovering Bombolini. In the end even Babbaluche was forced to admit that the wine seller possessed certain qualities that were surprising at least.

"But they won't last," the cobbler would say. "He's running on nerve and luck alone. You watch. Somewhere inside that fat bastard a clown lives, and sooner or later the clown will come out, because a clown is a clown and will always be a clown."

There were others, some of the old men who no longer believed in anything on earth except hunger and work and finally death. "He'll stop running," they said—there is a saying here: An ass's trot doesn't last long—but when Bombolini continued to run even the old men began to turn on Babbaluche.

"The ass is still running," one of them shouted at the cobbler. "Maybe this ass is a horse."

"An ass is an ass and will always act like an ass," Babbaluche said. "You wait. You'll see his long ears soon enough."

* * *

From his first day Bombolini seemed to have a feeling for the correct thing to do. The day after Vittorini had handed him the mayor's medallion a group of citizens went across the piazza to the Leaders' Mansion to ask Bombolini to surrender the office and put someone in it who wouldn't ruin the city.

"All right, Italo," they wanted to say to him, in all kindness, "the fun is over now; we've all had our good laugh. Now let's settle down and get ourselves a leader."

But they didn't find Bombolini home that day. They couldn't find him any place. When they finally went down to the terraces to tend their grapes Bombolini came out of hiding to tend to the town.

He had the streets swept. He had the fountain repaired and the water-catch cleaned of all its mold and moss and all the old glass and potato peelings that washed around in it cleaned out and thrown away. The third morning, the people woke up and found

that all the old slogans in Santa Vittoria had been changed in the
night. The one in the Piazza of the People that read

BELIEVE   OBEY   FIGHT

had been changed to

TRANQUILLITY   CALMNESS   PATIENCE
The three great virtues of the Italian people
A public service
(Signed) Italo Bombolini, Mayor

On the old fallen wall of the Chapel of the Bountiful Grapes the
old Fascist party slogan "I Don't Give a Damn" now read

WE CARE

In High Town where for years the sign had read

LIVE DANGEROUSLY
—D'Annunzio

Bombolini had added:

BUT DRIVE CAREFULLY
—Bombolini

Although there were no cars in Santa Vittoria then, it gave the
people a feeling of belonging with the times.

As you went down the Corso Mussolini it had been impossible
to avoid the sign on the wall of the house where the Corso curves
down to the left:

BETTER TO LIVE ONE DAY AS A LION
THAN 100 YEARS AS A LAMB

Today when you go down the Corso you read

BETTER TO LIVE
100 YEARS
—Bombolini, Mayor

After the third day, the group of men who had wanted Bombolini's resignation no longer tried to see him, and he began to show
himself in the streets.

It is impossible now to know whether the things the wine seller did came to him from study and thought, or whether they were the reactions of instinct. It doesn't really matter. The important point is that he did them.

The trouble with government in this country is that it is composed of the Ins and the Outs. There are blacks and whites, but no grays here. When the Outs get in, they kick all the Ins out, and the new Outs do everything in their power to destroy the programs of the Ins, even when they might help them. It is brutal and sometimes bloody and almost always exciting and usually no good for the town, but that is the way it always has been.

Bombolini's genius, for that is what it must be seen as now, was that instead of throwing people out he invited everyone in. He formed the Grand Council of the Free City of Santa Vittoria and in two days every faction that could be counted upon to be fighting one another, every family and every force in the city, had a member in the government. Everyone was an In or had a member of the family who was an In. Membership in the Council was almost evenly divided among Frogs and Turtles and Goats. Half of the members were young, and half of them were old, and every one of the large or powerful families was represented. The real secret was, perhaps, that if not everyone was In because that was not possible, almost no one was Out.

Giovanni Pietrosanto was made Minister of Public Waters, which meant that he was in charge of the fountain and the water tower. Under Giovanni's direction the spillways were cleared and the pump was put back in working order by Longo, and all the drains on the terraces were cleared and patched, and for the first time in twenty years there was water on the terraces for the grapevines. It isn't a great deal of water, but it is enough to keep a dry spell from becoming a drought, something that Someone greater than Bombolini had not seen fit to do.

Under his brother Pietro, the other powerful member of the family, the organization called Minute Men of Santa Vittoria was formed.

"Why do you want to waste your time on this?" Fabio asked Bombolini.

The mayor held up his hand. " 'The chief foundations of all

states are good laws and good arms.' I have no say in the matter. The Master says we must have an army."

At the start people laughed at the army, but as they drilled in the Piazza of the People after work and the twenty men got better at their drill, the people began to turn out to watch them. Pietrosanto has a voice that can break windows, and the drill was impressive. Every soldier was allowed to wear a red arm band on Sunday and to sport a hawk's feather in his hat, and soon every young man in Santa Vittoria was hungry for a feather, but the army was held to twenty because that was the number of weapons we had.

There were others. Commissioner of Sanitation, Master of the Scales, Minister for Bread and Pasta, Minister for Advanced Education, Minister for Affairs of the Aged.

He closed the second meeting of the Grand Council with these words. "A wise man once said, 'The first impression one gets of a new ruler and his brains is from seeing the men he has chosen to have around him.' " He put down his hand. "Men of Santa Vittoria. By these standards I submit that I must be judged a genius."

At first they felt that Bombolini was being egotistical, but as they went home and the words rolled around in their heads and they began to see what they meant, they were, of course, flattered. And as Bombolini had told Fabio, if you can't buy your way by money the next best way is to buy your way with flattery, because as every Italian knows, flattery will always get you somewhere.

There were mistakes. One morning Bombolini decided to please the people by bringing democracy to the water fountain. For several hundred years, for reasons no longer known, several families had had the right to go to the head of the line waiting for water at the fountain and to fill their jugs first. One morning the women found this sign on the fountain.

In The Eyes of God There Are No Preferred People.
First Come, First Served.

Order of Bombolini, Mayor

The proclamations were now signed with one initial only in the manner of the Caesars. The experiment in democracy went well until Rosa Bombolini came across the piazza with her seven-gallon aluminum jug, modern and progressive, the only one of its kind in Santa Vittoria, and went to the head of the line as was her privilege. Pietro Pietrosanto, as head of the army, was in charge of the new policy that morning.

"Back," he told her. "To the end of the line. You know the order."

"I know my rights," she shouted. She pushed against Pietrosanto with her large and powerful chest. "You go tell him this. Tell him that no fat-ass Sicilian ragpicker is going to come up here and rob the rights of any Casamassima."

"There is nothing to do," Bombolini told his general, "but to seize the offender's water jug."

A seven-gallon water jug is a true weapon, especially when it is used unexpectedly. The head of the army went down in the Piazza of the People exactly like a bull struck with a sledge hammer. Pietrosanto might have pressed charges. They might have taken her down the mountain to Montefalcone on the charge of intent to kill, but Pietrosanto's pride would not bear it and Bombolini was not yet ready for such a challenge to his young regime. The next morning the sign was down and the old ways were restored, and this was the death of pure democracy in Santa Vittoria. That night Bombolini had Fabio copy in his book: "There is nothing more difficult to carry out and more doubtful of success than to initiate a new order of things. For the reformer has enemies in all those who prosper by the old order." He was training Fabio to become mayor of the city when he would no longer be available.

This, then, was the way things were going in Santa Vittoria for Italo Bombolini. The people had trust in him, and then as the summer went on the harvest began to look rich and strong. The grapes were plentiful and they were fat; they had the look of healthy animals. When the grapes are good, things in Santa Vittoria are good.

If the failure of democracy at the fountain was his first error out of all the things that he did, I suppose it can be said that I was his second major error, since it was I who almost brought down his government. I came to Santa Vittoria the same morning that he was forced to take down his sign at the fountain.

91

THIS MUCH should be said at once. Although Fabio della Romagna, for a time at least, later came to hate me, if it hadn't been for Fabio I would have died. The first people to find me in Santa Vittoria that morning assumed that I was dead. One of them felt my legs and when he felt their coldness, since the blood had run out of them hours before, he took my shoes. When they sent news of the body to Bombolini he agreed with the people that it should be taken at once, before the sun was fully up, and buried some place in the rock quarry under the stones. Bombolini's fear was that the crime, if that was what it was, would be reported to Montefalcone and then the police would come, and the freedom of the city would be endangered. He woke Fabio, and Fabio came down the steps of the Mansion of the Leaders to see about taking me to the rock quarry, and he took one look at me in the grape basket and knew that I was alive.

They are funny about the dead in Italy. They are fascinated with death, but not with the body that death leaves behind it. Sometimes the people are so anxious to get rid of the body that errors are made. Babbaluche, who made coffins when he was not cobbling, has stories about the men and women who came to life at the sound of earth raining down on the roof of what was to be their last home. The fingernails left behind in the soft wood of the boxes, Babbaluche says, are the monuments to these silent struggles.

Instead of taking me to the quarry, they took me upstairs into the Mansion of the Leaders and put me in a bed. I have no idea of how long I stayed there. Three or four times a day the girl, Angela, came and held my head in her lap and spooned broth and pasta and soft sopping bread into my mouth, and sometimes she poured me a small glass of wine. I had no idea that I ever would get well, nor any hope that I would. I leaned toward death. The bone in my leg had joined together, but it had come together all wrong. I would lie on the bed for hours at a time in darkness and never make a move. When it was light in the piazza, I never knew whether it was because the sun was going down or coming up.

After some time, a week or two weeks, I began to realize that, with no effort on my part or any consciousness of it, I was beginning to understand all the shouting and calling that I heard from downstairs and from the piazza. The language of my father and mother was returning to me. I had learned it as a small boy, but later, although it was spoken in the house, I had unlearned it. I wouldn't speak to my family in anything but English and I wouldn't listen to them unless they spoke to me in what we called American.

I still dreamed at night about the boy, and the fat man or his daughter would have to come and restrain me while I would cry out and pound against the wall and hide beneath my blanket, which would go wet with sweat. But I knew that somewhere I had decided to try and live when one morning the girl was late coming with the broth and I was first hungry and then anxious and finally angry with her. And when she came, surrounded by all

93

her smells, hot broth and good bread and strong soap and the freshness of herself, I found I was smiling.

For some reason I was ashamed of myself for smiling, as if I had no right in the world to smile. I wanted to say good morning to her and to talk with her, but I was afraid to begin. During all of this time I had allowed no one to know that I knew the language. I knew it was a dialect and that my parents must have come from some village in this region, but I didn't even know the name of it. That's the kind of son I had been to them. It made me ashamed, not telling them about the language. I was deceiving people who had risked themselves to aid me. I had had no bad intentions at the beginning, it was only that I was too tired and too uninterested to want to speak, and also it was a simple form of self-defense. The people would talk in front of me the way they talk in front of idiots and the deaf and small children. Only once did I come close to revealing myself.

Bombolini and Fabio were in my room with some young men who wanted to look at me. Everyone in Santa Vittoria came to look at me at one time or another. There is very little to do here, and I was an object of curiosity. They felt my clothes, and some of them even rubbed their hands along my back or arms. I used to wonder which one of them had my shoes. I never have found out. Whoever took them will keep them in the family until I am dead, for fifty years perhaps, and when I am gone they will come out into the open with them, probably at my own funeral. That is the way they are here.

The young men were about to leave, I had bored them, when one of them looked down into the piazza from my window and said, "Oh my God, the Malatestas are back."

They all ran to the window and knelt down by it, since it is a low window and looked down into the piazza. The sound of their voices and the way they sucked in their breaths made me interested.

"It's the tall one," one of them said, "the snotty one. What's her name?"

None of them could remember at first. They all had a nickname for her, the Colt, Long Legs, the Icicle. Bombolini called her "the hawk"

"Caterina," one on them finally said.

"Caterina," everyone said. "Yes. Caterina."

She was crossing the Piazza of the People toward the street that leads down from High Town and because she was wearing city shoes on the cobblestones she didn't walk the way the other women here walk. The women here walk as if they were carrying a burden. It is not unpleasant to watch. They move slowly, with a kind of slow graceful power to the walk, and the motion of their bodies is as much side to side as it is forward. Both were graceful, the women of the city and this Caterina Malatesta, but their graces were of different kinds. This is not meant to demean the women of Santa Vittoria, because some of them are very beautiful, but the difference was that between a work horse and a race horse. Each has its use in the world, and its beauty, but one was meant to be used and worked and one was meant to be admired and to be ridden lightly.

She carried two suitcases and although they appeared to be heavy no one made any effort to help her with them, and she didn't ask for any. The women waiting in line at the fountain all saw her, but they gave no sign that they had seen her. I know little about clothes, but her clothes were of the kind that even a very ignorant person recognizes as the kind that cost money and are what is called high style.

"The Germans must be giving them hell in Rome," Bombolini said.

"They only come back when they're in trouble."

"They must have put her husband in jail. What was his name?" No one knew.

"They must have killed him," someone said, and they all nodded and were silent for a moment.

"Look at the way she walks. Zip zap zip. Like she's saying go screw yourself."

"She's a beast. She cuts the balls off men. She's no good for anything. If you married her you'd have fun in bed and starve to death," they said about her. There is a saying here: What you can't have, abuse. And this is what they were doing, but I didn't know it then.

"But she's very beautiful," I said, in Italian, and not one of them

95

noticed. She was the most beautiful woman I had ever seen.

One morning I awoke and found that it was cool in the room, and when I leaned out of bed and looked across the piazza and over the houses to the mountains beyond I could see that they were covered with snow. Sometime in the night, unseen and unheard by us, a great storm, a battle between the heat of the south and the cold of the north, had been waged up there, and now in the morning rivers of white flowed down the mountainside. When Angela came in with the broth I said, "If you go to my window you'll see something beautiful."

She put down the broth and went to the window and crouched down by it and that moment she looked very beautiful to me. I had not noticed that she also was beautiful in the way of simple things.

"I don't see anything," she said.

"On the mountains. There's snow this morning."

"Ah, the new wind." She turned back to me. "The new wind has blown summer away. It's good for the grapes." She spoke to me in dialect and was not at all surprised that I could answer her back or understand her. "Cool nights now and warm days," she said. "It brings out the sugar in the grapes."

"Aren't you surprised at my talking?" I asked.

"We were wondering when you would begin to talk," she said. "After all, you've been here for weeks."

"But I talk rather well, don't you think?"

She shrugged. "Little babies can speak at two years of age. You're a man."

However, she went downstairs and told them that I was now talking and while there was no surprise about the miracle of my tongue there was interest and even excitement, because now they could do business with me. Bombolini, followed by some other members of the Grand Council, came running up the stairs to my room.

"They say you talk very well," he said to me. "Good." He seized my hand and pumped it violently. He turned to the others. "What did I tell you? What did I say about him?" He shook my hand again so violently that it caused my leg to ache. "This is a very superior person. This is someone very special. We are in the presence of a superior human being."

He squeezed my hand and he went downstairs without ever hearing me say a word in dialect or in Italian.

Of all the people that I could hear downstairs only Fabio did not seem to be impressed by my language.

"It's a kind of trick really," he told people. He told anyone who would listen about an idiot they hired at the Academy to clean chamber pots who had learned German in one month.

"You see," Fabio told them, "the ability to learn languages in this way is in some cases actually a sign of idiocy."

No one understood what Fabio was trying to tell them, and neither did I then.

"Why do you keep telling us this?" Bombolini asked him. "You sound as if you have something against the man."

"I have nothing against him," Fabio said. "I only want to correct the record, to put things in the proper perspective. Learning a language this way is no sign of intelligence."

"But that's just it," Bombolini said. "I expected him to learn the language. You can see he's brilliant. It sticks out all over him."

What despair I caused Fabio in those days, and I should have known it.

Although the mayor had not stayed to listen to me speak on the first day, nothing could seem to stop him from coming back on the days that followed and I became sorry I had ever opened my mouth in the first place. He came in the afternoons when I was asleep and at night, and he stayed until I fell asleep in his face, asking me questions about how they did things in America, about the government and the setup of the states and the ruling of towns and the conduct of the police and the courts and the making of laws and the collecting of revenues—until I came to dread the sound of his step on the stairs. More than the intrusion and the effort involved was my shame at my ignorance.

"I don't know about that," I would say. "I can't answer that. I never studied it, I never found out about it."

"It's a wise man who can say 'I don't know,'" Bombolini would say. "Good man."

I would turn my head toward the wall in embarrassment.

"It is only the wise ones who know the extent of their knowledge."

The few answers I was able to give him he speared the way a beggar spears chunks of meat in his soup. He fished them out before they could get away from him and then he rolled them around in his mouth, savoring them, before finally swallowing them.

"Brilliant," he would say. "These are brilliant things you tell me."

It came so that I couldn't bear the sight of Fabio's face at such times. It was Fabio, however, who was finally able to figure out why Bombolini acted that way toward me. He had already figured out the reason for Bombolini's amazing success at government that had changed him from a clown to a prince in one night. What Fabio found was that Bombolini was no longer Bombolini at all but someone else who had lived five hundred years before him. When faced with any problem or any decision, Bombolini would not become alarmed by it but would go back to *The Prince* and *The Discourses* and have Niccolò Machiavelli provide him with the proper answer. It was from these books and this man that he drew his wisdom and his assurance and his poise and his strength. Bombolini was only a face and a body and a mouth for The Master. All of the answers weren't in the books, of course, but the important thing was that Bombolini felt they were and, believing that, he had no fear and suffered no qualms.

But somewhere along the line there were problems that even The Master couldn't provide answers for, and it was for this reason, and for no love of me, that Bombolini turned out to be such a formidable fighter in my behalf when the affair of Babbaluche the cobbler and Abruzzi the American threatened to tear the Free City of Santa Vittoria apart and bring down its government.

Life has changed little here since the days when Machiavelli went sourly through the streets of Florence, and yet some things have changed and it was these gaps in the Master's knowledge that frightened Bombolini. To close them he needed a representative of the New Ways, someone forged in the fire of the New

Culture, as Fabio says he put it. And who better than me, a dropper-in from the New World? For the purposes of Italo Bombolini, for his well-being and his assurance, it was essential that I prove to be brilliant and he made certain that I was. As soon as I was able to stand with the aid of a crutch the cobbler had made for me I was invited downstairs to sit in on sessions of the government and after a week I was invited to join the Grand Council as a full member, as a minister without portfolio, to advise on current affairs. I used to wonder what they would think in Benjamin Franklin High School, which I left when I was a junior, if they could see me sitting in the Grand Council as Minister Without Portfolio.

This was the state of things when Babbaluche came up onto the terrace of the Mansion of the Leaders one night during a meeting of the Grand Council and came into the middle of the meeting and began pointing his finger at me.

"Look at this son of a bitch," he said. "Feast your eyes on him."

They looked at me and I think I blushed, because I had always felt like a fraud at the meetings in the first place. I felt naked before them.

"Because of this son of a bitch each one of you stands to go to jail and to lose your vines."

It was the loss of the vines that struck fear in their hearts.

"Do you know who this bastard is? Do you know what he represents?"

I felt they had discovered that I had been a deserter, and I looked down, which didn't help my image before the people.

"This son of a bitch is an enemy of the state."

"He seemed like a good man to me," Giovanni Pietrosanto said. "That's all that I know."

"An enemy of the state."

The argument was that, despite the fall of the Mussolini government and the emergence of the Badoglio government, America was still at war with Italy, and by making me a member of the Grand Council each member was guilty of treason and infamous acts by collaborating with the enemy.

"You are collaborators," Babbaluche told them. "Do you know what they do to collaborators?"

Everyone knew what they did. They took away your home and they impounded your land and they tore up your vines by the roots.

"And even worse, you are guilty of consorting."

No one knew the penalty for consorting, but if that was worse than collaborating, no one needed to know. It would have been understandable for Bombolini to have deserted me then, and I have no doubt that he would have done so if his need for me had not been greater than the risk of being caught consorting. He could have put me in a cart and taken me to Montefalcone and turned me over to the authorities. It would have ended his troubles and even earned him some small favors, but he fought for me. They sent me from the room and I soon fell asleep, so I never heard the debate. The debate raged on during the night, and I understand that it was bitter, because no one has ever volunteered to tell me anything about it. Sometime early in the morning it finally became a question of confidence in the government and its leader. The issue was whether to turn me over and be safe or to keep me and run the risk of losing their vines and even their lives. Who could have trust in a government that had any doubt about which course to take? At dawn Babbaluche rose and began to read from a paper on which he had been writing.

Resolved, That the people of the glorious Free City of Santa Vittoria, having lost all confidence in the ability of the leader Bombolini any longer to lead . . .

They voted after this and no one has ever told me the count, so it must have been close. No one likes to tell me how close they came to putting me in the cart and taking me to Montefalcone. But whatever the count was, Italo Bombolini managed to do what Benito Mussolini failed to manage.

I have heard that there was not much honor in the victory. All kinds of things were promised in return for all kinds of votes. I have heard, for example, that I was described as a rich young man who might come back someday and in thankfulness endow the city with such things as schools and fire departments. But perhaps that isn't true; to this day I don't know. None of it has ever bothered Bombolini, because he had done the one thing all Italians learn to do above all other things: he had endured.

Why did Babbaluche bring the charge, he who hated the Germans and the Fascists above all the rest of us? It was, as Vittorini later told me, a curse of the nation and a curse of the blood. It is in Babbaluche's nature to embarrass and destroy governments. The nation is filled with people like him. In this way they find their dignity. It is their only business and their only true passion.

"They are the flies in the soup of state," Vittorini told me. "They are not very large but they must be taken out or they will ruin the entire bowl of soup."

For show they put me under house arrest and they sent notice of my presence to Montefalcone by way of Fungo, an idiot here, who would make certain to lose the message and lie that he had delivered it to the *carabinieri*. They took away my membership in the Grand Council and I became an ex-minister without anything.

There was never a serious challenge to Bombolini after that. I was his low mark but he had survived, and in surviving he strengthened himself. That next day, in a show of strength, he had himself named Captain of the People instead of Mayor, an old and honored title in this region, and after a time even Babbaluche came to call him Captain.

The Discourses of Italo Bombolini

Anyone can be great with money.
With money greatness is not a talent but an obligation.
The trick is to be great without money.

—ITALO BOMBOLINI

Anyone can make an omelet with eggs.
It takes a great man to make one with none.

—A saying of Santa Vittoria

THOSE MONTHS, the summer in Santa Vittoria, were good. There was hunger in Italy but there was no hunger here. There were shortages in everything but there was no true hunger. There was still good wine to trade and sell. Most of the wine here is vermouth, which is a blend of wines and aromatic herbs, and the vermouth we make is good. It is not boasting to say this or lying to say it. This is a history and it is a simple and recognized fact that the wine made in Santa Vittoria is one of the best in the world.

The vermouth is aged for a year or even two years, depending on the amount of sugar in the grapes and the amount of acid, on the time of month the grapes were picked, the position of the moon during the harvest and the whisperings of the gods of the grape into the ears of Old Vines, who alone here can hear them. Usually most of this wine is sold to the Cinzano family, who sell it all over the world, but because of the war the wine was still in Santa Vittoria. When we needed food three or four carts were loaded with wine from the Cooperative Wine Cellar and sent to Montefalcone, where there was always a market for our wine. The carts would come back up the mountain the next day filled with flour for bread and pasta, with bags of onions and salt and peppers, green peppers and red peppers, with tins of sardines and mackerel from Sicily, with balls of cheese and wheels of cheese, whole carts filled with artichokes, sometimes boxes of cherries and baskets of fruit from the north, dry pork sausage, salami, black olives and green olives, cheap black wine in big wicker baskets, since our own wine is too good to drink every day—one basket of ours for three of theirs—baskets of beans and lentils, and tins and jugs of olive oil to splash on our bread. When the carts came back up the mountain you would not know there was a war on in Italy.

But something was happening in Italy. The feeling could even be felt up on the mountain. There had been a time when two or three trucks in a morning was considered to be traffic on the Montefalcone road, but now the sound of trucks and half-tracks and even tanks could be heard from the River Road all day long and far into the night.

"You should see what's happening in Montefalcone," the men who went to get the food would tell the others. "There are more tanks in there than there are people. There are more Germans than our own people."

We felt it, but it didn't concern us. There was food and the weather was good and the grapes were fattening on the vines like pregnant women. The people in Santa Vittoria looked up at the sky as a source of danger, for the signs of a sudden heavy rain or even a hail storm, more than they looked down at the road to Montefalcone.

If the Italian nation was in danger of coming apart, the city of Santa Vittoria had never felt closer together. And for this, Italo Bombolini must take all of the credit. He had embarked the city on a program for greatness. Beside his bed in the Leaders' Mansion he had hung this sign:

Nothing causes a prince to be so much esteemed as great enterprises and giving proof of prowess.

It keeps the people's minds uncertain and astonished and it keeps them occupied in watching their result.

The mayor's problem, as he put it, was how to conduct great enterprises in a city where people trail oxen with a broom and pan in hopes of getting a free surprise.

How do you uncover greatness in a city so poor that a man will provoke another man into an argument just so that his donkey can be eating the other man's grass while they argue?

How do you give proof of prowess in a place where a man was observed to stand all of one morning waiting for a pear on a private tree to be blown off by a wind and dropped into the street, thereby becoming public property?

How do you accomplish anything at all when the city treasury is so bare that the addition of one coin to the vault would double the contents?

Bombolini began by changing the names of all of the streets. There were public hearings, there were contests among the children and the young and the old of the town, there were votes and re-votes, speeches and arguments, until the city was in a state of civic uproar and excitement.

In the end the Piazza Mussolini became the Piazza Matteotti, named for the first famous victim of the Fascist regime. It was a very popular decision. We were surprised to find after the war that five hundred other Italian towns had done the same thing.

The Corso Mussolini became the Corso Cavour, because it sounded good and every town must have something named after Cavour.

Then came the whole rest of the *Risorgimento*. There is never any problem naming anything as long as the names of the *Risorgimento* are recalled. Streets were named for Mazzini, for Garibaldi, for the Redshirts. One street was even named for Vittorio Emmanuele, and when no one was sure exactly which number was the good Vittorio the number was left off and now stands for any Vittorio Emmanuele you may desire.

104

The Street of D'Annunzio the Poet posed a problem, since no one, not even Fabio, knew of another poet to match D'Annunzio.

"What is the greatest book in Italy?" Bombolini asked Fabio.

"*I Promessi Sposi*," Fabio said.

"Are you sure of that? I have never heard of it."

"There is no question about it."

"Who wrote it then?" Bombolini said, and Fabio turned scarlet. The name escaped him and to save him further embarrassment the street was named Street of the Author of I Promessi Sposi, although the people still called it Goat Alley, as they always had done.

The effort was a great success. It had cost nothing, but had brought the people closer together. Perhaps the only saddened person was Bombolini himself. When the last of the streets and piazzas and lanes was named and there were no more left, Fabio found Bombolini sitting in the darkness of the large room in the Leaders' Mansion, which that morning had been renamed the Palace of the People.

"The people have entertained the vice of ingratitude," he told Fabio. I was coming down the stairs on my crutches.

"Never trust the people about anything," he shouted to me. "They'll show you the fangs of forgetfulness."

It was embarrassing to both of us, and we attempted to look away from the Captain without seeming to look away.

"Look at them out there, walking about, enjoying themselves. Do you know why? Because I carry their burdens for them, that's why. Ingratitude." He slammed the door shut and the room was dark again. "Do you know what ingratitude is? Ingratitude is the crack in the sewer that turns the sweet waters of life into a running shit pot. The sons of bitches." They could hear him pull back a chair and sit at the table. "They didn't even name an *arch* after me." We were glad we couldn't see him, because both of us felt he was beginning to cry.

In the morning it was as if nothing had taken place. He was as bright as the sun. It is said somewhere that the art of art is to make the work seem artless and this is what Captain Bombolini did with Santa Vittoria. With the exception of Fabio and occasionally myself, no one had any idea at all of the work and thought that went into the things that he did and how much of himself was in them.

"Fabio," he said. "Go and get your notebook. You are going to see a man make an omelet without any eggs and I want you to see how it is done."

* * *

It was Fabio who saved my life, and it was Fabio who was responsible for getting Caterina Malatesta to repair the bone in my leg. I didn't understand it at the time, but he wanted my leg made well so that I could go away from Santa Vittoria.

"You're a soldier and a soldier must make every effort to rejoin his own men so that he can continue the fight," Fabio told me. I nodded.

Fabio was not the person he had been before. Even I, a stranger, could notice it. He was moody and then sullen and finally openly angry almost all of the time, and he had begun to drink too much wine. In truth, Fabio was drunk a good deal of the time.

Everyone said it was the books. They begged him to give up the books because clearly his mind had been pushed to the breaking point. We didn't know it then, or for a long time afterward, that it was the sight of Angela Bombolini feeding me broth and the sound of Angela Bombolini talking to me while I stretched out on my bed in the People's Palace that was destroying Fabio before us.

Bombolini himself had gone up to High Town to see the Malatesta, as they called her, and she had laughed in his face. Even after that, as shy as he was, Fabio went to see her, and for reasons we don't know the Malatesta agreed to come and see me. It is a measure of how desperate Fabio must have been.

She was not a doctor in the sense that she had a license to practice in Italy, but she had gone to medical school in Rome until the final year, when her father, to save the family, forced her to leave school and marry a very rich young Roman, of a noble and influential family, who was a rising Fascist and a friend of Count Galeazzo Ciano.

Her family had once been a great family in this region. Once they held large holdings of land, but they began to lose it, plot after plot, in all the ways a family destined for disaster can find to lose its land. They had no love for the land, and worse, no greed for it, and no one can hold onto land around here without it. There are too many who want it too much. At the time of the marriage they were reduced to a few parcels of land and several houses in the region, one of which was in High Town and which various Malatestas retreated to from time to time to lick their wounds. When they would leave they would leave the house an unspeakable mess. The Malatestas didn't seem to know how to live any longer.

No one knew how the marriage came out. There is a picture of the rich husband in the Malatesta house, but it is assumed by all that he died when Mussolini was ousted. The face in the frame is one of those faces that it takes one thousand years of privilege and money to breed.

When she came into my room she never really saw me. She took off the smelly bandages that Dr. Bara had put on the wound, and took them off with no gentleness, and threw them on the floor. I was ashamed of my wound because it stank and I began to apologize for it to her. That is the effect she has on people. She didn't hear me.

"This wound will have to be opened," she told me. "The infection will have to be cleared up and the bone will have to be re-broken and set again."

"If you say that it has to be done."

"It doesn't have to be done. If you want a leg it will have to be done."

"I want a leg."

"It will hurt a great deal."

"It hurts a good deal now."

"It will hurt a *great* deal."

I shrugged and she smiled at me, which confused me.

"You don't know the pain I am talking about. I can't take you to the hospital, you understand."

"I understand that."

"Americans aren't prepared for pain. They think they have a right to avoid pain," she said. "The people here know different. They know that pain is the natural condition of life."

I didn't understand why she was telling me these things. Angela had come into the room and although the Malatesta was conscious that she was there she gave no sign of it until, without looking at her either, she ordered Angela to pick up my filthy bandages."

"Yes, signorina."

"Signora."

"Yes, signora," Angela said, and to my astonishment she made a small curtsy.

"I will come for you when I am ready," the Malatesta told me.

"Can't you give me some idea, to prepare myself?"

"When I'm ready I'll come," she said. "What are you going to do when they come?"

"When who come?"

"The Germans."

"I don't know yet," I told her. "People say they won't come here. I speak the language. Maybe they won't know."

She laughed at me. At the door she turned to Angela, although she still didn't seem to see her.

"You come to my house after you clean up here. I have some work for you," the Malatesta told her.

"Yes, signora." She made a curtsy again.

When the Malatesta was gone I was embarrassed for Angela.

"You wouldn't go up there," I said. "Not after the way she treated you."

It was Angela's turn to be surprised.

"Of course I'll go. We like to go. We charge her three times too much."

"But the way she talked to you."

I could see that Angela didn't understand what I was talking about. I could see what I should have been able to understand myself—how much a luxury pride and honor can be. It helps to be well-fed enough to nourish them both. And I should have been able to understand what they say about the peasant, that he needs two things here—a sharp mind and thick soles. The truth is that no peasant has ever died of a broken heart.

"Oh, yes," Angela said, picking up my bandages. The sight and smell of my own bandages made me turn away. "We milk her well."

The Malatesta was a hawk but if there was a pigeon in the room, I began to understand who it was.

The Malatesta came back several days later, with no warning. She came with some local anesthetic and a bottle of *grappa* with Fabio as a helper, and a half hour after she arrived she cracked the bone in my leg. There was, as she had promised there would be, a moment of "superior" pain (it pleases me to this day to think that she was impressed when I didn't cry out), and she began to reset the bone. During all of that time she never said one word to me to make me feel like a man or even as if she were working on a human being. At the end of it she said, "You lie in bed for one week and then you get up and try and walk. The sooner you walk on this the better it will be for you." She went to the door of the room and turned and looked out the low window into the piazza. "But I doubt that you will do it," she said.

It was this, of course, that sent me stumbling out into the Piazza of the People, my face stiff with pain and running with a cold sweat, exactly one week after the Malatesta had come into the room with her *grappa* and her rubber hammer.

The more I walked the stronger the leg would become. It had withered until it looked like the leg of an old man, and I began to go down through the streets and finally all the way to the wall and the Fat Gate and down onto the terraces.

The people liked me down there. I gave them an excuse to stop their work and talk. I had the strongest feeling that I had been in all of these places before, in the town and on the terraces. I seemed to know everything in advance, and there were no surprises for me. I think now it must have been caused by all the images left in my mind, even when I wasn't listening to them, by the talk of all the people from "the other side," from "the old country," who sat around the table in my mother's kitchen drinking coffee and wine and anisette and telling about the old days and how their children were falling to pieces in America.

In the end I would make it a point to go all the way down the mountain to the foot of the terraces and then to rest in the enormous ancient wine cellar at the base of the mountain before forcing myself to climb up again.

This was one thing that was different. I had never seen anything like the cellar before, and I came to love it for its coolness and quiet. It had been built by the Romans and then sometime in the Middle Ages it had been rebuilt entirely and so it wasn't the goal for tourists that it might otherwise have been. It had finally been abandoned in the eighteenth century.

There were two cellars actually, and one day this was to mean a great deal to Santa Vittoria. There was a small opening in the mountainside which led into an enormous room, hollowed out of the mountain itself, which was called the Great Room. It was as large as the inside of a cathedral, and I have no idea why they ever built such a room, unless in Roman times it had been used as a temple to some god of wine. From the back wall of the Great Room two long, deep wine cellars were cut into the bowels of the mountain. I didn't go into the cellars themselves, because they were humid and I could sense that they were filled with water, but the Great Room was cool by the entrance and I would lie on the dry sand and take a nap before going back up.

I soon found that I was the only person in Santa Vittoria who ever went into the old wine cellar. They were afraid of the spirits who lived in there. Everyone in Santa Vittoria has some story about some member of his family who strayed into the tunnel in a sudden storm and the terrible things that happened to them in there. They feared for my life, but when nothing happened to me it didn't lessen their belief in the evil spirits but only convinced them that Italian spirits and ghosts were not interested in non-Italian people.

During the week that I had spent in bed before walking I had worked on the radio of Vittorini, the mail clerk. They had brought it to me to fix because I was an American and Americans are supposed to be able to fix new inventions such as radios. I knew nothing about radios, but there is a certain logic about anything that is broken. Sooner or later there has to be something that isn't connected, and if it can be connected, as with my leg, then perhaps it may be made to work again. I finally got it to work. In those days we received an hour of electricity a day from the power station at San Rocco del Lago. Some days it never came at all.

But on one day when it did come I heard a broadcast from Egypt that was sent to Italy by the English. The Americans, they said, were almost all the way across Sicily and the invasion of the mainland was to be expected any day. I grew very excited about that, and I shouted out the news before I realized that the last thing I wished then was to be liberated. But it didn't matter in any case. Fabio had no interest, and Bombolini, even though he was from Sicily, listened to me without really understanding the words. He was far too interested in cooking his eggless omelet.

THE OMELET Bombolini was preparing was intended to feed the entire city, and he succeeded in doing it. He gave the people great enterprises and proofs of prowess, and he kept the people's minds astonished and occupied in watching their result at a cost of nothing.

The patron saint of this place is not Santa Vittoria, as you would have a right to expect. No one even knows who Santa Vittoria is, although it is thought that she is a corruption of some earlier pagan god who had to do with the wine. But the patron saint here, as our luck would have it, does not deal with the grape and has no special power or prayers to pressure God and make Him look after the vines or the rains or the condition of the soil. The patron saint here is Santa Maria of the Burning Oven, a local peasant girl who did the kinds of things that saints do to get themselves canonized and who was then thrust upon this city.

For example, once a baker here, while pulling out his loaves, fell headlong into his ovens. His screams could be heard all over the city, but there was nothing anyone could do for him except to hope that he didn't ruin the day's bread. But then the little girl Maria walked right into the blazing oven and picked up the baker and carried him into the street. Neither suffered a burn, and the bread that night was said to be the best ever baked in the city.

Another time, some pilgrims were passing through the city on their way to Siena. They had been caught in a snowstorm and were starving. There was nothing in the city to feed them—not that many would have parted with their pasta for the pilgrims—except a crust of bread, and they were sure they were going to die.

"You mock us. What good is this crust of bread?" the leader said to Maria.

"Eat of it," the girl told them.

They ate, and as the leader cut into the little crust at each cut a fresh slice of bread leaped onto the blade of the knife. They ate until they were fat with bread. It was said by all to be the best they had ever tasted.

One night the same baker, who must have been excessively clumsy, lost his wooden bread shovel in the oven. When Maria rescued the shovel from the oven it was only a charred crisp.

"How can I work without a bread shovel?" the baker asked.

"Weep not and God will find a way," the girl said.

In the morning the shovel had been restored. New wood had grown where the old wood had been burned, and it is said that green leaves actually sprouted from the handle. Many here believe the shovel was certainly a part of the wood from the True Cross.

Bombolini's plan, as simple as possible, was to turn Santa Vittoria into a national and then an international shrine for all the bakers of the world. Bakers from all over the world, who lacked a saint of their own, would want to come and pay homage to the Little Saint of the Bread Oven, as Bombolini began to call her.

What novice baker would wish to begin a career without first coming to Santa Vittoria and spending a few days, a novena perhaps, nine blessed days on the mountain, praying to God through Santa Maria to favor him so that he might make money in his new career? Old bakers would want to come and give thanks for their success. Bakers who were in trouble and going broke would want to come and get God and Santa Maria on their side for a change.

The idea of Santa Vittoria as a national shrine became a craze here. It was all that anyone talked about.

If a shrine was proclaimed, a road would have to be built up the mountain to accommodate the pilgrims; and if there was a road, there would be taxis and maybe even a bus. The pilgrims would need places to stay and places to eat. Every home was a potential inn, every woman a potential cook, every vine pruner a potential waiter going around in white jackets and soft shoes collecting tips for doing next to nothing. A cooperative bakery turning out bread from the Shrine of Blessed Bread (each loaf personally blessed by Polenta for a fee) could be started, and then there would be a need for curio shops selling such things as little wooden bread shovels and clay ovens and satin pillows with pictures of Santa Maria on them and wooden plaques that read Santa Maria of the Burning Oven, bless this humble bakery. It was felt by some that within ten years' time only a fool would ever have to go down to work on the terraces again.

Most leaders would have stopped there, but Bombolini knew things most leaders never learn. There is a dark side to man that needs a way out as well as the good side. The Master had written. "Hatred is gained as much by good works as by evil." As they say, if there is no acid in the grape the wine is tasteless and finally useless.

"The wise prince," Bombolini told Fabio, with his finger in the air, "must foment some enmity so that by suppressing it he will augment his greatness." It was this that led him to declare war on Scarafaggio and which also led to Fabio's leaving Santa Vittoria.

Scarafaggio! You have only to say the word and you can picture the town. There is no beauty to it. It sits across the valley on the other mountain, a feeble imitation of Santa Vittoria. It huddles over there like a sheep dog whose master beats her; it cowers there, filled with fleas and ticks and roaches. We have bedbugs here, but they only survive here; in Scarafaggio they flourish.

The people of Scarafaggio are known as the greatest fools in Italy, which is no easy title to claim. One example must suffice. Fifty years ago they found that their church was too small and since, of course, no one in the town was capable of enlarging it they were forced to go outside and ask bids for the work. No one would go there, of course, but finally they found a man who said he would *stretch* their church for them, and since his fee was so small they were willing to believe him.

He told everyone to go to bed, that his magic must be done in silence and in secrecy. And then he went in the church and locked the door and sometime in the night he took out the last pew of the church by the back wall and threw it over the wall, down into the bushes. After this he took strong raw soap and he soaped all of the floor along by the back wall where the pew had once stood.

In the morning twenty of the strongest men in Scarafaggio were blindfolded, since the magic must be done in secret, and they were led into the church and placed against the wall, facing it, with their hands on the stones.

"Now *push*," the stranger ordered. *"Push. Push. Push."*

And it was incredible. They pushed and they felt the wall move away from them. They pushed and pushed until the last of them was face down on the ground.

"Now take off your blindfolds."

When they did they could see that it was true. A miracle had been passed. They got up and ran down into the piazza outside the church. A miracle, they cried. The church had been stretched. The back wall was now a full five feet away from the back pew and there was room for another row of pews and more.

The people were pleased with their new church. "You could hardly tell it was stretched," they said.

They were so pleased with the results that they paid the church stretcher exactly half of what they had said they would pay him, which was considerably more than they had planned to pay, and to this day it remains a mystery in Scarafaggio as to how the newer, bigger church with the added pew holds exactly the same number of souls as the old one.

In the first week in September that year Bombolini called a

meeting of all the people in the Piazza of the People on a Sunday, and he asked the people to look out over the valley at Scarafaggio.

"They're laughing at us over there," he told the people. This was astonishing news. "For two hundred years they have been going around, every day, laughing at us."

It was hard to believe. He allowed them a few minutes to study the miserableness heaped up across the valley, and then the bell in our tower rang out.

"Do you hear that?" Captain Bombolini asked them. Everyone nodded, and then he pointed across the valley. "Well so do they." He allowed them to think about this.

"They get up by our bell. They go out by our bell. They go to Mass by our bell." The people were astounded by this. It had never occurred to any of them before.

"*We* pay for the bell and *they* use the sound. While someone here sweats to make it ring they lie in their beds and listen to it sing. They lie in their beds and they laugh."

If the best thing in the world is to get something for nothing it follows that the worst is to give away something and get nothing back for it.

"It is as simple as this," Bombolini told them. "Scarafaggio is stealing our sound."

The people were violent about it. Pietrosanto, for example, was all for calling out the Santa Vittoria army and marching on Scarafaggio. It became a little foolish after that, and everyone today is willing to admit it. But at the moment there seemed nothing foolish about it.

"Take down the bell," someone shouted, and that seemed like a very good solution. "Better no bell than to give away our sound." There was a roar of approval.

"Keep the bell, but cut the rope so no one can ring it," another man shouted. That made even more sense.

To his credit, Bombolini was able to restrain the excited people. He pointed to the new sign at the end of the piazza.

"Remember. The three true virtues of the Italian people. Tranquillity. Calmness. Patience. Restrain yourselves. Your captain has a plan for you. The old wrong will be righted."

So the city was excited after that. The people, as the Master said they should be, were astounded. That Sunday night three men left Santa Vittoria with a mule and a donkey and some of the old Etruscan vases from the room in the Palace of the People that had once served as a museum, and everyone knew it had to do with the Solution. Only Fabio, to whom Bombolini had already told the solution, was unexcited.

"If you go through with this I leave Santa Vittoria," Fabio said. "I resign from the Grand Council. I return to Montefalcone where I belong."

Bombolini was hurt by this, because Fabio, in a way, is the conscience of Santa Vittoria.

"It's an evil thing," Fabio said. "You know it is. It appeals to the people's worst instincts."

"That's not such a bad instinct, Fabio, to want what is yours."

"It's a rotten instinct and you know it."

"You forget one thing, Fabio. The people are the people, yes, but they also are only human beings. They are only Christians, not Christs."

Fabio put on his hat to show that he was leaving.

"You have no right to sell the Etruscan vases. They belong to the people. To all of us."

"No one ever looked at them, you know that. They sat in there covered with dust. You couldn't even carry water in them."

"The vases," Fabio said, with elaborate disgust, "happen to be two thousand years old."

"And what good is a vase if it can't carry water?"

The look of pain on Fabio's face was genuine.

"You hurt me deeply," Bombolini said. "You make me feel like some kind of evil person."

"If they come back up this mountain with that thing, I go," Fabio said, and he left.

It was not known at the time, no one could understand Fabio's ways then, but he wanted an excuse to leave the city other than for his own self, his own broken heart, and he had found it. If anyone should have been able to see it, it was myself; but I was young then and didn't wish to see things like that.

The men who had left Santa Vittoria with the donkey and the mule came back to the city early one evening a few days after they had left. The Etruscan vases were gone, but on the back of the mule was a large package wrapped in old sheets and tied around with grapevine. The people went down into the streets to see them come. They tried to touch the package, but the men pushed them away. Fabio came to see me in my room.

"All right," he told me. "I'm leaving. You can have her now. She is all yours."

I told him I didn't know what he was talking about. In a way I didn't, and yet in a way I knew what he meant.

"You know what I mean," he said. I had never seen him angry in this way before. He was cold and he seemed at once years older than before and years older than myself because he had suffered. If I had fought with Fabio then, it would have been the sort of fight that could not have stopped until one of us was dead or close to death.

"She eats you up with her eyes," he said. "She devours you. She falls all over you."

"I never asked her to."

"Oh, no. You lie there and lead her on, because you Americans don't have manners as we do. You take advantage." He was suddenly very generous toward me. "It's all right. I would do the same thing. Do I hate you for it? I envy you. It's nothing. I was simply born in the wrong place."

I was thankful that it was dark in my room and he couldn't see my face then. I had meant nothing by the little games I played with Angela, although something seemed to take place between us when we played them.

"Why do you think an American wouldn't marry you?" I would say to Angela.

"Oh, Americans don't go for girls like me. They want rich girls."

"It helps. But they like pretty girls, too."

"Then I'm not pretty enough."

"Maybe not," I would say. "Then again. Stand up there by the window and let me see you."

She was so simple and so sweet and of course she would stand by the window.

"Americans want women like the Malatesta."

"Oh, all men want women like the Malatesta. But if you can't

get the Malatesta you have to get someone else. Someone like
. . . someone like . . ." And she would turn scarlet.

I didn't know then that men and women didn't talk to each
other this way in Santa Vittoria unless they were going to be married, or that they didn't talk to each other in the same room or that
many of them never touched one another until the date of their
wedding was announced.

"She never sees me," Fabio said. "She has forgotten my name.
I'll tell you what she has done." He was close to shouting at me by
then. "For two weeks she has failed to bring me my plate of
beans." He went to his own room to pack his things.

* * *

The men with the package unwrapped it that night and did
what work they had to do so that it was ready for Sunday morning. On that morning Fabio della Romagna left the city for
Montefalcone. He did not take his bicycle, because it was dangerous to be on the roads with a bike without a pass from the Germans or without a good reason. The few things he took were in a
small, crude knapsack on his back. He reached the bottom of the
mountain and was crossing the flat fields toward the River Road
that leads to Montefalcone, when some men he knew from Santa
Vittoria came running toward him.

"Fabio," one of them shouted at him. "Fabio, Fabio, Fabio. It's
marvelous. Look."

He turned Fabio around so that he was looking back up the
mountain at the city. Someone on the Fat Wall was waving what
appeared to be Vittorini's flag.

"You see? You understand, Fabio?" the man said to him. "That
means it's ringing and we can't hear a thing."

"Nothing!"

"Not a Goddamn thing," a third man said.

"You should have seen them in Scarafaggio, Fabio. Their jaws
hanging open. 'What happened to the bell?' they ask. 'What's the
matter with the bell?' "

"And not a *sound*, Fabio," the first one said again. "The greatest
moment in the history of the city of Santa Vittoria."

None of them understood when Fabio broke loose and began to

trot and then ran to the River Road. They themselves began to trot toward Santa Vittoria to tell the people that it truly worked and to describe the silence over Scarafaggio.

In the Piazza of the People they didn't wait for the men from Scarafaggio before beginning to celebrate. It was clear from the first ringing of the bell that it was a success.

One of the Pietrosantos, whose back muscles could be seen through the shirt he was wearing, was in the campanile pulling the rope. They heard the old creak as the bell began to swing, but what they heard after that was something they had never heard before. The clapper met the bronze bell and there was a low muffled sound, not the good clear *bong* of before. It was the sound of a bell, but just barely. The people looked at one another and they began to smile and as the muffled sound went on they began to laugh out loud and finally to hit each other on the back while tears began to run down from their eyes.

The first of the runners came up from Old Town and down from High Town. You could hear the bell down there and up there, they reported, but only just barely. The sound ended at the town walls.

It was recognized for what it was, an act of inspiration, even an act of genius. The members of the Grand Council lined up in the piazza to take Captain Bombolini's hand, and soon a good part of the city was in the line. After shaking his hand they went up the steep winding stairs to the top of the bell tower itself to feel the clapper.

Cork! A cork clapper.

There could be no doubt about it. It was an act of inspiration, an act of genius. The Grand Council authorized some young men to go down to the Cooperative Wine Cellar and withdraw two hundred bottles of wine, and the celebration for the cork clapper began.

This much can be put down, not as a guess but as a fact. In all of the history of Santa Vittoria, in a thousand years at least, the people had never been more united or the government in better shape or the leadership in more capable hands.

3 VON PRUM

O<small>N THAT SAME NIGHT</small>, the night of the cork clapper, Captain Sepp von Prum, of the Financial Affairs Division of the Headquarters Staff of the Fifth Panzer Brigade, with headquarters in Montefalcone, was finishing the last of his letters. Every Sunday afternoon and every Sunday evening he devoted to doing his letters. He signed the last of them, and since it was not late he decided to take them down to the Piazza Frossimbone and have them stamped as censored by Colonel Scheer, his commanding officer. He wrote a good letter. He was conscious of that, and unlike a lot of other junior officers he did not mind having the letters censored. When the colonel merely glanced at them and stamped them "censored" he was sometimes disappointed.

He went down the narrow stone stairs of the house in which he was billeted more swiftly than he usually did and it caused him pain, since he was still recovering from wounds he had received the year before. All the men stationed with his unit in Montefalcone had been damaged in some serious fashion in North Africa or in Russia. Despite the pain, he continued to walk swiftly down the street of San Stefano into the piazza. There had been a rumor that the Americans and the English had made a landing somewhere south of Rome that morning and that the Italians not only had withdrawn from the war but were about to declare themselves in a state of war with Germany. At eight o'clock the news would come from the English in Cairo, and he wanted to be with the other officers when Colonel Scheer turned it on.

It is a fortunate thing for us that the letters of Captain von Prum have been preserved in the archives of Santa Vittoria, which actually is nothing more than the battered old gray file cabinet that von Prum was forced to leave behind when he left Santa Vittoria.

It is a fortunate thing that he made and preserved copies of everything he wrote, military records, entries in his diary and log, letters to his brother who was serving on the eastern front in Russia, and even letters to his fiancée, Christina Mollendorf, which were filed under the heading "Love Interest."

From the letters we were able to obtain a picture of the captain that might always have puzzled us here if we had not been able to have them translated and read to us. It doesn't seem out of place to print parts of several of the letters the captain wrote that day.

From the notes to his brother Klaus, we have been able to figure out that during an action along the Dnieper Bend several of Klaus's soldiers broke and ran in the face of Russian tanks, although they later returned to the field of battle. Despite this, the young men were shot, as an example to the others; and the officer who had reported them, Klaus von Prum, was badly shaken by the action.

Dear Father:

Mother writes to ask if I am happy. It can only be German mothers who write to ask if their sons are happy at war.

Actually I am happy. Happy to be alive, happy to still have my leg. I won't be climbing any mountains, but each day the leg grows stronger.

I am writing Klaus as you suggest. I too am worried about him.

As you can see I am now in the Financial Affairs Section, the Jewish Infantry as you used to call it. I am afraid that any chance of earning a medal now rests with Klaus. Actually we have little to do with finances. We spend most of our time cataloguing the assets of the area, and I will let you to guess what for.

You ask how it is here in Montefalcone and I answer you. Pleasant but dirty. If these people could be persuaded to keep their streets clean and their plaster from falling down, it might be called attractive and even beautiful. They seem to have an affinity for falling plaster.

My side job is that of Cultural Relations officer and it has been no easy task. It is no simple assignment to persuade these people that we come as friends and not as conquerors.

The money here comes from wine and I can tell you this much. Under sound German management the gross product of the region could be doubled. But they go on in their own old ways. They have a positive affinity for duplication and waste.

If nothing else, the work improves my Italian. I even speak the dialect now, to the amazement of one and all. When next you see me I will be spikking like a proper wop.

> Respectfully, your son,
> Sepp von Prum
> Captain, Infantry

I suppose by now you have heard of the rescue of Mussolini by the SS pilot or some such story. The fact that he wasn't put to death is so typical of the sentimental and disorganized Eytie. How such a clown ever got in control of the government in the first place is beyond a puzzle, but then history shows that these people have an affinity for clowns.

Darling Christina, ma petite chou:

You ask about the Italian women.

Do you recall last week when I described the inability of these people to plan for the future because they only live for the present?

Well. About their women. This is one case where they are right.

STOP. I can see that pretty face of yours flushing with anger. Let me put it in this fashion. Some of these women are beautiful. And some of them most decidedly seem to have an affinity for blond, light-skinned, blue-eyed men. But then one loses interest in them because there is always this feeling (I am sorry to be crude) that their underwear, if indeed they have any on at all, is not clean. And so one loses interest. Frankly I think their interest in us is just because we might have on clean underwear ourselves.

Do this for me. Put down this letter at once and go to your mirror and then look into it and know this, that little face in that glass, those clear blue eyes and those full lips and that soft white complexion belong to the kind of woman that appeals to me.

You may cease blushing now.

Lovingly,
Sepp von Prum

Klaus:

What kind of nonsense is this you have written home? You have upset your family. Let us try to isolate one thing. You are not young Werther in love, you are an officer in the Army of the Third Reich.

You ask what you should have done and I tell you. You do what you did. You do your duty.

If your commanding officer says they should be shot for the best of all, they are shot. It is as simple as that. You have lost your concept of duty.

Duty is what? Duty is one's responsibility to an idea larger than the self. This cancer of the self! The putting of one's conscience beyond one's duty is the true sickness of our time.

Look at this place. To coddle the self the people have lost the ability to perform the simplest collective actions. They cannot even keep their streets swept, Klaus.

You say you feel "chained" by the Germanic sense of duty. You have an affinity for the overcomplex argument.

Duty does not bind one, it frees one from personal responsibility. Duty liberates action. All kinds of acts become possible.

There is only one question: Does my act help the Fatherland or not? There is nothing complex about it. Duty *sticks out*.

Once you have done your duty you will eat better and sleep better and feel better, because self-doubt will have been put to death. You have always had an affinity for the morbid, and the time has come for it to cease.

Get on with your soldiering and do your duty and take care of yourself.

Your brother,
Sepp

A memorandum to a superior officer in the Cultural Affairs Section in Munich:

Your idea for the posters was a limited success. The people desecrated them. What they did was childish, of course, but it was also clever, in the manner of bright children everywhere.

You will recall the first poster, the one of the tall blond smiling German soldier holding out his hand and saying "Remember, the German soldier is your friend."

Someone here has gone about painting the hand red and dripping with blood.

All of them had to be taken down.

The second shows a German officer in dress uniform stopping by the side of a road to go to the aid of an Italian street urchin who has been hurt, although clearly his uniform will be ruined by the Samaritan act.

There are no words on this one, as you recall, because the picture tells the story. Someone has gone about writing on them: "Yes, but why did you hit him in the first place?"

We took those down also.

I think our basic error is that we have been attempting to treat these people as mature responsible beings, when our approach should have been to treat them as they actually are, that is, overage children.

The last paper is a memorandum to himself, under the title "Some Thoughts on the Italian Character."

In General: Italians act from emotion, not reason, in the manner of children.

Conclusion: Treat them as such.

Specific: Germans have a sense of cultural inferiority toward Latins. They appear quick and clever, whereas we seem dull and stolid.

Answer: Cause is not cultural superiority, but a lack of any values or beliefs. Since the Nordic functions from a firm set of values he is limited in the breadth of his movement, but not in *depth*.

Example: The German has an affinity for truth; the nation is a reservoir of truth.

When a German says he will be some place at six he will be there. No Italian will ever be at the appointed place on time, because he does not intend to be there. He will come late, but he *will* have a remarkable lie to tell as to why he failed to arrive on time. All Italians have an affinity for the lie.

Over-all conclusion: It is a mistake, then, to treat children as one would treat adults.

Persuasion and logic are a waste of time. During the occupation the leader must conduct himself as a father—stern but understanding. As the father, one can take advantage of the German virtues, of organization, of planning, of moral and physical strength.

As such, force, the usual method, is not needed except as a potential threat, such as the whip in the woodshed. We should rule by respect, as any father is respected by a child.

Such a policy should release thousands and thousands of men for active duty now tied down in occupation police duties. Police are not needed for errant children, fathers are needed.

Discuss these thoughts with Colonel Scheer.

The captain was disappointed when Colonel Scheer stamped his letter to Klaus as "Approved," without so much as glancing at it. It was the kind of letter a junior officer might wish his senior officer to see.

"And now, shall we tune in Radio Cairo? Just to see what lies they are telling, of course," the colonel said.

It was a standing joke, since it was accepted by all of them that the English provided the most reliable source of news. When the radio began to operate, officers from other rooms began to gather in the doorway.

The rumors had been correct. Landings had been made by the English and the Americans in a place called Salerno, south of Rome and Naples. The Italians had declared themselves out of the war and would soon, in a matter of hours, come in again on the side of the Allies.

"Oh, God, what good news," the colonel said. "No longer do we have to lose men saving the wops."

When the broadcast was finished the colonel turned off the radio and faced the officers in the room and at the doorway.

"There have been no official orders as yet, but you know what this means. As of this moment, Plan A is in effect. Unless I am seriously wrong, Operation Clutch will commence in a day or two."

Plan A was a full combat alert, in which the Italians would be treated like the people in any occupied territory, as the enemy and a source of potential danger. Operation Clutch was the formal plan designed to occupy Montefalcone and the rest of the outlying area.

Captain von Prum left the headquarters and went back to the building in which his men were billeted. He went up one flight of stairs and looked into a large cluttered room.

"We don't need formality," he said. But the soldiers were startled by the presence of an officer in their quarters and they got to their feet in confusion.

"Come to attention," Sergeant Traub shouted at them, and all of them, even the naked soldier, came to attention and remained that way until von Prum released them.

Along one wall of the room were buckets of glue and brushes and rolls of posters, this one showing a German soldier helping an old Italian woman across a busy street. The captain pointed to them. "You won't need those any longer," he said. "We are at war with Italy."

Some of the soldiers smiled, and some waited to see what the proper action was supposed to be. The captain took this chance to examine his detachment. It was the first time he had seen them all together, and it was not a reassuring sight. There were only eight of them, and all had been seriously wounded and were now on limited duty. The senior of them, Sergeant Gottfried Traub, had been hit in the face by shell fragments, and the muscles had been severed, so that the captain found it impossible to know what the sergeant was thinking from his expression. He had reached one conclusion, which was that the sergeant appeared happier when he wasn't smiling at which time his face became distorted.

"We're all going to become soldiers again. No more glue pots," the captain said. Once again the men didn't know how to take the news.

He took out the map of this section of Italy. It was so typical and correct, von Prum thought, that the only reliable map of the whole area had been sent to him by his father from Mannheim.

"You will note," he said, "a good German map and so we are safe. At least we will be sure to wind up in the town we have been sent to take."

His slender finger touched the city of Montefalcone. "We are here." The soldiers, who were timid about doing it at first, began to gather around the map. "We eventually will be *here*." He began to move his finger down the line from Montefalcone and out to the Mad River and along the red line on the map which marked the River Road. It was dark by then, and the noise of tanks and half-tracks from the streets and piazzas outside was so loud that he had to shout to make himself heard. They were wasting no time.

"It's on the mountain, as you can see."

The soldier who had been naked, Corporal Heinsick, had put on clothes and was leaning over the map. His thick, stubby finger touched the city and then crossed the map to the road.

"There's no line to it. There's no road."

"There's a road. It is a track, really. For oxen and carts. Our equipment will be equal to it. Are there other questions?"

The soldiers were silent because they were not accustomed to asking their officers questions. It bothered some of them and made them nervous. But one thing had been troubling them from the beginning and they looked at Sergeant Traub, and so he finally said it.

"Sir? There seem to be only eight of us, not counting yourself."

"That is correct."

Again there was an embarrassed silence and the man kept looking at Traub.

"Captain Pfalz has fifty in his command. They feel they need fifty to take and hold their town, sir."

"We need only eight."

They knew that it was the end to the questions, and they made a show of gathering around the map again to exhibit interest. Traub touched the name on the map.

"Sanda Viddoria," he said.

"Yes. Santa Vittoria," the captain said.

"Ah, yes. Sanda Viddoria," the sergeant said.

LONG BEFORE Fabio reached Montefalcone it had grown dark. Walking the River Road in the dark is hard, but the darkness had brought the traffic out, hundreds of cars and trucks and half-tracks moving by the little light of hooded parking lights, all heading south and he could see by them. He was forced to the side of the road, but he could see. A few soldiers riding the trucks shouted at him and made gestures at him and one or two actually aimed their rifles at him, but Fabio failed to respond. He was no fun for them.

At the gate into the city, still guarded by an Italian and a German, Fabio felt they would arrest him, but he didn't really care about that.

"You're not going to learn much at the academy," the Italian guard told him. "It's closed."

He only shrugged and they passed him through.

"Make Goddamn sure you check in with the prefect of police in the morning," the guard told him, and Fabio gave no sign of even having heard. Every foot of the city seemed to be filled with trucks and armored vehicles, pressed up alongside the walls of the houses for protection, some of them with men in them, sleeping under camouflage nets. A few of them said things to Fabio in German, but he didn't really hear them. He went to the *pensione* where he had shared a room with two other students, and he found that Germans were in it.

"What the hell do you think you're doing here?" the woman who ran the house shouted at him. "Don't you know about the curfew? Don't you know what's going on. You better get off the streets and out of here and stay out."

"What happened to my books?"

"They burned them. They used them to heat food. Page by page."

"Couldn't you stop them?"

She laughed at him. "Then they would have used my furniture. I told them to do it. You read too many books anyway."

He didn't know where he was going. He decided to try to reach the house of Galbiati, an instructor he had been fond of and who had been fond of him. He went down the Corso directly into the Piazza Frossimbone. Soldiers sitting in the darkness of doorways said things to him, but he walked on at his own pace. It is hard to frighten anyone who has no more use for life. At one side of the piazza a large sign had been put up and it was lit by a light that was shielded from the sky. A group of German officers and non-coms were gathered about the sign discussing what it said and taking notes and Fabio walked across to it.

The sign was a large, carefully drawn map of the Montefalcone region and on it, broken down into ten areas and twenty subareas, were the names of all the towns and villages that would be occupied within the next several days. The information included the names of the occupying units, the day they would take the town and the hour in which they would arrive. Fabio, even in the condition he was in, could appreciate the thoroughness of the work.

San Pietro would be occupied tomorrow morning. Garafano Maggiori tomorrow afternoon, San Rocco del Lago the next evening. Santa Vittoria and Scarafaggio were listed as being in Area R, Subareas 5 and 6. The Germans would come on Wednesday, at 1700 hours.

Three days. Not quite three days. At five o'clock in the afternoon. The bad time. How often things seemed to happen at the bad time, the seventeenth hour, Fabio thought.

"It's enough time for them," Fabio told himself. He wasn't sure if he said the words aloud. "They can ring their cork bell when they come."

He went through the little dark park in the center of the piazza and as he did he heard a girl struggling with a man.

"Don't do that to me," she said. "You promised. You gave your word to my mother."

"You little bitch," the man said—in good Italian, although he was German—and Fabio heard him hit her and then he heard her fall back through the underbrush and strike the ground and by the sounds he knew the German had run.

"You had better stop that crying," Fabio told her. He didn't know where she was, but the crying stopped and when he went to find her she had already gone. Girls who went with German soldiers deserved what they got, he thought, although as he said it he knew the soldiers sometimes went to the girls' houses and made it impossible for the families to refuse. All they could do was hope the German proved to be decent.

"Oh, God," he said aloud. Angela. They would do it to Angela. He knew at once, the same way he had known when he had seen Bombolini on top of the water tower, that he would have to go to Santa Vittoria and be the one to warn them. Now that he cared he found his heart was beginning to beat hard. He was excited, but his mind was clear and he knew exactly what he wanted to do. He got the rest of the way across the piazza without being seen and up into a dark narrow lane, and from this lane off into a series of lanes that kept him away from the Corso and the piazza but moving deeper into the city where the workingmen lived. He found the house he was looking for, and when his knock was not answered he tapped on the window, and when that went unanswered he was about to go away, when the shutter was opened by a young woman who did not seem to be wearing any clothes. Fabio looked down.

"Oh," he said. "I wanted Gambo. I was expecting Gambo."

"He isn't here, he's in the hospital. A rock fell on him in the quarry."

"Oh. I'm sorry." Fabio cleared his throat. "Is his bike here? He said I could use it whenever I needed it." She said nothing, but tried to make him out in the darkness. "I need it."

"Stand over here. Let me see you." She made him come near to the window and she held his head up. "Wait here," she said, and in a moment he could hear the chain coming down from the door. "Now come in."

When he went in he could see the bicycle chained to an iron ring in the stone staircase, and when he looked further into the room he could see the girl and was surprised to find that she was wearing only a shirt, one of Gambo's shirts. He was startled by her legs, because he had never actually seen a woman's legs before, and even more startled when he found he could see almost all of her breasts, because the shirt was not buttoned all of the way to the top. He turned back to the bike.

"A nice bicycle," he said. "Gambo always took good care of his bicycles."

The woman laughed and asked him who he was.

"Fabio. Just call me Fabio."

"Just Fabio? I can't loan a bike to someone called 'just Fabio,' eh?"

"Bombolini. Fabio Bombolini," he said. "From the Resistance."

She motioned him to come away from the door and into the room, and he looked at her quickly, because he had never seen anything like her, but when she sat down on the bed and turned back toward him he looked away again. The shirt was almost completely open.

"How long have you known Gambo?"

"Oh, for years and years and years," Fabio said. "How long has he been in the hospital?" She leaned back on the bed, and Fabio could feel his heart pumping.

134

"Oh, for weeks and weeks and weeks," she said, and he blushed. They talked about Gambo for a while, and Fabio found that the woman barely knew him.

"Why don't you ever look at me?" she said.

"I'm looking at you."

"No you're not. What am I doing now?" She was swinging a small key chain around and around. Her breasts were bare. "Why do you look away?"

"I'm not looking away. I'm looking at you. It's just that I was interested in the bike. I came for the bike."

"The bike is more interesting than me?"

"It's a beautiful bike," Fabio said. The nature of the silence, the coldness behind it, informed Fabio that he would have to say more. "You seem beautiful, too," he said.

"Then look at me for God's sake."

He took his eyes away from the bike and looked at her, as calmly he could, determined to examine her in all objectivity, as if she were in anatomy class or was a new shirt. But he felt that the pounding of his heart must be making a sound in the room, and then he found that his right leg was shaking so that anyone could see it.

"The key to the bike. See?" She held up the key chain. "If you want it you can come and get it."

He had heard about things such as this. There would be a game to get the key. Sex games, his father had called them. He realized he would have to play, but he didn't know how to begin and he didn't know the rules. She ended this by bringing his hand to her neck so that he could feel the chain.

"It's thin, you see, but very strong," she said.

The game went swiftly enough after that, although it was a one-sided game. She was expert at it.

"Why are you trembling?" she said, and he told her it was cold, although he was sweating, and she pulled back the sheet and pulled it over them, which made it somewhat better.

"What's this?" It was his holy medal.

"St. Anthony of Padua."

"Take it off," she told him. "I can't make love with a saint in between us. Your first time, eh?"

135

"Oh, no," Fabio said; but she laughed, nicely, at him.

"You'll have a good teacher," she said. "That's very important. You're awfully old to be beginning."

I will think only of Angela while I do this, Fabio promised himself. No, no, no. I will think only of the bicycle. I will remember that I am doing this as a duty in order to get the bicycle.

He was conscious of the woman but he did not allow himself to enjoy the consciousness. In a way, he was performing a patriotic act in the line of duty.

"Well," she said at last. "Fabio, you're a good student."

He wished she hadn't said it, because it implied somehow that he had invested himself beyond the point of duty.

"Someday you'll make some woman a good lover." He turned red, of course, and yet he found that he wasn't displeased. "And I'll tell you this, Fabio—Fabio *what?*"

"Della Romagna."

"I will tell you this, Fabio della Romagna: You may not be the best I've ever had, but you're the prettiest."

Despite himself, he found that he was smiling and could only hope that she hadn't seen him smiling.

"And one of the strangest. I think you are in love with bikes."

"Yes. I love bikes," Fabio said, and he got up from the bed at once. He had forgotten the chain and the key, and when he turned back to her with such a sadness she laughed aloud and said, "Oh, God," and reached up and worked the chain over her head while he looked away. She has no shame at all, he thought.

"When you bring it back we'll have lesson number two," she said.

When he got the bicycle out into the steep narrow street he was filled with elation. The bicycle rattled on the cobbles, and so he picked it up and put it on his back, and he barely noticed its weight. Near the bottom of the lane he realized he would have to go back and went all of the way back. When he tapped on the window she opened it. She was naked again, but this time he looked directly at her.

"My Saint Anthony medal, please. My mother would never forgive me."

When she came back with it Fabio was able to smile at her.

"You're not so bad at all," he said. She started to close the shutter, but he held it with his hand.

"One other thing," he said. "I suppose I should know your name. After all."

"Gabriella."

"Gabriella. What a beautiful name. It is very fitting," he said, and he trotted back down the narrow dark street. Fabio, he told himself, you are becoming a goat.

When he reached Santa Vittoria some of the older men were still in the Piazza of the People, seated around the fountain, waiting to hear the cork clapper strike twelve. They could not feed enough on the sound.

"Fabio. Oh, Fabio," Bombolini said when he saw him. "I knew you would come back to me." The mayor embraced him. "You're sweating like a pig, Fabio."

"I pedaled all of the way up the mountain. I have bad news."

"What could be bad news?" Bombolini said. "I want you to hear the good news first. Paolo, go and ring the bell for Fabio. I want him to hear it."

"No. No." Fabio stopped them. "The Germans are coming."

Once again Fabio experienced the blankness of the faces that he had seen the other time.

"I have seen the orders. Elements of the German army will arrive in Santa Vittoria at five o'clock in the afternoon on this coming Wednesday."

It meant nothing to them, even Bombolini. He threw his bicycle down onto the stones of the piazza.

"All right. I've told you. I have done my duty. I risked my life. I have stolen a man's bike. I have done all that I can." For a moment he had the wild idea of riding back to the arms of Gabriella, *his* lover; but he was too tired. Bombolini came after him.

"We know it's important, Fabio. We appreciate your coming and telling us. It's just that we have expected it all along and there's nothing much to be done about it."

"You could put your women away some place."

"If they touch the women they'll pay for it and they know it."

"You could get that Abruzzi out of town before he gets us all shot."

137

"No, he's going to stay. He'll be dressed like one of us. No one will be able to tell."

"Do you think all these people can keep a secret like that?"

"We can be a very loud people," Bombolini said, "but when it is to our advantage to keep a secret we can keep one. Keeping a secret is a form of lying you understand."

They were almost all the way across the piazza by then, and at the edge of the Corso Cavour, where it drops down from the Piazza of the People into Old Town, Bombolini took hold of Fabio's arm.

"Don't go away again, Fabio," he said. "We need you here."

"Oh, I don't know. I'm thinking of going into the mountains." He hadn't thought of it before. "The Resistance, you know."

I shall go to the hills, Fabio told himself, and I shall stay in those hills even until I am the last one left, but I shall be unbowed.

"When the Germans come, the policy here is going to be one of accommodation, do you understand?" Bombolini said. Fabio made a face, but Bombolini didn't see it and didn't hear the sound of disapproval, because men generally seem to hear and see the things they wish to hear and see.

"When they push, we will give. We'll be like quicksand."

And I intend to be a rock, Fabio said, but to himself.

"We don't intend to be heroes here. We don't want or need any heroes. We intend to do something a little better. We intend to survive. Thank you, Fabio, and now you get some rest."

He tried to answer the goodnight, but he could not force his lips to say the words. The only words in his head then were the ones of Petrarch he had memorized at the academy.

Valor against fell wrath
Will take up arms; and then be the fight quickly sped.
For sure the ancient worth that
In Italians stirs the heart, is not dead.

It was midnight. It had been a long day. He was tired. He had come back to save Angela, and they had no desire to save their women. So be it. They wanted to accommodate themselves to the Germans. So be it. The day hadn't been all wasted. There was

Gabriella, his lover. What was it she had said—someday you'll make someone a good lover. If he hadn't been concentrating so hard on the bicycle he probably could have shown her a thing or two. At last now he knew where his destiny rested. Up in the mountains.

And just then, since it was twelve o'clock, the cork clapper began to ping against the metal of the bell, weak and thin and colorless.

"Oh, God, what a people we are," Fabio said aloud.

$\mathbb{S}$ERGEANT Traub looked down in the Via San Sebastiano and shook his head. "It's not very much equipment, sir," he said.

"It's what the colonel would authorize," Captain von Prum said. "It's enough for our needs."

In the street below them, parked up against the walls of the houses across the way, was one small truck capable of holding four soldiers in the back and two in the front. They would have to find a way to fit two more in. Behind the truck was a motorcycle with a sidecar that appeared to have been used in the First World War. Behind the truck, as an afterthought, trailed a small, battered 20-millimeter dual-purpose gun which had been designed

for use against tanks and airplanes and people and which now
was used mainly to frighten street mobs.

"In Russia they would have authorized us three times as much,"
the sergeant said.

"But this isn't Russia, is it, and these aren't Russians, are they?"
von Prum said.

The soldiers nodded and one said, in a low voice, "And thank
God for that."

"And we aren't going up there to wage war."

"That suits me," Traub said. The captain looked at him closely.
It was possible that the sergeant had lost his nerve in Russia, although his record showed that he had been a man of not just
ordinary courage but unusual courage. The officer and his sergeant were still in the process of feeling one another out.

"What do you think of the Italians?" von Prum asked, in a very
offhand manner. It was, however, a crucial question to him. He
had chosen all of these men because of their understanding of
Italian and it had been part of his reasoning that a man doesn't
learn another man's language in order to despise him.

"They're all right," Traub said. "They're people. People tend to
be people if you let them be," the sergeant said. "They want their
supper like I do."

"And you," von Prum said to Corporal Heinsick. "What about
you?"

The corporal had been cleaning his equipment and his back
was to Captain von Prum. The captain could see that he had hairs
on the back of his neck like the bristles on the back of a boar. He
had been cleaning a bayonet and it was cleaned and he slapped
the blade against his knee and slid it into the scabbard with one
harsh movement. There was violence in the man, a reservoir of
anger, but it also seemed to be controlled. Von Prum had been
worried about him.

"The wop is all right," he said. "In some ways I like the wop. I
just have no respect for them."

One of the other soldiers nodded openly then.

"That's the word for it, sir—no respect. I saw them at Smolensk.
They went charging across the field on the attack and then the

Russkies stopped and held and turned around, and you should have seen those sons of bitches come. Excuse me, sir."

"I've been in barracks before."

"Those bright-green uniforms and those crazy hats with the feathers! You never saw anything like it."

"They were fast though. You have to admit that," Heinsick said. "You could have formed a fine Olympic squad from that bunch. I can live with them, I just got no respect for them."

When the others nodded, the captain was well pleased. It was what he had wanted to hear.

"I am not one given to generalizations," he told them, "but there are certain truths about certain peoples that simple observation will bear out every time."

And he told them what these were. The average Italian, he told them, had no stomach for battle. It was not so much a matter of courage as much as having nothing worth dying for.

"What man chooses to die for decay and corruption?"

They all nodded.

"A basic observation, then, is that the Italian, *when given the chance,* will at every turn choose to manipulate and bargain and make deals to protect what he has rather than fight for what he has."

"They fought up at Castelgrande last night, sir," Traub said, in a voice as respectful as he could make it. "They had five or six dead up there."

"And you missed four words I said, Sergeant," Captain von Prum said. "What were they?" When the sergeant was unable to answer the captain said them. "*When given the chance.* Do you understand now? Captain Moltke marched into Castelgrande and began to take things without even asking for them. There was nothing for the people to do but to fight. That's going to be the difference with us. We aren't going to take, they're going to give."

It was a secondary part of the captain's theory that the Italian, even when he could get something in a straight and direct manner, wanted to get it by conniving for it. For a time, he said, this can produce results, or seem to produce results, but in the end, because the Italian lacks self-discipline, when conniving is pitted against a direct but disciplined opponent, conniving comes apart.

"In one last word, then, every Italian scheme contains the seeds of its own destruction, the Italian himself."

He wasn't sure that the men understood, but he knew they were impressed by his talk.

"They had fifty men at Castelgrande, sir," Traub said.

"And we have eight," von Prum said. "And eight is all we will need. But I want no man to go with me who has no confidence in me or in my approach."

They backed him with shouts of approval. He was moved to smile then.

"This is the difference between them and us," he told them. And they smiled. "Ours will be a bloodless victory," Captain von Prum said, and he knew at once that this was the title of the report he would write.

BLOODLESS VICTORY

A technique for the conservation of manpower and equipment during the confiscation of enemy assets

> A report on the occupation of the city of Santa Vittoria under command of Sepp von Prum, Capt., Inf.

He even took time to write it down while the men were still standing about him.

"The only red I expect to see is the red of their wine," Captain von Prum told them.

* * *

When Fabio had gone and the bell had rung for the last time that night, Bombolini went back across the piazza, but all of the men had gone home. He turned toward the People's Palace and then turned away because, although he was tired, he knew he couldn't sleep then. He decided to walk through the city. He liked to walk through the city at night, because he thought of it then as his city and of the people as his people. They could sleep, because they knew he carried their burdens on his back. It was the price the leader paid and one he was happy to pay.

He walked down past the Memorial Glade, and it was sad to look at the trees. During the other great war the people had planted one beech tree in a little plot of land for each man who had gone away to the war. Each tree carried the soldier's name and a little picture of him. There was a belief that as long as the tree lived the soldier would live. But then people who had grievances against another family would sneak into the grove at night and cut down that family's tree, or at least take off a limb in the hope that a member of the family would lose a leg or an arm at least.

He went back up the Corso Cavour, because he knew he could sleep, and went inside the Palace of the People and to his room. Before going to sleep, however, he stopped at Roberto's doorway.

"Do you think the Germans will come here?" he said.

Roberto was annoyed. It was three o'clock in the morning.

"I don't know. I don't know about those things. I was in the air forces."

"There's nothing for them here."

Roberto nodded. "Only your wine," he said, and he was sorry to be disrespectful, but he closed his eyes and fell back to sleep.

"There's no road up here at all," Bombolini said. But the sound of Roberto's breathing told him that his argument was being wasted.

"I'm sorry. Sometimes I get to be a bore," he said, and he went to his room and to bed.

When he woke again the sun still had not risen and so he knew he could not have slept for more than an hour at the most. Something had been troubling him and he found a candle and a flint to light it with and began going through *the* book.

"Men are apt to deceive themselves in great things while being scrupulous about the small ones."

He felt a cold hand rest on his heart and begin to squeeze it. He put the book over his heart as if that might stop it. He knew what the words meant. It was only that morning that Babbaluche had said to him, "We lie about the truth, that's what ruins us here. And do you know why we lie about the truth? Not because we like to, but because we are scared to death of it. If we looked the truth in the eye nine out of ten of us would run to the graveyard and demand to be buried at once."

He got up then and walked by Roberto's room and was going to wake him but decided against it, even though it was Roberto who had seen the truth.

Man sees what he sees and hears what he hears, he thought, and the few who don't are generally considered to be mad. He went downstairs and out into the Piazza of the People where one of the madmen was already in the piazza, on his knees by the fountain, screaming at him, Bombolini. "You son of a bitch," he was screaming. "Do something. Do it now." It was Old Vines.

Bombolini trotted across the rough stones. "Get up now," he said. "I know. There's no sense in terrifying the people before we have a plan."

Others had heard, however, the ones who get up in darkness before the sun even, and they were coming across the piazza.

"Tell them the truth," Old Vines shouted. "Don't lie to us." He got up from his feet then, his face as red as any wine he had ever aged, and turned to them. "The Germans are coming," he shouted, "and they're going to take our wine."

To the south there is an old Roman city that was buried in the ash of a volcano. Although no one here has ever seen it, people say that in this city there are figures of people who are locked forever in the ash at the moment of their doing. Those who were about to eat will forever be a spoon's length away from eating and those just reaching for the wine will never taste it. It was this way in the piazza in Santa Vittoria that morning. When people heard the words, they recognized them as the truth at once and they seemed, for a time at least, to be turned into stone and to be so stiff that if they moved they would crack and fall into pieces on the stones.

Bombolini was the first to move. He turned away and started back toward the Palace of the People.

"They're going to come and take our wine," Old Vines screamed.

The mayor continued to walk away from them as if he didn't hear.

"What are you going to do?" someone shouted.

"What can we do?"

Bombolini closed the door behind him and locked it and went up the stairs and woke Roberto.

"You have to help me now. Don't let anyone in. I must rest. I must go to sleep," Bombolini said. "It's all that I can do."

* * *

Traub was one who rose with the sun. It was a habit that had begun on the family farm and continued with him into the army. He believed it was a sin to be down when the sun was up. "The early sun is gold in the mouth," his mother said to him. "Yes, the bed is a thief," his father would say.

He was worried. In two day's time they would be going up a mountain into an unknown city with one officer and two non-coms and six privates, all of them limited-duty soldiers because of previous wounds. He waited for an hour and finally knocked on Captain von Prum's door.

"I want to put a reconnaisance up in Santa Vittoria this afternoon, sir," Traub called through the door. He could hear that the captain was up but he wasn't asked into the room because in the German army it wasn't considered good for morale and discipline for soldiers to see their officers in their underwear.

"No," Captain von Prum said.

"But the book says, sir," Traub said.

"I'm not interested in the book. This is not a military problem. It's a psychological problem. Do you understand that word?"

The sergeant said that he did.

"I want to make the strongest possible first impression on these people. If we arrive there with nine men it will impress them. These people lay great store on first impressions."

"But, sir, if there's a road block . . ."

Von Prum opened the door of the room and looked at his sergeant.

"The German army has not yet become a debating society," von Prum said.

Von Prum smiled, because the words had the same effect on the sergeant that they had had on himself the night before when Colonel Scheer shouted them at him. The colonel had had second thoughts about the wisdom of the bloodless victory.

The bastard is making me pay in blood for my bloodless vic-

tory, von Prum put in his log, but when the colonel summoned him he had gone at a run.

"No, it all stinks of an experiment," the colonel had said. "It's all right to experiment with Poles. It's all right to try things with Jews. It's not all right with the grandson of Schmidt von Knoblesdorf. If anything happens to Captain von Prum, Willy Scheer will be the one to hang for it."

Scheer was a rare case, the peasant who had risen through the ranks to a position of power without discarding his peasant ways. His manner was rough and direct, his speech was filled with folk sayings, most of them coarse, and he looked as if he had been carved from a potato. It amused him and it flattered him to have aristocrats around him and beneath him.

"No, I can't let you go," Scheer said. "The cream of our culture, the flower of our people." He was being sarcastic but good natured. "If your name was Schwartz you could go. But a blood relation of Alfons Mumm von Schwarzenstein? Oh, no. It's not your ass I worry about, it's Willy Scheer's ass."

The captain had stared at him. Von Prum knew it was the correct thing to do then. For reasons he didn't understand, Scheer enjoyed being stared at in a cold haughty manner.

"You look at me as if I was manure in the field," he said. "Like I was shit." But he smiled. "You heard what happened at Castelgrande," the colonel said. "They went in with fifty men."

"And Moltke," von Prum said. Captain Moltke was famous for his short temper. When he had encountered a small road block, Moltke had ordered his men to fire on the people of the town and they had no choice but to fire back.

"Well take a tank at least," Scheer said. The captain shook his head and continued to stare at the colonel.

"What are you going armed with," he finally asked.

"The culture of the German people," von Prum said. "Our national sense of purpose. Our genius at working with disciplined order."

"Oh you are such a *good* boy," Scheer said. "My God what a fine noble boy." He was shaking his head by then. "Do you really believe this."

147

"I really believe it," von Prum said. "It isn't the idealist's way. It isn't the dreamer's way. It's the only sensible, practical way to do it. You'll see."

These were the words that angered the colonel and this was when he told the captain that the army had not yet become a debating society. What the captain said went against all the rules Scheer had had to learn so painfully in his life.

"You listen to me," Scheer said. "We don't learn much in the turnip fields but we learn some things that are never forgotten, and one of them is that the one thing that gets respect, the only thing that gets respect, is strength. The weak respect the strong for one reason. Because they're not weak like themselves." The colonel thumped his hard brown stubby hand down onto the hard wooden table. "Here's one of those quaint peasant sayings, Captain von Prum. 'One must be either the anvil or the hammer.' You think about it. There is no other way."

But in the end von Prum had won, as he knew he would win, because in the end he was what the race aspired to, and he knew this and knew that Scheer knew it and approved of it. His Nordic bleaching, as the colonel called it, the blondness and whiteness and the cold blueness of him, was not just the symbol of racial purity but the fact of it. Most Germans, like most of the people of the world, are dark and short, but unlike other people the Germans despise their darkness and their shortness and they don't believe in it. It is von Prum they put on all their posters, and when they have a baby it is von Prum they hope to produce.

"You push me too Goddamn hard," Scheer said, "but then again the German army has not yet become a place where officers go back on their words." They smiled at one another then. "Take a tank," Scheer said. Von Prum shook his head.

"My God you're stubborn," Scheer said. His voice became hard again.

"This experiment has only one solution, and that is that it must work."

"I understand."

"If it doesn't, I come up there and do things in my way," Scheer said. Von Prum nodded his head.

"Because I'm committed for that wine."

"You will get your wine."

The colonel began to walk toward the door of his office and by this the captain knew the interview was over.

"I want the wine, I want it soon, and I want all of it." He stopped at the door. "When you are ready you let us know, make it soon, and we will come and get the wine."

"But that's all part of it," von Prum said. "When the time comes I intend to have the people bring it out themselves."

"You expect the people to collaborate in their own robbery," he said. His voice was bitter.

"Yes," von Prum said, so quietly and with such little doubt that his arrogance finally caused the colonel to laugh aloud.

"You know one thing that isn't right for a Schmidt von Knoblesdorf?" He ran his stubby fingers down the front of the captain's tunic. "You're a virgin here. No decorations."

It had bothered von Prum's father. Once he had even offered to lend the captain several of his before they went to church.

"I will tell you what I will do," Colonel Scheer said. "If you can get the people of this place . . . what's the name?"

"Santa Vittoria."

"If you get these people to bring their own wine to the railroad here I will recommend you for the Iron Cross."

Von Prum smiled at this.

"Third class, of course," Scheer said, "but an Iron Cross nevertheless."

The captain was excused then, but at the foot of the stairs he turned back to the colonel.

"As for you," he called up, "I'll put your name on the cover of the *Bloodless Victory*."

"No, to hell with that," Scheer said. "After the war you invite me to your home for dinner. Let me come in the front door." He smiled his hard tough smile. "Have me with that fellow you're always quoting."

Von Prum was puzzled.

"Nitcha," Scheer said. "Your friend Nitcha."

"Nietzsche," the captain said. "He's dead."

"Oh, I'm sorry to hear it," Colonel Scheer said. "Have me with all the ancestors then."

"I'll do that," Captain von Prum said. "And I'll toast you in the wine of Santa Vittoria."

* * *

Considering the state of things in Santa Vittoria they were good to Bombolini; they allowed him to sleep until eleven o'clock, and then they told Roberto to go and wake him. When he looked in the door he was surprised to see how peacefully the mayor was sleeping.

"They're waiting for you down there," Roberto told him.

"Yes, I know that. I can sense them."

"The whole piazza is filled with people."

"They don't know what to do. They don't have their leader."

The mayor rose from the bed and moved very slowly and easily, and the manner in which he moved convinced Roberto that he must have found an answer during his sleep.

"The Grand Council is downstairs."

"I can sense them," Bombolini said. "I can feel them. I can smell them. They say a horse can smell water before he can see it when he needs it. I can smell them and they can smell me. Do you know what I did, Roberto?"

"No."

"I had a good sleep." He tapped his head and at the same time attempted to brush down his mane of hair, which was wild, so wild that Babbaluche once claimed that a bird could nest in it and Bombolini would never know it until he got egg on his face. "God came to me, I think. He put something in here. Let's go down."

They went down the steps into the large room where all of the members of the Grand Council were gathered.

"God put a story in my head. I want to tell it to you and you can tell me what it means. I think the answer is in the story."

They sat down along the walls and stood against the walls, and Italo Bombolini told them the story of the peasant Gagliaudi.

* * *

A thousand years ago, some invaders from the north called barbarians came to conquer Italy under the leadership of a man named Barbarossa. Everything fell before the barbarians until they came to one walled city to the north of here that refused to lie down and surrender. They tried everything to make it fall, but when they failed they decided to surround the city and starve it out. Winter came and the people began to go hungry and everyone knew it was only a matter of time. It was then that the peasant Gagliaudi went to the prince with a plan.

"Give me all the wheat that is left in the city and give me all the grain that is left, and I will save the city. If I don't, then kill me."

"Don't worry, I won't have to do that. They'll do it for me." But against his better judgment, because there was nothing else to do, he gave the wheat and the grain to the peasant. The people were shocked and outraged when the peasant began to feed the precious food to his cow.

"Now bring me the last of the water," Gagliaudi ordered. The people by then were chewing stones to keep their mouths wet, but the cow drank and drank.

"Now bring me the last of the wine."

They watched in rage as the peasant sat before them and drank the last of the wine and got drunk before their faces. When he was drunk enough, early in the morning just before dawn, a little side gate in the wall was opened and the drunk peasant and his bloated cow slipped outside the city's walls. Once outside, along the road where the enemy camped, Gagliaudi began to sing and laugh and roar, and he kicked the cow so that it mooed and bellowed in protest. The enemy could not believe their eyes any more than the people of the city, who were peeping from the tops of the walls, could believe theirs.

"We have been made fools of," they all agreed.

The guards of Barbarossa realized at once that only a madman or a drunk could behave in this manner, and when they seized the peasant he fell to his knees.

"Oh God help me, what have I done?" He wept. He cried aloud. "I was taking my cow to the grainery and I opened the wrong door. Oh, don't harm me. Please. Take me to Barbarossa. I have a proposition for him."

They dragged the weeping drunk to the warrior, and he looked with astonishment at the drunk man and the fat sleek cow.

"I have a proposition for you," Gagliaudi said. "Don't kill me. Please don't harm me."

"Italians always have propositions," Barbarossa said.

"It's how we survive," the peasant said. "We're weak. But if you will let me go I will promise to go back inside the walls with any soldiers you select and bring you back my twelve cows."

"Twelve like this?"

"No, not like this." He kicked the fat cow. "Twelve that are fat and filled with meat and milk. Not this beast. I was treating her, sir. Can't you see? She's sick."

It was Barbarossa who was sick, sick at the sight of all of that beef on the hoof.

"Do you mean to tell me you have twelve more like that inside the walls?"

"Only my own, sir. Just my own. All of the others belong to someone else and I can't give them to you."

Barbarossa was above all things a good soldier, and a good soldier recognizes when he is beaten. The city clearly had enough food to last them for two more years at least. That afternoon he packed up his army and he left. The city was saved.

* * *

They all looked at one another. It seemed to be saying something to them. The answer was in the story, everyone felt that.

"It's in there," Bombolini shouted to them. "Otherwise why would He have put it there, eh?"

But they were silent. It was a strange story; every man in the room felt that the answer was flitting about inside his brain waiting to fly out on his tongue, but when it came time to open the mouth nothing came out.

"It's like those parables in the Bible," someone said. "Just when I seem to understand and have it in my hands it hops away from me."

They looked at each other as if by staring very hard into one another's eyes they would unlock the answer in their minds. A long time passed. They heard the thin sound of the bell telling that it was midday, and no one in the room was any closer to the secret of Gagliaudi.

152

"To hell with all this," Pietro Pietrosanto suddenly shouted. "To hell with this bum and his cow. I say fight."

There was a cheer from the others. Their minds were tired from the pressure of the thinking, and the idea of fighting seemed good then. At least it was doing something.

"I say dig in down in the rocks by the big bend in the road in the terraces and the sons of bitches will *never* get us out."

Another cheer.

"Sometimes you make people spill a little blood for what they want, and you find they don't want it so much any more."

The problem with Bombolini was that he was torn between voices.

Men often deceive themselves in believing that humility can overcome insolence. Any way that you read that, it meant to resist, to fight.

"I say this to you," a young man shouted. "The German who touches my wine or my wife pays for his touch in blood."

A very big cheer then.

And yet The Master had also said: *Cunning and deceit will every time serve a man better than force.*

Bombolini was confused and, even worse, he began to feel a kind of fear dancing in the back of his mind like cold needles, like the sun, cold and brilliant, on ice. The Master was failing him.

"Fabio was right, he was the one who knew," another young man was now shouting. "What good is it to save yourself and then crawl around your own country like a dog looking for a bone?"

"*Mussolini* was right. Better to live one day as a lion than one hundred years as a lamb."

A great cheer then and the eyes turned on the mayor, because it was he who had painted out the sign. All these brave words, these cries of valor. How to answer them? He thought of one more saying of Machiavelli: *Deceit in the conduct of war outweighs valor and is worthy of merit.*

How could that be explained to them? How to tell a bunch of men bent on becoming heroes that it would be more heroic of them to practice being cowards?

Just as Fabio had once been saved by Babbaluche, now Tommaso Casamassima, Rosa Bombolini's uncle, stood up in the room

153

and struck the floor with his mulberry stick until there was silence.

"You forget who you are," he shouted. "You forget where you come from. You think you're warriors and you shout like heroes and you are a bunch of grape growers."

There was silence, because everyone knew what Tommaso said was so.

"A bunch of grape growers."

Silence.

"We have no heroes here. This is no country for heroes. If you want to be martyrs, go be martyrs somewhere else. We can't afford martyrs in Santa Vittoria."

Silence.

"Tend to your grapes."

Silence.

"Because you forget the one lesson that every Santa Vittorian has known for the last thousand years: Brave men and good wine don't last long."

*   *   *

Everyone went outside after that. All idea of the fight was ended. The people were waiting for them in the piazza.

"We're thinking. Don't worry. We're coming up with something."

As if it were a command, they began to go across the Piazza of the People and down the Corso Cavour to the Cooperative Wine Cellar. In the absence of anything to do they were making a pilgrimage and performing an act of faith in the wine, the way people in other places might go into a church and pray for guidance.

They filed in through the narrow door, into the cool dimness and smelt the incense of the cellar, that sweet sharp smell of the herbs that go into the vermouth, and went down through the tiers of wine which look like tall pews in an attitude of reverence.

It is a true sea of wine in that cellar, a rich dark-red sea held in bottles. To the south of here there are towns where people make the sign of the cross over each crust of bread before they eat it, and we are the same way with the wine. To say something loud or vulgar, to utter an obscenity in the presence of the wine, would be the same as urinating in a cathedral. The sight of so much wine, all that wine to be stolen, was too great for Bombolini to bear, and he went out of a little-used side door and back up a narrow back lane until he reached the piazza and the Palace of the People and found Roberto.

"Have you figured out the story yet?" he said.

Roberto looked puzzled.

"The dream. My dream. What does it mean? You're the American. You know everything." He was shouting at Roberto, but then he stopped and sat down. "What are you doing?"

"Arithmetic. My arithmetic. I'm figuring out the hours until they come."

Bombolini didn't want to know. He preferred it that way. Without any plan it was better to just let them come when they came, unprepared for and unannounced.

"All right," he said finally. "How many."

"They'll be here in fifty-three hours."

When he heard the hour now it began to flash in his mind in large block letters, as bright and clear as the lights on the theater in Montefalcone, flashing on and off—53 · · · 53 · · · 53 · · · 53—and it was minutes before the glow of the lights would leave his brain.

He went to the window of Roberto's room and looked down at the people standing in the midday sun in the piazza, and he looked at the wall and at a picture of St. Sebastian being rent with arrows.

"Quick, now. As fast as you can say the words. If you were me what would you do with the wine?"

"Hide."

"What?"

"Hide it."

"You would hide it?"

"Yes, hide it," Roberto said.

"Oh, Roberto. So simple and clean and beautiful that it's almost stupid," the mayor said, and he struck Roberto such a blow on the arm that it was weeks before the American could raise it without feeling pain.

Oɴ ᴛʜᴀᴛ same afternoon, Captain von Prum wrote
this, the second letter to his brother Klaus.

Klaus:
You falter, you lose sight again.
I cease to preach to you. Don't take a brother's word, take instead
the words of a man you profess to admire.
"You say it is the good cause that hallows even war.
I say unto you: It is the good war that hallows any cause."
Need I say more, Klaus?
"It is a sad fact, but a fact, that war and courage have accom-
plished more great things than love of thy neighbor. Not your
pity but your courage will save the unfortunate."
Need any more? One more, then.

"What is good?" you ask. "To be brave is good."

Your men were not brave, Klaus, and for that they paid the price, as any evil person must pay.

I finish with Nietzsche.

"What matters long life?
What warrior wants to be spared?"

Your brother,
Sepp

Klaus: We move out within two days, as I intimated to you. I have my duty, you have your duty. Wish me luck, Klaus, even as I wish you the same.

* * *

The effort to hide the wine was a failure. Within the first half hour of the experiment, before twenty thousand bottles had been taken from the Cooperative Wine Cellar and brought up into the Piazza of the People it was clear to anyone who wished to see it that the experiment was no longer worth going on with. But people sometimes are more willing to go on with the work than face up to the failure.

They piled the bottles in the piazza and then the different families began to hide them in their houses. They put them in closets and under beds and behind pictures and in the backs of fireplaces and then in the drains and on the roofs and under loose tiles and then in the manure piles and on grapevine hung down the chimneys.

"Keep the wine in the shadows, the sun is bruising it," Old Vines shouted at the people. "Would you put a newborn baby in the sun? This wine isn't even born yet. Don't shake the wine. Would you shake a newborn baby? This wine isn't born yet."

Sometime in the early afternoon Bombolini summoned the courage to ask the keeper of the wine how many bottles remained to be hidden, and when Old Vines told him, it was a matter of several minutes before he could make himself hear the figures, and when he did he wrote them on a card—"1,320,000."

Each time he looked at the number he found it hard to comprehend. He held the card up first on one side and then on the other, as if somehow, if he twisted it in enough ways, the value of the numbers might change. Even if they hid 100,000 bottles, which was impossible, it was only one thirteenth of the wine and by enormous effort they would have achieved nothing. At four o'clock there was to be an inspection of the hiding, and the teams went out even though all of the people knew what they would report. A few minutes later the first of them came back.

"It's no good, Captain. It isn't working right," Longo's son said. "You can see bottles everywhere. Everytime you turn around in the Pietrosanto house you sit on a bottle, you step on a bottle, you break a bottle. The beds are lumpy with bottles."

It was the same everywhere.

"Bring the bottles back out," Bombolini ordered, and he felt at that moment the dread of failure. To the credit of the people he passed, none of them said anything to him. He went back across the piazza, passing the bottles piled on the cobblestones and piled in carts, seeing and not seeing at the same time the people going into the houses and starting to bring the wine back out. He had the weight of the city and of one thousand people and now one million bottles of wine to carry. It was too much for any one man, he thought. He felt someone pulling on him and he turned to look. It was Fungo, the idiot.

It is said that when a man is drowning, just as he goes down, he will grab at a twig in the water and for that moment really believe that it will hold him; and so, at this moment, Bombolini stopped to listen to Fungo.

"I have something to tell you," Fungo said.

"Tell. Tell me."

Out of the mouths of babes and idiots and drunks— Who could tell until he listened?

"Tufa's back," the boy said.

"Oh, Christ above!"

"You have a filthy mouth," the boy said.

"Excuse me. How do you know?"

The boy told him how he had gone to Tufa's house to see if he could find any bottles and he had found Tufa there, in the dark, lying on the floor.

"He's dying," Fungo said.

"How would you know that?"

"Someone told me."

'Who?"

"Tufa. And he should know."

I will attend to Tufa, he thought. It was at least something positive to do. I will make every effort to save Tufa's life. He thought for a moment that he was crying, and then he looked up and was surprised to see that it was raining.

The people were running past him, getting out of the piazza before the full force of the rain reached them. The people here love the rain and they love to see it rain. It is not going too far to say they adore the rain in Italy, but as soon as they see a drop they run from it.

Old Vines caught up to Bombolini. "Stop them," he shouted. "You have to order them to stay. We can't leave the wine out here. The rain will wash the dust from the bottles. The rain will chill the wine."

Bombolini looked at the old man as if he came from some other town. "Who cares?" he said. "Do we have to have the wine at room temperature for the Germans when they come?"

"Wine is wine no matter who has it," the old man shouted. "To abuse wine is to abuse life itself." Now he was shaking Bombolini by the shoulders and shouting something about killing him.

"Then fuck the wine," Bombolini said. Old Vines fell away from him.

"Oh, you sin," he said. Neither of them felt the rain that was falling hard by then. "You sin against the wine."

I fully expect the next bolt of lightening to strike me in the heart, Bombolini thought.

He pushed the cellar master to one side and started down the Corso Cavour to Old Town and Tufa's mother's house. He had made up his mind to keep all of his thoughts on Tufa.

There were strange things about Tufa. He was, for one, an officer in the army, and that should have separated him from the people here, but it didn't. Even worse, he was a Fascist, but this had never stopped him from being a hero to the young people here and a person to whom the old were not afraid to turn for help when he was home.

The thing about Tufa was that he was a true Fascist, a real Fascist, who believed all the glorious words and tried to follow them, and that had made him a very strange person here and in all of Italy. As a young boy he had been chosen from all the rest in Santa Vittoria to go away and be trained as a Young Fascist Scout. He had believed every word he heard at the camp. Later he became a soldier and after that was made an officer in the Sforzesca, one of the aristocratic regiments, a very rare thing to happen.

When he came home on leave people would go to him and ask him to intercede for them with The Band or with the Fascists in Montefalcone.

"What is this I hear you are doing to Baldisseri?" he would ask them. "Only Communists would do a thing like that."

It must have been a mistake, they always told him, and it would certainly not happen again.

"Well of course not," he would say. "*We* don't do things like that."

"No, we don't," they would say. They were afraid of the innocence in his eyes and the anger that could replace it. He was a believer in a nation of nonbelievers, people who believe that to believe in anything is dangerous and even evil itself, since believing limits one and to be limited is to court disaster. None of the Fascists in the region could wait for Tufa's leaves to be over, and they breathed easier when he was gone and hoped to God that he would meet a glorious end in Albania or Greece or Africa.

The room was dark and it felt wet and it was dirty. It smelled bad. Tufa's mother had never been able to run a house.

"Where is he?" Bombolini asked. The soldier's mother pointed to one end of the room, where the mayor could eventually make out Tufa's shape lying on the floor facing the stone wall.

"He's going to die," the mother said. "I can see it in his eyes. All the life is gone."

Bombolini crossed the room and stood over Tufa's body, not knowing what to say to him. Tufa had never liked him because he had been a clown and Tufa didn't understand clowns. With a terrible slowness Tufa turned away from the wall and looked at Bombolini.

"Get out of here," he said. "I have always despised you."

The mother was wrong about the eyes. There was the recognition of death in them, but there was also hatred, which had not been seen there before, and beneath both of these a kind of terrible hurt.

"You had better get out," the mother said. "He means what he says. He always means what he says."

"Tufa? Can you hear me?"

"Get out of here."

"I'm not a clown any more, Tufa. I'm the mayor here now. Can you hear me? Can you understand that?"

"Get out of here."

The hatred was so strong that it defeated Bombolini. He backed out of the house and stood in the Corso Cavour and allowed the rain to fall on him until his hair was streaming with water. The people looked at him from the doorways. Now there wasn't even Tufa as a reason for existing. He started back up the Corso. Before he reached the piazza, Pietro Pietrosanto came down the steps toward him. "We can't put it off any longer," Pietrosanto said. "We've got to do something with The Band."

Bombolini took in a large breath. Pietro was correct, the time had come. It was the one problem he had been unable to face since the day he had taken office. He knew the words of The Master: "Men must either be caressed or annihilated and the injury must be such that the victim cannot pay you back for it. Whoever acts otherwise is obliged to stand forever with knife in hand." At night he could hear the words tumbling through his mind and he would resolve in the darkness to do something about them, but in the morning when the sun lit the walls along the piazza and the people went down to work, another day would pass with the problem unanswered. Now, with the Germans coming, there was no room left for the luxury of indecision.

"Do away with them," Bombolini said.

Pietrosanto found this hard to believe.

"I am tired of standing with my knife in my hand."

"I don't understand you," Pietro said.

Bombolini took Pietrosanto by the arm. "Do you have a rifle? You own a rifle, don't you?"

"Shoot them? Is that what you mean? Shoot the sons of bitches?"

"I don't mean to caress them," the mayor said. "Come." They both went back up toward the piazza. "Try and look as if we have a plan," Bombolini said. "It gives the people heart."

It had stopped raining. It had been a good drenching rain. As Old Vines had feared, the rain had washed all of the dust off the backs of the dark-green bottles, and in the greyness of the light the wetness caused them to sparkle as if the stones of the piazza were strewn with jewels.

"I don't know about shooting," Pietrosanto was saying but Bombolini didn't hear him. Now that he had ordered the final solution to the problem of The Band it didn't concern him any more. He looked instead at the wine.

"What do you think they would think if they were to come now?" Bombolini said.

"That we were trying to butter them up. That it was a gift for them."

He was probably right, the mayor thought.

"They'd take it as their due," Pietro said. "It's the way they are."

"Yes, that's how they are," Bombolini agreed.

THAT EVENING Bombolini asked Roberto to go and ask the Malatesta to take a look at Tufa. "She'll listen to you," Bombolini said. "You're not from here, and she thinks you're brave."

"She doesn't think I'm brave," Roberto said. "She thinks I'm afraid of pain."

"Ah, but that's just it. *Because* you're afraid of pain, the way you acted to it makes you a brave man," he said. "Besides, I think she has an eye for you. She thinks you're handsome."

"How do you know?"

"I heard her say so once."

It was a lie, a complete and shameless lie, which Roberto recognized as a lie and treated as one, and yet it made his heart beat faster. Despite himself, the heart beat faster.

He dressed and went into the rain and crossed the Piazza of the People. It was the first time he had seen all the bottles in the piazza. At the wineshop he decided to stop and get some cheese before making the hard climb up to High Town and when he thought of facing the Malatesta he ordered a full bottle of wine as well.

"What's all the wine doing in the piazza?" he asked Rosa Bombolini.

"Do you think I know? Do you think I care? Do you think I give a shit what idiot tricks that boob is up to?"

He determined never to ask her a question again. When he came out it was dark and he felt a little drunk from the wine, but it made the ache in his bone feel better. At the street that runs up into High Town someone whispered his name. It was Fabio.

"I thought you were up in the mountains." Roberto said.

"I am in the mountains. Five of us. The Petrarch Brigade, formally. The Red Flames, informally." He named four young boys who were with him, none of whom was over fifteen years of age. "They're young, but they can fight," Fabio said. "They also are hungry."

With some of his own money and some of Fabio's, Roberto went back to the wineshop and bought two loaves of bread for the Red Flames.

"Now you do a favor for me," Roberto said. He made Fabio go with him to face Caterina Malatesta. They walked up the hill in silence for a long way.

"How is she?" Fabio said at last.

"Who?"

"Angela," Fabio said.

"I don't know. I haven't seen her. That's why I was buying cheese. She doesn't bring us our meals."

"I suppose you two have a lot of fun together when he isn't around."

"Angela and me?"

"Yes, Angela and you. A lot of fun together, if you know what I mean."

"Oh no, nothing like that. Angela isn't like that."

Fabio made a sound like a mule. "They're *all* like that," he said.

"Don't tell me. I know them from top to bottom. Put a grape basket over their heads and turn them upside down and—"

"Oh, do they say that here, too? We say 'Put a sack over their heads.'"

Caterina lived in the next to the last house on the mountain. It was a long way.

* * *

Neither one of them wanted to knock on the door, but it was Fabio who finally did it, and when she came to the door and opened it they were surprised to see her. She was wearing long slender pants and little slippers and a sweater that revealed the outline of her breasts. None of these things are worn by the women here, even today. She had pulled her hair back and tied it with a scarf the way the peasant women do, and yet it looked nothing like a peasant's. She didn't wish to come and she resisted, but Fabio was persuasive and there is something about Tufa, even to those who had barely known him, that was special. She got a raincoat that looked like the kind of coat army officers wear, and she went with them down the dark winding back lane into Old Town.

She didn't knock at the door of the house, but opened it and went in and put down the medical bag Roberto had carried for her. She took a lamp from the bag and when it was lit she could see Tufa, not lying down any longer but propped up against the wall looking at her the way a wolf looks at someone coming for him from the back of a cave. In the light his teeth were as bright as his eyes, and he looked very sane and very mad at the same moment, like someone who could kill or become a martyr with equal ease.

He frightened Roberto. He had never before seen a man who seemed to burn. Caterina had known him from when she was a girl, but when she saw him she made a sound, a stifled sound of astonishment. She was not able to take her eyes away from him.

"You are hurt," she said.

"You aren't going to touch me." Tufa has the finest voice in the city, sweet and yet strong. Sometimes it sounds as if Tufa was whispering through the pipe of an organ.

165

"You're badly hurt. I can help you. You'd like to die, but your body won't allow you to."

He said nothing.

"It's the fate of your kind," she said. "My kind die easily."

All of this while Caterina kept moving toward him. Somewhere in this book it tells of thunderbolt love, but this was something different. There was an awareness of each other that was so acute and powerful and immediate that it went beyond anything we know as love. It is an understanding of each other so immediate and so total that there is nothing they don't know about one another and they are able to share things with each other at once, even in front of others, that they have never been able to share with anyone before.

They have *always* known each other, at once. Some people feel that this is proof that people must have lived before, people such as this are playing out again a love affair from some other age. Except for one thing: There is no love; it goes beyond love. They exist totally for one another, and nothing else exists. The attraction supplants all else, and yet there is no love, not even any tenderness, only the attraction and the understanding of one another. They are like vacuums, and when they meet the crack is formed and they rush into each other, each into the other, the souls are sharing one another, the way the wind rushes into the wine cellar when the door is swung ajar.

When she touched him he stiffened. She didn't move her hand for a moment, but then she began to take off the officer's jacket he wore to examine the wounds in his chest and upper arms that he had received the week before from an exploding grenade.

"They told me you were a good man," she said. Roberto brought her the medical bag. "How can you be a Fascist and a good man at the same time?"

For a long time Tufa said nothing, but it didn't seem to bother her. She was willing to wait. She dressed several of the wounds.

"You can be," he said at last, "if you are a fool."

Caterina finished dressing the last of the wounds. Most of them were not deep, but several of them were infected and the flesh was ragged around them.

"You're not going to get better here," the Malatesta said. "You're going to have to get out of this room."

"Where are you going to take him?" Tufa's mother asked. "He can't go to the hospital."

"Some place where he can get better."

The mother got up from the box she sat on and began collecting her son's things.

"I don't want him dying in here," she said. "Besides, you know what I have to feed him?" She tapped the side of an earthen pot. "I have ten or twelve olives. I can't count. I have one piece of bread and no oil to drip on it."

Caterina looked at Tufa. "Do you want to go with me?"

"Oh, yes. You know that," he said, and he began to get to his feet. When she helped him she was surprised to find that he was silently crying.

"The first time," he said. "The first time ever."

He didn't know why he cried, but he wasn't ashamed of the tears. Later he was able to figure that he cried because he was giving up the death he had planned for himself and he knew that he was going to have to enter again into the life that had fooled him so terribly and that he had wanted to give up. He went past his mother and out into the Corso Cavour, where Fabio and Roberto were waiting in the rain.

"You don't say goodbye to your mother?"

"No, we don't do that in this family," Tufa said. Tufa, although he was weak and sick, led the way up the Corso, which is the way it is in this town. He was forced to lean against the walls and gasp for breath, but he led the way up. Finally he had to lean on Caterina.

"I apologize for that," he said.

"You don't have to apologize to me," she said, and it caused both of them to laugh because it was a truth, and when you hear the truth it makes you laugh. They had at the moment recognized the truth between them: because they knew everything about each other, they would never have to apologize to each other and they would never have to or be able to apologize for themselves.

At the Fountain of the Pissing Turtle, although the rain was falling heavily, Tufa was forced to stop and sit on the wet edge of the fountain.

"I like this rain. It's been a long time since I've been in a real rain."

"You were in Africa?"

"There and Sicily, yes." He looked up and allowed the rain to run down his face, and she was able to see how beautiful his eyes were, the thick lashes, the dark brows, the large soft brownness of the eyes themselves. It was said that every woman in Santa Vittoria was jealous of Tufa for his eyes.

"I can feel the dust of Africa washing off me," he said.

It made Caterina laugh, and she could see that it hurt him.

"Why do you laugh?" he said. His voice was annoyed.

"Oh, it sounded so dramatic. You must go to a lot of movies."

"I never go to movies."

He was silent after that. He let the rain wash down his neck, and then he lifted his face to it once more.

"The other officers in my mess were always laughing at the things I said, and I never knew why." He looked at her. "You're like them."

He didn't say it with any anger or any sadness about it, but as a fact. "Not inside, maybe, but like them." It was, she knew, a matter of class, the education of people who were trained to respond to innocence with scorn or anger because they were terrified of what innocence might see. Although she understood him, there were things she would have to do differently.

"Do you think we can go?" She was becoming chilled and wet.

"In a moment."

"Then tell me the story of the fountain while we wait." Tufa looked up at the fountain and smiled, and it was the first time she had seen him smile. She had seen him laugh, but a laugh is something different from a smile.

"It's an old story and not a nice one," Tufa said.

"I think I can bear it."

"It's very dirty."

"You're apologizing."

"No, I'm warning you." He took her hand. "Here, help me up." They started to walk across the piazza once again. "I don't think

I'm going to tell you. Don't you know that that story is told to women who are thirty years old and who no longer are virgins?"

"I qualify then," Caterina said. He gripped her arm then, very hard, so hard that it took her by surprise and hurt her.

"No you don't," he said. "I know when you were born." She was amazed by this.

"Your father gave my father a cup of wine, a tin cup of wine and some coins, on the day you were born," Tufa said. "Do you think I would forget that?"

"Yes."

"My father didn't want them. He was insulted. And when my mother heard my father had turned down the money she made me go up to your house and tell your father that my father was wrong, that there was something wrong with his head and that we wanted the money."

"And you were ashamed."

"Of course I was ashamed. Everyone laughed. They never heard of such a thing before. So they gave me the cup of wine and put the coins in my pocket and then they put a chicken around my neck for my father."

He was silent, and she said nothing. There was no reason to apologize for her father, and both of them knew that.

"He never forgave my mother and he never forgave me," Tufa said. "We ate the chicken and he sat there and looked at us and went hungry. Then he went away and never came back. I was eight then. Do you think I would forget?"

"No."

"I was eight and I am thirty-four now, and that makes you twenty-six," he said.

"Why did you do that to my arm, grip me like that?"

"I don't want any lies. Even little lies. I want no more lies of any kind."

"I'll try not to tell any lies," Caterina said. "I don't know if it will be easy or not. I don't think I ever tried before."

At the end of the piazza they came upon the last of the rows of wine. "What the hell is all this?" Tufa said.

"The Germans are coming." She could feel his body stiffen and then relax once more. "They were trying to hide the wine."

"How do you know?"

"The mayor here, what's his name? The fat man. Bombolini. Italo Bombolini. He used to run the wineshop."

"I refuse to believe that that fat bastard is the mayor here," Tufa said.

"Does that telling lies apply to yourself as well? Because he is the mayor. The Captain of the People they call him."

"O God! O Maria!" Tufa said, and both of them were laughing again. He looked at the bottles glistening in the rain.

"No, I believe you," he said. "This is the work of some kind of idiot."

They went up the long hill and it was midnight when they reached the door to the Malatesta house and Tufa stopped to regain his breath before going inside it.

"I never thought I would go inside here again," Tufa said. "I never thought I would go inside of my own choice."

He hesitated at the door.

"I never ate chicken again. I have never had a piece of chicken in my mouth from that day," he said, but then he went through the door.

It was cold inside and dark and when Caterina managed to light the little lamp that was fed by ox fat she found that Tufa was trembling from cold and wet and from exhaustion. The lamp light made the room seem warmer, but he could not control his shaking.

"Take off your cothes and get into that bed," Caterina said. "My bed."

"I'm not used to taking orders," he said. He made no move of any kind.

"Do you want me to turn away?"

"Of course." He sounded annoyed. "Of course."

She waited until she heard him get into the bed before turning around. Next to the bed was a small porcelain stove that had been brought to Santa Vittoria by some Malatesta from some foreign place when there was money. There was no fuel for the fire, but she burned the stump of a broom and it gave good light, and for a while it heated the room. She found a bottle of anisette and the liquor warmed them both, but there was not enough of it to sustain them and he wanted to talk to her.

"I'll borrow a bottle," she said. When she returned he was asleep, but he awoke at once when she came back through the door. She had a bottle of good vermouth and she uncorked it and handed it to him.

"The bottle is all wet," Tufa said. "Oh, you went back down?" He shook his head. "They would have hung you from the fountain by your heels if they had caught you."

The story Tufa had to tell is not an uncommon one in Italy, although it is possible that Tufa would tell it with greater hurt than most of the others, since Tufa has more pride than most. The story is the same, over and over, only the facts are different and the names and the places.

He had wanted to be a good soldier and a good Italian. He had wanted to act with courage, he had wanted to keep his integrity and live with honor. It wasn't a great deal to ask of a state, to be able to serve it and to live and even die for it like a man. But they wouldn't allow that, although Tufa wasn't prepared to admit it. He lied to himself about the failures in Albania and the disasters in Greece. He continued to encourage his men to die for a cause they couldn't believe in, but which he could not make himself admit was not worth dying for. Through his example, young men, for him alone as a man, stood and fought and were maimed or killed for it. And then one night, in North Africa, near Bengasi, some of the men, his own men, shot him in the back.

"I'm sorry," the one who did the shooting said. "We have to do this to save ourselves."

Even then he wasn't willing to admit everything to himself. When he rejoined his regiment in Sicily the soldiers were frightened by the officer who was so brave that he would kill them to prove it. During the first attack his men deserted.

"*We* stay," Tufa had shouted at them. "The others run. We stay. We stand like men, we go down like men."

But they ran. They ran at him and past him, and he lifted his rifle as he had been forced to do before, and they kept running, and for the first time he lowered the rifle and knew that they were

171

right and he was wrong and that to shoot them would be to murder them. That night he himself ran, across Sicily in the night, to the Straits of Messina, where he used the rifle to force a fisherman to take him to the mainland, and he had run in the night like some wounded animal trying to make his way back to his den to lick his wounds in secrecy and darkness or to die.

When he was through the fire had gone out and the house was cold again and it was Caterina who was shivering.

"I'm going to have to come to bed. I hope you will allow this," Caterina said. It was a matter of courtesy only.

"There is no choice, is there?"

She took off her clothes and came to the bed, and neither of them said anything after that. Tufa had begun trembling once more, from the cold and his tiredness and from the story he had told. The heat of her body warmed him and calmed him and the trembling lessened, and after a time he slept. It wasn't sleep but a gaining of rest, because when he really slept he would not be easy to wake again. After a short time he awoke and they made love to each other. There was no surprise about it and no surprise about each other, they were exactly what they had expected of each other. When they had finished they lay back on the bed and looked at the darkness of the ceiling.

"I know everything about you," Caterina said, "except one thing. I don't know your first name."

"Perhaps we should keep it that way. You know what they say here: 'Love, but make sure to keep a wall between you.'"

"No, I want to know it. I feel I am entitled to that."

"I don't like my name. Carlo," he said.

She tried it several different ways. "It doesn't suit you."

"It's German. It comes from *Karl*. I've come to despise it."

They could hear the rain running down from the roof tiles and the filled gutters, splashing down into the shutters outside the windows and onto the cobblestones of the street.

"We have no wall between us," Caterina said.

"Maybe that is bad. Maybe that will destroy us."

"Why do you bring that up?"

He said that he didn't know. He said that he had lost faith and was no longer sure. "They say something else you should know, 'Love as if one day you will hate.' Maybe they're right."

"Why are they so mean and hard?" Caterina said.

"Because life is mean and hard. That's my trouble, do you see. I only learned that when I was thirty-four years old. The oldest child you will ever meet."

The shutters began to slap against the stone walls of the house. The rain began to come hard against the window pane. The wind was changing, Tufa said, and that meant the rain would pass.

"I think I'm also entitled to hear the story of the fountain now," Caterina said. She wanted to end this concern with themselves, it was too much for one day, but it didn't matter, because Tufa had surrendered himself to sleep at last. She lay beside him, fearful of moving but not able to sleep.

"Tufa? Carlo?"

She knew he wouldn't answer, but she wanted to talk to him. She had been watching his face and she found that looking at it moved her. She found she wanted to touch it, but she was afraid to.

"You're going to make me be in love again," she said.

The idea frightened her, because falling in love is dangerous. She thought of the Germans' coming. What was meaningless the day before was suddenly full of meaning. They had been nothing then and were everything now. They could take her, they could take Tufa, they could end what had already begun. In the end, however, she slept and like Tufa surrendered herself so completely to sleep that she didn't hear the soft thin pounding of the bell or peoples' steps on the cobblestones or the slamming of the doors, or even the shouts of those who were beginning to fill up the piazza down the hill below them, or the thumping of the carts going down the hill into the piazza.

ROBERTO had left them, Malatesta and Tufa, in the Piazza of the People and had gone to the People's Palace and to bed. He had slept for perhaps an hour or more, when Bombolini woke him. "God has come to me again," he said. "I want you to hear the new message."

Roberto was reluctant to move or even to lie there and listen to the story.

"Would you like some onions? I have some onions," Bombolini said. "*Please.*"

Roberto got up then because it frightened him to hear Bombolini beg him, and together they went downstairs. There was a pot of onions simmering in olive oil over the small fire the mayor had built.

"God clearly is trying to tell me something and I am too stupid to understand it," Bombolini said. "The answer is in here. I feel it in here and I can't get it out—like a rabbit in the back of a hole." And he told this story about the famous family named Doria:

They were famous sailors from Genoa, but at the time of the story they had very little money. One day the king announced he would honor them with a visit for dinner to their house.

"Turn down the offer. Find some excuse," the brothers of Andrea said. "We have no silverware, we have no decent plate, no dishes worthy of a king. We will be ashamed."

But Andrea told the king to come and then he went to a rich neighbor and borrowed all of his gold and silverware, and as proof that he would return it he left his oldest son as a hostage. If the plates were not returned the rich man could do as he pleased with the boy, even kill him.

The king arrived and he was impressed with the meal and with the service and with the gold and silver plates and platters and with the marvelous view of the sea and the harbor.

"You've done well for yourselves," he said. "You know how to live in the royal way."

"Our house is small because as seamen we prefer to live lightly so that we can move swiftly," Andrea said. "Sometimes, for example, when we are about to sail, we don't bother with the plate. We simply throw it off the terrace and into the sea."

And he flung a solid-gold goblet over the side of the terrace and down into the sea far below. The king's mouth was open.

"You can throw them over your head or you can drop them like this." He dropped a heavy silver tray into the sea. "I like to throw them myself." He threw a gold fork over his head and off the terrace.

"Like this?" the king said. And he flung a gold plate.

"Like that, yes. It's very handy," Andrea said, and he dropped a silver pitcher into the sea.

Even for a king it is not an everyday occasion to cast a fortune into the sea. They threw the plates and they threw the bowls and the knives and the forks, and when there was nothing left to throw at all the king turned to the Dorias and said: *"Great* men. You are great men, capable of the great act. I salute you."

He made them dukes on the spot. They are dukes to this day. They have been rich from then on.

* * *

"It's in there, Roberto," Bombolini said. "The answer, the solution, it's hiding in there."

"It was a high price to pay to impress the king," Roberto said. "What happened to the boy?"

"What do you mean what happened to the boy?" Bombolini said. "He went home to his father."

"But the treasure. All of the treasure was gone in the sea."

Bombolini looked at Roberto as if he had never really seen him before. "The gold and silver was in the fish nets they had stretched all along the bottom of the sea the day before. They only lost a silver cream pitcher."

"Ah, the fish nets." If the answer was in the story it lay somewhere in the fish nets, Roberto realized.

"Of course, the fish nets. You don't think they would throw the gold off the terrace without fish nets down below?"

He realized one other thing. That although he spoke the language he would never understand the mind of these people. Any peasant would know there was a fish net down below, and the point of the story was not how to fool a king as much as what a clever way to use a fish net.

"Do you see it now?"

Roberto had to admit that he didn't see it.

"Come and eat and maybe it will come to you." He ladled out the hot browned onions and he poured the bubbling olive oil over bread, and while he did that Roberto told him about Tufa and the Malatesta.

"You know there's only one bed in the house, don't you?" Bombolini said. Roberto shook his head.

"*One* bed. Can you imagine it?" he said. "A Malatesta copulating with a Tufa? You don't know what it means. A revolution, a new world entirely. A Tufa copulating with a Malatesta in the house of Malatesta."

"How do you know they are doing it?" Roberto said.

Once again Bombolini looked at him as if he had not seen him before. "They're in the same bed, aren't they?"

It is an Italian belief that if two people are in the same bed they must be making love to one another, not from desire necessarily, but because man is weak and unable to resist the natural urge. There is no court in Italy that is prepared to believe otherwise.

Roberto watched the mayor wiping the olive oil from his cheeks and chin and realized only then that he was crying, quietly but steadily, exactly as he had been eating. When the last of the bread and onions had been eaten Bombolini turned to Roberto.

"Don't let it alarm you," Bombolini said. "But, Roberto, tell me this one thing. What am I going to do?"

"Something will turn up. You watch."

"Americans always say that," Bombolini said.

"Will you listen to a story from me?" When Bombolini nodded Roberto told him a story he had learned from a soldier who had come from Arkansas.

One day, Roberto said, a man was hunting for bear and he came to the middle of a great open field and he found that his gun wouldn't work. There was no tree to climb, no rock to run behind, no cave to crawl into and all at once an enraged bear came out of some distant woods across the open field directly at the hunter. It was a very close call, Roberto said.

"What do you mean, a close call. What did the hunter do?"

"He climbed a tree."

"But I thought you said there was no tree."

"That's just the point. There *had* to be, there *had* to be."

Bombolini had listened with respectful silence, and when the story was over he shook his head and made a face.

"That's the difference between us, Roberto. You think there has to be an answer. But we know different. A thousand years has taught us differently. *That's* just the point. There isn't always an answer. Your people will learn that some day."

The mayor began to shed tears once more, very quiet and with no movement of his face, and Roberto felt he should turn away.

"Like with your idea about hiding the wine," Bombolini said. "It seemed like a good idea but it didn't work."

He said it as if it were an accusation and it angered Roberto, as if somehow America was responsible for the wine in the piazza.

"Of course, if you had put it where I told you . . ." Roberto said.

"What do you mean, where you told me?"

"In the place I told you about," Roberto said. "It might not work but at least you might have tried."

Bombolini did not want to ask him. He was becoming used to the idea that there was nothing that could be done to save the wine. It was comforting to him to admit surrender, and he wasn't willing to have the idea challenged.

"Where?" he said, in a voice as thin as the sound of the bell.

"In the Old Roman wine cellar."

Bombolini said nothing. He had an enormous urge to yawn.

"Down below the terraces," Roberto said. "At the foot of the mountain. The place with the two wine cellars."

"The two wine cellars," the mayor said.

"Put the wine in one of them and brick it over."

"Put bricks over the opening." His voice remained as thin as before, but it was a little higher.

"Yes. So it looks just like the wall. Seal it off," Roberto said. "Instead of an opening you'll have a false wall."

Bombolini said nothing for a long time—so long that Roberto grew impatient with him.

"It's all brick back there. You must remember it."

Bombolini nodded but the truth was that he had not been in the cave or seen the wine cellars in many years.

"That second cellar doesn't even look as if it belongs in there. The one at the far end. It looks like an afterthought, you know."

"Yes," Bombolini said.

"As if they built the first cellar and found they didn't have enough room and had to add a second one."

"Yes."

"So if you bricked it over it would all look like part of the wall."

"Yes." He looked numb now, although his heart was racing and he was conscious of blood rushing through him, as numb as the old oxen, the eyes large and staring, the body stunned but not moving, waiting for the next blow of the sledge hammer.

178

"They'll find it out," the mayor said.

"I suppose so."

"They'll see through it at once."

"It's a chance, that's all."

"They aren't stupid people."

"I suppose there are stupid Germans and smart Germans, just like here," Roberto said.

"They want the wine," Bombolini said. "They'll do anything to get it."

"You want it too," Roberto said. "I thought you wanted to try anything to save it."

Bombolini had been looking at the wall, afraid that if he looked at Roberto his line of reasoning might break down. Now he turned and moved toward him.

"I'm sorry," Roberto was saying. "I thought it was worth the try."

"Worth the try, Roberto? Worth it?"

He moved so swiftly toward Roberto that he struck a chair and knocked it over and didn't seem to notice it.

"Christ, Roberto," Bombolini said. "Christ above, Roberto," he said, and then he did something that is hard to put on paper because it is hard to make sense of. He struck Roberto such a blow in the face that the American fell to his knees and stayed there for a moment before going the rest of the way down to the stones on the floor.

"We'll build such a wall that God Himself won't be able to see it," he said aloud. He came back to himself then from wherever he had been. There was blood on the stones and for a moment he made a gesture of stopping and helping Roberto, but he turned and started instead for the door.

"I'm sorry, Roberto, but there's no time for you."

He ran. When he reached the piazza he kept running until he got to the campanile, and when the bell tower door wouldn't open he pulled on it with such fury that the old iron handle came off in his hands and he was able to work the latch. He felt for the bell cord in the darkness and when he felt the greasy hemp he began to pull on it as hard and as swiftly as he was able. There was the thin and muffled tone.

"God damn this miserable bell," he shouted. "God damn me for this miserable bell."

But it was strong enough to carry around the edges of the piazza and at least the people there heard it and they lit the olive-oil lamps and the tallow lights and they began to get out of bed, although it was an hour or two before it was time to get up. It was black in the piazza then.

Bombolini had no watch. "The time?" he shouted at the first people to come into the piazza. "What is the time? Tell me the time." At last someone came who owned a watch and they crowded around him and he held it up to catch the light of the moon. It was two o'clock in the morning. They watched Bombolini while he counted. He used his fingers for the hours and his fist stood for an entire day. He did it over several times because he wanted to be certain.

"Thirty-nine hours," he told them. "The Germans will be here in thirty-nine hours."

4 THE WINE

BEFORE the sun got into Santa Vittoria that morning, while all the cocks in the city were crowing as if they were inventing the morning, it was no longer possible to cross the Piazza of the People in a straight line.

Every person in Santa Vittoria who was able to walk, every man, and every woman and every child was in the piazza. Every cart in Santa Vittoria was in the piazza. Everything that could be pulled or pushed or had wheels was in the piazza. Every animal that could carry a bottle of wine was in the piazza. Every donkey and every mule and every ox in Santa Vittoria was in the piazza.

When Bombolini and the members of the Grand Council came out of the People's Palace into the piazza they were forced to nudge the people to get by them and finally to push them out of the way to reach the Fountain of the Pissing Turtle and start their inspection tour down the Corso Cavour.

Everyone wanted to say something to Bombolini, to touch him, to hit him on the back. A woman took him by the arm. "I want to tell you this, Italo. You are a great man," she shouted at him, and she kissed him full on the lips while her husband stood there and smiled and approved.

That is the way it was in the Piazza of the People, all of the way across it. The mayor didn't want to smile, he wanted to impress on the people the importance of the day and the work that lay ahead of them, but when they shouted at him and blessed him the smile would come and he could not get it to go away from his face. They stepped around the big wicker grape baskets the people had carried into the piazza and past the women with the large-throated water jugs that would receive bottles and over the buckets and tubs and laundry baskets that were spread over the cobblestones. Up on the fountain itself, Pietro Pietrosanto, as head of the army directing traffic in the piazza, was shouting orders.

"Get all of the people with the shoulder yokes and bring them to the fountain," he was shouting.

"Shoulder yokes, shoulder yokes," the men shouted, and in every corner a push and a shove began as the people with the yokes began their fight to get to the fountain.

"Will you ever get it organized?" Bombolini shouted to Pietro.

"I got it organized," Pietro said. "I know what I'm doing up here."

It was hard to see it, the way it is hard for an outsider who sees the harvest here to realize that out of all this chaos was actually a kind of secret and complex order that only those involved in picking the grapes can understand and that in all the pushing and shouting and shoving there was a shape and a form. Already, for example, all the young men and the strong men had been lined in a file, so that when the time came to pick up the bottles and begin carrying them down the mountain to the Roman cellars they would be the first to go because they could do the most.

"When you're ready for me down there," Pietrosanto shouted, "I'll be ready up here."

By the time Bombolini and the men reached the Corso and

started down it the young men were clapping their hands in time and shouting *"Let's go, let's go, let's go, let's go . . ."* and the sound followed them down through the street as if a mob were bellowing through a pipe at them. At the Fat Gate they stopped.

"Now where the hell is Polenta?" Bombolini said. "It's no good without the priest."

They waited for him and before they left they saw him coming down from a side lane into the Corso, his silver cross bobbing up and down over the heads of the people around him as he came, running.

"I'm sorry. They all want to be blessed on this day," Padre Polenta said.

"There's no time for blessing," Bombolini said.

"There is always time for God's blessing." When Bombolini saw all the men begin to nod he dropped the matter. The shouting from the piazza drove them on.

"We could move the whole city today," Vittorini said.

"We could move the whole mountain," one of them said.

When they trotted around the sharp corner in the Corso just past Babbaluche's house and shop, Bombolini for one brief moment felt a sensation of chill, the way it happens on an autumn day when a cloud passes over the sun and all at once it is cold. Bombolini said it was as if a cold hand slipped over his heart and squeezed it, very gently and coldly.

But they ran on. There is going to be trouble here, Bombolini said to himself, but he didn't hear himself. They went through the Fat Gate and started down the track that goes through the terraces to the foot of the mountain. They were walking fast, and then they were running down.

"Pietrosanto will be starting now," one of them said. The sun came up then, all at once, and it touched the walls around the city and then the roof tiles, and it glittered off the red-and-blue sign on top of the Cooperative Wine Cellar so that the sign was like a sun itself.

"You're certain you know how to do it, Padre?" Bombolini said. "It won't take long, I hope."

"It's in here, right here," the priest said. He tapped the book he held in his hand along with the cross. "All the rules of God."

After such a rain it should have been cool, but the wind had shifted and was coming from the south. The door to furnace of Africa that we thought had been closed for the year was open again. By afternoon the fresh snow on the high mountains would have melted and the slopes would be running with fresh water and the fountain in the piazza would be spurting ice-cold water. But down here the mud would harden and then cake, and by late afternoon the caking would explode into dust.

"A very fine day for the grapes," one of them said. Heat after rain is said to cause sugar to form and turn fat in the grapes. No one mentioned the other thing, that it would be a bad day for people. The sun already had a hot look to it, flat and hard and white, like a plate hung in the sky, and no cloud anywhere to soften it along the way. After that they went in silence until they reached the opening in the mountain that leads into the Big Room and the two cellars built into the back wall of the room. None of them would enter it then until the priest had gone in first.

"Hurry up, Padre, please," Bombolini said. "Run in there and sanctify the place."

"God's work will not be hurried," Polenta said, and he opened the black book and licked a forefinger and started through from page one.

"The index, Padre," Babbaluche said. "Can't you study the index. Look under 'D' for 'Devils.'"

The priest didn't look up. He went on the way he was going. The first men were already starting down the mountain with their loads of wine before he was halfway through the book.

"Can't you make up a prayer, Padre?" Vittorini said, in a gentle voice.

"I think that God would like that," someone said. They nodded.

"Something new and fresh for a change," Bombolini said.

"Something from the heart, not from a book."

"Yes," Bombolini said. "God would like that. If I were God I know that *I* would."

"There is a right way to cast out spirits and there is a wrong way," Padre Polenta said. "It's all in the book, and God goes by the book."

The first of the men had put down their wine on the sandy flat outside the entrance to the cellars and started back up the mountain when Polenta found what he was looking for.

"Exorcise," the priest said. He looked up at them. "Not under 'devil.' Not under 'ghosts,' not under 'spirits.' Under *'exorcise.'*"

Polenta waved his finger at him, and the mayor leaped forward to seize the book.

"Don't lose your place, Padre, in the name of God," he said.

It wasn't easy even after that. The priest read to himself for a long time and then announced that he needed water. There was no water and they offered him wine, but since the book said water it must be water. It was fortunate that it had rained the night before and the drainage ditch alongside the cart track to the road was filled with muddy water. They got the water in Vittorini's leather hat and the cock feathers were limp with water and clogged with clay. Bombolini handed the hat to the priest.

"Now go in there and start blessing, Padre," he said.

Polenta went inside the entrance and several of the braver men went with him, staying behind the cross and the aspergillum and the priest while he flayed and scourged whatever evil spirits were hiding in the darkness of the Big Room. When he started further in, back toward the two wine cellars built into the back wall and dug far into the mountain, even Bombolini lagged behind, and so the priest was all alone when he stepped down into the first of the cellars and fell head first into the water. When he came up again and shouted for help no one went to his aid at once, because it was felt that the battle between evil and good must have been joined there and that good was losing to evil, as sometimes happens. Finally Bombolini and Vittorini crossed the room and found the priest standing waist-deep in the water and they led him out onto the dry sandy floor of the Big Room.

The ice-cold hand had slipped over Bombolini's heart once more and his heart, or perhaps his soul, which he felt was associated with his heart, was as cold as the priest's skin.

"It's all over now," one of them said. "There's nothing left to be done."

The cellars were flooded with four feet of water. Men began to come into the Big Room, although no one would go to the cellars. Some of them had been afraid even to stand by the entrance, for fear that the spirits, chased out of the cave by the holy water and the cross, might somehow fly down into them.

Five people at least now claim to be the one who first suggested what to do. "Get Longo," someone said. "If anyone can do anything now it is Longo."

When you write a history and look back you see there are many points and times when everything might have changed if it had not been for some one act. If Fabio had not gone to Montefalcone that evening, if Gambo's bike had not been available because Gambo had been hit by a rock and Gambo had not shared a room with a woman like Gabriele and Fabio had not been pretty enough to please her, and if Tommaso Casamassima had not made his speech about brave men and good wine—Longo belongs to one of these moments.

They seized his name and began to shout it in the Big Room, booming it off the rough stone walls, "Longo, Longo"—a miracle in their midst, one more twig for people who were drowning. One of the youngest men ran out of the cellar and started up the mountain. He ran until his legs would not go any farther, and then he cried out Longo's name to one of the men coming down. There was now a steady line of people coming down the mountain with their burdens of wine, and the man turned and called the message back to the man behind him and that one called it back to another, and in this way the message flew up the mountain from mouth to mouth, leaping up at fifty feet a step. By the time Bombolini and the priest came out of the cave and into the sun and looked up at the city, Luigi Longo, as puzzled as most of the people in Santa Vittoria, was already on the way down.

Longo is an example of something that can happen to a man here. When he was young he had somehow managed to get away and go to Switzerland and become an apprentice electrician. But he came home one day for his father's funeral, and a few months later there was a letter from Constanzia Casamassima telling him that she was carrying his child and that he had better come back and make her honest or her father and her brothers would go up there and make him something she would rather not describe. Longo came back, and then there was the grape harvest and the baby was born and he had inherited a piece of a terrace and some vines, and one day Longo woke up to find that his visa had expired and he couldn't go back to Switzerland and he was bound to the soil of Santa Vittoria as securely as were the roots of the vines he tended in a subdued rage.

We were spoiled by Longo here. He never lost the dream of wires and when he was sober he was a genius with electrical things, a first-rate electrician with tenth-rate equipment. There was no piece of wiring that Longo had not at some time restored or re-created. The wiring here was our Lazarus, sickly and dying and dead, and to them Longo was our Christ, performing a miracle a week.

He looked at the first of the two wine cellars, and he went into the water and walked along the walls, and in total silence he came outside and drew some pictures in the sand and then he stood up and brushed the hair out of his long, tired, ravaged face and said: "I can do this thing."

There is no need here to put down in detail all of the things that Longo did or started. There was an old generator here which was kept in the cellar of Santa Maria of the Burning Oven and which had been left behind by a traveling circus when a juggler had attempted to kill a tightrope walker over the love of a twelve-year-old acrobat, a boy, which confused the people here, and everyone had cut everyone else and gone to the hospital or to jail, and we were left with a set of Indian clubs and the generator for the lights. He told them to get the pump from the water tower and to cut down all of the electric wires that ran from the foot of the mountain to the Fat Gate and to bring the wire to the Big Room and after that he ordered the two best bicycles in the city to be brought down the mountain with four or five of the best young riders.

Bombolini went back outside of the cave, because he didn't understand what Longo was doing and it made him nervous not to understand what was happening. The wine was now spread out all over the flat sandy place and was piling up back across the flat part of the valley.

"How's it going?" the men who were carrying the wine would shout to the mayor.

"Fine. It's going well. It's going well."

They would smile then. They were happy and excited. They were doing something and had some work to do. Bombolini also made marks in the sand. There were 18 hours left in this day and there were 17 hours left in the day ahead. The total was 35. He added them over and over again, as if by coming up with some new answer he could change the order of the hours. He looked very sad then.

"What's the matter?" Vittorini asked him.

"Nothing is the matter. Everything is good," Bombolini said, but the anguish was there, in the numbers: 35 and 0.

The Germans would arrive in 35 hours. Not one bottle of wine had as yet been hidden.

ND when they put up the plaques, next to the one for Bombolini and Tufa, alongside the eternal green flame that already burns in the piazza for Babbaluche the cobbler, there should be one for Longo. The things Luigi Longo did that morning are remembered here and will always be remembered here.

By seven o'clock the pump had been pried loose from the base of the water tower and the generator had been cleaned and the old fire hose had been carried down the mountain as if it were an old tired python and the bicycles had been taken apart and readjusted so that, when they were pumped and their wheels, which were elevated from the ground, were turned, they caused the drive wheels on the generator to turn and power was created and a dim light began to appear in the bulbs, which grew brighter and brighter as the young men drove the bicycle wheels. Fabio was among the bike riders.

"*Now* you have come back," Bombolini said.

"Only for today and tomorrow," Fabio said. "I won't be here to humiliate myself when the bastards come."

"We're going to do it, Fabio. We're going to save the wine."

"Even if you lose your honor."

Bombolini was hurt by the boy's bitterness.

"You get on fire, Fabio. It's no good. Fire in the heart only ends up causing smoke in the head."

Babbaluche, who was fashioning the leather belts that connected the generator to the bicycle wheels, had heard them.

"It's more peasant wisdom," he said to Fabio. "Don't listen to him. It's more smooth words. What did my father say? 'Beware of the man who makes cream with his mouth; he winds up making butter with his nose.' You watch him, Fabio. When the krauts come he'll wind up with butter all over his nose."

Fabio was disgusted. He turned away from Bombolini, who disgusted him.

"Where are the real Italians?" he said but no one heard him, or if they did no one answered.

"That's exactly what I plan to do. When they come I plan to have butter all over my nose," Bombolini said.

When the generator had built up a store of energy Longo connected it to the pump. At first, for the first few minutes at least, there was terror in the Big Room because nothing happened to the pump. The moving parts were heavy with old oil and stubborn like an old ox, but then Longo began to move the parts by hand and they began to move on their own after that, grudgingly, only as far as they had to go, the way a snail moves when it is prodded, but then to go a little more swiftly each moment and then to gurgle and cough and burble and finally to thump now and then and all at once to go *thump, thump, thump, thump,* and water began to gush from the mouth of the hose. They heard the cheer from the Big Room all the way up the mountain, because the hollow roars went up the ancient air shafts out into the pastures above the cellars, and they could hear them in the town.

When the old hose broke, which happened often, it was Longo

who fixed that as well. He sent boys up onto the terraces and they came back with grape leaves and vines, and they tied them over the breaks in the tired old fabric of the hose, like crude bandages to stop the bleeding of a wound.

Longo came out of the cave after that, and he sat down with Bombolini in the warm sun.

"We're going to do it," Longo said. "The first cellar will be empty in an hour."

Bombolini rose and took Longo's hand and he kissed him on both cheeks. "He says we're going to do it," he said to Vittorini.

"Yes. I heard him say it. We're going to do it."

Old Vines came out of the cave after that. "That was clever of you," he said to Longo, "using the grape leaves. So the grapes will save the grapes. It is fitting."

"We're going to do it," Bombolini said.

"Yes, we're going to do it," the cellar master said.

Bombolini started back up the mountain then for Santa Vittoria, and he was conscious that never in his life had he ever felt happier than he felt right then.

TUFA was like the others here. He had come awake with the sun, and in the end he couldn't stay in bed with the sun up. He wanted to stay in the bed, next to this woman, but he heard the sounds in the piazza and the oxen in the lanes and he felt that he must get out of the bed. Before he did he was conscious that she was awake also, lying next to him, looking at him.

"You should go back to sleep," she said. "It's very important for you. You should lie here for days and get your strength back."

It caused him to laugh and that offended her. One of them was always laughing at something the other had not meant to be funny.

"Do you really think I'd get my strength back lying here next to you all day?"

"Oh, that. Oh, I see. Soldier talk. It was uncalled for."

"Why? You have no shame. You told me."

She smiled at him then. "It's true. I was born outside shame. It used to worry my teachers at school. They always felt I was going to get in some terrible trouble."

"And did you?"

"Of course not. Since I had no shame I wasn't attracted to the kind of people who get you into trouble."

"Which is why you are here in bed with me."

"I don't know why I'm here in this bed with you. Except that I want to be." It was she who got up.

"What are you doing?" Tufa said. "I'm the peasant here. I'm the one who gets up."

"I'm going to get us something to eat," Caterina said.

"I'm not hungry for food right now."

"You're the one with no shame."

"I'm the one who is starved," Tufa said.

He watched her come back across the room toward him. She had no clothes on and there was no consciousness of herself, and he knew that no other woman in Santa Vittoria would ever be able to walk that way or do such a thing.

"You're so honest," Caterina said. "I could never say a thing that way. I haven't learned to talk that way yet."

He reached up and brought her to the bed.

"No, I see it," Tufa said. "It's true. You have no shame."

When they were through he did sleep again, and it was her turn to listen to the sounds of the city and the morning. She sat in the bed and looked at his uniform, black, stained, dirty, torn. It would have to be done away with before the Germans came. The sight of the uniform saddened her, because it told by itself the ordeal Tufa must have endured. Very quietly then she got out of the bed and went into a back room and came out with a suitcase full of clothes that had once belonged to her husband. He had left them there in the event that one day he might be forced to run. They were good clothes for Tufa, outdoor clothes, estate clothes, hunting clothes.

She went back into the room and looked down on Tufa and at that moment knew real fear. Through Tufa she had invested in life again, and to the degree you invest, to that degree are you in danger of losing your investment.

There was no fear for herself—not that she was brave but because she was confident that men would not abuse her or be able to take advantage of her. Men were afraid of her kind of beauty. Tufa was beautiful, also, but his kind of beauty was different. Because he was a challenge to other men, she knew that he was a type that men were driven to destroy. She began to clean up the room, because she knew he would like that, and even to sweep and she was thankful that he wasn't awake to see her handle the twig broom. When he finally did awake again he said he was hungry, truly hungry, not for her but for bread dripping with olive oil, for some good black olives and for an egg. Caterina put down the broom and went to the door.

"I am going to get you an egg if I have to sell myself to do it," Caterina said. She was conscious that he didn't approve of her joke.

"I'm going to go with you," Tufa said. He began to get out of bed, and for the first time she was able to see him.

"Aren't you going to turn around?" he said.

"If you wish."

"It's what the women here do. When the man gets up they turn around."

"I didn't know," Caterina said.

"I don't see anything wrong with it," Tufa said.

"I'll make it a point to turn around," Caterina told him.

But she had seen him and he was the way she expected. Had he been born rich he would have to be described as beautiful, the kind of model a sculptor would use. But time had done things to Tufa. The body now showed the effects of life on beauty, the way life attempts to destroy it and bring it down to its own level. The body was too hard in places and too damaged. The arms were too heavy, too veined and muscled from too much hard work, the wrists were thick, the texture of the skin was rough from too much sun and wind and too much sweat. Everything about the body was bone and sinew, and hard. But still the beauty was there, beneath it, especially in Tufa's face and eyes.

"If you will look by the bed you will see some clothes," she told him. "They belonged to my husband. I didn't think you would mind."

"Mind? No, why should I mind?" He began to pick up the clothes. "He had good taste," Tufa said.

"He had money."

"You can turn around now," he said. He was wearing brown corduroy pants with leather patches on the inside of the knees and a white linen shirt that opened at the neck and a large brown leather belt and a soft dark hat. He was very handsome and he knew it.

"They'll think I'm a landowner," Tufa said.

"It's better than knowing you're a Fascist officer. Come. You must be starving."

"I am starving."

When they were halfway down the hill that goes into the Piazza of the People they were able to see the piazza itself, and Tufa stopped in amazement. "What in the name of God are they doing down there?" he said.

"Something to do with the wine we saw last night," Caterina told him. She wanted to take the lane that cuts down and around the back side of the piazza so they would be alone and quiet, but Tufa wouldn't allow her. When they came down into the piazza itself he stopped and watched them.

"Look at the way they're loading those carts," he said to her. "They should take down the sides and then put the wine in and put the sides up again. They could go twice as fast. And look at this one over by the front of the church."

"Come," Caterina said. "It's not our concern." She looked at him and made him take his eyes away from the scene in the piazza. "We have so little time, you know?"

'Oh, you're right," Tufa said. "It's a habit. You see them doing it wrong and you want them to do it right." He took her by the hand, in the daylight, something that isn't done here, and they started around the outer edge of the piazza. Not many noticed them. It was hot in the piazza then and loud, and the ox manure and mule droppings steamed on the cobblestones and there was the smell of people and wine from broken bottles and the sound of them all mingled into a thick soup.

"I can smell this town miles away," Tufa said. "Every town has its own smell."

"I don't know if I like it or not," Caterina said. "I used to hate coming back here."

"I like it."

"Then I think I'll try to like it," Caterina said. "I'll make an effort to cultivate the smell."

They were in the part of the piazza where the oxen had been put, and the smell was very strong then and they pushed their way in and out between the animals.

"Then you'll have to fall in love with an ox first," Tufa said. "That's the first step."

"No it isn't," Caterina said; but he didn't understand her.

They went around the far side to one of the lanes that leads out of the piazza down into one part of Old Town to where the dung heaps are and the chickens are and where they might be able to get an egg. Before going down it, Tufa stopped to study the scene once more.

"Whoever is running this is an idiot," Tufa said and turned away from it, and so he failed to see Bombolini with several of the other leaders come up into the Piazza of the People, although they saw Tufa.

"Look at them," the priest said. "Everyone in Santa Vittoria knows there's only one bed in that house."

"Who would have believed it?" Bombolini said. "It's hard to believe your own eyes. A Tufa with a Malatesta in one bed. That's democracy for you."

For the past several hours Bombolini had refused to believe the evidence of his eyes. He had come all the way up the mountain lying to himself. The traffic in the Corso Cavour had by then backed up so far and so deeply that the river of wine had become a trickle. It was because of the turn in the road and because the men were becoming exhausted from the loads they carried and the trips back up the mountain. The ox carts locked wheels in the turn and the traffic going down had to stop entirely to allow the traffic to come back up.

"It's all going wrong," Pietrosanto said. "I don't know what's happening, but it's all going wrong."

"It will work its way out," the mayor said, and although he felt the cold hand on his heart again, he believed it at the moment. The Italians have made an art out of their ability to deceive themselves, a German once wrote about us. "And why not?" Babbaluche would say. "It's the only thing that keeps the poor bastards going."

"It's the thing that destroys us," Fabio once said. "We have to face the truth."

"And do you have a gun to put to your head?" the cobbler said.

There is no way of telling how long the mayor would have gone on this way if Pietrosanto had not seen Tufa pass through the piazza. "I'm going to ask Tufa," he said.

"We don't need people to come in from the outside and tell us how to run our affairs," Bombolini said. He was openly hurt.

"Outside?" Pietrosanto shouted. "Outside? Tufa's one of *us*. Tufa's a Frog. Tufa's our blood. What are you? A Sicilian . . ."
He didn't say the rest, but began running for the back lane, pushing and shoving people as he went.

Caterina and Tufa were already far down when Pietrosanto reached the head of the lane but they didn't stop or turn around.

"No one looked at us in the piazza," Caterina said. "I thought they liked you here."

"They saw. Under the veils, behind the oxen. They don't know what to say to us. They don't know how to speak to us. They don't know whether to call me *signor* or *don* because I'm sleeping with the Malatesta."

"Do you think they know about last night?"

Tufa looked at her first with astonishment and then with real humor, and he began to laugh as he hadn't laughed for a long time.

"Do they know? My God, Caterina." It was the first time he had used her name. "They know how many times."

"They must think I'm terrible."

Tufa was serious then. "No, no, they think I'm lucky."

Pietrosanto seized him by the shoulder. His face was as red as a pot and he was taking big breaths, because Pietro is not young.

"I saw you looking in the piazza. Do you know something? You know something to do?"

Pietro put his hands on his knees and bent over to get his breath and stop his heart from pounding, and Tufa took a long time in answering. "Yes, I have a plan."

Pietrosanto stood up then. "I knew he would have a plan," he shouted at Caterina. "He's smart, do you understand? He has a head. A head. A head." Pietrosanto isn't one to hold back when he is excited. He hit himself on the head with the heel of his hand so hard that if he had done it to someone else it would have begun a real fight. He hit Tufa in the head and he would have hit the Malatesta if Tufa hadn't blocked his hand.

"It's very complicated," Tufa said.

"Will it save the wine?"

"If it works it will save the wine."

Pietrosanto took off his hat, the one with the tall hawk's feather that marked him as the leader of the army of the Free State of Santa Vittoria, and put it on Tufa's head, and he took off his red arm band, which read Commander in Chief, and pinned it around Tufa's arm. Tufa looked at Caterina.

"What can I say?" Caterina said. "You look good in the hat."

"If it was anything else but the wine, do you understand?" Tufa said. "But it's the wine. It's blood here, you know, and it's my blood as well as theirs."

"I'll go and get you the egg," Caterina said, and started down the lane.

Pietrosanto and Tufa started back toward the Piazza of the People. Tufa's name ran ahead of him the way they say it happens in Rome when the Pope passes.

Tufa . . . Tufa . . . Tufa's here . . . Tufa's back . . . Tufa . . . Tufa . . . Tufa's in charge . . . It's going to be all right, Tufa's back.

When they reached the piazza, although no one had been able to move before, a path was somehow opened in front of them. Give this credit to Bombolini. He was able to see the piazza as it was, the mess that had been created in the city. The Master would have approved of him. He came forward to meet Tufa. And give credit to Tufa. He could have seized command then with the approval of the people, but he deferred to the mayor, whom he knew only as a clown.

"Will you ask the people to clear the piazza?" Tufa said.

"Tell them to go to their homes and wait. Tell them to get something to eat and to rest and to wait."

At first it appeared to be a failure, but then a few people got into the right lanes and started down them and as they left the jam began to lessen and soon the lanes going up and down from the piazza were filled to the walls with people and animals and carts. While they waited they heard good news. The water pump had lowered the level so that it revealed the top of the ancient drain, and a boy named Rana, which means frog (because he is shaped like a frog) was sent swimming down the darkness of the pipe with a grappling hook. He found a tree in the drain which must have been there hundreds of years, since there are no trees here anymore, not down in the valley. They pulled it out and the water began to rush down the length of the drain as if a giant toilet had been flushed.

"God has a purpose. God knows. He sent us the frog twenty years ago for just this purpose." Everyone nodded. There had never been any other use for Rana during all that time except to make jokes of him.

While Rana had been swimming in the drain they had found the old ventilation shafts, and cleaned them of the bones of sheep who had fallen in, and all of the things that had blown in over the centuries, so that the hot African wind which was burning on the side of the mountain began to rush down into the cellars and through the Big Room, and Old Vines could say that they would be ready to lay the wine within an hour.

Tufa's second order was to take down the wall of the Cooperative Wine Cellar that faced the Fat Wall and the little opening through it that we call the Thin Gate. Some of the men were not sure about the next move.

"Are you sure you want to do this, Tufa?" Bombolini asked. Tufa nodded that he did.

"Take down the wall," the mayor ordered.

The men were not strong about it at first. They chipped at the bricks and stones with mattocks and hammers and iron bars, and they were delicate because they didn't like to break down something which had been built with so much effort and cost. But when the first bricks came out they began to throw themselves into the work, because there is always something exciting about destroying something and about tearing something apart.

"The Corso is a pipe, you see?" Tufa said. "As with any pipe, it can take so much water and no more, no matter what the pressure behind it."

"I see."

"You thought you could push it through by desire, because you wanted it. But there are laws—laws of nature."

"I see."

"Now we have to find a stream that can handle a larger flow."

"I see."

"Call out the people now. Leave the carts and leave the animals and bring the people down."

The wall was down then, and the wine in the cellar could be seen inside, naked, exposed, looking out of place, like a woman caught with no clothes on in a place she has no right to be.

"Ring the bell," Tufa said.

They looked at one another.

"The bell doesn't play so well." One of them said to Tufa. "Something happened to the bell."

"It's a very complicated story," Bombolini said.

They rang the bell, what there was of it to ring, and they sent boys running through the streets and lanes, and the people came out of their houses and gathered first in the Piazza of the People and then in a long file down the Corso Cavour right to the door and the broken wall of the Cooperative Wine Cellar. Some of them had managed to sleep for a few minutes and to eat, and they rubbed the sleep out of their eyes and the bread from their beards and lips.

As they came down, then, Tufa and Pietrosanto and the soldiers and Bombolini began to make a line of them beginning at the open wall and running down across the open area where the grapes are pressed at harvest and down to the Thin Gate and through the wall and then down the steep track that the goats take down the mountain.

"It's going to take courage," Tufa said to the women. "It's going to take all your guts."

"We have guts," a woman answered him.

"When it comes to the wine we have guts," another said.

"I'm going to ask more of you than I ask of soldiers," Tufa told them.

"I would hope so," someone said. There is no respect for soldiers up here.

Down they came then, filing down the Corso from the Piazza of the People, the true army of Santa Vittoria in the service of the wine.

"Some of these are babies," Tufa said.

"When it comes to all-out war," Vittorini said, "you use the troops you have." It caused Tufa to laugh.

"I'm supposed to say those things," he said.

They mixed the old with the young, and the strong with the weak, so they could spell each other and make up for each other's weaknesses. If people were too old or sickly Tufa would take them out of the line.

"A chain is only as strong as its weakest link," Bombolini would tell them, but they would curse him, to his face anyway. When Caterina came down the line Tufa stopped her. "Let me see your hands." She held out her hands. They are so long and beautiful. He sent her back up the mountain to get gloves.

When the last of the people had passed, Tufa ran down the line to make a last inspection. The line now ran from the back of the wine cellar to the wall and through it, and down the mountain to the entrance to the Roman cellar. Tufa came back up, placing the people where they would be of the most value. In a place that was steep the taller people were positioned since they could reach up farther and lean down lower. The older people were put on the flat places, where the strain would be the least.

At a few minutes after one o'clock on Tuesday afternoon Carlo Tufa was able to stand on the floor of the valley, one hundred feet from the entrance to the ancient wine cellar, and look back up the mountain, over the terraces, all the way to the city wall and to the Thin Gate, and even a few yards inside it, and see one continuous line of people. And he was able to know that the line continued all of the way beyond that into the heart of the cellar. He ran across the flat sandy stretch in front of the opening.

"Are you ready in there?"

The men inside shouted back that they were hot to go. He ran outside then and back away from the base of the terraces so that Bombolini would be sure to see him and he gave the sign by a motion of his arm.

"Start them going," he shouted. "Let them go. Pass them on," he called out, even though he couldn't be heard.

But you could hear the people on the mountain then, shouting and cheering when they saw the sign, very loud in the valley and perhaps all the way to the river and over it in Scarafaggio.

"Pass them on, pass them on," the people began to shout, and the word flew up the mountain, it shot from mouth to mouth, and it was the start of the rhythm.

The bottles began to flow then, hand to hand, a stream of bottles at first, out of the cellar, down to the gate, through the wall and then down the mountain, a stream at first until they found the rhythm of the flow and then it was a river, a river of wine running down the mountain.

$\mathbb{T}$HE SHOUTING stopped soon enough, because the day was hot and the work was hard, but the wine kept coming so that three teams of men were finally needed to put down the wine.

It isn't easy to describe how they lay the wine here. It is a simple-looking job, but outsiders never learn to do it well. It is something you grow up knowing how to do, the same as spooning soup into your mouth. No one remembers learning how to use a spoon, it is something that is learned and not taught. It was the same with the wine. The first row of bottles is laid on the ground, and then long strips of wood, just strong enough to support a second row of bottles, are laid on top of the bottom row. The second row is placed in the opposite direction, one row of corks, one row of butts, and this goes on, tier after tier, eighteen and even twenty tiers high. All of the while long thin strips of wood are worked down through the rows of bottles, to the left of the neck of a bottle in one row and to the right of the neck of the bottle below, so that the bottles pull and push against each other and in the end provide the very force that holds them all together. It is very simple and very strong, and it can be put up or taken down as fast as men can put down bottles.

At the beginning the wine-layers were gay also, shouting to each other to move it, move it, slapping the bottles from hand to hand, the rows rising and going back into the dimness of the deep cellar to where Longo's pale lights could barely reach, but they soon ceased. As the wine kept coming they began to feel that they were running just ahead of a flood that in the end would drown them. Some of the men who worked in the cellar that day and night have never put down another bottle of wine, because the memory of it was so painful to them.

In the first hours the enemy was the sun, which sat on the people's backs as if it were a hot iron pressing down on them, but later it became the mountain itself. To keep from falling off it, the people were forced to brace themselves with one leg and step up the steep flank with the other, and more than any other part of the body it was the legs that began to tire and then to sting with fatigue and finally to cramp and knot. Tufa worked out a good plan. At a blast from the horn of Capoferro, every ten minutes, the people passed one more bottle and then stood up and massaged their legs and moved up the mountain to the spot above them. This gave the people a sense of going somewhere and it changed their positions and different muscles were put into use.

After that, the problem was water; and there was a second plan. At two blasts from the horn the wine passers put down the bottles and walked across the terraces to the concrete spillways that run down through the terraces and waited for the water to come. They got five seconds, and the water came down hissing and rushing like a runaway train. Some of the people put their faces in the spillway and caught what their mouths would hold and some caught water in shirts and hats and broken bottles and some climbed into the spillway itself and let the water run over them.

After the second hour the bottles began to break. There were tired hands and sweaty hands, and the bottles would slip or swing against a rock and there would be the sound of breaking glass and a groan from someone on the line and then the smell of wine, good and sweet at first, but then sticky and sour as the sun reached it. Then there was blood. Many of the people had no shoes, and although their feet are as tough as ox leather, glass will finally cut through leather, and blood began to run with the wine and the whole length of the line to glitter with glass.

In the late afternoon, when the sun was not so direct and when a cooler breeze began to slip up from the shadows in the valley, the people passing the wine had settled into a true rhythm; they gave into the bottles then, not seeing but only feeling them, swinging to the left and right, slapping the bottles from hand to hand, so that at times it sounded like a regiment of soldiers marching on the mountain.

When the boys came down from the mountain where Tufa had sent them to cut pine branches to use for torches in the coming night he had another plan for them. He sent them into the line because they were fresh and still strong, and the people they replaced were allowed to get out and to crawl under the thick green shade of the grapevines and to rest and even sleep there for a little while. It was only a taste of rest, but it was enough to keep them going.

The men were mixed with the women and there was something personal in the passing of the bottles, in the rhythm of it, in the swaying of the bodies, in the smell of each other and in the touching of their hands. Fabio, for instance, found himself next to a woman he had hardly ever noticed before, and as they worked he began to appreciate a kind of stubborn beauty about her in the calm, passive set of her face and the smooth solid strength of her arms and the sureness of her touch and the way her solid full breasts rose and fell with each passing of the wine. Up above him in the line, he could see Angela working and it didn't bother him. She was a girl and this was a woman.

"What are you looking at?" the woman finally said to him.

"You," he said. It was the kind of thing that a week before

would have caused him to turn scarlet and sent him running down the mountain.

"Well, keep your eyes and your hands where they belong," the woman said.

"I will make an effort, but it will be hard," Fabio said, and he smiled at her. Fabio, he told himself, you are becoming a goat.

Up the line, beyond Angela, he could see Caterina, and he decided that when the chance offered itself, he would work next to her. She was surrounded by women. She was the only one who wore gloves and in spite of the rough clothes she wore, ones designed for hunting or riding, it was easy to see that the Malatesta stood out from all the other women. The other women were black with sweat, but Caterina didn't sweat, there was only dampness on her brow and beads of wetness on her upper lip.

"Even when they work the rich don't sweat like the poor," a woman said and it was true.

From time to time Tufa came down the line to encourage the people on it and to change positions and to keep the bottles flowing, and when he did he took her place for a few minutes and allowed her to crawl under the vines.

"Why don't you sweat?" he said to her. "It would be good for you."

"Malatestas don't sweat," she said. "They must have forgotten how. They gave it up a long time ago."

"The dream of every Italian is some day not to sweat," someone said.

"And who will grow the grapes?"

"We'll hire people to do that," the cobbler told them. "We'll hire Germans to do it. They like to work," Babbaluche had said.

One time when he had to go on, Tufa found Caterina asleep under a vine. He kissed her then, in front of others.

"You have to get up," he said. "But I am proud of you." Later, Tufa realized that it was the first compliment he had ever given to a woman, because the men don't learn to do that here. The sun at the time had been partly hidden by the tall mountain to the northwest of here and then swiftly, in a matter of moments, it went behind them completely and the mountainside and then the city itself was thrown in shadow. There was a sigh then all along the line, mixed with the *slap, slap, slap, slap* of the glass against flesh, because at once it was cooler and also because many had promised themselves that if they could last until the sun went down they could make it through the evening and perhaps the night.

* * *

In the beginning of the night it was better. The cool winds had come and after that the fog. It clung to the dew on the grape leaves, and it moistened the ground and cooled the rocks, and it softened the skin that the sun and the wind of the day had dried and cracked. But the fog got thicker and there was new trouble on the line. When someone fell out it was hard for the replacement to find where the chain had been broken.

"Here . . . Over here . . . Down . . . here . . ." the people would call, but at night and in the fog voices are strange and distances are obscured. People stepped on the glass and fell on the stones, and the bottles began to break again. At ten o'clock Tufa made a mistake. There had been no food, and a tiredness was beginning to settle on the line like some disease that paralyzes the muscles so there is only numbness left. To bolster the spirits he decided to allow every other person on the line to open the bottle he was passing and to share it with the person next in line. Because they were so starved, the wine made many of the people drunk, and the bottles began to break even worse than before.

The night gave us protection from the eyes on the road and although the idea of morning was desired by the people it frightened them as well. But what frightened the people most of all was the knowledge that as hard as they had gone—and each hour they were going slower and slower—the Cooperative Wine Cellar on the mountain was still more than half full.

Some time after ten that night, when the wine was moving badly, Tufa decided that the time had come to risk the use of light. The pine boughs that had been cut that night were bound with wire and dipped into barrels of ox fat and lengths of rope were dipped in the same barrels and they were lit and passed down the mountain, one every fifty feet or so. It was dangerous. Beneath the fog the light of the flaming torches was magnified and the line glowed like some flaming arrow pointing down from the city to the ancient cellar below. It was dangerous, but it gave the people heart again. The people here are afraid of the night. Many of the men were afraid to step off the line and go into the vineyards to relieve themselves, and the women also worked in fear and pain both. The lights gave them courage.

And it was these lights which drew Roberto down to the wine-passing line. He had recovered from the blow and gone to bed, and when he awoke he went out of the Palace of the People and, not finding Bombolini, took a walk in the piazza to clear his head. He had thought the city was asleep until he saw the lights. He went down the Corso to witness what his words had begun.

"What happened to you?" Bombolini said.

"You know what happened to me," Roberto said.

"Oh, yes," the mayor said. It seemed to have taken place weeks before. "It was excitement. I know you understand. A blow of admiration. A blow of love. I am Sicilian, you understand."

"Being Sicilian must be a very strange thing," Roberto said. "It provides an excuse for everything."

He watched the wine going down the mountain and he knew what was taking place, and then he went back up to the Cooperative Wine Cellar. He could see that almost half or perhaps even more than half of the wine was gone by then and he could also see that the people on the line were working by instinct, at the level of the lowest animals, like blind mules grinding grain at harvest.

"It's good that you are almost done," Roberto said. "The people can't go on much longer."

"What do you mean, done? There's still half of the wine to go," the mayor said.

"But you wouldn't take it all. You have to leave some of it for them."

"We don't leave a drop for the bastards," a man shouted to Roberto from the line. "Don't give away *our* wine, friend."

He felt guilty not helping, and although his leg pained him to work he took a place in line from a woman and was pleased to find that he could do the work and that he was near Caterina Malatesta and Angela Bombolini, although he knew he shouldn't think of such things. The work helped, but it bothered him, because he knew they were wrong about the wine. While he passed the bottles he remembered something from his youth and he knew he was right and that he also could tell it to the people in a way that they could understand.

It was the Rabbit Garden that since has become famous in Santa Vittoria. When Roberto was a boy his father put in a large vegetable garden in the back of the house, because no Italian could stand the sight of soil going unused. Roberto was ashamed of it, filled with broccoli and other goomba foods. At night the rabbits came from the woods along a parkway and stole from the garden. The first year the garden was a failure, until some people told his father what the Americans did. They made their garden and they fenced it in, and then they made a second garden, smaller, with a low fence around it, for the rabbits. The rabbits came and ate the rabbit garden and they never touched the main garden again.

"That's America for you," his father would say, and he would tap his head. In Italy, he would say, they would put boys in the garden all night if they had to, but they never would build a garden for the rabbit.

"Signora," Roberto said. "You have to take your place again." She was disgusted with him.

"You Americans, you have no guts," she said. "You have forgotten how to work."

He went to Bombolini and he told his story, and Bombolini knew at once that it was true, that Santa Vittoria, if the Germans weren't to tear it apart brick by brick and stone by stone, needed a Rabbit Garden of its own. The only question was how large the garden should be.

The mayor told it to Tufa, and Tufa was impressed, and Pietrosanto was made to understand, and so they stopped the flow of wine and allowed the people to rest, and by the light of the pine torches they held a meeting of the Grand Council.

The council members looked into the wine cellar, and some of them walked around the bottles and tried to count them in their heads, and they came back outside with long faces.

"Ten thousand bottles," one of the older men shouted.

"Ten thousand. It's enough," another said. "Not a drop more. It's all that we can afford."

Everyone knew the number was wrong, but none of them wanted to be the one to give the wine away; it goes against everything in the blood. Pietro Pietrosanto is tougher than the rest and a realist, and it was Pietro who began the bidding again.

"One hundred thousand bottles," Pietro called out.

One older man clapped his hand over his heart as if a knife had been put in it. "Jesus, Mary and Joseph," he said, and he made the sign of the cross.

For a time after that, no one dared to talk, because although there was not much time shocks such as these need time to be absorbed. Tufa and Roberto knew that a hundred thousand bottles were not enough, but it was Babbaluche who let them know it in the manner they could understand.

He began by calling them bottle-grubbing bastards and penny-pinching peasant pigs and he ended by saying things that in Italy it is forbidden to put on paper, even in one's own home, and in the end he named a proper figure: 500,000 bottles.

He was correct and at the same time he was wrong.

No bearer of the blood of the men who cut the terraces an inch at a time out of the stony sides of the mountain, no sons of those whose sweat watered the vines that had first been planted here a thousand years before, was capable of giving away 500,000 bottles of wine, even if it was the only correct thing to do. There is a limit to how far men will go even to save themselves. But the figure had the virtue of making the figure that was finally decided upon seem believable. After more minutes of bidding and debate, during which men wept and threatened to put themselves to death first, it was agreed to plant the Rabbit Garden with 300,000 bottles of wine.

It is possible that at any other moment in the city's history such a figure would have led to rebellion, but the people were then too tired to rebel, and the truth, which was not admitted for a long time afterward, was that to many it meant 300,000 fewer bottles to carry down the mountain. It gave the people on the line a second or third or last source of energy, the way it must be with a runner when he finally sees the tape ahead of him. There was at last a goal in sight and it was one that could be reached.

At a little after four o'clock in the morning, when the sun had warned of its coming by making the torches useless, Tufa stepped in front of the man who had just bent once more and picked a bottle off the floor of the Cooperative cellar and he took it out of his hands.

"This is enough," Tufa said. "You can rest. This is the end. This is the last bottle."

The last bottle. They started it down the line with tenderness, they handled it with enormous delicacy. "Don't drop it," they said, "this is the last." People expected it to look different from all the rest, but it was the same, and it was hard to believe that one more would not be coming after it. They passed it along the way women pass around the newborn child or as if they were passing the Holy Eucharist, the Body and Blood of Christ, down the mountain, which in a manner they were, since this was the wine of God and the body and blood of Santa Vittoria.

It was strange when the bottle had gone past. There was no sense of joy, but only one of emptiness.

"What do we do now?" a woman asked Tufa.

"We go home to our beds," he said to her.

"But it's time to get up."

"We go home to our beds."

They began to leave the line, the young helping the old, many so bent over they could not then straighten up. They went up the Corso Cavour and off into the lanes and were lost in the corners and dark pockets of fog in the piazzas. It was agreed that the city should sleep until four o'clock in the afternoon, and then some of them should go down onto the terraces so that the Germans would not be suspicious and some should be in the piazzas and the streets.

Tufa waited for Caterina to come up the line because he was too tired to go down after her.

"This is the man who saved Santa Vittoria," Bombolini said to the Malatesta.

Tufa doesn't like this kind of thing. "We aren't saved yet," Tufa said, "and if we are, the people saved the people."

"We know," Bombolini said. "Everyone knows."

"Oh Christ, he can be a bore," Tufa said.

"And Christ, he can be true," Caterina said.

"Don't use language like that," Tufa said.

They stayed behind the others in the cellar and rested, because they were too tired to climb up through the city without rest. She slept again, but he woke her.

"Let's go," he said. "They'll be here in twelve hours."

"And what if they come sooner?"

"They won't come sooner," Tufa said. "If they're supposed to come at five o'clock, they'll come at five o'clock."

Everyone had gone by then, except the men who couldn't be seen who were still laying wine in the Roman cellar and the men who were preparing the mortar and the brick to build the false wall. The street ahead of them was empty and the street behind, and when they went through the Piazza of the People it was empty as well. If it is possible to hear a city sleep, Santa Vittoria slept.

Caterina slept when she reached the bed. She had taken off her gloves, and he could see the soreness and the blisters of her hands. On the table was the egg she had found, a small one, a jewel of an egg, still stained by the dung heap in which she had found it. He broke the shell and drank the egg and put his head back on the bed. He had no idea whether he had slept or not when there was a shout at the door and he tried to get up and could not and then someone was beside him.

"Tufa?" He shook him. "Tufa, you got to get up. You hear me?" Tufa nodded.

"Something terrible has happened on the mountain."

Caterina didn't hear him get up and go.

THE EXPEDITIONARY force to Santa Vittoria. They were ready to go by ten o'clock that morning. They could have left and been in Santa Vittoria before noon, but they remained in the street that leads into the Piazza Frossimbone and waited for later in the afternoon. They wanted to move while it was still light, but late enough in the day so that any planes that might strafe them would have gone home for the night.

There was the motorcycle and behind it the small truck, and behind the truck the 20-millimeter dual-purpose gun. They were dressed not for war, but as if they were going on parade.

"If I had flowers I would put flowers in your buttonholes, is that understood?" Captain von Prum had told them that morning. They had all nodded.

They were restless. They wandered from the convoy out into the piazza and back into the shadows and out into the sun again, and as they waited they began to talk with the informality that boredom can induce. From the piazza it was possible to see from Montefalcone across the river to where several villages and towns, much like Santa Vittoria were hanging far up on the sides of their mountain.

"Why did they build them up there, sir?" Sergeant Traub asked the captain.

"People like us," von Prum said. The sergeant didn't know whether to laugh at that or not.

He tried again later, however.

"I have to admire those terraces, sir," Traub said. "It must have taken work."

"Yes, hundreds of years work," von Prum said. "Back-breaking work."

"I didn't know the wops had it in them," the sergeant said. At a glance from the captain he changed that. "The Italians," he said.

"That's better, Sergeant."

Because of that, Traub decided to bring up one thing which had been troubling him and which he might have kept to himself.

"Sometimes it seems like a shame to take their wine," Traub said. The captain looked at him and so he was forced to go on. "They work so hard for it, I mean. It's what Schnabel was saying, sir. He worked in the vineyards. 'A bottle of sweat for every bottle of wine.'"

"And then we come and take it."

"Yes, sir."

"And then you had better think of it this way. We are engaged in a war, and wars aren't pretty things to be engaged in."

"No, sir."

"What we do we do to aid the state, the Fatherland. Whatever aids the state is good."

"Yes, sir."

"And now let me tell something a very wise German once wrote, Sergeant. To put your mind at rest."

The others had come around them, which pleased the captain.

He wanted to give a lecture at this time, but without making it seem to be one.

" 'The essence of life is a taking over.' Do you understand that?"

Not only Traub, but the others too nodded. He repeated the words.

"We don't invent this fact. This is life itself." He paused to allow them to think about his words. "The people who are rising in the world take over. The ones who are sinking are taken over."

"The Germans and the Italians," Traub said.

"It is the natural order of things. Nothing can alter it. The strong take; the weak surrender. Do you think that is wrong?"

None of them was sure how to answer.

"It isn't right *or* wrong. It is nothing. It is the way of life. The fact of life. The truth of all life."

He was through and knew that it was a good time to get away from the soldiers and let them accept the truth themselves.

"Let's get going and take over then," Heinsick said.

"The orders say five o'clock," Sergeant Traub said. "If it says five o'clock it means five o'clock, and we will be there at five o'clock."

"Do you believe that?" Heinsick said. "What he said?"

"Yes, I believe that. There are those who are born to be on top and those who are born to be on the bottom. Like officers and soldiers. There's von Prum and Heinsick. Von Prum is better than you."

"Yes, it's true," Heinsick said.

"But then you're superior to most wops."

"Yes, that's true."

* * *

They met him in the Piazza of the People—Bombolini, Pietrosanto, Fabio and Roberto—and started at once down the Corso Cavour.

"It can't be described to you. You have to see it. All at once," Bombolini said.

Down through the Fat Gate, down the track that goes through the terraces. The sun was well up then. Fog still clung to clumps of grape leaves and tried to hold on to the vines, but they were only shreds of fog, the sun had burned the rest away.

"Don't turn back," Bombolini said. "I want you to see it all at once."

On the sandy flat before the entrance to the Big Room the bricks had already been brought down and were stacked on the sand. Some men were taking the first bricks inside, while a second group was beginning to mix the cement and lime and sand and water that would be used to seal the bricks together.

"They might as well stop that now," Bombolini said, but the men didn't hear him.

"It's not going to do any good. It's all a waste now." They didn't hear him. In the morning Bombolini seemed to have grown smaller than he had been in the night. He touched Tufa on the arm. "Go ahead. Look. You might as well see it now."

Tufa was unable at first to see what was causing the concern, and when he did see it he felt that it might only be some trick that the early morning sun was playing or that his own eyes were playing on him even though it was clear to him that the others had seen what he saw.

From the Thin Gate down the goat path, down through the terraces and directly into the mouth of the cellar ran, unbroken, and growing darker and wider as it went, a brilliant purple stain.

"The wine," he said.

"Yes, the wine," someone answered him.

And making the purple even more brilliant to the eye, dazzling in truth, was the glitter of the sun on the pieces of glass from a thousand broken bottles.

"If God Himself were making a sign to where the wine was hidden He could not have done a finer piece of work," Bombolini said.

They could not take their eyes away from the stain. Each moment, as the sun rose higher and the mist burned away, the color grew in strength and in depth and the glass shone more brightly to match the sun itself. Old Vines came out of the cellar and looked at the mountain.

"We never should have disturbed the wine," he said. "This is His curse for disturbing the wine."

When they could stand looking at the stain no longer they went back across the sand to the Big Room. Cavalcanti the Goat, who wanted to be a professional bicycle rider and who claimed he could pedal a bike for two days without stopping, was turning the generator and the lights were glowing and the men with the bricks were ready to begin to lay them, but when they saw the faces of Bombolini and Tufa and the rest, they stopped what they were doing.

"There is no sense going on," Bombolini said. "To home and to bed. There is a purple arrow in our heart."

They didn't know what the Captain was talking about. They sat in the dim coolness and looked into the dark mouth of the second cellar where the tiers of wine sat.

"We came a long way," one of them said. "We made a try. We didn't quit without a fight."

Suddenly Vittorini got to his feet. You see Vittorini in the dim light, because he was already wearing his uniform so that he might stand at Bombolini's side in the piazza when the Germans came, a representative of tradition, the kind of man another soldier might respect.

"Everybody to his feet. We have a solution," the old soldier said. "We shall wash the mountain."

They tried to think of ways that it wouldn't work, because they had given up and the effort to save the wine once more was too much then to face.

"There is no water," Guido Pietrosanto said. "We used the last of it last night."

"We'll pump some more," Vittorini said. "Longo? Can you get the pump back up the mountain?"

Longo was asleep against the wall. When his work was done he had drunk a good deal of wine. But when they woke him he said he could get the pump and the generator up the mountain and that the bricklayers would have to go on by torchlight.

"I don't want to be the one to wake the people," Fabio said. "I couldn't bear to look at them."

"They've had two hours' sleep. It's all they need," Pietrosanto said.

There were the carts and oxen which had brought down the

bricks. They got in the carts, and on the way back up most of them slept. When the oxen stopped—since some of them were as tired as the men and had less to gain for their work—they kicked them, and when the kicks no longer worked they burned them on the bellies with the pieces of rope that had been dipped in tallow.

It would be good to say that the people responded to the crisis with good humor, but it wasn't true. Most of them were angry at being awakened. "You lied to us," they said.

"Come on, get up," the men would say to them. "Get your water jug, get your chamber pot, get your buckets. We're going to wash the mountain."

They got up, but they were angry. Once again there was a line on the mountain. This time they lined up along the spillway and when the water came they filled the jugs and bottles and walked back across the terraces to the goat path.

At first it was no good. The water didn't thin the wine, the wine here is so heavy and dark, but it spread the wine and made it brighter and the air was thick with the smell of sour wine. There was nothing to do, however, but to go on and finally at ten o'clock in the morning, after perhaps a hundred thousand gallons of water had been poured on the side of the mountain the wine began to thin and the earth began to swallow the wine and the water. Young boys had been coming down the path with grape baskets strapped to their backs and these were filled with glass. The people's spirits kept rising, because in another hour, if the sun stayed out and the wind held, the earth would begin to dry and by noon no one would be able to tell what had taken place there. It had rained the day before, when it shouldn't have rained, and now clouds were swarming up from the south. If they brought rain again it might do good, but if the clouds only served to hide the sun it could prove fatal.

"Send for the priest," Bombolini ordered. Before Padre Polenta was brought down from the bell tower, Capoferro was already in the little piazza before the Fat Gate rolling his sticks on the goatskin drum and shouting at the sun.

"Come on, you bastard up there, burn us," he shouted. "Bake us, fry us, boil us, singe us, dry us up."

Capoferro is one of those here who believe that God lives in the sun, just as there are those who believe He lives in the moon, although they never tell that to Polenta. When they brought the priest down the mayor seized him.

"We need your prayers," Bombolini said. "Say the prayers for sun."

"There are no prayers for sun," the priest said. "People always pray for rain."

"When Noah was in the Ark I suppose the people prayed for rain?" Babbaluche said.

"That was before organized religion," Polenta said.

"Ah, all *they* had was God, the poor bastards," the cobbler said.

In the end, however, they came to a sound religious compromise. The priest agreed to read the prayer for rain and everytime he came to the word he paused and the people said "sun." At times the prayer made little sense, but God must have been able to understand what the people were trying to tell Him, since mysteries are nothing new to Him, and not too long after the prayer was said the clouds slid over Scarafaggio on the other mountain, and our wet earth began to bake again.

After the prayers it was a time for listening again and for waiting for the false wall to grow and for re-laying the wine in the Cooperative Wine Cellar.

It was Fungo the idiot who thought of the last, and perhaps Fungo too deserves a plaque as things turned out. There are many ways to put down wine, but in general there are two ways, the tight way which we use here and the loose way which is used in wineries that have a great deal of room to spare. In the loose way, the bottles are placed in such a fashion that they don't touch one another. It takes a good deal of room, more room than we have here, but it reduces the chance of bottles breaking when accidents happen, and so it is used when there is room. Where Fungo learned of it no one knows, because Fungo wouldn't say. Some people think that Fungo hears holy voices that direct him; and who is prepared to prove they don't? Instead of going home to bed the wine-layers were put to work in the Cooperative cellar and all that morning and afternoon they spread the last of the bottles, so by midafternoon the 300,000 bottles almost filled the great room and were made to look as if they were at least 600,000.

The listening was for the boys who were stationed in the drainage ditches and in the reeds and rushes along the side of the River Road with high-pitched little whistles carved from reeds by Babbaluche and his family in the night. The boys were spread out along the road as far apart as they could go and still hear the next whistle down the line. When the first of them saw the Germans approach he was to blow on his whistle and it would be picked up by the next along the line and all the way up to Santa Vittoria so that we would have an early warning of their arrival in case they came too soon or in case they came late under the cover of darkness. In that way we would have some chance to put away things and to hide signs that might be revealing, to sweep the sand around the entrance to the cellars, to put back up the brick wall of the Cooperative cellar, to get the people out of the piazzas and to get people down onto the terraces.

But most of the worry was with the wall.

"How does it grow?" the people asked.

"It grows, it grows," Bombolini would say. But the work went slowly. The light of the flares was bad and it caused smoke, and the men were on the edge of exhaustion. But, as Bombolini said, it grew and it wouldn't stop growing. It was two feet by eleven o'clock, and six feet by noon, and eight feet by the time the people had had their bread and soup and the old people at least and some of the women had fallen asleep. At one o'clock a boy rode up the mountain on a mule and he had good news to tell the town. The wall would be finished no later than two o'clock that afternoon, three good hours before the Germans came.

At fifteen minutes before two o'clock, Italo Bombolini and Tufa and Pietrosanto and Vittorini and Fabio and Roberto and twenty other members of the Grand Council of Santa Vittoria went through the Fat Gate and started down the mountain. Every so often they stopped to listen for the sound of a reed whistle, but when they heard nothing they went on.

The men had done a good job. They had done a fine job. It is not too much to say that it is doubtful if such a wall could have been built in such time and under such circumstances in many parts of the world. It is not to boast, but it is a fact and part of history that Italians have a genius for stone and brick.

From the floor of the cellar entrance in the back wall of the Big Room to the arched ceiling, the bricks had been fitted with enormous care, shaped and fitted to the old bricks of the wall so that they looked as if they had grown there and not been laid by the hand of man.

"You have done a great thing for yourself and for the people of Santa Vittoria," Bombolini said. He cried. What had been that morning a gaping entrance to a great ancient wine-filled cellar was now one solid blank wall. The cellar and the wine were gone.

Many of the men were already asleep on the floor and others, too tired to listen and even to sleep, rested against the wall, so almost none of them, the first time at least, heard what Tufa said.

"The wall will have to come down," Tufa said.

The ones who heard him, or wanted to hear him, turned around.

"Why did you say that, Tufa?" one said.

"The wall will have to come down," he said again. Tufa at times can have such a voice, so cold and hollow and distant that it seems like an echo from the back of a cave.

"It's no good," he said. "The wall won't do. It will have to come down."

No one noticed Luigi Casamassima, who had been the leader of bricklayers, get up from along the wall and come behind Tufa and put his hands around his neck.

"You're crazy, Tufa," Luigi shouted. "You're a Fascist. You're in the pay of the Germans." He turned to the rest of them. "Don't let Tufa say things like that."

"You're doing that, Luigi, because you know it's true."

Casamassima took his hands away then, but Tufa turned to him and his voice was low and not cold.

"You should have stopped, Luigi. You should have had the courage to stop."

"We couldn't stop," Luigi said. "We were too tired to stop. All we could do was go on."

When they turned back to the false wall, all of them could see it then.

"It stands out like a new grave," one of them said.

"Like a priest in a whorehouse," Babbaluche said.

CAPTAIN VON PRUM'S convoy was scheduled to move out of the Piazza Frossimbone and start down toward the Constantine Gate at 2:30 P.M., and at 2:25 Sergeant Traub gave the order to start up the engines. The truck motor started but the motorcycle was silent. Sergeant Traub climbed off the saddle of the motorcycle and apologized to Captain von Prum who was sitting in the sidecar and got down on his knees to examine the engine. Heinsick was looking over his shoulder.

"The spark plugs," the corporal said. "Some son of a bitch has stolen your spark plugs."

Traub looked defeated. "It will take me two days to get some plugs," he said.

Heinsick put a hand on the sergeant's shoulder. "Field expedi-

225

ency," he said. He walked down the lane that leads out of the piazza until he came to a line of vehicles pulled up in the shadows of the lane hiding under camouflage nets. He looked both ways in the lane and then slipped under the netting and several minutes later came back up the lane juggling several spark plugs in his hand.

"When in Italy," Heinsick said, "do as the wops do. Rob the bastards blind."

Only one minute late the convoy started down toward the gate. The motorcycle was at the head and behind it came the truck, driven by a soldier under the command of Heinsick. In the back of the truck, squashed tightly, were five other private soldiers and behind the truck was the dual-purpose gun. At the gate they were forced to wait for clearance.

"I wouldn't want to be going up there," one of the German guards said. "Eight men."

The Italian guard was very upset about it.

"Not enough men," he said. "An insult, don't you see? Fifty men, a hundred men, what can anyone do. But eight men. They have to fight if only to defend their honor."

"Maybe they have no honor," one of the Germans said. The Italian was hurt.

"You insult them," he said. "I'm warning you. You insult me." They laughed at him.

"Even so, I wouldn't want to be going up there," a German said.

"Shall I tell them about the Bloodless Victory, sir?" Traub said.

"No, let them read about it in history," von Prum said.

At a little after three o'clock a sergeant came out of the guard house at the gate and handed Sergeant Traub their convoy clearance.

"Santa Vittoria, eh?" he said.

"That's right, Sanda Viddoria," Traub said.

They drove down the long steep hill that leads from Montefalcone to the River Road and there they turned left toward the city. There was no traffic along the road, and although it was filled with small potholes from aerial cannon fire they made very good time. The road from Montefalcone is said to be very beautiful.

The tourists today come and get out of their buses and take pictures of it and so there must be something beautiful about it. But the people who are born here never notice it at all. The road represents an enemy who must be overcome; the road is so much sweat and so many hours.

Captain von Prum enjoyed the ride. He was glad to be moving and he was anxious to begin putting his ideas to the test.

"And so begins the first phase of the Bloodless Victory," the captain said, and Sergeant Traub nodded.

"We can find a place for ourselves in history up there, Sergeant," the captain said, and Traub nodded again. And a grave too, he thought.

When the convoy was a mile from the road—it is a cart track, really, made for oxen and carts by the feet of oxen and the wheels of carts—von Prum raised his arm and signaled, and they came to a stop under the shade of a beech tree that for some reason had been allowed to stand.

"We're early, we must wait," the captain said.

To the left of the road were low hills, and the captain and the sergeant got out of the motorcycle and walked across to the hill and went up it and when they were near the top they were able to see our mountain and Santa Vittoria on the top of it. A few of the clouds that had frightened the city that morning were over the city then, and for a moment it would be thrown into shadows and then the cloud would pass and it would spring back into the brightness of the sun so that from a distance it looked very clean and sparkling and to some people, since it is so high up and remote from the world down around its feet, even mysterious.

"That's it," Captain von Prum said. "That's your city."

"It's like all the rest," the sergeant said.

"Except it's *our* city."

He had binoculars and they were good ones and he could see things all along the road and up the road and among the terraces and he could even make out the faces of people who were gathered about the Fat Gate.

"There are people going up the road, a whole group of them," Sergeant Traub said. His eyesight was keener than the captain's, and he had been handed the glasses.

"Our welcoming committee."

"If I knew the language that well I could read their lips," Traub said.

"I'll tell you what they're talking about. About the weather and about the grapes and about wine. It is all they talk about."

The sergeant had moved the glasses down the mountain and along the road and on the cart track, near where it turns off the River Road, around a corner from it, he could see some obstruction in the road.

"They've put something on the road, sir," Sergeant Traub said.

"Is there anyone around it. Any sign of anyone?" Traub studied the area with the carefulness of a good soldier. There was no sign of any kind of life.

"It's a cart. Just a cart along the track."

It caused von Prum to smile.

"What a splendid Italian gesture," the captain said. "Obvious, childish, annoying and ineffective."

They started back down the hill toward the River Road and the convoy.

* * *

The men they had seen on the mountain were Bombolini and Tufa and the others coming from the Roman cellar. They were halfway up the mountain then, and none of them had said a word. They were too tired then and too disappointed. They had come that far, they had come that close to succeeding, they had licked it and so they knew the taste of it, and now it was denied to them. All of the pieces had fitted into place except the last one, the main one, the doorway to the wine.

"Let's not tell the people," Bombolini said. "It won't do them any good to know."

"Tell them," Tufa said. "They know everything else. They have a right to know."

Fabio was forced to smile at hearing the ex-Fascist putting his trust in the people. When they reached The Rest, the place where everyone always stops on his way up the mountain, they stopped as much from habit as from desire and looked back down behind them into the valley.

"Now you want to quit and I won't let you quit," Tufa said to them.

"Why do you tell us now?" someone asked him.

"Because I hope the shock of the wall has died in you," Tufa said.

"The shock of the wall will never die in me," Bombolini said.

"If the Germans don't look in the entrance on their way up, if the Germans don't look in the entrance tonight, if the Germans don't look in the cellar tomorrow the wall will be built."

"Ah, yes," Bombolini said. No one wanted to believe Tufa. It was too much to believe and too exhausting to hope. "The Germans won't look in the tunnel. They'll go right by the tunnel and not look in." He turned on Tufa. "You yourself told us how thorough they were."

But the false wall was coming down. Even from where they were on the mountain they could hear the first of the bricks being dropped into the great copper kettles that we use here to blend all the wines and ingredients that go into our vermouth. The kettles, the most valuable property in Santa Vittoria, had been brought down the mountain to be hidden behind the wall along with the wine, so that they wouldn't be taken too.

The problem with the wall had been the bricks. They were not new, they were very old bricks, but they were bricks that had been bleached by several hundred years of sun and leached by thousands of winter rains and scoured by winds too numerous to be considered. As Babbaluche had said, they stood out in the darkness of the rest of the back wall like a monk in a house of pleasure. Now they were being dyed. The credit for this belongs to Old Vines. The bricks were being dumped into the huge copper kettles which had been filled with several hundred bottles of our best red vermouth, a painful way to use good wine.

Bricks drink. They absorbed the wine, they drank it into their open pores, and they turned a deep, rich, dark red, as dark and rich as the wine itself. While the bricks drank, the bricklayers were painting the rest of the wall around the opening with the wine so that when the false wall rose again, the bricks would blend and belong to one another.

"It's as I said," Old Vines said. "The wine will save the wine."

They got up from The Rest and were started back up again when Tufa saw the cart along the cart track.

"What is that?" he said. "Who put that along the road?"

"A cart," Bombolini said. "My cart to be exact. I allowed Fabio della Romagna and the Cavalcanti boy to put it there this morning."

Tufa's face was annoyed and finally angry.

"As a gesture of defiance, you know," Bombolini said.

"If that cart makes them late, do you know that it will make them angry?" Tufa said. "Do you know they like to be on time? Do you know they hurt people for things such as that?"

"It was only a gesture, a small thing," Bombolini said.

"So was the answer that the man gave them at Rocca di Camera," Tufa said.

"They asked him which direction the enemy was and he said, 'Why, I thought the enemy was you,' and for that they shot his wife and they shot his children and they allowed him to live with his joke."

"I could go down and move the cart," Fabio said, but Tufa told him there wasn't time for that now, and that it was better that no one be near the cart when they came.

They went up in silence after that. There were some people among the vines on the terraces and a few were working, but a great many of them had fallen asleep in the shade beneath the leaves.

"We should wake them up," someone said.

"No, let them sleep. It will only confirm what they already think of us," Tufa said, "that we're a bunch of lazy bastards."

When they neared the Fat Gate some of the people came down the track to meet them.

"How's the wall? How does it look? Is it all grown up?" they asked.

Bombolini looked at Tufa and Tufa stared back at him.

"It still grows. They're still working on the wall."

The people were astonished and frightened by what they heard.

"But they said . . ."

Bombolini shook his head.

"No," he said. "They were wrong. The wall still grows." It made him sad to say that. "I wish we had Mazzola back," he said to Pietrosanto.

"I wish we had Copa," Pietrosanto said. Although they had not done much work in recent years both Copa and Mazzola had once been the very best men in Santa Vittoria with stone and brick.

"You did what you had to do?" Bombolini said to Pietrosanto.

"Yes. The problem is solved. The Band is all taken care of."

Bombolini put his hands over his ears. "Don't tell me," he said. "I don't want to hear about it." He looked at Pietrosanto with a new respect, however. "Was it terrible? Did you find it hard to do?"

"No, it wasn't hard to do," Pietrosanto said, and then he stopped very suddenly, almost locked in motion, as if he had come face to face with an invisible barrier.

"Did you hear it?" he asked. "Do you hear it now? Quiet," he shouted.

The people by the Fat Gate and the people around them and they themselves were quiet, and then they heard, all the way down the valley, not just one whistle but many of them, high and thin and reedy, across the valley and up the mountain, as high and clear as the cry of a wild bird.

They were coming.

They were moving on the River Road, they were rushing along the Mad River, they were looking for the turn to the cart track that leads to the foot of our mountain, they were taking the turn and coming into the valley.

Bombolini had run up the Corso Cavour for several hundred feet when he heard the reed whistles, but then he turned around and started back down the street until he found Tufa.

"Tufa?" he said. "What shall I wear?"

"Wear what you have on," Tufa said. "Be yourself."

"What should I say to them?"

"Nothing. Answer what they ask you."

"But how do I act? I don't know how to act."

"Like yourself," Tufa said.

"But I don't know how I act."

Tufa started up the Corso and Bombolini, since Tufa was walking swiftly, was forced to trot behind him.

"Tufa?" he called after him. "*You* know what to say. *You* know how to act."

Tufa continued to move away from him.

"I want you to be the one to meet him," Bombolini called to him. "I want you to take command. I'm not enough."

Tufa stopped then.

"I'm not the mayor of Santa Vittoria, you're the mayor—the Captain of the People. Isn't that what they call you?"

Bombolini nodded. Still they could hear the fine sharp notes of the whistles blowing and blowing.

"The people chose you, Bombolini, not Tufa," he said. And then he said something remarkable, which Bombolini never forgot and didn't understand. "You'll make a much better mayor than I could ever make."

He was tired. The running had winded him and he could only walk now and do that slowly.

"They're coming, eh, Bombolini?" someone in a doorway said. He didn't turn to look.

"Yes, they're coming."

"There's nowhere to run to now, eh?"

"No, there's nowhere to run."

"All we can do now is stand here and wait."

"It's all we can do," Bombolini said.

WHEN THERE WERE ten minutes less than an hour left, since Captain von Prum had estimated it would take them fifty minutes to cross the valley and go up the mountain, he struck the flat of his hand against the sidecar, making a hollow *boom*, and raised his hand and shouted "Forward," and the convoy moved out of the shade of the beech tree and onto the River Road. It is difficult to see the track that turns off to Santa Vittoria, since it dips down off the road so suddenly, but Sergeant Traub saw it in time and turned off the road a little faster than he would have liked, steeply down, and at the first turn in the track, far sooner than he had expected it to be, was the cart, and he was forced to apply his brakes so sharply that von Prum was almost thrown out of the sidecar and the truck behind them came close to hitting them.

Traub got off the seat to examine the cart. "I never saw one like it before," he said. He spun one of the heavy iron-rimmed wheels. "Oak," he said. "Like iron. It's as heavy as a tank."

"Can we get around it? Can we lift it off?"

Traub told the captain no.

"Can you hit it with one shot?"

"I can hit anything with one shot if it isn't shooting back at me," the sergeant said.

"I'm sure they're all looking from the town," von Prum said. "This will be a lesson."

They unhitched the light dual-purpose gun from the back of the truck and they ran it up onto the edge of the River Road to give Traub aiming room. He was careful about it, a little longer than von Prum would have wished, but he made the first shot good. It hit near the heart of the cart and it split the oak grain and a shower of splinters flew out. He hit it again and again after that, until it came apart and looked naked and disgraceful in the sand. They lifted the pieces up then and threw them alongside the track, and it was the death of Bombolini's Sicilian cart.

"It's been a long time," Traub said. He was proud of his work. "I like the way it jumps when it cuts loose."

The road was dusty, and when they had gone perhaps a half mile more across the valley they stopped to clean the dust from their eyes and mouths and to put on glasses. The truck behind them was buried in a cloud of fine white chalk.

"They should pay for things like that," Traub said. He motioned back toward the cart. He had liked the feeling of the gun and the smell of oil and the powder and the hot metal under his hands and the feeling of satisfaction he had felt when the shell had entered the oak and split it apart.

"It's like with a puppy, sir. You aren't cruel, but you make them pay for their annoyances."

A kind of reasoned ruthlessness, the captain thought. An enlightened ruthlessness. A civilized ruthlessness. He wrote that down later.

"You want to hit something else?" the captain asked.

"Yes."

Out of all the grays and the dull reds and oranges, out of the sun-bruised brick and stone and plaster, the coloring of stone and smoke and old age that is Santa Vittoria, one piece of color stands out above all the colors of the city, the red-and-blue sign of the Cinzano company on the roof of the Cooperative Wine Cellar.

"That?" von Prum said. "Do you think you could hit it?"

The sergeant nodded.

The first shot went over the top of the sign and landed someplace up on the mountain behind the city. He told us later that he fired this way so that no one would be hurt. By that shot he was able to adjust his fire, and the second shot struck the sign and exploded against it. When it didn't go down right away, he fired a third shot and the sign started down then, falling off the roof like a goose or a wild swan that has been hit with shot but is unwilling to die at once because of it.

"I think we've made our first impression," Captain von Prum said.

They moved slowly after that, to keep down the dust and because the road was not fit for a speed much faster than that of an ox. One of the children who was to blow his reed whistle had come out along the track and was blowing it so that his face had turned red. They stopped and watched him.

"What's the matter with him do you think?" The child continued blowing so that at one time it appeared that his eyes would come out of his head.

"I think he's crazy," the sergeant said. "They have these little boys tend the goats all alone and sometimes they go crazy."

In another ten minutes they had reached the bottom of the mountain where they saw Fungo, who in truth looks crazy when he smiles, sweeping the sand in front of the entrance to the Roman cellers.

"Another one," Sergeant Traub shouted. They had turned and started up through the terraces, the first motor vehicle ever to attempt to come up the mountain, when the captain looked back once more at Fungo and the cellar entrance.

"A place to examine," he said, and Traub nodded. "It might make a good place for an air-raid shelter."

When they were halfway up the mountain they stopped to allow the engines of their vehicles to cool. Among the vines and beneath the leaves they could see people hiding in the shadows or people sleeping.

"Now prepare yourself for the Italian pageantry," Captain von Prum told the sergeant. There would be the mayor of the city in his one black suit stained with wine and manure, and several old men holding flags and with their medals from the other war dangling from their worn shirts, and there would be the members of the Fascist party swearing undying allegiance to those who had come to conquer them, the captain told him. It was ten minutes before five o'clock.

Just before they started up again Captain von Prum sampled some of the grapes that grew alongside the cart track and they were bitter. Paolo Lapolla had the bad fortune to be near them.

"What's the matter with your grapes?" von Prum asked Paolo.

At first Paolo found it impossible to find his tongue. "They aren't ripe yet," he finally said. "You came too soon."

It caused the Germans to laugh. "When would you have wished us to come, next year?"

"Later, later," Paolo said. "Much later."

"Your grapes are bitter. How is your wine?"

"Ah, the wine," Paolo said. "The wine is something else. You must try some of it sometime."

"Ah, we will," von Prum said, "we will."

Paolo was frightened by the loudness of their laughter.

"You speak very good Italian," Paolo said.

"So do you," von Prum said.

"Yes, I was born right here, Your Excellency," Paolo said.

At the Fat Gate and wherever they could see down into the terraces they were fearful about Paolo and what he might say, but Bombolini, when they told him, had no fear. As the Master said, it is sometimes the highest form of wisdom to simulate folly, and at this Paolo was a master, for it is something every Santa Vittorian learns by the time he leaves the breast.

* * *

236

All up the Corso Cavour and up into the Piazza of the People the people were in the doorways and along the edges of the street and around the fringes of the piazza, because it was foolish now, after the destruction of the cart and the blowing down of the sign, to pretend they knew nothing of the Germans' arrival. They were silent and they were composed, on the advice of Bombolini, who said that they should treat the arrival as they would treat the passing of a hearse; no one would go into the street and run after the hearse, and no one would turn away from it, either. There was even a quiet kind of elation among them, because the tunnel had been seen and the tunnel had been passed.

Only Fabio seemed to be upset. "Eight of them and an officer, against one thousand of us," he said. "What has happened to my country?" When the sound of the engines could be heard coming up the Corso Cavour, Fabio left the piazza and went up to High Town and over the wall and into the mountains.

The Corso is bad for traffic, because it is, as Tufa said, a pipe, but it is good for sound. The noise of the engines thundered up the pipe and roared in the piazza and even the people at the far corners found themselves becoming stiff.

There were, in the center of the piazza then, only two people: Italo Bombolini, the mayor, and Emilio Vittorini in the dress uniform of his old regiment. And behind them was the Fountain of the Pissing Turtle.

The motorcycle was the first to come into the piazza. Because of the steepness of the Corso the people could not see it until it had come up onto the lip of the street where for a moment it seemed to waver and hang suspended, half in the piazza and half in the Corso. Then it seemed to catch hold of the cobblestones of the piazza and to explode out into it.

They must have seen the two men but they didn't go directly toward them but turned to the right and circled the piazza, roaring along the rim of people, who were pressed back against the walls of the houses, and going all the way around the piazza and back to where the Corso begins. Bombolini and Vittorini kept turning with them so that they would always be facing them, much as the matador does when a bull is on the loose in the arena.

237

Once was not enough for them and they went around the piazza a second time, until the truck and the little cannon had ground up into the piazza and could follow them. They went faster this time, with a great noise of engines and the crying of rubber on the stones. It was impressive. It was terribly impressive. There had been a great many who had denied that any motor vehicle could ever come up the Corso and get into the piazza. At a sign from the officer, the truck pulled to one side of the square and the soldiers leaped from the truck and unhitched the gun and pointed it out across at the people. And when this was done, the motorcycle very sharply turned and only then headed directly toward the two men.

Vittorini's wife shouted for him to jump, but everyone knew Vittorini would never move. It seemed to us then that Bombolini would be forced to break and run if the machine was not to hit him, but he too stood in the piazza as if this was the ordained thing to do. Some in the piazza at that moment turned away, but the motorcycle, with a terrible screeching of brakes, came to a stop less than a foot away from the two of them and actually at the edge of Bombolini's shoe.

"Welcome to the Free City of Santa Vittoria," Bombolini shouted above the sound of the engine. "We of this city know that in times of war . . ."

It was the last they heard, as Traub raced the engine and the mayor's voice was lost beneath it.

"Pay attention," Traub shouted. He shut off the engine. Captain von Prum rose in the sidecar.

"Have sixteen mattresses delivered into this piazza within the next twenty minutes," von Prum ordered.

Vittorini now had come to full attention and was beginning the execution of a formal military salute.

"We know that in time of war—" Bombolini began.

"Quiet," Sergeant Traub shouted.

"Sixteen," von Prum said to Bombolini. "Did you understand that?"

Bombolini nodded his head.

"I want you to know, sir, that we are willing and anxious to cooperate with you as guests of the city, exactly as we would do if we were running an inn."

"With no bedbugs," Traub shouted. "With no lice. With no ticks. With no bugs of any kind."

Bombolini continued to talk, but they didn't hear him. The sergeant had gotten down from the seat of the motorcycle and had gone around and opened the door of the sidecar for the captain.

"Words flow out of his mouth like piss from that turtle," Captain von Prum said. They began to walk toward the fountain.

"Go ahead," von Prum called to Bombolini. "Keep talking."

They walked around the fountain and examined it carefully and came back past Vittorini, and the captain touched the old soldier's epaulets.

"Do you know that a museum would give you good money for these?" he said. Vittorini was still at parade salute. Von Prum stopped in front of the mayor.

"Why did you stop talking?" he asked.

"I had nothing further to say," Bombolini said.

"Do you expect us to believe that?" von Prum said. "Would you like to hear what the sergeant said about you?"

Bombolini nodded his head. "He said you were like the piazza; very large and very empty."

He had said the words very loudly, and someone in the piazza laughed. It was Babbaluche.

"And what is he doing?" von Prum said.

"He is waiting for you to return his salute, sir." Vittorini's arm and even his body were now trembling from the effort of holding the salute.

"But why should I do that?" von Prum said.

"Because he is an old soldier, sir."

"Oh, is that what he is?"

Von Prum took several steps away from Bombolini and came to a stop in front of him and came to attention. He lifted his arm and shouted "Heil Hitler."

"Long live Italy," Vittorini said.

"It is my hope that we can find a way of living here that will be profitable for both of us," Bombolini said.

239

"I will *insist* on it," the German said.

He was back in the sidecar then, and Traub started up the motorcycle. It made a great noise, but it did not start at once. It seemed to strain to release itself, much like a young horse held to a stake, and then it broke loose. As it did the foot pedal on the left side of the cycle struck Bombolini's leg and it sent him moving backward. Had he fallen at once there would have been nothing funny in it, and it might have even alarmed the people. But he didn't go down at once. He began to fall and to run backward at the same time, going a little faster at each step, trying to keep his balance but losing it a little more at each step, going backward and down, clutching the air to hold him up. There must have been twenty desperate steps in this way before he was moving at such a speed and was bent over backward so far that in the end nothing could support him and he went down, flatly down, fully down, on his back, so that his legs flew up in the air and hovered there as if he were about to do a backward somersault.

He was stunned by the fall but not hurt by it, and then he could hear them beginning.

Please God, Bombolini said to himself, don't let them do it. Not in front of them.

But they did do it. It began as a titter and it ran around the piazza but it didn't remain a titter long. It became a laugh, and because of the way sounds carry in the Piazza of the People, it became a gigantic laugh, a thunderous, booming laugh, that fed on its own noise, laughter creating new laughter until it went beyond anything that had to do with Bombolini lying on his back in the center of the piazza, but must have been a cry at everything they had done and knew they were going to have to do.

The Germans heard it, although they were already down in the Corso Cavour making their first reconnaissance of the city.

"I don't understand these people at times, sir," Traub said.

"It's because in many ways they are like children," Captain von Prum said, "and so they react like children."

"I don't understand them."

Get up, Vittorini was saying. You can't lie there. The mayor was on his knees looking at the stones he had fallen on.

"Right here," he said, aloud. "In this place. On this rock."

He got to his feet and he marked one cobblestone with the sole of his shoe. He looked at the people and nodded his head at them, over and over.

All right, he was saying to himself, you can laugh. Laugh now. One day, right here, on this stone, you will erect a monument to me.

5 THE SHAME OF SANTA VITTORIA

T HOSE FIRST DAYS of the occupation were good ones for the people of the city. They had set themselves for something bad to happen, and nothing bad had taken place. The weather for the grapes had turned good again, and when this happens things are always good in Santa Vittoria, no matter what else may be happening. But beyond that was the fact that we all were after the same thing. The Germans wanted us to cooperate with them, and we couldn't find enough ways to do it.

At the start it had been Captain von Prum's policy to show a strong, hard hand and then, when the people were properly conditioned, to show them that the rock in his breast was actually a heart and that he was human. He wrote about it. "My plan is to

245

be a benevolent despot up here," he put in his personal log, "but to be benevolent one must first be the despot."

On that first night, for example, a curfew was set for eight o'clock at night. It was too late to warn the bricklayers, and when they came up the mountain at ten o'clock, after finishing the second wine-dark wall, they were jailed for breaking the curfew and they were whipped.

"I am sorry to have to do this, but these men have broken the rules and must be punished for it," the captain said.

"It's only correct," Bombolini said. "They have been bad and deserve it."

The bricklayers didn't mind. They were so tired they were numb, and later said they had barely felt the blows. Nothing mattered to them. Some of them slept all through the three days of their confinement and never missed the food they were supposed to be deprived of.

Padre Polenta was arrested and brought down from the bell tower for using his light at night.

"And what was your aim?" Captain von Prum asked him. "To guide the bombers in?"

"I was at God's work," Polenta said.

"One week on bread and water for God's work," the captain said.

"Why not a few strokes of the lash as well," Bombolini offered. "He might have gotten us all blown up."

These weren't the only ones. Many people were arrested that first week and treated roughly, but it was the fines that bothered the people most. They cleaned up the dung hills in Old Town and they fined people who emptied their night jars in the streets outside their doors. They beat the people who opened their doors after eight o'clock or who showed a light of any kind. At the end of that first week Captain von Prum wrote this letter to his father.

So far so good. It goes better than we ever hoped or dreamed. I keep my fingers crossed. I try to keep in mind that saying from Clausewitz that you always quote: "The first rule. Never underestimate the nature and the quality of the enemy."

I had not intended to work with the mayor here, but he is so available and so willing to please and carry out our requests that I find it useful. He is a clown and, as I think I wrote you before, these people have an affinity for clowns. But he also seems to get things done. I'll try not to underestimate him. I try to remind myself that even clowns can possess a kind of cunning and even widsom, although I must admit that in *this* case it is hard to see.

He wrote that he had been stern and that he had twisted the screw tight and that now he was going to release the pressure a little—"If things go right the people will be grateful for small treats," he wrote.

It was one of the captain's beliefs that decency not backed by superior force was merely a symptom of weakness. "The weak have to be decent, while the strong can choose to be decent. This coming week I will choose to be decent."

He had taken over the Palace of the People that first day, but it was too large and gloomy for his needs, and Bombolini had persuaded him to cross the Piazza of the People and move into the home of Constanzia Pietrosanto, which was small but well built and clean and airy and light.

Constanzia wept and cried, and she shouted at her brothers and sisters. "Why me? Why did he have to go out of his way to send the German to me?"

"Quiet," they told her. "Bombolini has a reason. It's for the cause, for the wine."

And then one morning, at the end of the week, she was delivered an envelope by Corporal Heinsick and in it was fifty lire, and they came every week after that. Under the rules of war the German had no need to pay, but he chose to pay.

The rest of the soldiers were quartered in the office of the Co-operative Wine Cellar, all except Sergeant Traub, who had a room with the captain in Constanzia's house. He might have put them in private homes, but he didn't want his men to go soft or to face the temptation of corruption, and he paid the city of Santa Vittoria for the use of the wine cellar office. Each week he gave Italo Bombolini fifty lire, and it was the only source of income in the entire city.

"You see?" Sergeant Traub would say to Bombolini. "He's firm but he's fair. You watch. You have a friend here, whether you know it or not. Just so you cooperate."

It was always that word.

"I think I'm winning them over," the captain wrote to his fian-cée Christina Mollendorf. "Each day a little more I earn their co-operation."

He didn't know then, and he never did know, that Bombolini's policy, which he had actually written down, was named Creative Cooperation. We didn't just go along, we tried to do the German one better. We didn't grudgingly do what was asked, we did it eagerly and willingly.

There was a great deal of smiling going on in Santa Vittoria those first weeks. We smiled at the soldiers, and although they were supposed to be firm, they began to respond and smile back. There was a great deal of saying "Good morning" and "Good eve-ning." We learned the name of the captain and used it. "Good morning, Captain von Prum," "How are you today, Captain von Prum." When he walked down the Corso Cavour they said his name so often, von Prum, von Prum, that it sounded as if someone was filling a barrel with apples.

And then we had the Good Time Boys. These were groups of younger men whose job it was to drink with the German soldiers and to play cards with them and smile at them. They met in the soldiers' quarters, in the wine cellar office, and it was a convenient place. They were next to the source of wine and, as Babbaluche said, what better place for rabbits than the edge of the rabbit garden.

The people would say, "Are they in it? Have they gone over the fence?" And the Good Time Boys would tell them, "They're look-ing. They're nibbling."

They would look at the wine and rub their jaws, but they never took any of it. The Good Time Boys went in shifts. Some dropped around in the morning to share an eye opener of *grappa* and some in the middle of the morning for a little pick-me-up of vermouth and some to bring wine for lunch and an after-nap refresher, and in the evening the serious drinking began with the card playing. The result was that the Germans and the Italians became friends, and the Germans were drunk a good deal of the time and some of them drunk all of the time. They would fall on their blankets at night and smile at us with those cowlike drunk blue eyes of theirs.

There is a saying in this country and it must be true. "No one knows his own servants as badly as the master." Captain von Prum saw none of it. Tufa put it this way: "Until his own life is at stake an officer can never know what is going on with his own men."

Von Prum's mind was on other matters. He was exuberant about the way the first phase of the Bloodless Victory was proceeding. It was going beyond his highest hopes. It was so successful that he finally felt he must speak to the Italian mayor, and he summoned Bombolini to his office on the evening of his eighth day in Santa Vittoria.

"You are so cooperative with us. Why?" von Prum said. "There must be a reason." He had intended to shock the mayor.

"The obvious one," Bombolini told him. "It is selfish, I suppose. If we help you we hope that maybe you won't hurt us. We hope that you might even help us."

There was nothing for the captain to say except that it was a very realistic way of looking at things, and very mature.

"We don't see this as our war," the mayor said. "It doesn't matter to us who wins or loses, all we stand to do is get hurt by it."

"But you're Italians."

"What does that mean to us?" Bombolini said. "All we want to do is act in the way that's going to cause us the least harm in the end."

The *proposition*, which was always at the back of Captain von Prum's mind, was going to be easier to propose than he had hoped.

"So you're willing to work with us even though we are Germans," he said.

"We don't care who you are," Bombolini said. "Look at it this way, sir. We don't love you and we don't ask you to love us. This is like a game and you hold all the trump cards and so we have to play our hand so at least we lose as little as possible."

The German told the mayor once again that it was very realistic of him.

"You scratch my back, I'll scratch yours," Bombolini said. "Something for you, something for me. You lend me your mule, I'll lend you my ox."

All of these things are in the captain's notes. He liked the one about the mule and the ox. "Use this one," he wrote down.

"Self-interest is their motivation," he wrote. "Appeal to their sense of self-preservation. They love themselves more than their country."

* * *

It wasn't the only time they talked. Each time they met, the German pushed the conversation one or two steps nearer to the proposition.

"So you would be willing to cooperate with the German if it meant preserving yourself?"

"The first duty of every Italian is to preserve himself," Bombolini said. "What good does it do me or my country if I get killed? Right?"

"Very mature way of thinking," von Prum said.

"They are marvelous in their way," von Prum wrote to his father. "They are disgusting, of course, and yet at the same time there is a realism about them that can't be denied. This afternoon the clown, this Bombolini, had a proposition for me. He would cooperate with me in *anything*—his word, *anything*—if I would let him in on it first, so that he could at least offer his views on how it might be done so that it would work and yet cost them as little as possible. He becomes riper by the hour. I have prepared a little test for him to test the quality of his sincerity."

The test was to make an inventory of Santa Vittoria; to count all the houses and all the people, to list all machinery, to count all tools, and to report the number of bottles of wine in the Cooperative Wine Cellar.

"The wine?" Bombolini said. "Why the wine?"

"Yes, the wine. It's a property," the German said. "What makes you surprised about that? It's what you make your living on."

"Yes, but the wine . . . you see, the wine here . . ." Bombolini said, and then didn't go on.

"You wanted to cooperate," von Prum said. "You came to me."

Bombolini shrugged his shoulders. "There's a lot of wine," he said. "We don't count so well."

"Then *we* can count the wine. You count the other things."

"No. Oh, no," Bombolini said swiftly. "We'll count the wine. It wouldn't do for the people to see you counting it. It makes the people nervous."

* * *

That night the captain put in his log: "He has the bait and he is running with it. Traub says that he will lie and lie and lie. I don't know. I suspect Traub is right, but we can only see. The counting begins tonight."

"How many are you going to tell him?" Old Vines asked Bombolini.

"How many bottles are there?"

"Three hundred and seventeen thousand," the cellar master said.

"I don't know. I'm not sure," the mayor said.

"Tell him two hundred thousand," Pietrosanto suggested. "He'll never know."

Everyone agreed that Pietrosanto was right.

It was very strange. At first everyone had been concerned with saving the wine in the Roman cellar and had already given the wine in the Rabbit Garden away. But as the days went by and the Germans didn't go down the mountain and look into the cellar, they began to hope that they could get away with saving half of the Rabbit Garden too. Bombolini was a little wiser than the rest of them. He went to the captain's headquarters the next night.

"Three hundred and two thousand bottles," Bombolini told him.

The German smiled at him. "Your counting isn't very accurate," the captain said. "The right number is three hundred and seventeen thousand bottles. We counted them last night."

Bombolini pretended to be greatly embarrassed. "I warned you that we don't count so well."

"Isn't it odd that the number would be too few and not too many?" Captain von Prum said. But they both smiled at one another and Bombolini knew he had done the correct thing. It was only natural that he would lie. It was expected of him; it was in truth, he knew, required of him. Everyone is fearful and suspicious of the too-honest man. He had lied, but just a little bit. For the most part he had told the truth.

When Bombolini had gone, the captain called his sergeant in.

"He's a liar like all of them, but he's just a little one. I couldn't expect it any other way. He has to protect his people, too, you know."

"I don't know, sir," Sergeant Traub said. "You know what they say, never trust the wop."

"That can limit you, you know. You can become so suspicious of people that you can do nothing with them in the end. Fifteen thousand out of three hundred thousand bottles is about right, Sergeant. I'd do the same myself, I think."

So he wrote that night in his log, it is dated: "He can be trusted to work with us. I will have to stand on that. He passed the test."

Ａｆｔｅｒ ｔｈａｔ the relations between the two men, the German commander and the Italian mayor, changed very swiftly. They lent each other the ox and the mule and they scratched each other's back, and what was good for one they attempted to make good for the other.

And the attitude of the people changed. At first they were afraid to look at the Germans for fear the Germans could read the thoughts in their heads. Most of the people were fearful that they wouldn't be able to keep the secret, that in some way their tongues would slip and the terrible words would be said. But as the days and then the weeks passed and the secret held, it became a habit. If the secret had been held by one person alone it might have been hard to keep, but the fact that all of the city shared it made it somehow bearable and even simple to hold. There was such a total combined silence about the wine that some people began to forget that it had ever existed. Some of them developed such confidence in themselves that at times they came close to arrogance.

"How do you like our wine?" Pietrosanto asked Corporal Heinsick.

"Very good wine."

"Help yourself sometime," Pietrosanto said. "Take a few bottles sometime. Even when we're not here."

"I'll take you up on that some day," Heinsick said.

"I am sure you will," Pietrosanto said.

In the beginning, in those first fear-filled days, we followed von Prum around the city with our eyes, from behind windows and half-opened doors. He never moved without being watched, and it was known where he was every minute of the day. He was known as the Rabbit then, and the first question anyone coming up from the terraces would ask was "Where is the Rabbit?"

The Rabbit was in the Piazza of the People, he was counting houses, he was in Constanzia's house writing in a book.

"Has the Rabbit seen the garden? Has he been in it? Has he been nibbling?"

As the days went by, many of the people began to believe that perhaps the Rabbit wasn't interested in the garden after all.

"Maybe he doesn't like lettuce," people would say, and nod as if they heard some word from God Himself.

"All rabbits eat lettuce," Babbaluche would tell them.

"But this is a German rabbit," they would say.

"Rabbits are rabbits are rabbits. They eat the same thing and shit the same shit," the cobbler said. People hated Babbaluche for saying things like that.

We called the secret wine, the secret wall, the entire secret, "the thing."

"How's the thing getting along?" someone would ask someone who went to the Roman cellar.

"It's all right," he would answer. "It's growing older. It's growing a beard."

They worked on the wall every day. Men were stationed all the way down the track in the terraces to sound an alarm if the Germans were to come down, but they never did. They continued to paint the bricks, until even to those who knew and worked on them there no longer was any way to tell which part of the wall was real and which was false. "Right here. Here's where the wall starts," they would say and tap the stones and find they were wrong.

The cellar was filled with lichens and mosses and fungus, and they had taken these growths and transferred them to parts of the new wall, and some had taken hold of the stained bricks. This was the beard that the thing was growing.

The people had confidence in their thing, and the feeling grew so strong that some of them began to object to the way Bombolini acted with the German.

"I know he has to deal with him, but does he have to crawl before him?" a member of the Grand Council said.

"It's not manly," one of the Pietrosantos said. "No man with any real eggs could do such a thing."

"If we have *him* for a leader," one of them said, "what must the Germans think of *us?*"

"I agree with what Fabio said," a young man said. "It's time we got our honor back and showed them we can be brave too."

Babbaluche and Tufa stopped that kind of talk—Babbaluche only because he had come to hate the words courage and honor and Tufa because he knew where they led men to.

"If you want to be brave you had better go up to the mountains and start being brave," Tufa said.

"But don't be brave here," Babbaluche said.

"Go up to the mountains and be brave on your own, but don't be brave at other people's expense," Bombolini told them.

Even Vittorini agreed. It made him sad to say it. "Tufa is right," he said. "This is no country for brave men now. We have better things to do."

"You should bless the butter on Bombolini's nose," Babbaluche said.

It had been a meeting, and after the meeting the men went out into the Piazza of the People, where they saw the soldier who we called Private Impossible, because no one could pronounce his

255

name, putting up a strange-looking machine at one end of the piazza.

"What is it?" Bombolini asked.

"You turn the handle, see," the soldier said, "and sausage comes out the other end. Try it."

The mayor turned the handle and a terrible sound, a scream of loneliness, filled the piazza. It was a sound that one might expect to hear from the cave when the evil spirits controlled it. Von Prum had joined them.

"An air-raid alarm," he said. "Now all we need is the proper shelter."

He said afterwards, Bombolini, that at that moment there was the feeling of a shadow passing over his mind.

"The church would be good," Bombolini said. "It's strong and there's a deep cellar and, besides, they never bomb a church. God won't let them bomb a church."

It caused the German to laugh and then he looked at all of them, and it was a look of disdain.

"There is a better place than that," he said.

When he left they looked at each other, and none of them said anything, but they looked at one another and the words formed on their lips.

He knows. He knows.

"We should kill him now," Pietrosanto said.

"No," Bombolini said. "Not now, not yet."

He tried to work that afternoon. He was putting down the rules that would guide his policy with the Germans. There had been many rules and ideas, but he had reduced them to three.

All men can be reached by flattery, even God can. (What, after all, is prayer?)

All men can be led to believe the lie they want to believe.

All men can be corrupted, each in his own way.

He wrote them down on the back of a photograph, the last clean piece of cardboard he could find in the city. It was a picture of himself taken on the day of his marriage to Rosa Casamassima. He no longer liked to look at it. In the picture they appeared to be in love, as much in love as people here are likely to be when they marry. They were not an unbeautiful couple. At the bottom of the picture is printed: "May this marriage become a vine and produce a bountiful harvest." The words always caused Bombolini to wince and turn away from them. It had produced one grape, sweet and beautiful, and a wine barrelful of bitterness.

When he finished the three rules he lay down and tried to sleep, and the thought wouldn't go away from him. *He knows.* He was not surprised when Heinsick came to the Palace of the People and told him the captain wanted to see him.

He crossed the piazza and he realized that it was the same way he had gone years before, when they came and told him his brother Andrea was injured in the rock quarry and that they wanted someone to sign a paper and he knew at that moment Andrea was dead and yet he went pretending he wasn't.

Von Prum came to the point at once. "You have one of the finest air-raid shelters I have ever seen and you mention the church to me," the captain said. "I'm surprised at you."

Bombolini said nothing to this. He looked at the stones of the floor as if they were the most important objects in the world. He turned his head to the left and to the right, and he bent down to look at the stones again.

"Sometimes it takes an outsider to see things an insider cannot see," von Prum said.

"We don't go in there," Bombolini said. "It's filled with evil spirits."

"Oh. So you know where I mean?"

Why must he play this game? the mayor thought. "Yes, I know," he said.

"It used to be an ancient wine cellar, I believe," von Prum said. "Roman, perhaps. Or even Etruscan. I would not discount Etruscan."

"I wouldn't know. No one goes in there."

"Someone goes in there," von Prum said. "*Someone.*"

The mayor said nothing. There was no further use for a fight or for lies, he felt.

"There is a string of electric light bulbs in there." Von Prum's voice was harsh now. "What are you hiding in there?"

Bombolini was only able to lift his hands in front of him as if the German was about to strike him.

257

"Who uses it?"

He could bring himself to say nothing.

"The Resistance," von Prum said. "You allow them in there. You harbor them."

"No, it isn't true," Bombolini said, but it was a shout.

I must not laugh. Oh, God, I must not laugh aloud.

"It's true," the German said, and Bombolini lowered his arms and then his head. Von Prum looked at the mayor and finally laughed at him.

"They say the Italians are good liars, that you are all good actors. It isn't so. You're a rotten liar."

Instead of laughing, Bombolini found that he wanted to weep.

"You will get them out of there and keep them out of there."

"Yes."

"You lied to me about the wine."

"Yes. Not much of a lie."

"You *lied*."

"Yes."

"And you lied about this."

"Yes." Then he looked up at the captain and was serious. "I am not a good liar," he said. "I won't lie to you again."

"It does you no good."

"I am ashamed," Bombolini said.

*   *   *

He went out into the piazza and he saw no one and heard no one. Once there was a man in this city who was dying of some strange disease and they took him to Montefalcone to die. When he got there they found nothing the matter with him and he came back and danced through the piazza because he was alive again. "I am born again."

It was this way with Bombolini. It was the happiest he had ever felt in his life. He had died and been reborn. The Roman cellar would be used as an air-raid shelter and it was frightening, too, but he was alive again.

That day wasn't over for Bombolini, however. That night he got drunk. By nightfall the story was known all over the city and the entire city drank wine and drank wine and told the story again and again. It was the secret drunk of Santa Vittoria. They drank, but they kept their mouths closed except to drink or to talk in low voices. It was a drunk that was owed to them all. A soldier came to get Bombolini while he slept drunkenly in his bed.

"Despite your behavior I have decided to continue the policy of informing you about affairs. Tomorrow night we will commence using the cellar at the foot of the mountain as a shelter."

"I understand. I am grateful to you."

"You should be grateful," von Prum said.

"But it is the evil spirits," Bombolini said. "You must understand. The people would rather face the bombs."

What Bombolini was unable to understand then was that von Prum needed the people as much as he himself did. Without the people there would be no Bloodless Victory.

"I have thought of that. I am going to have your priest—what is his name?"

The mayor told him.

"We will have this Polenta sanctify the place first. There is a ritual, you know."

"No, I didn't know."

"They say it is very beautiful and very impressive and very effective," the German said. "We will have a ceremony and we will purify the place."

"I am grateful to you."

"We will clean it out."

He wrote that night: "I have a man here now who is grateful to me. He owes me everything. The time is right."

BUT THEY DIDN'T get into the cellar, not then at least, because something happened the next morning that was to change the whole course of events in Santa Vittoria, not only for then but in some ways for generations to come and perhaps for all time to come, as long as this city clings to its mountain. A little after sunrise a messenger came up the cart track and stopped at the Fat Gate, which was guarded by Private Impossible, and he held out the message.

"To be delivered by hand," he said.

"You'll never get that motorcycle up there," Impossible told him. "I'll take it up if you want. I'm going up there now."

The young men looked up the length of the Corso and at the rows of stone steps, and handed over the message.

"By hand," he said.

"I heard you," Impossible said. But he didn't go up then. He stopped first at the wine cellar office and had an eye opener of *grappa* with some of the Good Time Boys, and in the end the message went up the Corso in the hands of Paolo Lapolla. He took it, of course, to Bombolini first. They could not read a word of it. With his knowledge of English, Roberto was able to figure out a few of the words.

"All I can tell you is this, that it's about the wine," Roberto said.

Babbaluche was beside himself. "O Christ above!" he cried out. "This is the kind of country we are. We deserve to die. We deserve everything that happens to us. Here we are, handed the plans of the enemy and we are too Goddamn dumb and stupid and uneducated to *read* them."

We only found out later what they said and I can print them now.

Von Prum:
  Here is your chance to earn your medal!
  The time of the wine is upon us.
  May Schmidt von Knoblesdorf have reason to be proud of you.

                                                              Scheer
  I must admit that you have surprised me. I was certain that you would send a call for help and for reserves. What do you do to them up there?
  But the real test, of course, is now.

The second paper was the official order authorizing the taking of the wine.

They waited all of that morning for von Prum to make his move. In the afternoon he summoned Bombolini.

"Sit down," he said. It was the first time he had ever allowed the mayor to be seated in his presence.

"I think that so far we have worked together well," von Prum said. Bombolini was forced to admire the direct manner in which von Prum was able to come to the point of his business. It would have taken an Italian six *aperitivi* to arrive at this stage of the talks.

"I think we have been able to act in a mature and realistic fashion," the German said. He stressed the word realistic. "You told it to me and now I tell it to you. One of the reasons has been that I have lent you my mule and you have lent me your ox."

Except, you son of a bitch, Bombolini thought, you want to steal *my* ox. Bombolini nodded. The captain picked up the official orders that they had been unable to read.

"Can you read this?" Bombolini said that he couldn't. "It is a pity, since it would make my work easier." The captain got up and turned away from Bombolini. "It is your fate to be a civil authority and it is mine to be a soldier. What do soldiers do?" Bombolini didn't answer. The German turned around then.

"Soldiers take orders. I want you to remember one thing now. I do not want to do this personally. This is not my business. I can only follow my orders because I am a soldier."

An *aperitivo* or two would help right here, Bombolini thought. The wine of the night before was still throbbing in his temples.

"It is also true that we are at war with one another."

"I forget," Bombolini said.

"And in a war someone gets hurt. Someone loses things and someone pays a price."

Bombolini dropped his head then. "I know who pays," he said.

"I am asking you to be mature," von Prum said.

"Mature, yes," Bombolini said. "What is it they want?"

The directness of the question had upset the order of the captain's approach and he was for the moment off balance. Many men might not have recovered it, not in the manner that von Prum did. In the end he turned it to his advantage.

"Some wine," he said. "Are you strong? Are you able to hear it?" Bombolini nodded.

"They want your wine."

It is not necessary here to put down all the things Bombolini did after that. He did what was expected of him, he did what he had been rehearsing every night in his sleep since the day they had hid the wine. He slapped his hand over his heart as if he were suffering a stroke and shouted, "The wine!" and he gripped the region of his heart as if he were squeezing a grapefruit.

"They want our wine?" he cried, and he fell to the floor.

It was only the start. It is embarrassing today to put down all the rest that he did—the running into the piazza and the bathing of his head in the fountain, the cries and the tears, the hitting of his head against a stone wall, the drinking of a bottle of wine without taking the bottle from his lips, always with cries of "No . . . Never . . . No . . . No . . . Never . . . No . . . It is too much . . . too much," and finally running back into the headquarters with eyes as wild as those of a calf who has been hit with the sledgehammer and who has not died but has gotten loose from the ropes that hold him. In the end he collapsed, as he had planned, on the floor of Constanzia's house, where von Prum could talk to him.

It was the signal, of course. Everyone knew then. The Rabbit had gone over the fence. The Rabbit was in the garden. The Rabbit was eating. The Rabbit was gorging himself.

"In the name of God," Bombolini shouted. "The wine is *us*."

"You must stop," von Prum ordered him. "I trusted you, as a mature man."

"But my God above, the wine. The *wine!*"

The German leaned down toward him then. His voice was almost a whisper. "It is not all that you think," he said. "You must hear me."

"The body and blood of my people." He tried to sit up. "Captain von Prum. I want you to shoot me, to destroy me now."

The captain wouldn't listen to him. Instead, he would try the last trump, short of violence, that he held in his hand.

"I have a proposition to make to you," he said.

Bombolini succeeded in sitting up.

"Didn't I know when I said that," von Prum wrote later, "that the wop would listen? His face lit up, the tears went away, his tongue hung out, his eyes bulged at the word. They are all alike; they are Arabs in their souls."

And the captain told him. In payment for the cost of occupying and thus protecting their town, the town would be required to surrender its stock of wine.

"It's like paying an intruder to sleep in your bed with your wife," Bombolini said.

Part of the wine would be considered a payment, but part

would be considered a loan to the German government which would be returned with interest when the war was won.

"What if you lose?" Bombolini said.

Von Prum went on then to the proposition. Because transportation was becoming increasingly hard to obtain, any city that would volunteer to bring its own wine to the railhead at Montefalcone could retain for itself some part of the wine.

"How much," Bombolini said.

They began at twenty per cent.

"I can't ask my people to rape themselves for that amount," the mayor said.

"I could force them."

"No, this can't be done by force," Bombolini said, and the German knew he was correct.

"I ask you one thing. Has this been done by any other town?"

The German was honest about it. He told him that it hadn't.

"Then the price will be fifty per cent for you and fifty per cent to stay with us."

"It's high," the German said. "I don't know if they will accept it." He went to the window of Constanzia's bedroom and looked down into the piazza. Bombolini hoped the people weren't gathered in the piazza looking at the house. At last he came back in and when he did he was smiling.

"An ox for a mule and a mule for an ox," the German said. "We help each other."

There was a good feeling in every part of Santa Vittoria that night. Von Prum, of course, was consumed with joy which he was forced to conceal.

"Do you know what this means?" he asked Sergeant Traub. "Can you conceive of what this means?"

Traub was more worried that the card players and the wine drinkers would never speak to them again. He had gotten to like their company and along with the rest he looked forward to the games and the drinking at night. He didn't like this stealing of their wine. And so he was pleased and even amazed when they came to the wine cellar office that night.

"We know that you're soldiers and you have to follow orders," one of them said. "We don't hold it against you. Who has the cards?" They even got out the *grappa* that night.

There was good feeling, and it remained in the city until the morning we were due to carry the wine to Montefalcone. The feeling remained even when it was found that the order which von Prum had shown to Bombolini had required him to requisition only fifty per cent of the wine in the first place.

Maybe we are realists. We were content with our victory, it was more wine than we had counted on, and we were content to let the German have his.

N̵o one here likes to look back on the journey to Montefalcone. It began as if we were going on a picnic, and it ended in misery. Tufa tried to tell us, but no one listened to Tufa, because no one wanted to hear what he had to say.

"Have you made any arrangements for anyone dying?" Tufa asked Pietrosanto, who was the leader of the march.

"Why should anyone die?"

"You had better plan for someone dying," Tufa said.

We should have known better, but Tufa alone seemed to know what was involved in carrying 150,000 bottles of wine so many miles by so many mules and donkeys and oxen and carts and people and backs all the way over the hills to Montefalcone. Some of us can still recall Tufa's words as we started through the Fat Gate and down the mountain for the River Road. The sun was not quite up then and it was cool and damp, and we felt light and as if we could go on forever.

"This will be a terrible day for Santa Vittoria," Tufa said.

"Do you know that sometimes you are a troublemaker," Pietrosanto said. "You've seen some bad days and think that all of them are bad. We were all right before you came along."

The people were actually gay at the beginning.

"They should be crying," Sergeant Traub said. "I tell you, I don't understand these people."

"They have accepted what can't be changed," Captain von Prum said. "Why not make the best of it? As this Bombolini says, the people are realists."

"I don't know," Traub said. "I don't know." By his standards it was carrying realism too far.

The trip down the mountain, even in the dimness before dawn, was easy, because the people know the mountain and how to take it and they know every stone on it and every turn and hole where one might twist an ankle. When we reached the River Road the sun was up and the column began to spread out along the road. The wine baskets on the people's backs began to get hot and heavy even then. Many of the people had never been to Montefalcone before, and they looked ahead toward it as an adventure although Montefalcone was many miles away and out of sight.

When we passed Scarafaggio the people all stood in the Piazza of the Brass Urinal, their mouths gaping open wider than usual, and pointed down the hill at us and then began running. I could tell you the story of how the piazza got its name, how they came to Santa Vittoria and stole a huge brass urn we used for the wine during the harvest festival and how they used it for a public urinal and how we then went down and put dynamite in the pot and blew it into a thousand pieces so that every home in the city had some brass chip of Santa Vittoria in it, but the story is too long and involved and sad. They came down their mountain and across their part of the valley until they were lined up along the opposite bank of the Mad River, where they stared at us.

"What do you think you're doing?" one of them finally shouted to us. "What are you doing with the wine? What are they making you do with it?"

No one bothered to answer them, because they were Scarafaggians and because breath already was becoming valuable and because how do you explain to people that you are helping to steal your own wine?

When the column began to fall apart and the older people to drift back through it like pebbles sifting down in the water, still being carried along by the tide but sinking all of the time, Tufa, from habit as much as anything, attempted to keep the long march organized. It was the first time the Germans noticed him. There was a manner about him, the way he controlled himself and the quiet, sure way that he gave orders, a sense of keeping within him a stronger power than he chose to reveal, that made itself apparent.

"That son of a bitch is a soldier," Traub said. "We're supposed to turn them in."

Von Prum had been watching. There was a kind of control about the man and yet at the same time a kind of wildness hiding just beneath a mask of discipline that the German recognized as very Italian and which he found interesting in a man, and almost always fatal—one of the men destined in advance to commit the destructive act that ruins.

"Meanwhile he's doing our work," the captain said. "We'll watch him."

"There's something wrong about the other one as well, sir," Sergeant Traub said. Tufa had been talking to Roberto who was attempting to make the march. "He has hands like a girl. I went to have some boots fixed . . ."

The argument had no meaning to Captain von Prum. He also had hands like Roberto. There was nothing unmanly about them; it was merely that they had never pruned vines in the wet cold autumn or dug in piles of manure or strung the wires for the vines or worked the harvest or washed dirty clothes in cold water with soap made from ox suet and strong lye. The women were envious of the hands of Roberto and Captain von Prum.

It is something the men of Santa Vittoria don't like to admit about their women, but it is true. Whenever the German went through the streets the women didn't look at him directly, but when he passed they followed him and undressed him with their eyes. They peeled him like a Sicilian orange and devoured him. He was so clean, which our men are not, so clear and pink and white and blond and cool, with even a sensation of silver, shining and swift and delicate, like a trout in clear water.

We must face a truth. The men here have skins the color of copper pots, reddish brown and as tough as leather. If a brush could be made from the hair on their legs and arms and chests, it could be used to curry a water buffalo. It is possible that the women, if given the choice, would finally choose to go to bed with a hairy copper pot because it is what they know, but it is also possible that they would at least dream of trying once someone with the white clean softness of von Prum.

It has nothing to do with the war or loyalty, it has to do with the truth that in this town, where everyone is known by everybody, when even the chickens that run in the street are known and have names and are talked about, that someone like Captain von Prum becomes an unbearable curiosity walking in the streets. He was in truth all that the women talked about for some time.

"I wouldn't do it with him, you understand, but I'm curious, you know. You wonder how it must feel with that, it must be different, do you understand?"

There is one other thing that must be told: In Italy all of the men are unfaithful, because, as is known by all Italians, all Italian men are by nature and birth great lovers.

And, of course, just because they *are* such, all the women are faithful. The faithless woman can be killed and no one will lift a hand to defend her, because she has committed the unpardonable sin, the worst of all crimes, she has dishonored the man. And then the seducer must be harmed and punished and sometimes killed to restore the honor of the man who has been made to wear the horns. If he can't do it alone, his brothers will help him, his family, his whole section of the city, because the honor must be restored. It is naturally because the woman must not so much as look at another man that they do look at him, that they dream of him, that they fall in love with him at a distance, that they commit rape with their eyes and adultery in their dreams.

There is only one question that has never been answered: If all Italian men are faithless and sleep with all the women in the town, how is it that all the women, except one or two, are faithful? Either the men are not the great lovers they claim to be or all of them must wear the horns; neither of which any Italian man is willing to admit. It is a very great mystery.

At the first of the hills the first of the people began to fall out of the line of march. The Germans had made some effort to keep order on the way.

"I don't care where it is or what it is," Sergeant Traub said, "a line of march is a line of march." But at the hills it was no good. The soldiers stopped prodding the people with their rifles. "I take it back," the sergeant said. "A line of march is a line of march everywhere but in Italy."

By midday those who could march had settled into themselves and had developed a rhythm, an almost silent, shuffling cadence, that pulled people along with it, the same way it had been on the day of the passing of the wine. There was the sound and then the smells that chained the people to each other, of sweat and leather and salt against the wicker of the baskets, of urine and oxen and manure and the stale water of the drainage ditch alongside the road, and the sound of the Mad River itself, rushing against the stones and boulders in its bed.

People came down along the road to look at us, the *cafoni* who for shares worked the vegetables and the corn of the landowners' farms along the river bottoms, but they said nothing to us, not one of them, and we said nothing to them. They would never understand.

Sometime in the evening, fourteen hours after we had started in the coolness of the morning, the first of us started up the steep side road that leads to the Constantine Gate and then Montefalcone itself.

This was the cruelest part, the last long hill before the end and, after that, the people who met us. The word had gone down the river that the people of Santa Vittoria were surrendering their own wine and bringing it in on their backs. The streets of Montefalcone were lined with people and they were making a great noise, and for a moment we thought they were cheering us in. How simple we must have been. Why should we have thought they would do such a thing?

The first one was a butcher. He broke away from the sidewalk along the main Corso and out in front of us, his apron spattered with blood, and he was holding the skull of a goat in his hands, and he was screaming. "Tell me these are lying." He put his bloody hands to his eyes. "Tell me I'm not seeing what I see."

"Don't look at him," Tufa said.

"Tell me, just tell me. I will believe you," he screamed at us. "Because I cannot believe what I see." He shoved the goat's head into Tufa's face and tried to pull the wine off his back. "No son of Italy could be doing what I see you people doing. Tell me you are Greeks."

And this was the beginning. It is too painful to tell the rest. They spat on us, on our heads and in our faces, they grabbed our hair and lifted up our heads so that our faces, looking down at the stones, could be seen by everyone. The priests in the streets turned away from us and one of them encouraged a boy to urinate on our heads from a terrace of the rectory. An Italian soldier in the pay of the Germans aimed his rifle at our heads.

A woman who appeared to be a respectable woman broke through the line of German soldiers, who now were needed to protect us from our own people, and she ran to Tufa, who was in the lead, and she seized him by his private parts.

"Did you see?" she screamed to them. She held out her arms and then turned her palms downward. "Nothing," she cried out. "I swear to you, *nothing*." She ran along the line of people. "I felt nothing. No eggs," the woman shouted. "They have no eggs."

We have never lived it down. Even later, when they learned why we had done what we did we were not excused. "I don't care," they would say. "Only bastards could do it." When people from here go to Montefalcone they don't tell where they are from.

"Santa Vittoria?" they would say in Montefalcone. "Oh yes, that's the place where the men have no eggs. It's been proven."

In the end, to add to the shame, it was the Germans who saved us and they despised us for having to do it. Captain von Prum had sent a soldier ahead, so that when we came into the Piazza Frossimbone (where none of us can bear to walk) on our way with the wine to the railroad yards in back of the city, Colonel Scheer was on the terrace of his headquarters with other officers of his command. We marched in front of them with our wine, now *their* wine, in the same manner that Fabio tells us the slaves were marched in front of Caesar when the armies came back from their wars.

"I salute you," Colonel Scheer called to Captain von Prum. "We all salute you."

The people of Santa Vittoria, bent with their loads and with their shame, filed by the German officers.

"I don't know how you have done this," the colonel called to the captain. He sent a young officer down to pinch one of our people to see if it was real.

The officer pinched Guido Pietrosanto's face. "Yes, they're real people," he said.

When Captain von Prum passed in front of the steps on which Scheer stood, the colonel stopped him. "Unless I am mistaken you are soon to be Major Sepp von Prum. How does that sound?"

Captain von Prum told him that it sounded very pleasant.

"And about the other thing"—Colonel Scheer tapped the region of his chest where a medal would go—"I haven't forgotten. I don't go back on my word."

It was one of the few times that we ever saw the captain openly smile.

* * *

The journey back was even worse because many of the people had planned to spend the night in Montefalcone and rest before turning home. But that was now impossible, and we began to pray for darkness both for the coolness it would bring and the cover of secrecy it might provide.

The long march back is remembered now as the time when Captain von Prum first met Caterina Malatesta. The captain had promised that he would use his truck and his scarce gasoline to help carry the women and the children back to the foot of the mountain, and he was true to his word. The Malatesta, against Tufa's wishes, had helped carry wine and because she wasn't used to such work her feet had become a mass of blisters so that even without shoes she was no longer able to walk.

"I'm going to have to go with the German," she said to Tufa. "Don't be angry with me. I don't want to leave you."

"I can't carry you; its all right," Tufa said. But when the truck came back down the River Road he didn't feel that way. The back of the truck was filled with women, and when it stopped the officer motioned for Caterina to get in front with himself and Sergeant Traub.

"Get in the back," Tufa said. When the German again motioned to the seat beside him, Caterina looked at Tufa and then climbed into the front of the truck.

"Go the next time," Tufa said. Caterina pulled away from him and sat down next to the officer. Tufa looked into the cab at them. "I *asked* you," he said to the Malatesta, and the truck pulled away.

"Did you see the eyes on that one," Sergeant Traub said. "He's one to watch."

"Find out his name and find out what he does," the captain said.

They rode in silence for miles until finally von Prum put on the little running light inside the cab of the truck and was able to see the woman beside him. She had worn the clothes of a peasant woman, but the effort to pass as a peasant had been in vain. There are women who are so beautiful by nature that they do not know what to do to make themselves less beautiful. The roughness of the cloth only served to exaggerate the fineness of the lines of her face.

"I haven't seen you before," the captain said.

"Oh, yes. Many times," Caterina said.

"No," he said.

Just that, she thought. No. The perfect Germanness of it, blunt and uncharming. The fact that he was correct did not concern her.

"I assure you of one thing," von Prum said, "had I seen you I would not have forgotten you. Thus, I haven't seen you."

She shrugged her shoulders. How German of him and how Italian of me, Caterina thought. To her annoyance she realized that she had been speaking to him in Italian and not in the dialect. It had been a tactical error on her part caused by tiredness. But also to her annoyance she found that she liked to talk in good Italian, clean and clear, and that she found she was enjoying sitting next to someone who was so clean and who smelled so clean.

"You aren't like the others here," he said.

"These are my people," Caterina said.

"No, you aren't like them. Any more than I am like them."

She shrugged her shoulders once again.

"We're strangers here, you and I," the German said. Even his breath seemed clean and almost sweet. She knew that hers was heavy with the wild scallions they had found along the river.

"You're more like me and I'm more like you than you are like those women in the back," Captain von Prum said. Several times the truck had been forced to stop suddenly to avoid pot holes in the road, and when it did it sent the women in the back sliding forward and they groaned aloud and even sobbed in fear.

"Do you hear that?" the German said. "You don't groan. Our kind don't do that. *They* do that."

"They aren't really groaning," the Malatesta said. "It's only a way of expressing themselves."

"Of course it is," he said. It angered her that she had made another error.

When they could see the mountain and they neared the foot of it, von Prum touched Caterina on the arm. "Now I'm going to tell you something," he said. "One is that you are extraordinarily beautiful; but you know that, and it is merely a formality to get out of the way. The other is that some time this winter, when it has been raining for days and everything is rotten with wetness and you have had no fuel for days and nothing to eat for weeks on end and your body is chilled so that you become afraid to touch anything, on that day you will look down on my house in the piazza and see the smoke coming from the fireplace and you'll think of the brightness of the rooms and the beds with sheets and the hot water in tubs and warm, clean clothes and someone to cook for you the way you deserve, and at that moment you'll want to be there."

They had stopped then and she pulled away from him.

"Not because of me, not at first at least. But because that will be where you belong," von Prum said. "It's the only way that people like yourself can live. Life owes that to people like yourself. The oxen can survive, but not the race horses of the world."

When she got out of the truck he opened the map compartment and handed her a pair of gray woolen socks.

"You'll need these to get up the mountain," he said. "It's all right. You can bring them when you come."

When the truck had gone and the Malatesta and the other women had started up the dark track they turned on her.

"What did he say to you," one of them demanded.

"The German would talk to *you*," another said. "You Malatestas are all alike."

It didn't bother her. She had long ceased to feel or to take personally the feelings of hatred some of the people held for her because of crimes committed against them by members of her family whom she never had known. The socks felt good and warm on her feet. She was angry with herself that she had nothing to say to him when he had finished saying what he had said. They stopped at The Rest, and most of the women forgot their anger with her, because they wanted to know what the German had said. She told them that he had said that he liked it in Santa Vittoria, and he hoped that they liked him in return.

"Don't listen to him," a woman said from the darkness. "No matter what he says all he wants to do is get into your pants."

She could hear the others agreeing with her.

"They're all the same, *all* of them."

"It doesn't matter, wop or kraut, all they're good for is the same thing."

They started up again after that, and Caterina found herself wondering if it really was that simple. This thing that she and Tufa had found in each other, was it in the end as simple as that? This attraction she felt for the German, against her will, was it only that? She was sorry she had accepted the ride. The thing of being beautiful, how safe the others were behind those broad brown masks. Maybe this was part of their wisdom. But a beautiful woman will have people tear at her, not for her but for themselves, and because she is what she is she can't escape it. Beauty very rarely brings wisdom, the Malatesta knew, and very often danger.

After the wine had been taken, the days continued good. Each day the grapes grew fatter. Old Vines told us that he could hear them growing in the warm nights, fattening in their skins, pushing out against their sides. The wine had been taken and even if the false wall was noticed, which no longer seemed likely to us, there would be no reason to be concerned about it. Why should anyone be looking for something, we asked each other, when nothing was missing? Santa Vittoria could be said to be confident of itself. Italy might be falling apart, but that was Italy's problem.

One of the strange things was the growing friendship between Captain von Prum and Italo Bombolini. It is said that every German has a desire to sweep his neighbor's dirty steps, and in this sense von Prum was no exception. He began by remaking the mayor. He saw to it that the mayor shaved each day and that his hair was cut and kept trimmed. In September, on Bombolini's forty-eighth birthday, the German sent his measurements to Montefalcone and a few weeks later a suit came back purchased with von Prum's money.

"If you are going to share the leadership of the city," von Prum said, "then I want you to be worthy of me."

The captain was then at work on the first draft of "Bloodless Victory," and it was then that the two of them began to discuss the ways of the people here and the reasons for things.

"Now tell me, in your own words," the captain would say. "Exactly why were you willing to cooperate with us?"

"Because the people here aren't idiots and you didn't treat us as idiots," Bombolini said. "As a result you took some of our wine but we still have half of it."

The little talks between the two men gradually grew into longer ones and finally even into mild debates.

"There is something rewarding about a debate," Captain von Prum wrote to his father, "when you know that in the end your view will prevail. In this way you get to share another's view without the debate getting out of hand or losing its final discipline."

The subject that seemed to interest him above all others was why the star of Germany was rising so high and why that of Italy had sunk so low.

Why were the people of Germany so vigorous and virile and young, and those of Italy so decadent and corrupt and tired?

"Look at your soldiers. Item: Why do all Italian soldiers run away in battle?"

At times like these Bombolini would study the floor. There was a certain truth in these things. Even Tufa now had left the battlefield and was in bed in a woman's arms.

"Perhaps it's because our soldiers love life more than your soldiers do," Bombolini said.

It caused von Prum to laugh. "But what good is life without honor?"

"I don't know," Italo said. "I don't think I ever tried one with honor yet. It's a very great luxury for people like us."

On another day he complained about and then studied the Italian lack of organization and civic responsibility. "The streets," Captain von Prum said. "Why are the streets falling apart and filled with filth? Why is that? Your sewage disposal: a stream through the middle of your town. Why is it that we have toilets and you have ditches? Why is that?"

At times Bombolini grew angry at his inability to answer the captain's questions, and the captain would give the screw one more turn.

"We may not be good organizers," Bombolini shouted one day, "but we're good improvisers. That's why we make bad soldiers but good partisans."

"Is that some kind of threat?" the German said, and they didn't talk for several days afterwards.

One afternoon von Prum announced that Italy had not won a major battle in over six hundred years.

"What can I say to things like that?" the mayor asked Babbaluche.

"Tell the son of a bitch that we are easy to conquer but hard to defeat," the cobbler said. "Tell him he'll find that out."

"Sometimes I die to tell him about the wine," Bombolini said. "Just to see his face. Sometimes I think it would almost be worth the price."

"The difference between the German and the Italian is that when the wop walks into a room he wonders how many people in it are going to like him, and the kraut wonders how many will despise him. I don't understand why it is, but all Germans despise themselves," Babbaluche said.

"Should I tell him that?" Bombolini said.

"Yes, and then report to Padre Polenta for Extreme Unction," the cobbler told him.

One morning, very early, the morning of the day on which Captain von Prum received the message that was to change things here so swiftly and so terribly, he actually came to the Palace of the People to visit the mayor.

279

"I think I'm on to something," the captain said. "It is as simple and direct as this: a matter of sex. Germany is the Fatherland. Italy is the Motherland. A matter of sex. As simple as that." He grew very excited about the discovery. "I am amazed that I have never read this before.

"Male and female. What is the male? The male is aggressive, the male takes. What is the female? The female is passive, the female gives. Give and take. Strong and weak. Do you know that one of the reasons things have worked out so well here is that we make a good marriage?"

"You might ask him when we can have a divorce," Babbaluche said later in the morning, before the messenger came.

"Man is reason. Woman is emotion. One reason you can't organize anything properly is that organization is an act of reason. Can you see that? We in turn probably don't feel things deeply enough. It's not *all* on our side."

"Yes, we tend to act from the heart," Bombolini said. "It's the trouble with our soldiers. They tend to act like people. You can't have a real army and people at the same time."

"Yes. Well," the German said, "in any case, this is what I have been leading up to, I think I have the answer. The ultimate answer." He read from some notes in his hand: "The Italian exists by emotion, and emotion exhausts energy. This is a fact of simple observation. For a time it sustained you and you flamed briefly and brilliantly. And then you used up your source of energy, you burned yourself out, you wore yourself thin, and now you are old. Italy is old."

"And you, then, are young," Bombolini said.

"Because reason attaches itself to nothing, it never wears itself out. Reason is restless, adventurous," Captain von Prum said. "It's why the whole spirit of the race, the thing we call the German soul, remains a repository of youth. We are as young now as we were in the beginning, while all the rest of Europe is dying of old age."

There is no question that it bothered Bombolini. He was telling these things to Babbaluche in the hope of finding an answer, but before he had come down the Corso Cavour to the cobbler's house he had taken one tour of the Piazza of the People. He had walked along the old broken cobblestones by the edges of the houses and tried to see the old things in a new way—Santa Maria of the Burning Oven, built hundreds of years before; the fountain of the Pissing Turtle, the last piece of constructive water engineering, done almost four hundred years before. Roberto Abruzzi was always asking the question:

"How were you able to build all these things then when you can't even repair them now?"

It was what had always driven Tufa wild. Where had all the money gone, and the energy? What happened to it, who took it away, where did we lose it? Why was everything broken?

Bombolini had just finished explaining the German's view to Babbaluche when the messenger's motorcycle shook the window of the house. He forced women to jump to one side, and a girl with a basket of laundry was sent sprawling and the clothes fell into the street. They went to the door and they saw Sergeant Traub come over the top of the Corso and come down the street to get the message even before it arrived.

"Something is up," Bombolini said. "Somthing big."

They went back inside after the motorcycle had passed down the Corso again.

"You tell him this," Babbaluche said. "Ask him this. We may be old, but just when do they plan to grow up?"

* * *

Traub stood in the doorway with the message in his hand and von Prum did not look up. He was working on "Bloodless Victory," and his notes were spread over the packing case he used as a desk. Although Traub was aware that he was not to interrupt when the captain was at work on his report, he decided this time to risk it.

"I think I have good news, sir," the sergeant said.

"Then it can wait," von Prum said.

"I think by this time tomorrow I might be calling you Major von Prum, sir."

He heard the pen drop down onto the packing case, but still the captain did not come out.

"One thing I have learned," he said, "is to rely on nothing. Do

281

you know your Clausewitz? 'The only true plan in war is that plan which plans for the unplanable.' Something like that."

He worked for another fifteen minutes—a good discipline, he felt—and finally he came out into the other room.

"If I forget to call you major at times," Sergeant Traub said, "please forgive me. It will take time to learn."

"I will give you a month," Captain von Prum said, and they both laughed then.

Inside the envelope were two messages. One, from his brother Klaus, had been forwarded from Montefalcone.

Dear Brother:
  Everything. It is all there is.
  This one.

                                                    Your brother
I think that I am going mad. What do you have to tell a young German boy who is going mad?

Because he knew that the other message contained good news, he was sorry that he had opened Klaus's letter because it took some of the joy away. It also annoyed him that he couldn't recall his previous letter, since it was clear that Klaus was answering questions; but he was grateful that he had made a habit of keeping copies. He found the letter. Nietzsche's two questions: what was life to the soldier, and what soldier didn't wish to die for a glorious cause. The question of Klaus's madness, in which he believed, he decided he would have to think about later. He opened the second letter and was surprised to find that his hand was trembling. It was not an official letter and it was written by hand.

Von Prum:
  This is not what you expected to receive; it is not what I expected to send.
  I submitted your name for promotion and decoration as promised. Both requests were rejected.
  They have ridiculed your performance and through it my endorsement.
  A study of sales figures for the past 20 years obtained from wine wholesalers in this city and from the Cinzano company reveals the fact that your quota of wine should have approached 600,000 bot-

tles and not the 150,000 bottles that you so "miraculously" brought to Montefalcone.

The question is very simple: Where is the rest of the wine?

An accounting will be expected from you by ten o'clock tomorrow morning.

Scheer

He went into his room and closed the door, and he was not seen again until evening. There were obvious conclusions. They would claim that he had managed to get the people to carry the wine by letting them keep most of it. A check of the remaining wine would answer that.

It could be claimed that it was a simple case of thievery and collusion—that, in return for money or rewards to be paid after the war, he had taken the wine not for the Fatherland but for personal gain. The wine in that case would have to be hidden somewhere and it could be found.

It could be a case of cowardice as happened at San Pietro di Camano, where the people had warned the officer in command that if the wine went, no matter what, he would die, and he believed them and turned in false reports about the wine. The Germans obliged him by doing the killing.

Or there could be wine hidden somewhere in the city and he had been fooled. There was wine and he had been made a fool of, there was actually wine and he was the fool of Italo Bombolini. He was not ready to believe any of this. The answer, he was convinced, lay somewhere else.

He made a mistake that afternoon. He left Constanzia Pietrosanto's house and began to walk through the city, looking up the lanes, sizing up the city, moving swiftly and restlessly, an intelligent curiosity, the expression of the fox looking for a proper hiding place before leading the hounds on a chase informing his face and so informing us.

Everyone knew. So the element of surprise which every good soldier covets was lost to him. In the evening he came back up into the piazza of the People and everyone knew and was waiting, and when he saw Italo Bombolini with the others around the fountain he went, as was his way, directly toward them. He didn't want the mayor alone, he wanted the eyes of the others as well. His own eyes were hard and cold, and yet disinterested, as if the question was one of curiosity and not of importance. His voice was just as cold and as level and as impersonal.

"I know now," he said. "Where is the rest of the wine?"

"The rest of what wine?" Bombolini said. His face showed shock and anger.

"The rest of *all* the wine."

"You can't have the rest of the wine," Bombolini said. He was beginning to shout, and the men around him were angered. "That wine is our wine. You promised us. Are you lying? Is the word of a German officer nothing but shit?"

"You know what wine I'm referring to."

"We will fight for the rest of the wine, Captain. We will fight because there is nothing left for us but to fight."

"We will die then," Pietrosanto said, "and God damn you, you will die with us."

Someone stopped him and put his arms around Pietro and pulled him back across the piazza.

"He didn't mean it that way," the man shouted to von Prum. "It's only that the rest of our wine—it would be death to us."

It has been said here and it has been said by others that all Italians are actors and all of them know the subtleties of the good lie and perhaps again this is true, because all of them played their parts so well.

"Not that wine," the German was forced to say. "We don't take that wine. My word is my bond on that. The other wine."

And they came back around him then with their mouths open and their eyes dazed as if trying to see something and not being able to make it out, none of them with as much wisdom on their slack faces as was owned by Fungo or shouted aloud by Capoferro.

And so the German had to tell them about the records of the wholesalers and the records of the Cinzano people and the one million or more bottles of wine, and as he talked they looked at one another and their mouths fell open and they said, in low bewildered voices, "No, oh no, it couldn't be . . . there is some-

284

thing wrong. . . wrong . . . wrong . . ." When he was through
one of them said that no people in the world could be that
rich; and they all nodded and were silent.

* * *

It is a pride of many men who make it a habit to tell the truth
that because they possess this virtue they are qualified to know
when another man is telling a lie.

In von Prum's case, it was a belief that if you watch a man's lips
as he talks and if you seal your eyes on his eyes, the man who is
lying must falter and stammer and then turn away, because truth
and honesty when confronted with the lie must overcome in the
end. He should have known that a good lie is always better than
the truth, because a lie has been tailored to look like the truth,
but the truth is just its clumsy self. If you look at an Italian in the
mouth when he is telling the truth he might stammer, but never
when he is telling a good lie. The Master himself has said: Never
tell the truth when a lie will do as well.

And so they convinced him. He already believed them, when
Pietrosanto apologized for saying what he had and then asked the
question, "But if we had a million bottles—*if*, mind you, Mother
of God, *if*—where in the name of God would we put them? How
do you hide one million bottles of wine?"

The captain went to his room and he immediately wrote this
letter.

I say this much with no fear of contradiction.

For reasons that I am now unable to understand I am forced to
conclude that you have been falsely informed and that any further
investigation by you can only bear this out.

On the following I stake my professional reputation, my personal
reputation, my good name and that of my family which, as you
know, is considerable.

Upon my word of honor: There is no other wine in the city of
Santa Vittoria except that which the people have been authorized to
keep.

The letter was sent to Montefalcone that evening and an answer was returned that night.

Dear von Prum:

Upon receipt of your letter I myself am forced to conclude that I have been misinformed and that a further investigation by our office can only bear this out.

Sleep well this night at least.

Scheer

Before going to bed he answered Klaus's letter as well as he could. There was, he said, nothing to tell a young German going mad except not to do it; that madness was often a simple display of weakness and that character would prove to be stronger than the mind if only the person had the courage to try it.

After that he read Colonel Scheer's letter to Sergeant Traub, and it was so ridiculous to the sergeant that he was forced to gasp and then to laugh aloud.

"There's no wine," the sergeant said. "There's no place to hide it, and if they did hide it they couldn't keep a secret. You have to know them sir. They'll tell you everything there is to tell about and anything there is to talk about."

6 THE NOOSE GROWS TIGHTER

I T MIGHT BE THOUGHT that the question of the missing wine would have separated the Germans from the Italians and made them suspicious of each other, but that wasn't the way it happened. It became as important to the Germans as it was to us that there be no other wine.

We discussed it with each other; for days thereafter it was the only thing we talked about, and we went over it and over it again the way a person does who is injured in a ridiculous way, trying to make some sense out of something that is senseless. For a time we talked about where they thought we could have hidden it.

"The logical place," Bombolini actually said, "would be the old Roman wine cellar. It's the only place big enough. But the wine isn't there."

After that, the talk advanced to the question of why someone would want to say that we had hidden the wine; and finally an answer came forth. It was decided that some of the wholesalers and some of the Cinzano people had altered their figures so that after the war they could file some kind of claim with either the Italian or the German government for confiscated wine which, of course, had never existed. It sounded so sensible that many of the people here began to believe it. And then we stopped talking about it entirely, because there is a belief here that if you dwell on one subject too long it can be harmful to the brain, and that just like a pool of water, the brain must be refreshed with new thoughts or it will become polluted and turn sour.

Something was happening with the war, but it didn't concern us. Electricity was coming back to Santa Vittoria for several hours a day, probably because the Germans in Montefalcone had the power plant going again for their own needs and didn't know how to shut us off, and Vittorini's radio began to play now and then. But the River Road was now filled with traffic going south all night long, and we could hear the trucks in the convoys slamming into one another when they hit in the darkness. One afternoon before dusk we saw a regiment of Italian soldiers moving at a swift march down the road going south.

"It won't be much longer now," Babbaluche said. "The Italians are in it."

From time to time, when the wind was just right we heard from far away the booming rolling sounds of heavy guns. It interested the people, because if the Americans and the English came it meant that we were safe. But still there no longer was any real fear for the secret, because the feeling was strong that we had been tested and found not lacking, and that if any slip was to occur it would have happened long before this. We had learned to live with our secret.

One evening what Captain von Prum had feared took place. The people had come up from the terraces, which is what saved most of them, when some planes came over the city and dropped some bombs. Most of them landed down in the terraces and damaged some vines, although not many, and several of them dropped among the houses in Old Town. We never knew who bombed us, the Germans or the English or the Italians or the Americans. Two or three old people were killed by the bombs and seven or eight other people were badly hurt. Since the hospital in Montefalcone had been taken over by the German army for their own wounded being sent up from the south, there was no room for our people and Tufa turned the Palace of the People into an emergency hospital and put it under Caterina Malatesta's direction. It was not very nice there. She worked with the help of Bombolini, who could not bear to look at the wounded, and Roberto Abruzzi and Angela Bombolini. There were no drugs to help relieve the pain and no medicines to stop infection, and it was not satisfactory work.

"You will have to go to the German and make him get us supplies in Montefalcone," Caterina told the mayor.

"I don't think he wants to do that," Bombolini said.

"You tell him that as commander of the city he is responsible for the health and welfare of the people in it under the articles of the Geneva convention of war."

"I couldn't tell him all that."

"Tell him that if he doesn't do it he will be held accountable as a war criminal when this is over," the Malatesta said.

"You should tell him this. You're the one he will listen to," Bombolini said. "Haven't you seen the way he looks at you?"

"I will never go across the piazza to beg anything from any German," Caterina said.

The captain went that same day to Montefalcone, and he returned with most of the things that were needed. After that he came every day to help in the hospital. He was capable and quick, and he had no fear of blood, unlike Roberto and Bombolini. Tufa had never come back after the first day, because he couldn't stand the sight and sound of the pain and the cries of the people.

During the time that he worked in the Palace of the People the captain did his work and took his orders, and the two of them, von Prum and the Malatesta, almost never exchanged a word that didn't have to do with the people they were treating. There was no outward sign at all that the captain was slipping into love. But he began to write about her in his log and then in his letters to Christina Mollendorf, which is a certain sign that a man is falling in love.

"There are things to admire about her, but at what a price. She is what you would call a New Woman, the liberated woman we were all talking about before the war broke out. Thank the Lord that era is over and gone with. God spare me from the liberated women and God be praised for the likes of you. You may commence blushing now."

Another time he wrote about Caterina's darkness, the deep olive color of her skin and the darkness of her hair, the blackness of her eyebrows, beneath which the eyes were so dark that they couldn't be said to possess any color at all.

"We don't raise people such as this. It is interesting and at the same moment repelling. One feels that this darkness doesn't stop at the surface but extends all the way into the spirit or the soul, whatever you call it.

"I suppose, however, I am hopelessly smitten with the idea that all real women are fair and blond and soft and white—with a soul or spirit or whatever you call it to match. If you think that's a good description of yourself, Christina, you may commence blushing again."

The letters that came back to him began to be filled with pictures. In several of them, the later ones, she had unpinned her hair and it flowed down over her white shoulders like a field of ripe grain flooding down the side of a snow-covered hill.

It was the night after the bombing that the Roman cellar was turned into the air-raid shelter for the city of Santa Vittoria. At first the idea had been that in the event of a raid the people would be roused from bed by the air-raid siren and would take a blanket and start down the mountain, but for two reasons it was plain this wouldn't work. If the raid was a true raid the people would be dead before they ever reached their shelter; and if it wasn't, the journey down, the lack of sleep, the trip back up the mountain with the grapes growing fatter and needing more work and the harvest looming upon us, would kill the people just as surely as a real air raid. It was decided that the people would take down bedding and a few things to heat food in and the city of Santa

Vittoria would be moved into the Roman cellar at night, within breathing distance of their wine.

The afternoon before the move Bombolini went down with Sergeant Traub and Corporal Heinsick and Captain von Prum.

"It's a remarkable place," the captain said. "It could take direct blows from any airplane in the world and everyone would be safe. Why is it so large?"

"It is said that it was the collection point for all of the wine in all of the region," Bombolini said. "It all belonged to one man. I think it was Julius Caesar. Yes, that's who it was."

"The large room is here, and then there is the wine cellar that goes back off it," the captain said. "It's a very peculiar shape. I wonder what was the need of all that wall along there?"

Bombolini said that he didn't know.

The people started down that evening, after working all that day. They carried mattresses and straw mats and blankets and anything that anyone could lie on. It was a mass migration of lice and bedbugs probably not equalled in this part of the world before. They took down jugs of water and bread and bottles of wine and pots of cooked cold beans and baskets of onions and jugs of oil to pour on the beans and the bread. Longo started up the lights again, and this was a good thing to happen. By those pale dimming lights the false wall looked more natural than ever before.

At first the people who camped along by the false wall were afraid to talk loudly, as if the vibration of their voices might cause a brick to pop loose. They were even afraid to look at the wall. But that passed. As the cellar become crowded with pots and pans and kettles and chamber pots and bedclothes and people, the old Roman wine cellar ceased to be a wine cellar at all and became solely an air-raid shelter, run like some monstrous underground inn from the Dark Ages.

Other things helped. Captain von Prum did not come down to the cellar but stayed in his room and worked on "Bloodless Victory." Von Prum was given to questions and curiosity. His soldiers were given to drink. We set them up in a running card game well away from the wall, and in such a way that their backs were almost always toward it. The Good Time Boys would come down with the vermouth and the *grappa* and the game would begin, *tre setti* from sundown until far into the night. Such precautions were not a waste of time. It was just this arrangement that saved us from ruin the first time.

It must have begun early in the evening, because the lights were still on. By agreement the lights would be on until nine o'clock and after that the soldiers and the card players had agreed to play by lantern light so the working people could sleep. Even inside the tunnel we could hear the planes this night. There were more than usual and they were bombing somewhere in the area. It is our belief that they had no interest in Santa Vittoria but were going after the River Road and some of the bridges over the Mad River. There was a moon and the bridges would stand out over the white waters of the river.

We heard the bombs begin by the river and then we heard them start coming across the valley floor, giant strides of bombs, coming in our direction. There was no fear for ourselves, although there was fear for the people in the Palace of the People and there was fear for the grapes on the terraces.

Several of the German soldiers stopped playing and went outside and came back again when the bombs came closer.

"These are the big ones," one of the Germans called to us. "The big bastards. Americans."

"Yes, that's right," Roberto said. "B-24s." It was his only slip in all his time in Santa Vittoria. They didn't hear him.

After that they came louder and louder, and their force was stronger. We could feel the explosions then, through our feet, and dust began to fall from the arches above. The cellar was rumbling from the pressure of the explosions, and there was a shaking of things and even the mountain seemed to shake.

And then everyone seemed to see it at once, everyone was looking at it, everyone except the card players, all of us incapable of any movement, the way people are supposed to be before a poisonous snake—frozen, frightened, unable to take one's eyes away from it. The bombs were dropping on the side of the mountain and as they exploded, as if the shock were coming down through the rock veins of the mountain, the false wall began to swell and to puff out, and the bricks actually bulged and then all at once to sink back into place again until the next bomb landed on the mountain.

The false wall billowed out and sank back again, each time the bricks barely holding, as smoothly and almost as regularly as the swells at sea.

Then there was one great explosion, the heaviest of them all, and this time the bricks swelled out so far from the rest of the wall that it seemed impossible that we didn't hear the sound that we dreaded more than any in the world then, the *snap*, the first dry sound of the first brick popping, springing out from its framework in the wall.

The next explosion was a little less than that and the one after that far less, and we waited and waited until finally there were no more sounds at all and they were gone and it was over.

"It's all over," one of the Germans called to us. "They won't come again tonight."

The sigh from the people was like a wind that comes a night just before the rains begin. The next morning all of the people of Santa Vittoria went to Mass.

"And what is this?" von Prum asked.

"Deliverance Day," Bombolini said. "Every Santa Vittorian gives thanks to God for protecting the fruits of the harvest."

"I thought you weren't a religious man," the German said.

"I have become one today," Bombolini said.

They found that morning that the mortar that had held the bricks in place had shivered itself apart. If one man, an unknowing German, had leaned against the wall, the entire structure would have come down on top of him and the treasure been exposed. Later in the morning some of the men took a cartload of bricks out through the Fat Gate and into a field where one of the ventilators was located and they dropped the bricks down the shaft on the inside of the false wall. After that they took out enough of the bricks to allow three or four men to step inside the cellar, and then they put the bricks back and rebuilt the wall from the inside, twice as thick as before, except for one little section they crawled back through.

We learned something else that day. The bricklayers came back up from the field with the empty cart. The bricks were gone.

"What did you do with the bricks?" Private Zopf said.

"Fixed something," one of the men said.

"That's good," the guard said. "It's always good to fix something."

They weren't really interested in what we did. They really only cared about themselves. They didn't really see us as people at all. As Babbaluche once put it, when the Italian looks into the mirror he sees the pimple on his nose, but when the German looks in the mirror he sees those blue eyes and tries to look through them into his soul.

* * *

It was this same Zopf, one day before the wine began to explode, who came closest to exposing the wine. He had been drinking in a corner of the cellar and smoking his pipe. On the way back across the cellar to the card game he stopped and tapped the bowl of his pipe against the brick. When the tapping failed to dislodge the tobacco he took a few steps more and tapped the wall again. He tapped once and he went back and tapped again.

Hard tap—*tap*. Hollow tap—*poonk*. *Tap, poonk, tap, poonk.*

"Do you know something?" he said. "You could play a tune on this wall."

They got him very drunk that night. They played a game where the winner was to be treated with drinks and they made certain to lose. When Zopf woke up the next morning he had no memory of the wall and the pipe at all and only a vow, which he broke that night, never to mix *grappa* and wine again. There was one positive result of the Zopf affair, however. It was decided the morning after that if any soldier, or all of them, discovered the false wall, he or they would have to die, even if it meant the deaths of fifty or a hundred of us, since without the wine we were as good as dead in any case.

On the fifth day of October the wine began to explode. Not all at once—a bottle now, several a few minutes later, a long pause perhaps, and then a succession of explosions. It was fortunate for us that they began in the early afternoon. The sounds of the explosions came up out of the air shafts and carried across the terraces and up into the streets of Santa Vittoria, as if someone were throwing little hand grenades or little hollow glass bombs, somewhere in the valley.

Something had gone wrong with the weather. In October it is dry here, hot in the day and cool at night, but on this morning the wind began to come from the southwest, hot and steaming and moist, and it settled down on the streets and lanes of the city and clogged the piazzas as if a wet hot shawl had been dropped on Santa Vittoria. The people sagged with sweat, and the mules looked as if they had been lathered with soap. By afternoon the moist heat had worked its way down into the air shafts and had settled on the valley floor; and when it was hot enough the first of the bottles, for reasons we don't know, began to explode. We only guess that it was the result of some kind of imbalance in the fermentation process, caused by layers of cool air and layers of hot moist air.

After the first several bottles exploded, they dropped Rana, our frog, on a line down one of the air shafts, and he told us that the bottles had become beaded with sweat and that some of them, especially the special bottles of *spumanti,* a bubbly kind of wine that some of the growers experiment with, were boiling inside. Beards of white fungus hung down from the corks like hair on the chin of a goat. Sometimes only the cork would go, and then there would be a hollow pop that could be heard through the wall. When the cork held, however, and the drive of the wine was strong, then the bottle gave, and the sound of the explosion was a sickness and a terror in our hearts.

When they first heard it in the Piazza of the People, Bombolini felt that he knew what it was. Fabio and the Petrarch Brigade, the four or five young boys who made up the Red Flames, must have decided to fight.

Sergeant Traub came across the piazza toward them. "What the hell is that?" he asked.

"From the rock quarry," Pietrosanto said. "Someone is shooting off blasting caps. Some kid is wasting them down there."

The answer satisfied the sergeant then.

"It was a very good answer," Babbaluche said. "I didn't know you could think that fast." A compliment from the cobbler was a very rare thing.

"What? Isn't that what it is?" Pietrosanto asked.

With the setting of the sun and the cooling of the day the explosions stopped and we felt we were safe, at least until the next day. But when the people came in from the terraces to settle for the night the heat of their bodies was enough to make the heat rise once more and cause the first of the bottles to explode.

And once again, to most of the people here at least, the only explanation for what took place is that a miracle occurred. On this night, as if stationed there by God, spread out along the floor of the wine cellar just in front of the false wall, were the families of Constanzia Muricatti and Alfredo del Purgatorio, who were preparing for their marriage. The families, using sheets and blankets and the canvas covers from the grape carts, had set up two large strange-looking Oriental tents. In one of them the women were all working and sewing on the bridal gown and their own dresses. In the other tent the men were singing and dancing and drinking. The people were very gay and very loud because everyone was very happy about this marriage. It had long been conceded by the Muricatti family that no one would ever marry their Constanzia, and it had long been conceded by the del Purgatorios that it would be a miracle if Alfredo, who was very small and very shy, would ask a woman to share a bed with him.

When the bottle exploded behind the false wall, several of the German soldiers turned around from their cards and looked back into the cellar.

"What's going on back there?" Corporal Heinsick asked. One of the Good Time Boys winked at him.

"The celebration has begun," he said. "They're popping the corks. There will be some action in here tonight."

They sent wine to the soldiers, and a little later, when the music began and the dancing started, we knew we were safe. At the start there was a mandolin and an accordion, and while this worked well as a cover for the sound, Bombolini ordered every musician in the city to play. There were tambourines and one old man with his pipes, there were Capoferro's drums and, finally, the singing and the dancing and the clapping of hands. If you listened with your ear to the wall you might be able to hear a bottle explode now and then, but this was the only way it could be heard.

At nine o'clock that night the dancers, who had worked all day in the vineyards, grew tired and the wine was having its effect and the musicians wanted a rest.

"Play," Bombolini ordered. "Dance," he shouted at the men and the women. "Sing," he told us, "and clap your hands while you do it."

"We can't go on," Tommaso del Purgatorio complained. "We've danced our legs off."

"You'll go on because you have to go on," the mayor told them. "The whole city is depending on you now."

"And look as if you're having fun," Pietrosanto said. "Get that long look off your face."

At eleven o'clock, when they would normally have been asleep for hours, the dancing still continued. It went in shifts now, fresh dancers every fifteen minutes or so, and when the mandolin player stopped, the tambourines beat a little more loudly, and they pounded Capoferro's goatskin drum with heavy wooden spoons. At midnight, while taking a walk in the Piazza of the People, Captain von Prum heard the noise of the gaiety and went down the mountain to see what it was. No one knows how long he might have watched us from the entrance to the Big Room.

"They don't seem to be having very much fun," the captain said.

"They're tired now, but they'll get a second wind, you'll see," Bombolini said. Pietrosanto and some of the others went around the back of one of the tents and gave out new orders.

"Get a smile on your faces," the people were told. "Get some spring into your steps. Start having fun, and don't you dare forget it," Pietrosanto warned them.

"Now, you see," Bombolini said. "Now they're perking up. They can go all night."

And they did.

The dance, Bombolini explained to von Prum in the morning, was a tradition in Santa Vittoria. It might go on for days, he said, through night and through day, until the bride and the groom were exhausted and were too tired to be embarrassed in each other's presence any longer. When the moment was reached they were put to bed together, where they often slept for a day or two at a time, but when they finally woke they were strangers no longer.

"It's not beautiful, perhaps," Bombolini said, "but it is very effective."

"What happens to your work? You can't dance all night and all day and do your work."

"What does it matter about the work if it helps to create a beautiful marriage?" Bombolini said.

"The Italian mind," von Prum said. "You jump from realism to romanticism in the middle of one sentence."

"Oh, it's realistic," Bombolini said. "It keeps up our population. It grows future grape growers." And the German was forced to admit that there was a hard peasant wisdom behind it all.

And then began some of the hardest days and nights ever spent by the people of Santa Vittoria. As long as the city sat stewing in the heat wave, the party would have to continue, all the time, dancing at eight o'clock in the morning, singing and dancing in the heat of the day, people coming down hot from the terraces to take their places at the drums or in the singing, wine flowing until people were sick of wine, and throats raw from singing and faces frozen from smiling.

"One more night of joy and I shall go mad," Angela Bombolini said. Her thighs and legs cried out in pain from the continual dancing, and she was no different from all of the rest.

On the fourth day of the wedding celebration, because they were forced to do it, the people began to take chances with the bottles. They would sit by the instruments and not move for fear of raising the heat, and when a bottle would go, but only then, they would all get to their feet and hit the tambourines and begin to sing and shout in a tired and mournful way and to shuffle about in the sand.

"The gaiety has died down, the laughter has cooled," von Prum remarked.

"It's coming to that time now," Bombolini told him. "The bed time. We begin with the lullabies, the siren songs, you see. Soon they will sleep."

But it wasn't to be for another two days. The mandolin player wore pruning gloves and he hit the strings with his knuckles. Several members of the del Purgatorio family had already had fights with Muricattis. The sound of the tambourine grew more painful than the crashing of glass behind the walls. If there had been a vote then, it is possible that the people might have surrendered the wine, anything to stop the wedding party.

One night we thought we heard the bombers coming and we were pleased because the sound of the engines and the roar of the explosions would drown the sound of the bottles. Then we felt the first of the wind coming into the mouth of the Big Room, and after that we heard the rain and the thunderclaps and saw the flashes of lightning. And then came a hard, cool wind with a hard, cold rain.

The bottles didn't stop right then. If anything, for the next hours it was worse than ever before, and we feared that all the effort was in vain, that there couldn't be a bottle left to save; but we also knew that the heat was gone, that the autumn was back with us and that in the morning the party would have ended. So we danced then with some wild last source of energy called from the very bottom urge of desperation, beating the tambourines until they split and strumming the mandolin strings until they broke and striking Capoferro's drum until the goatskin burst.

In the morning we held the wedding of Constanzia Muricatti to Alfredo del Purgatorio. We shivered in the cold in the Piazza of the People, pleased by our goose-pimples, our backs turned to the cold wind that was blowing over Santa Vittoria, the city washed bright and shining by the cold hard rain, and it was the most popular wedding ever held in our city.

They had earned their right to bliss, and it was a wedding that we would never allow to fail. Because this was truly a marriage made in heaven and ordained by God Himself.

"They are very sweet," Captain von Prum said, "and very tired."

"Very tired."

"Now you have no music? A week of music and just when they're married the music ends. It's just the opposite with us."

"Now is the time to sleep and to sleep and to sleep. There's no more need for music. The party is over, you see."

THE CITY still slept when the Germans came, two cars of them, four Germans and four Italians in each car. The cars were unable to make it all of the way up the mountain and they were parked at The Rest and the men proceeded up the rest of the way on foot. The Germans walked ahead and the Italians trailed along behind them. The Germans were all officers and looked as if they ate a great deal of meat. The Italians were all civilians, dressed in little thin dark suits stained with wine and pasta and they looked as if they lived on field greens and pebbles. Word had gone up the Corso Cavour to Captain von Prum, and by the time they arrived at the Fat Gate the captain had already gotten dressed and gone down the steep street to meet them. Colonel Scheer made no response to his greeting.

"They say the wine is here," the colonel said. He pointed to the Italians.

"With all respect, sir, they can say what they wish, but I am forced to stand on my statement," Captain von Prum said.

"It cost them a lot of teeth to say that and to stand by it," Colonel Scheer said, and he went across to one of the Italians and he forced open the man's mouth. His gums were torn and his teeth were gone. "We took them out one by one and he stayed with his story. I'm inclined to believe a man like that."

There was nothing for the captain to say.

"So I decided I had better come and see for myself." Scheer turned to the youngest and most intelligent-looking of the Italians. "Show the captain the papers, the documents," he said.

At first the young man was shy with Captain von Prum, but as the papers began to tell the story of the wine he found courage in them and he grew excited by what the papers revealed. There were receipts from the cellars of wine wholesalers for years past listing the amount of wine received and stored and shipped. There were warehouse receipts showing bottle deliveries in the north of Italy, there were bills of lading and transportation orders and there were the books of the Cinzano people showing how many bottles had been received each year and how many stored and how many shipped and to where and how many sold. In every case they told the same story. In some years the amount of wine ran as low as 800,000 bottles but in good years it ran to a million bottles, and even more. Because of the war, since deliveries had not been made the season before, it was safe to assume, the Italian said, that well over a million bottles, perhaps 1,500,000 bottles, could be found in Santa Vittoria. Von Prum studied the papers as carefully as possible for some kind of weakness in them or at least an explanation, and finally he faced Colonel Scheer.

"There can be only one explanation," he said. "The papers are a fraud."

The Italian, who had grown arrogant now, answered for the colonel. "In order for these papers to be a fraud it would take hundreds of people to be involved in the deception. It would take people in the wineries, in the warehouses, in the railroads, in the Cinzano company." They stopped the Italian at that point. It was

303

apparent that he might have gone on for a long time. He was very convincing.

"Now they want to see the wine you have," Scheer said; and they started up the Corso to the lane that turns off into the Cooperative Wine Cellar. Bombolini had been warned, and when they turned into the lane von Prum saw him and told him to come along in case questions would need to be answered. In the darkness of the cellar none of them could see the wine well at first, but when they could see the bottles the Italians began to smile at one another. Bombolini tried to catch their eyes and shake his head. As Italians perhaps they would rise to the moment against the Germans, but he knew it was hopeless. The sad little clerks were what are called Fascists for the Family, men who felt for their jobs a love no greater than their fear of hunger.

"It is what you would expect," one of them said. Bombolini felt an urge to get out of the cellar then and begin to run, but he stayed where he was.

"There are two ways to put down wine," one of them began. "Ah, well, we will show you."

They knew their wine and how to handle it, and they began to put down the bottles in the tight way, and when they had finished several rows it was as clear as if someone had painted a picture of it, a picture of before and an after, that the cellar had been made to handle ten times the amount of wine that it now held.

"Do I need to go on, sir?" one of the Italians said.

"No, there is no more need to go on," Colonel Scheer said, and he turned to Captain von Prum. "The question being then, Captain, what happened to the rest of the wine? Where is it? What have they done with it? How did they fool you?"

He turned to the young officers who were with him. "Get me a wop," he said. "From the town."

"There's one right here," a lieutenant said.

"The mayor," von Prum said.

"Who could be better than the mayor?" the colonel said. "Come over here."

Bombolini was afraid and he tried not to show it. To his surprise, however, he found that he was not afraid for himself or what was about to happen to him, but only afraid that he might reveal something even against his wishes.

"We are not a cruel people," the colonel was saying to him. He tried to listen to the words, but since he knew he would not be answering the questions he found it hard to listen. He was more interested in preparing himself for what was going to happen.

"So if you are honest and generous with us you will find that we are honest and generous with you. Now, then. Where is the wine?"

Bombolini held out both of his hands, palms upward. His eyes were as wide open as his mouth.

"This is our wine."

Scheer raised his dark hard fist and struck the mayor in the mouth. "Where is the wine?"

When Bombolini held out his hands again the colonel hit his face once more, as hard as the first time, breaking his nose and breaking one tooth loose from the bridge of his mouth and causing him to fall on the stone floor of the wine cellar. The first blow had caused a lump the size of a pigeon's egg to form below Bombolini's eye, and the colonel touched it with the sandy tip of his boot.

"Now if you want to lose your eyesight to protect something that will be found out in the next few hours, I will oblige you with my boot," the colonel said. He turned on von Prum. "Don't turn away," he said. "Is this too crude for someone with such fine blood as yours?"

"It isn't that," the captain said. "It's the failure of what I wanted to do here. We wanted to rule without violence."

"Well your rule has been shit," Colonel Scheer said. "What do you think of that? Do you think this is ineffective?" He slammed his hard fist into the palm of his other hand. "You would be surprised how well it works."

"It wasn't the way I wanted to do it."

Scheer was angered by the statement. "You may think you're different, but you're one of us," the colonel said. "You are a German. Don't you ever forget how many fists have been used on how many faces by men who haven't been afraid to use them to make fine people like yourself. We fought for that, and I am not ashamed of it. Those who can use the fist have a right to use the fist, they have a responsibility to use the fist if the fist can help the Fatherland. Who do you think you are?"

The colonel's anger and harshness and scorn were very difficult for the captain to take. He lowered his eyes at last and he looked at the floor not conscious of the mayor's body lying on it.

"Get him up and hit him," Colonel Scheer said. Several of the soldiers lifted Bombolini to his feet.

"It isn't the hitting, Colonel. I can hit." He surprised them by pulling back his arm and smashing his fist into Bombolini's face. He hit him on the swollen lump and it split on the impact like a grape between the fingers, and blood splattered from it.

"You have been baptized," Scheer said. "Now you are one of us." He was easier toward the captain now.

"I believe you now," Captain von Prum said. "The wine is here. I am humiliated. Now I ask one thing of you."

"Will you hit him again, good and hard? Would you knock an eye out?"

"Yes," von Prum said.

"Then ask."

"I want a chance to restore my honor in my own way," the captain said. "I want to find the wine and bring it to you by myself."

"And if you don't?"

"I'll find it."

"I give you five days."

Von Prum was overjoyed. "You will have your wine," he said, "and if you don't I shall resign my commission."

Scheer laughed at him then. "That's generous of you," the colonel said. "If you don't, you'll find your ass on the eastern front—excuse my peasant manners, von Knoblesdorf. What kind of war do you think we're running here?"

They went outside then, and as von Prum wrote in his log that evening, he was surprised to find that the sun was out and it was still day.

"Five days, then," Colonel Scheer said. "Do you know, I am a very generous man."

"Now that I know the wine is here there's no question of its being found, but I am thankful to you, Colonel Scheer."

The colonel put a hand on the captain's shoulder. "And if, on the fourth night, you still haven't found the wine, when it comes time for pulling out fingernails, you'll pull them out, and when it comes time for crushing testicles, you'll crush them, and if you have to kill, you'll kill."

Von Prum said nothing. He gave the impression that he believed, but within himself he denied it, not because he couldn't do it, but because he wouldn't need to do it.

"You'll do it," Colonel Scheer said, "because you're one of us and this is the way we do things. You will surprise yourself, von Prum."

When they were gone Captain von Prum went back to the wine cellar. Some women were already washing the mayor's wounds.

"I had to do that, do you understand?" the captain said. "It was required of me, a matter of form."

Bombolini was facing away from the captain toward the wall. He was in great pain, and yet he was pleased with himself. He had discovered that he wasn't afraid of the punishment and that he would say nothing despite the pain of it.

"It was unworthy of you," Bombolini said.

"It was a matter of form," the captain said.

The mayor turned toward the captain. His face was badly battered and, as von Prum later wrote, it was almost disgusting to have to contemplate.

"After all of the things you told me," Bombolini said.

"I still believe them," the captain said. "Now the wine will be found. I try to force no answer from you. I ask you as a reasonable man to save both of us effort and pain. Now that they are gone, where is the wine?"

Bombolini smiled at him, although it was painful to smile and the air that touched the broken tooth caused him to gasp aloud.

"There is no wine."

To his surprise, the German found that his hand was opening and closing and that he wanted to smash Italo Bombolini's eye.

H E WAS confident, and his confidence passed to the men. Now that he had no doubt that the wine was in Santa Vittoria he had no doubt that it could be found.

"It is a matter of reason and logic and science," Captain von Prum told them. "I want no force and no violence."

The matter of violence had become important to him, because of the "Bloodless Victory," which only the day before he had contemplated giving up, and because of the beliefs he had invested in it, and—something he wasn't prepared to consider then—because of Caterina Malatesta and the respect he wanted from her, and the love.

He wanted to find the wine easily and gently, he wished to find it wittily, to touch the right place, almost sadly and say, "The wine is here. I'm very sorry, it was a good effort but it wasn't quite enough. I'm truly sorry about it."

Because he was certain of finding the wine, he had time on his side and instead of beginning the search at once, in a haphazard fashion, they sat down and constructed a detailed map of Santa Vittoria, which is still the best map ever made of our city, and they divided the city into sections and quarters and into logical geographical situations that would lend themselves to the hiding of one million bottles of wine. There were only five or six of these.

"It is a simple process of logical anticipation followed by logical elimination, which in the end will leave no other possibility except the place where the wine *must* be and, so, *will* be." Von Prum put this down in his log and then, finding it good, read it to his men.

"Oh, we'll find it all right," Corporal Heinsick said. "If *they* hid it, sir, then *we'll* find it."

This was the true logic: that if the Italians had been smart enough to hide the wine, then it stood to reason that the Germans must be smart enough to find it.

The first "logical anticipation" was the Roman wine cellar, as the most obvious and convenient place to put the wine, and it was the first to be eliminated. Sergeant Traub told the other soldiers, "Even the wops are too smart to put their wine down there." And they went on to the second anticipation, which was the Fat Wall around the city. It was a possibility that had to be checked, that the wall or some stretch of it had been hollowed out and was being used as a massive container for the wine. In the morning they began going over the wall almost brick by brick, striking the sides with their trench knives and bayonets, listening for that hollow sound that would tell them that the brick front was false and the wine was hiding behind it. By the middle of the morning they were still not halfway around the city. It is very hard to explain to someone who was not there on that day, how ironic the tapping on the bricks was to the people of the city.

When Heinsick suggested ways to speed up the process, the ways were rejected by Captain von Prum.

"Carefulness is the keystone of our method here, Corporal," the captain said. "Thoroughness. Time is on our side, not on theirs. Each time we finish one area the remaining areas grow smaller. The noose draws tighter."

They were good words, and the soldiers liked them. *"The noose grows tighter."* It offered a satisfaction, even when the search found nothing. It proved that nothing indeed was there; and *that* in itself was something. The captain and the sergeant found a true satisfaction in inking out the sections on the map that had been found wanting. Each failure only meant that they were that much closer to the end.

When they were through with the Fat Wall they began to investigate the possibility that the wine was in some fashion buried in the very bowels of the city, and that there must be some old storage place, probably built in ancient days as protection against marauding armies, that could be reached by old stairways and trap doors in the floors and cellars of the old houses or through the church or the Palace of the People. Late on the first afternoon they began a step-by-step, door-by-door, systematic, logical examination of every house in Santa Vittoria.

They began in High Town and from there they started down the lanes to the Piazza of the People, down from the Goats to the Turtles and, if needed, to the Frogs in Old Town, where the wine would almost surely lie.

They picked up the beds and the mattresses on the floors, and the rush mats, and they tapped the stone floors and the earth floors, and they tapped the tile floors (of those fortunate enough to have tiles) with metal rods and wooden sticks and stone hammers.

The search of the houses took longer than they had thought, and although time was on their side time also was fleeing from them. Von Prum began to urge them to go a little faster and a little faster, and the stop for lunch was only ten minutes long and there was no rest, and then they ate their supper while they worked. At night we still went down the mountain and, since the evenings were becoming cool, it was comfortable in the Roman cellar. The Good Time Boys played cards by themselves, and if we were quiet we could hear the sound of the stone hammers all the way down the mountain. Young men went up and watched the Germans' progress and told us where they were—now in Francucci's old house, now in del Purgatorio's, now in Vittorini's, tapping, tapping, tapping, until the lights went out in the Roman cellar.

We woke to the same sound. They were at it before the sun was up.

* * *

Bombolini never heard the tapping on the stones, because all of those days he slept. At times he awoke, but then he would sleep again. They had carried him up to his old bed in his old home above the wineshop, so that Angela Bombolini could take care of him. On the third day he was able to sit up and take some soup, and they made him a chicken soup in which an entire chicken had been used, a very great thing here. When he finally awoke for good, although he could not see because of the swelling of his face, everything seemed clear to him. He felt that he could see things as if they were written on glass through which a light was shining, and all of the answers were simple and clear. It was he, for example, who knew at once what must be done with The Band.

As the Germans neared the houses in Old Town, Pietrosanto came to him in terror.

"So you didn't kill them after all," Bombolini said.

Pietro hung his head in shame. "I tried to. I had my rifle ready, and then I looked into those big stupid ox eyes of Francucci's, and I couldn't make my finger pull the trigger."

"I'm ashamed of you. What would The Master say about you?"

"Yes, it is shameful." Instead of killing them, he had hidden them in the cellar of one of the oldest houses by the wall at the bottom of Old Town.

"As soon as it is evening take them out of the cellar and up the back lane around Old Town and put them in the cellar of Copa's old house. They'll be safe there. The Germans will never come back."

Because of the systematic manner of the German search we

always knew where they were going and where they had been. A criminal might have stayed one house ahead of them or one house behind and been perfectly safe all of the while.

And when Fabio came down from the mountains, Bombolini knew what to do with him.

"This act must be avenged," Fabio said. "The time for crawling has passed, the time to act is at hand."

Fabio had grown a beard in the mountains, and since it was the same color as his hair, so deeply black that when the light struck it it was blue, the beard against the long whiteness of his face made him look more like a martyr than before.

"It isn't the blows to you as an individual," Fabio said.

"No, of course not," Bombolini said. He allowed his fingers to touch the swelling of his face and his tongue tipped his broken tooth.

"It is to you as our leader," Fabio said. "This is what hurts. These blows to you wound us, the damage to you demeans us. When they strike you, they wound me. I am the one who is insulted."

He then went on to outline the attack he planned on the Germans, on von Prum and on the drunken soldiers in the cellar.

"I agree with you, Fabio," Bombolini said. "The time to act has come."

A plan was made at once. The Red Flames would come down out of the mountains that night and gather in back of Copa's house, just outside the Fat Wall. At two o'clock, at the sound of a goat, Pietrosanto and the other soldiers would drop ropes and pull them up over the wall into Santa Vittoria where they would join forces and prepare the assault on the enemy. Fabio was moved to tears.

"You don't know how long I have waited for this," Fabio said. "The hour has come when we will pay acts of dishonor with deeds of honor."

It is embarrassing, after what happened, to write that Fabio then kissed him on both swollen cheeks.

And it was Bombolini who began the silent evacuation of the city. They got Padre Polenta's parish list and began to write down the names of all the people they felt could not keep their silence if the Germans turned to violence. These people would be allowed to work in the terraces but never to come up into the city. In the next two days they sent down almost all the women of the city and they sent the old men and people like Fungo the idiot, and Rana because he was wild and Capoferro because he was crazy and Roberto Abruzzi because they were afraid he might cry out something in English if they tore out a fingernail. And because the Germans were the way they were, because they didn't really know what we were doing, they never noticed the women gone, the children vanished, the old out of sight.

Because of what happened to Bombolini there was a good feeling in the city about the prospects of physical violence.

"If he can do it, if *Bombolini* can take it, then I can take it," the men said.

Only Tufa, who said nothing aloud to all this, had no faith. "They don't know," he told Caterina Malatesta. "They don't know what's going to happen to them."

"Then why don't you tell them?"

"It won't do any good. They feel good now, and why should I spoil that? They may not turn to it after all, so why should I frighten everyone?"

He told Caterina then what they would do. The soldiers in the city now wouldn't do it. They would send for the professionals, for the Gestapo or the SS secret police.

"Then they all break," Tufa said. "No man can stand it. They do things to men that it is impossible for men to believe even when it is happening to them."

"But Bombolini stood it," Caterina said.

"No, no, no, no. He stood *nothing*. After five minutes with the SS he will beg them to break his jaw or put out his eye if only they will stop doing what they are doing to him."

In the end she persuaded him to go to Bombolini and tell him. And what the mayor heard saddened him, because he had been feeling confident about himself and about his people.

"But it takes time to break a man, isn't that true?" Bombolini said.

"Sometimes it takes two minutes and sometimes ten and sometimes an hour, although they don't generally live after that."

"I was nothing then?" He was very sad.

"You were brave, Bombolini, and you were nothing. This goes beyond bravery. They *all* break sooner or later."

"So there is no hope."

"There is no hope."

And then Tufa was astonished and even angered to see that Bombolini, to the best of his ability, was trying to smile at him.

"I have some people no one in the world can break," Bombolini said.

"They all break," Tufa said. He almost shouted at the mayor. "You must believe me and be prepared for it."

But Bombolini only shook his head and continued smiling, like the statues of some saints one sometimes sees, gentle and all knowing and at peace with the world.

"I have some men who won't break," Bombolini said, and fell back to sleep then.

* * *

That night he told Caterina about it.

"I tried to tell him, to make him understand, but he wouldn't listen," Tufa said. "He kept insisting he had men who would not break."

The two of them did not go to the shelter—Caterina because she was excused to care for the people in the Palace of the People, and Tufa because he chose to be defiant. She had been asleep when he came in, but he did not get into bed with her. He sat on the edge of the bed and looked at his hands in the moonlight. He didn't know that she was watching him.

"Why are you looking at your hands that way?" she asked him.

He said nothing, but finally decided to tell her. "Because I'm afraid," he said. "It's my nails. I'm afraid what I might do if they pull out my nails."

"There's no reason to be afraid," Caterina said. "There are only ten of them. You should try to remember that."

Tufa turned on her. "My God, you're hard. A man reveals his

314

fear to her and she tells him there are only ten of them. Do you have any more advice like that?"

"I didn't say it to demean you," Caterina said. "I meant to make the pain understandable. It's only human pain. People lose nails all the time."

"Not this way."

"Have you seen it?"

"Yes," Tufa said, and after a pause he admitted that he had done it, in Greece, and to Arabs in North Africa.

"Did they die?"

"No."

"Then you can bear it, Carlo. You only imagine the pain because you feel guilty about what you did."

"They told us what we wanted to know," Tufa said.

He went to the window and looked at his hands, and it was while he was there that he saw the first of the Petrarch Brigade, Fabio's Resistance movement, come up over the wall and drop down into Grapebasket Lane, where they were met by Pietro Pietrosanto and led down the lane to Copa's house.

These must be the ones that Bombolini was counting on not to break, the young idealists, Tufa thought.

"The ability of our people to deceive themselves is the highest art of the nation," Tufa said aloud.

It was almost dawn when Pietrosanto went down into the Piazza of the People and reported to Bombolini what they had done with Fabio and the rest of the Red Flames. They had led them to the cellar, the same one in which The Band was hidden, and they had bound and gagged them and put them in the darkness beneath the house.

"How did they take it?" Bombolini asked.

"They vowed to kill first you and then the Germans," Pietrosanto said.

"Did you explain that it was for the good of the wine, for the good of the people of Santa Vittoria?"

"I told them."

"And how did they react?"

"The same as a pig I once told that he'd be more help to everyone as bacon," Pietro said. "He didn't want to understand me."

Bombolini smiled his painful smile. "Well I feel safer now," he said. "This was no time for valor."

"What gets into people like Fabio?" the head of the army said. "He knows this is no place for honor."

"In some ways Fabio wasn't raised right," Bombolini said.

THEY FINISHED the search of the houses on the evening of the third day with the very last house pressed up against the side of the Fat Wall in Old Town. It was clear to all of them that nothing could be hidden around or beneath that hovel, but Private Zopf and Private Goettke searched it so that the record was perfect and every house in the city had been searched from top to bottom.

"So much for *that*," von Prum said. "Now the noose grows truly tight."

They had a good meal that night for the first time in several days, but the captain found that even though he was hungry he could not eat and although he was tired he could not sleep. He allowed himself a nap, and it was while lying on his bed, in between the worlds of sleep and waking, that he received the first of his inspirations. He got up very swiftly, moving directly and silently as if he were stalking an animal that would break and run from him if he made an unexpected sound or move.

"Traub." He woke the sergeant. "The bell tower. Where else but the bell tower?"

They crossed the piazza, moving swiftly and silently.

"The entire middle part of the tower could be filled with wine," the captain said. He spoke in a low voice, as if the wine could hear him or someone could do something about it if he was heard.

Sergeant Traub pounded on the door and when the priest was slow in answering the knocks, since light was not permitted in the tower, Captain von Prum told the sergeant to shoot the lock off the door. He fired three shots in all, and then Padre Polenta opened the door.

"We should have looked here first," the captain told the priest.

Traub was already running up the steep stone stairs, but when he could see well enough to realize that he could see all the way up the tower to where the bells hung and all the way down to where the captain stood, he came slowly back down and then they went out into the Piazza of the People and back across it to Constanzia's house.

"It was worth the effort," the captain said. They got out the map of the city and with a good deal of satisfaction they eliminated the campanile from the list of possible hiding places.

Sometime during that same night, although they had already searched Santa Maria of the Burning Oven once before, the captain woke Sergeant Traub and sent him down the Corso Cavour to the wine cellar to get the other men. It was something that Bombolini had said, about the church having been built on the ruins of an even more ancient church, a Roman temple which, in turn, had been built on an Etruscan foundation. It stood to reason, von Prum told the sergeant, that there was an ancient cellar, down below somewhere, which they had overlooked. They searched the rest of the night until the dawn.

At dawn he thought of the water tower. It had not even been on the list. It was almost painful to watch the things they did that morning. It made people tired watching the work they did. Ever since the people here have been willing to admit that a German is a person capable of a great amount of painful work. It was Private Zopf who made the climb and he regretted all the stories he had told about the days he had spent traveling with a circus through Bavaria and how at one time he had had a bright future as a high wire walker. He went up the narrow ladder of the water tower in surprisingly swift time, but at the iron catwalk he stopped.

"Go ahead," von Prum shouted. "What are you waiting for?"

"I'm tired, sir. I've run out of strength, sir," Private Zopf called down. "I haven't slept in two nights."

"Take a rest, but hurry," the captain ordered.

Eventually the soldier worked his way onto the catwalk and then up onto the roof, where he found a small door. By a great effort, since the door handle had turned to rust years before, he opened it and looked down into the tower.

"It's only water, sir," the soldier shouted down.

"Have you tasted it?"

"No, sir. But I know it isn't wine. It doesn't smell like wine."

"Are there any bottles in the water? There must be bottles in the water. Thousands of bottles in the water."

In the end Zopf dropped through the doorway and suspended himself over the water by his feet. It was a dangerous thing to do. If he had slipped he might have drowned in the tank.

They didn't wait for Zopf to come down but went instead, at a very fast pace, back up to the Piazza of the People. The sun was up by then and another day was well underway.

"Allow me to ask him," Corporal Heinsick said to Traub.

"He doesn't want to hear things like that," Traub said. But in the end he allowed the corporal to speak to the captain.

"Let me have one of them, sir," Heinsick said to Captain von Prum. "Let me take charge of one of these people."

The captain looked at the corporal as if seeing him for the first time.

"What do you mean, *have* one?" the captain said.

"We've got to start hitting someone soon, sir," Heinsick said.

"I'll take some woman or some child. It won't take much, sir. It will be all over this morning. I'll just stick someone's hand in the fire, sir."

Von Prum almost struck the corporal. As it was, he shouted at him. He told him that they didn't do things that way, that the Russians did things that way and barbarians acted that way, but that Germans didn't act that way because Germans didn't need to act that way.

"We don't use muscle, we use the mind," Captain von Prum said. "It's the difference between us and all of them."

Sometime in the morning Sergeant Traub thought of the priest and he went to Captain von Prum.

"A priest *can't* tell a lie, sir," the sergeant said. "Ask him where the wine is, and he has to tell you. Otherwise he goes to hell when he dies."

"In Germany the priests don't lie," the captain said, "but in Italy the priests lie. But go get him."

Polenta was frightened when they came to get him because he is afraid of physical punishment and he feared what they might do to him.

"A lie is a sin," von Prum said to the priest, "and as a priest of the Holy Roman Catholic Church you are forbidden to lie. Do you know where the wine is?"

Polenta stared at them with amazement.

"Notice, Father," von Prum said, "I don't ask you to reveal where the wine is. I merely ask do you *know* where it is?"

Polenta shook his head and waved his hand in the direction of the Cooperative Wine Cellar.

"There is the wine," he said.

They got a Holy Bible after that, and they told the priest to put one hand upon his heart and to lay the other hand upon the sacred book.

"I ask you once again, as a man of God, as God's representative here on earth, who can knowingly commit no sin in the face of God: Do you know of the wine?"

"No," Polenta said. "As a man of God I give you my sacred word. I will do better."

He had brought along a cross as a shield to hide behind, and he

320

held it up and made the sign of the cross, and he also blessed them with the cross.

"This cross is made from the wood of the True Cross," Padre Polenta said. "I paid five hundred lire for it and it ought to be sacred. Upon this cross, as God is my witness, I tell you there is no other wine."

Von Prum struck the cross from the priest's hand.

"May you burn in hell for that lie," he said.

But it bothered the men after that morning. It bothered them that the captain had struck the cross, and it bothered them the way that Polenta had answered the questions.

"They can lie," Sergeant Traub told them. "Priests are only men wearing skirts."

"I don't know. I don't understand it," Heinsick said. "He stood right there and told us, a man of the cloth, 'I tell you there is no other wine.'" Heinsick shook his head.

"How could he hold the sacred cross like that, the True Cross, and lie?" Private Goettke said.

"They can lie, but not when they hold the cross," Private Impossible said. "If you lie on the cross or the good book, God sends a sign so everyone can see. Your tongue turns black. The words strangle in your throat. It's like telling a lie in the confession box. They always know."

"It is impossible to deceive the cross," Heinsick said. "Do you know what I'm thinking? I think there is no wine here."

Zopf had come down from the tower, and because he had done the dangerous thing he was allowed to say things the others wouldn't say.

"I think someone is going out of his mind," the soldier said, and several of them, when Traub was not looking, nodded their heads. Heinsick had been drinking wine, and on the wall of the room with charcoal from the fireplace he wrote:

Ein feste Burg ist unser von Prum.

It can still be seen there. We found out much later what it meant. "A mighty fortress is our von Prum."

"You had better take that off," Traub said. "Men have died for less than that in this army."

But Heinsick only shrugged. He was a good judge of human nature.

"He'll be flattered by it," he said, and that afternoon, when von Prum came running down the Corso with another inspiration, he read the words. He looked around at the men, who were hiding the wine bottles behind their backs. For one terrible moment they knew terror.

"Thank you," the captain said. "It reinforces me."

That afternoon they began to dig around the burial vaults of the Malatesta family in the burying grounds beyond the city walls.

* * *

It was educational to the people of Santa Vittoria to watch what was happening to Captain von Prum. He became a lesson to us; and to this day, when a person runs about trying vainly to do the impossible we say that he is "doing a von Prum." We didn't understand it then, but his trouble was that he didn't know how to fail. Roberto said that he hadn't been raised that way.

When the people here want something and find they can't get it, which happens all the time, they convince themselves they never wanted it in the first place. After that they become scornful of the thing they wanted and spit on it. It's a matter of being ridiculous. To want something that you can't have is to be ridiculous and in a town such as Santa Vittoria to not look ridiculous is sometimes all that one has.

Von Prum became ridiculous. He could not believe he couldn't find the wine his own way, he could not believe that sometimes men, even himself, can fail, and so he didn't know how to stop what he was doing.

He changed in those five days. In that one week he appeared to us to age ten years. He didn't eat and he didn't sleep, and he lost weight, and all at once the fine lines of his face appeared not fine but bony and old, and we had a look at what he would look like if he ever grew old. Because his clothes had been tailored for him, when he lost weight the uniforms so tightly fitted before sagged on him.

322

"If he lasts one more week," Constanzia Pietrosanto, who did his cooking, said, "he'll die of old age."

We began to worry about him then, not for himself but for us. If under the pressure his mind were to break, we would be the ones to suffer for it. We tried our best to calm him down and to help him sleep and eat. If someone was fortunate enough to stumble on something good to eat we gave it to Constanzia to cook for him. She made him little dishes, the way one gets a child to eat, a little fresh salad from the field, green beans cooked in melted cheese, a live trout from the Mad River they brought up in a pail, pigeon eggs, a rabbit which was stupid enough to come down on the terraces, frog legs, and then, since it was late October and the songbirds were flying south, the people netted little finches and wild canaries and nightingales and cooked them to a crisp in olive oil so the little bones would crunch in the mouth. He looked at the plate of finches and he cried for them.

"He's like a toy now that's been wound too tight," Babbaluche warned. "One more turn of the key and the spring will snap. The son of a bitch will fly apart."

The captain began to write things down all of the time, letters he didn't send, notes to himself, notes to the soldiers.

"They want me to act like a barbarian and I refuse," he wrote to someone, perhaps his brother Klaus. "Nations with a culture need not do things that way. I will remain true to myself."

He turned, instead, to bribery. In the late afternoon of the fourth day he called the soldiers together.

"What above all things do the people here hate most?" he asked them.

"Us, sir," Private Goettke said.

The captain ignored him. The thing we hated most, he said, was the mountain. It was the mountain that kept us poor, that destroyed us, that robbed us of our youth and our strength. At the end of a day's work there was the exhausting climb back up the mountain, the daily enemy.

"And what shall we offer them?" He looked at them with a triumphant smile, the first smile they had seen in many days. "We offer them something to overcome the mountain."

They rolled out the motorcycle with the sidecar, and they put it in the center of the Piazza of the People, and then they invited the people to sit in it, sit on it, and even feel its power while the engine roared and throbbed beneath their legs.

"Yes, look at them," Captain von Prum said. "They adore that machine. They hunger for it, they lust after it. They can't wait for the cover of darkness to come and tell us their secret."

There were many ways to tell it. Soldiers were stationed in the dark quiet lanes; and the back doors to von Prum's house and the Cooperative cellar were left open. And no one came.

It was not a matter of virtue. It would be good to pretend that it was. But bribery is a good tool to use on a people who have nothing. If flattery will always get you somewhere in this country, then bribery will do the same if the price of the bribe is right. There were people who went to bed that night sweating and dreaming of flying up the mountain past all their bent-over brothers, seeing themselves sitting around in the piazza picking songbird bones out of their teeth after their supper, when the rest were just stumbling their way into their houses and starting up the fires for their soup.

The captain stayed at his door, sitting alone in the darkness all of that night, and no one came to him.

"I don't understand it," he said to Sergeant Traub in the morning. "I don't understand it."

Traub said nothing, but he knew. The price of the bribe was not correct. With the key to the motorcycle went a shroud and a coffin.

"It is a very good offer," Heinsick said to the sergeant, "just as long as you have a regiment to guard you."

"He'll turn to muscle today," one of the soldiers said.

"He'll break some heads today," Heinsick said. "It's all that he can do. And when he does I know who I want. I want that cobbler, that Babbaluche."

"No, no. The one with the big eyes, the soldier. The one that looks at you that way."

"Tufa," Sergeant Traub said. "He's the one to get."

"And her," Heinsick said. "The one who looks at you as if you were scum."

324

* * *

It was the fifth day, and on that afternoon, as they expected and as we expected, a messenger came from Montefalcone. There were two messages in all, and they are in the archives of the city.

One was from his brother Klaus. It is not a letter at all, but a card, on the top of which, in black crayon in the hand of a child, is drawn a dark wing.

> The angel of death calls me and I fly to her.
> Goodbye, Sepp, my brother.

It is signed only "K."
The other was from the office of Colonel Scheer.

> The hunting season is over.
> Bring in your pelts or bring in yourself by sundown tomorrow evening.

It is not signed.
He read the letters several times, and when he was through reading them he put them in his files. After that he took the pages of the "Bloodless Victory," and he ripped each one in pieces, one after another, and then he burned them, and after that he began to cry. It was still light when he began to weep, and he cried until it was dark, and we could hear him at the far end of the piazza. He cried for his brother, but most of all he cried for himself, and we were frightened then because a man who cries is capable of any evil.

THERE ARE five things that were written in the captain's log that night. They are offered to you for what they are worth. No one here is sure of what they mean, but others might be wiser than ourselves and they may have meanings that others understand. Most of the people here only think that von Prum, for that time at least, was mad.

1. HAMLET HAS DIED.
2. I determine now to rejoin Old Fritz.
3. "Deep in the nature of all these noble races there lurks unmistakably the beast of prey, the blond beast, lustfully roving in search of booty and victory."
   Nietzsche is right.

4. Question: What is God?
   Answer: God is a German corporal.
5. I go to offer Bombolini and the people of this city a last bribe. I offer them the bribe of fear.

He must have gone out right after that. He left Constanzia's house and crossed the piazza to the wineshop and without waiting or announcing himself in any way he ran up the stairs to Bombolini's room, where he found him in bed, with Roberto seated by his side. He was very excited and he spoke swiftly. He was smiling then, even though it was still possible to see tears in his eyes.

"I am a sportsman," the captain said.

Bombolini could only stare at him. We don't know what a sportsman is here.

"I am dedicated to the principle of fair play and adhering to the rules. I see this all as a game."

Silence.

"I think we have played a good game. We have tried to be fair with one another. I think you would agree to that."

"Oh, yes," Bombolini said.

"But we won't lose the game," he said. "We are not allowed by law or by God to lose it."

Silence.

"But the game is almost over. The referee has the whistle to his lips. You won't win, you understand, but you can save yourself from a terrible defeat."

There was another long silence, so long that Bombolini felt required to speak.

"I don't understand what you are saying."

"You understand, and I am going to make the final play. Where is the wine?" Von Prum had been sitting on one side of the bed and now he stood up. "Would you like to play?" he said to Roberto.

Roberto shook his head.

"All right. That's the way it is, then." He made a motion as of putting something in his mouth, and we supposed it was a whistle that he had in his mind.

"The game is over," the captain said. "I did my best. I have played fairly. My hands are clean."

He appeared to be relieved.

"I want you to remember that I gave you your chance until the end, Captain Bombolini." It was the first time he had ever honored the mayor with his title. "Tomorrow the new team comes."

He turned then and went out of the room, and when we saw him crossing the piazza toward Constanzia's house his stride was strong and rapid. He seemed to be a new person. Perhaps an hour after that we heard the sound of the motorcycle engine and Captain von Prum left Santa Vittoria.

"It's time for me to get up," Bombolini said. He asked Roberto to tell his wife to bring him his clothes and to leave him alone for a while. When she came with the clothes he was already out of bed.

"You heard what he said," Bombolini said. "You had better leave before the captain comes back."

"No," Rosa Bombolini said. She began to help him with his clothes. His entire body was sore and stiff although only his face had taken the beating. She pointed at his face. "If you could take that I can take it." She stood before him with her arms crossed, those broad powerful arms.

"Do you care at all for me?" he said.

"No." She was aware that she had hurt him.

"You couldn't bring yourself to say something good, something nice at a time like this?"

"Because your face looks like an ox stepped on it does that mean I should care now?"

He sighed both at the effort of dressing and at her words, and he put his arm on her strong shoulder and told her that she would have to help him down the stairs.

"Well did you ever care?" It embarrassed him to continue, but he finally said it. "Did you ever—" It was difficult for him to say the word. "Did you ever love me?"

"I don't know," Rosa said. She turned away from him. "There was a time, I guess. Then you became a clown, and a woman can't love a clown."

"Not one like you," Bombolini said. "Some of us are going to get killed here tomorrow. You know that I might be one of them."

"That doesn't make me tell less than the truth," she said.

"No, I could have counted on that," Bombolini said. When they were in the room with the wine barrel he leaned on it and asked for a glass of it.

"So you don't think then, when this is done, providing of course that I am here, that you and I might, oh, come back to each other?"

"No."

He was hurt once more. On a night such as this, he thought.

"Oh, stop being hurt. Can't any of you hear the truth without being hurt? Do you all have to lie to yourselves all of the time?"

He drank a second glass of wine, and then he asked her why she had ever married him.

"It was a mistake," she said. "I didn't know any better. It's something every Italian woman has to learn by herself and then it's too late."

"And what about her?" He pointed in the direction of Angela's room. As always, the wine made him feel better, and he reminded himself that in order to get through the next days it might be good to be a little drunk through most of them.

"She's going to marry the American."

"Roberto? Abruzzi?"

"Is there another one?"

It caused Bombolini to laugh, because it was so perfect a response from his wife. All of their life together she had done it, and he laughed because he knew the words she would say before she said them. When they were young he had not noticed, and when they were older he had not listened.

"He doesn't know it yet but he's beginning to fall for her," Rosa Bombolini said. "I see to it that they're together. I push her at him, and she doesn't know it and he doesn't mind it."

Bombolini was angered by that. "You don't even know what kind of man he is," he said.

"He's good enough for her. He'll take her to America," Rosa said. "What does it matter what kind of man he is, just so he takes her to America?"

"And Fabio. Have you ever considered that Fabio della Romagna is sick with love for your daughter and that he is a fine boy and that I have promised him anything he wants for saving my life?"

He drank an entire glass of wine after that, without taking his mouth from the glass.

"Fabio is an Italian. As such he is no good for my daughter. Go on, have more wine. Get drunk."

He poured more wine.

"There is no Italian man who is good for a woman."

It made him laugh. "I don't feel so all alone then," he said.

"To feel like a king it is necessary for them to make the woman into an ox."

"I didn't do that to you."

"You couldn't."

"I didn't do it by choice. I didn't want you to be an ox."

She laughed at him. "You tried," she said. "I escaped."

Roberto had gone ahead with the word about von Prum, and they were waiting for Bombolini in the piazza. All of the members of the Grand Council were at the fountain, not talking to one another but feeling the need for each other's company.

"A man should choose a woman and an ox from his own country. My mother told me that."

"You should have told it to me," Rosa said. He put down his glass. He had drunk enough. They were waiting for him, although he had nothing to tell them.

"You win," he said. "You never came close to losing. In the world of love the one who can run away is the winner. Goodbye."

She nodded goodbye. When he was at the door to the shop he turned back to her.

"Tell me one thing," Bombolini said. "These past months. I did surprise you, didn't I?"

It made her smile, because it was true. "Yes, you surprised me," she said. He had picked up the glass and he held it out to her before going outside, and she came to take it.

"You know," he said to her from the doorway, "that was the best thing you ever said to me."

*　*　*

330

He joined the men in the piazza and they began to drift along the sides of it, none of them talking, looking at the old buildings they had grown up with, making what some of them felt would be a last tour of the town. It was very quiet then. The sound of cannon to the south of here, which had become a daily sound, like living along the sea, had ceased. There was a dog wailing in Old Town, and there was smoke from fires where the old women were cooking the meals ahead of time so they would only need to be heated in the morning. Someone suggested that they go inside Santa Maria and offer a prayer, but others said no, it would only frighten people to see men in the church. They walked to the Corso Cavour and decided to go down it. They were stretched out behind one another in the darkness.

"I have never been more afraid in my life," one of the men said. "I am sick and trembling with fear."

"It might help you to know that all of us are sick with fear," Bombolini said. "You were the only one courageous enough to say it."

"But you've already felt it," the man said. "You know the taste of it. You know if they do it again you will be able to bear it again."

"Are you afraid for yourself or for what you might say?"

"What I might say."

"Then you won't tell," Bombolini said.

There was the sound of thunder in the south, but the moon was out, so we knew the cannons had begun again. The sound was very big, much larger than ever before. Despite the sound we could hear the Germans drinking inside the wine cellar office. They no longer asked for the wine, they took it as their due.

"I'm glad it isn't the rain. It would hurt the grapes now," someone said. At the Fat Gate we looked down on the terraces in the moonlight and then started back up the Corso, and when we passed the cellar Heinsick opened the door and came out into the street. He was drunk.

"I suppose you think that's going to help you," he said. He motioned toward the south. No one answered him.

"It might," he said. "It might. But it might be too late then, too." He smiled at us and we could see that it was a fraudulent smile because his eyes were as cold and as distant as the moonlight that lit them.

"Wait until you see who comes back with him tomorrow," Heinsick said. "Wait until you see them."

We turned away from him because he made us sick and because he frightened us at the same time.

"Wait until you *feel* them," Heinsick called. He laughed at us. "Then you'll know what it's all about."

He came after us, holding a bottle of our wine, following us up the Corso Cavour.

"These are the professionals," Heinsick said. "These aren't the poor little bastards like us. They won't even let us touch their tools."

He stopped and we went ahead of him, moving away from him as swiftly as possible without appearing to be running from him.

"Knives and scissors, fork and candle, little children must not handle," the corporal called.

We were far up the Corso now, but not so far that we still couldn't hear him.

"You'll tell them. Oh, yes, you'll tell them." He was laughing once more. "You'll beg them to let you tell them."

When we reached the Piazza of the People Padre Polenta came running across the piazza toward us.

"You should see it," the priest said to us. "Thousands of lights, millions of lights. Something big is taking place. Something tremendous is underway in the south."

It meant nothing to us. It was too late to help us.

"It's time we got some sleep," Bombolini said. "If they're going to burn us tomorrow we should be ready for the burning."

"Padre?" one of the men said. "Say a prayer for us. Make us a goodnight prayer."

Most of them kneeled in the piazza, and Polenta blessed them. The sound of the war was very loud then, so loud that the sound of the water flowing from the fountain could not be heard. The great attack had begun, some great attack. We didn't even know by whom.

"Did you see Heinsick's face?" Bombolini said. "Did you see the hatred? Why is he filled with so much hatred? Where do they get it from?"

There was no answer, of course. The men shook hands with one another, every man with every other man, and when each had touched all of the rest they went their own ways home.

7 THE RAT IN THE THROAT

WHEN WE SAW them come up the mountain from Montefalcone early the next morning, there was almost a sigh of relief from the men. When one has steeled oneself for an ordeal it is sometimes best that the ordeal take place at the proper time.

There is always the memory of Lupo, the last of our great bandits. He was scheduled to be shot to death before the people in the Piazza of the People for savage acts. Before the shooting he shouted obscenities at God and the judge and the people, and then for some reason he received a stay of execution. One month later they had to carry Lupo into the piazza and tie him to the fountain, because he could not stand. He trembled and held the priest's hand. The one month of hope had whetted his appetite for life and destroyed him. He should have known that in Santa Vittoria the only safe policy is to never hope for anything and then there is nothing to be lost. Lupo had committed the sin of hope.

The men were passing around the *grappa* bottle, drinking deeply from it and encouraging the others while being encouraged, when Bombolini surprised them by telling them each to hide in a house that faced on the piazza from which they could watch the piazza but not be seen from it. They were to stay there until he waved them to come out. Some of them were disappointed and even angry.

"I thought we were to be courageous?" one of them said. "Now you have us running and hiding."

"I'm ready," another said. "I'm ready for the sons of bitches. I'll take everything they can hand out."

But he sent them away and they went, and so it was that when they came, the four of them, von Prum and Traub and two young soldiers from the SS, Bombolini was alone in the Piazza of the People, this time without even Vittorini to stand behind him in his uniform. They came on the motorcycle and they were followed by a small compact truck that held the SS men's equipment. Sergeant Traub stopped the motorcycle near the edge of the Corso Cavour, and Captain von Prum stepped out of the sidecar and as he came across the piazza toward Bombolini, even the most unobservant among us could see that some change had taken place in the captain. The age that had altered his face seemed to have passed in this one night and he walked with an easy confidence and his motions were slow and controlled; the stiffness that had caused him to move like the overwound toy was gone and with it the wildness about the eyes. We didn't know then that he had made a sixth and a seventh entry in his log that morning, on the page that follows the other five.

6. Much that is dreadful and inhuman in history, much that one hardly likes to believe, is mitigated by the reflection that the one who commands and the one who carries out are different people. The former does not behold the sight and does not experience the strong impression on the imagination. The latter obeys a superior and therefore feels no responsibility for the acts.

—Nietzsche

7. I give myself up to Old Fritz. I prepare myself to perform my
duty and I feel a happiness about it.

—Sepp von P.

"So. You put everyone away this morning," Captain von Prum
said. Bombolini nodded.

"Or did they run away?"

"No, sir. I hid them."

"The same as your wine."

"No, Captain."

"We'll soon find out." The captain began to walk across the piazza toward the Palace of the People and so Bombolini went
along with him. "I'm going to use your place, because it's bigger."

They stood in the doorway of the Palace and examined the
large dark room, and Bombolini found himself wishing that he
had kept it more neatly because he could see von Prum's disap-
proving face.

"And because it's very filthy," Captain von Prum said. "They
bleed and vomit, and all of the rest of it. I'm told that every orifice
comes into use."

Bombolini understood that this would be his one opportunity to
do what he had to do, and although he could see that the captain
didn't wish to hear him he seized the chance.

"Which is why I have this one thing to ask of you," Bombolini
said. "I don't want to have to be responsible for picking any man,"
the mayor said.

"I'll do the picking if you wish," von Prum said.

"I told the people not to come into the piazza until after you
had come," Bombolini said.

"And? What about it?"

"The first one who comes into the piazza is the one who will
have to taste it first."

The captain was interested, Bombolini could see that.

"In that way I don't have to have his blood on my head. And
you don't have to be the one to choose, Captain. God will decide.
Or fate. I don't know if you believe. The first who walks into the
piazza is the one fate has determined to choose."

339

"I would have said the devil, not God," von Prum said. But he was smiling. The idea appealed to him. Sergeant Traub had come into the room then, and he was followed by the two SS men. Bombolini was surprised to see how young they were. They were boys. The captain turned back to Bombolini.

"So you can control who faces these men," von Prum said. "You have all of your brave boys ready to walk into the piazza by fate."

"No, it isn't true. Have *them*"—he nodded toward the SS men— "try me if you don't believe me. I have no one ready for you."

Von Prum then explained the situation to the younger of the two soldiers who, despite his age, appeared to be the leader.

"It makes no difference," the soldier said. "It makes no difference at all. They all talk."

He was very casual and totally confident in his work, and his voice had the unconcerned quality that those who possess the truth often use.

"No. It doesn't matter," the second soldier said. "A matter of time sometimes, a few minutes this way or that. But they break."

"Yes, they all talk."

"We never fail," the older one said.

"No, we have never failed."

Captain von Prum turned back to Bombolini.

"All right. It's in the hands of God," the German said.

"My hands are clean," Bombolini said.

"And mine," von Prum said. But he was smiling. "God has the dirty hands now." Both of the soldiers gave the captain a questioning look and he decided that he had gone far enough in that direction.

They were very young and very clean. When they laughed, which was often, their teeth were even and clean and strong. If one word alone could be used to describe them, it would be clean, and after that young, and after that strong. They weren't dressed the same as the other soldiers. Their uniforms were black with white piping, and the darkness of their dress made their skins seem fairer and their eyes bluer and their blondness more striking. The men had studied them from behind the doors and from the roof tops around the piazza.

"They don't look like devils," someone said.

"Devils come in all disguises," Pietrosanto told him.

They unloaded their equipment from the back of the small truck, and even von Prum helped them with it. It was pleasant outside in the early morning and the captain suggested that perhaps they would prefer to do their interrogations outside.

"No, it will be better inside," one said. "The sun will be up and it will get hot."

"It's hard work, you know," the second said. "Hot and tiring."

"*You* try pulling teeth all morning long."

"When the people don't want them pulled."

They smiled at one another. It was an old line of their own; they had many of them.

It was impossible for even Bombolini not to admire the neatness and precision of their work. In a very short time they had cleared out the truck and set up their equipment. The last piece was a wooden table, a narrow, thin plank of wood not much wider than an ironing board, which folded into sections, very much like a portable operating table. From the sides of the table hung three black leather straps, very wide and strong and three large, strong metal buckles.

At one side of this table was a battery-operated portable generator to which they began attaching coils of wire with little metal clips that had rows of teeth like ferrets. On the other side was a smaller table on which rested pincers and pliers, hooks, rubber hoses, a large funnel, surgical scissors, metal clamps, an iron grappling hook, a gouge, a hammer with a long thin head and claws like the horns of a ram, handcuffs, a blowtorch.

"You're young but you know your business, you interrogators," Captain von Prum said.

"We like to think of ourselves as a truth squad," the youngest of them said. "Going about the land uncovering truth."

Again they smiled at one another. There was nothing solemn about them.

"Now hand me the gloves, Hans," the younger one said. They had already put on black rubber aprons over their black uniforms, and now Hans handed the younger, who was named Otto, black

341

rubber gloves. "Sometimes it gets a bit messy, you see," Otto said. "You haven't even seen this before?" he asked von Prum. The captain shook his head.

"After a while you get used to it," Otto said.

"After a while you get to like it," Hans said.

"I have a special treat for you, Captain Bombolini," von Prum said. "I am going to allow you to watch it all. *All* of it."

Otto looked up at them. "Uh, uh, uh," he said. "That's not very nice, Captain. Sometimes it's harder to look, you know."

"Sometimes the one who is looking does all the talking," Hans said.

"You don't look very happy," Otto said to Bombolini. They both spoke very good Italian. "We'll put on a good show for you, don't fear."

Bombolini went to the window and looked out into the piazza. It was still empty. For a moment he was happy for that, but by then there should have been some sign of Pietrosanto in the far edge of the piazza or coming down the hill from High Town. He tried to keep looking into the piazza, but against his will his eyes kept going back to the table of instruments, the hard cold metal of them, the sharpness and hardness of the things, the hooks and hammers, the silver pliers—he knew, for toes and teeth and fingernails—the fat rubber hoses, the torch. Captain von Prum was looking at them as well, and his tongue kept wetting his lips, which would have surprised him had he known it.

"Do you actually use these?" he said. It seemed to be a stupid question to Bombolini, but he was wrong.

"No, not often," Hans said. "We have used them, but this does the job, you see." He pointed to the generator to which a magneto had now been attached. A wire ran from the magneto to the handle of a metal hammer to which the wire was clipped.

"Are you ready to test?" Hans asked. Otto nodded. The older soldier nudged the brass arm of the magneto, and there was a sputtering sound, and sparks began to shoot from the head of the hammer, and the hammer itself actually began to leap on the wooden table.

"They do the same," Hans said to von Prum. "The people. They leap."

"And scream, I'm afraid," Otto said. "That takes a bit of getting used to."

"They hit high C sometimes," Hans said, "but you won't like the lyrics they sing."

So they smiled at one another again. Otto pointed to the instrument table.

"All the while it's going on they never stop looking at these," he said. "The pain is unbearable, of course, but they look at these, like these pliers, for example, and think we are saving the worst for last."

"And so they talk."

"They can't wait to talk. They demand to talk. They cry out to talk. They beg to talk."

"And sometimes we let them."

Von Prum noticed that he was wetting his lips with his tongue, and he stopped.

"How long," he said. "For how long?"

The two soldiers studied one another.

"A minute sometimes. Five sometimes. Three or four minutes on an average, wouldn't you say, Hans?"

"Three or four, yes. We ask them later sometimes, the people we have treated, and they think they have been on the table for hours."

"Time is strange," Otto said. "Pain stretches time."

"Time is strange. We do something to it. Sometimes when we're through we're surprised to look up and find it's still day. I'm ready. Are you ready?" He looked at Otto and then at Captain von Prum.

"There's a final question," the captain said. "How do you know when they're telling the truth?"

"Because they always do. But we make it a matter of numbers," Hans said. "When we really put the juice to them, when we cook them good, you know."

"When we set fire to their hair, you know."

"They tell you. They always tell you, but we aren't allowed to take just one man's word. Even when we know what the patient has said is true, we have to do a second and a third. Sometimes we do five. Just to look good."

343

"Although one would be enough."

"Oh, yes. One is enough," Otto said. "But it makes *them* feel happier." By "them" he must have meant the officers who order the interrogations.

"We'll do five," Captain von Prum said. He turned to Bombolini. "Did you hear that?"

"If one will do . . ." the mayor began.

"Five," von Prum said. "I want five." His voice was hard and cold.

"Do you want him?" Hans asked the captain, nodding at the mayor.

"No, I like him where he is."

Hans tested the leather straps. He pulled them hard and they snapped; they were strong and they held. He tried the blowtorch, and the hot blue flame licked out. There was a branding iron, which Bombolini had not seen before, and Otto held it in the flame of the torch.

"No, we don't use it," Hans told von Prum. "That would produce evidence. But people hate the brand."

"They hate the idea of burning. Of the brand sinking in."

"Especially on the soles of the feet."

"But this," Otto said, patting the magneto, "this hurts more. Still they're more afraid of the hot iron."

"Some day when they've all had more experience," Hans said, "they'll come to respect Sparky more." It was their name for the magneto. "They'll beg us for the branding iron."

"But we'll just give them Sparky." They smiled at one another again. "Where are they, sir?" Otto said. "We're ready for them."

Bombolini found that he was trembling and that he felt sick, not as if he were about to vomit, but sick in the entire self, in the heart and the soul and the brain. There was no one in the piazza but Germans.

"All right," von Prum said. "We'll give fate a minute or two, and then we'll have to go and get someone."

They waited after that in silence broken only by the metallic sound of Otto moving the instruments in a kind of nervous irritation.

344

"I always get just a little excited before we start," he said. "You never know what you're going to get."

"And how they're going to react."

"Just don't send us any heroes," Otto called to Bombolini. "It's boring, you know, these heroes."

"They come in with their jaws sealed together like this," Otto said. He was on his feet and he imitated the face and the posture of the hero. "They set their eyes like this and they spit at you with them."

"Then we put the clamps on them and give them a little juice and all at once they want to talk," Hans said.

"They want to lick you with their eyes."

"It's very sad and boring, actually."

"It's very disgusting, really."

"I will send you such cowards," Bombolini suddenly said, surprising even himself, "men who will tell you such lies, who will beg you and try to please you in so many ways, you won't know what is true and what is false."

"The more they talk the more truth they reveal, even when they're lying," Otto said.

Traub came up from the piazza on to the terrace and called in through the door.

"Here comes one," he said. "We've got one coming across the piazza now."

They went to the door of the Palace of the People and they looked out at what fate had delivered to them. He had come down the steep hill from High Town and paused for a moment at the edge of the piazza. When he saw the Germans he made no effort to avoid them, but instead went directly toward them.

"A martyr. It's one of the martyr types," Hans said.

They watched the man say something to Corporal Heinsick and then he began to bring the man across the piazza to where they were.

"You lied to us," one of the Germans said to Bombolini. "You sent us a hero."

At the stairs up to the terrace Heinsick stopped and then pushed the prisoner up the stairs.

345

"He says he's glad to see us," Heinsick said. "I told him *we* were glad to see *him*."

It was Giuliano Copa, the former mayor of Santa Vittoria. When he saw Captain von Prum he made a Fascist salute. "Long live the Duce. Long live Hitler," he said. "What took you so long?"

"Oh, God. *This* kind," Hans said. "The loyal, true Fascist." He turned to the others. "He was really for us all along, you see. *Now* he will tell you."

They laughed at Copa. His eyes grew large with suspicion and with fear. Bombolini made an effort to stay in the shadows of the room. When he saw the interrogation tools Copa began to shout.

"I am a loyal Fascist," Copa shouted. "I am a member in good standing of the party. There has been a mistake—"

"*Quiet,*" Hans suddenly shouted at him. It was easy to understand then how Hans had been entrusted with the kind of work he did. "There is always a mistake," he said to the rest. "Take off your clothes," he shouted at Copa.

"I don't understand," Copa said.

He was brave. He was still in command of his voice, and his body gave no outward sign of fear.

"You don't understand the words 'Take off your clothes'?" Otto said. "Does this mean anything to you?" He seized the top of Copa's shirt and in one sudden motion ripped it from his body.

When Copa was naked they placed him on the narrow wooden table and they strapped him to it with the leather straps.

"What are you going to do to me?" Copa asked.

"If I were to answer that," Otto said, in a quiet, gentle voice, "you wouldn't believe me."

"And then you'd lose the chance of finding out for yourself," Hans said. They smiled.

"You take their clothes off," Otto was explaining, "because it makes them feel defenseless. If you put a naked soldier in the front he won't fight, but if you dress him he will fight until he dies. It's all been tried. It's all been tested."

"You have it down to a science then," von Prum said.

"Oh, yes, it's a science."

"Do you hear that?" von Prum said to Bombolini. "This is a

science. It's the difference between you and us." Copa was praying aloud then.

They moved the magneto closer to the table, and when Otto tested it for the last time the little clips that would be attached to Copa jumped about like little frightened toads.

"You never let the client feel human, do you understand," Hans said. "You always look at them as if they were roaches, and when they talk to you you never understand them. In this way they feel all alone."

"Like turds. Most men feel like turds deep down, you know. Like something disgusting that was dropped into the world," Otto said. "Those aren't my words. The psychologists, you understand."

"Did you hear that?" von Prum said. "The psychologists. It's all been figured out."

Otto was leaning over Copa then.

"We don't want to do this to your body. It will be more terrible than you know. At the moment it begins you will want to die. You will beg us to let you die. Sometimes they do die. He looked up at Captain von Prum. "The heart explodes in the chest. The brain is shattered; shocked to pieces, you understand."

"You are getting an education, Captain," Hans said.

"We don't want you to die, and you don't want to die."

To Bombolini's horror he saw that Copa was nodding yes, yes to the German.

"Sometimes they tell us the truth before we ever touch them," Hans said to von Prum.

"And you allow them to get up?"

"No." Hans seemed disappointed in his student. "We burn them. We put them on Sparky. How else would we know?"

"Now," Otto was saying. He began attaching the wires to different parts of Copa's body. He would press the clamps so the teeth were bared, and then he would allow it to close around the flesh of a toe or an ear lobe or the nipple of his breast, like a wicked little animal.

"We only want you to *feel* this pain so that you want to tell us the truth."

"Yes, I want to tell you the truth. Now," Copa said. "I'll tell you what you need to know."

"Now, you see, we'll see if he is telling the truth," Otto said. He looked up at the captain again with an embarrassed smile. "What was it we wanted to know."

"About the wine. Where is the rest of the wine?"

He asked and Copa said that he didn't understand the question and that he didn't know what they were asking him.

"Now?" Hans said. "Now," Otto said.

He made a movement with his finger on the magneto, a very slight movement with the brass handle, and at that same moment Copa came flying up from the wooden table against the leather straps as if the straps must cut him apart and during this same instant he opened his mouth and after what seemed a long passing of time, a little lifetime of time, he released from the depths of himself a scream so terrible in its fear and agony and horror and worst of all, disbelief, that both von Prum and Bombolini found themselves shouting aloud in some kind of cry of recognition of the human animal.

T HERE ARE people here, since this is a history, who want a description of every action that took place in that room that morning, so none of it will ever be forgotten, an accounting of every burn and every scream, a listing of every tooth destroyed and nail ripped out, but it isn't needed or even desired, because as Bombolini told us later, he who saw all of it, when the assault on the flesh reaches the point where death approaches, all of it becomes the same.

Toward the end, it is deadening to everyone involved and, as the Germans say, in some ways even boring (if that sounds possible), because all the torture, no matter how administered, becomes the same and all the torturers are the same and all the tortured become the same man—so many shrieks, so many sobs, so many wishes to die, so much blood, so much urine, so much excrement, so much courage and so much cowardice—and finally it even took an effort for Bombolini to remember which of the men he had grown old with was lying strapped there to the wooden plank.

When they were through with Giuliano Copa (because there was no way to revive him) it was the turn of Mazzola, another of The Band. A few minutes before, Pietro Pietrosanto and Vittorini had released Mazzola from the cellar in High Town, and he went down, as he thought, to meet with Copa in the Piazza of the People. In the name of justice he should not have been allowed to see Copa's body lying against the wall before it was his turn to be put on the table, because it should be each man's right not to know the extent of what will happen to him until it happens. It is enough to say that so hysterical did Mazzola become—and Mazzola was no coward—that when they put the metal clamps down inside his throat and he had bitten off the end of his tongue when the electricity was applied to him, Mazzola had actually said "Thank you" to the soldiers. It was during this time that Bombolini found that he was crying for the people who had been his enemies.

He had tried to tell himself that what was happening to these men was only what they deserved, that in one sense true justice was being carried out and that they had brought upon themselves what they were receiving and that it was right and that it was the will of God or else God would not allow it to take place. But even as he convinced himself, he knew that what he was saying was a lie, because he knew that what was happening to Copa and Mazzola should never happen to any man and there was no reason in the world that could justify it.

For much of it Captain von Prum managed to stay apart from the suffering in the room. What was being done was not being done by himself. But before they turned to the old baker Francucci they went back to Copa once more, because Copa had regained consciousness.

"This is the time to get them," Hans said. "If there is anything to get. I only do this because you insist the wine is here."

"The wine is here," the captain said. But he found himself wishing that they would go on to someone else who would break more easily rather than return to the wreckage of the man Copa.

"Sometimes a child with a pair of squeezers can extract a confession when a man reaches this state," Otto said. "You let them cool, and when you come back, before you say a word, they are talking."

After that they did things with the blowtorch on Copa's body that cannot be written down. After the torch they cooled him with water. He was still conscious and they put the funnel in his mouth so that it went far down his throat and they bent his neck back and brought him to the point of drowning.

"He's too brave," Captain von Prum said. "My God, some people are too brave for their own good." He did something unlike himself. He went to the table where Copa was drowning and began to shout at him. "What are you doing to yourself? You have no right to be this brave." He turned to Bombolini. "In the name of God, Bombolini, tell him to tell us."

Bombolini could only hold his hands palms upward and turn away. "Do you think if there was anything to tell you that I wouldn't have told you now?"

With the wires that brought Mazzola surging up against the leather straps, turning the voltage higher and higher, placing the clamps in places they had never tried before, in ways and combinations that are not believable and which we have come not to believe, they brought Mazzola up to the doorway of his death.

"Do you still insist there is wine?" Hans said.

"There is wine," von Prum said.

So they began to treat Francucci. We have since learned how valuable it is, in a situation like this, to be a coward, and perhaps it is a good way to go through the world. By honestly being a coward, how many things a man is spared and how little is expected of him. Before they could ever make Francucci feel what they wanted him to feel he had fainted, several times. They threw Francucci along the wall with the others. Although he suffered very little, Francucci was the most convincing of all.

"If there was wine this one would have told us," Otto said.

"Exactly where and how much and how we could get to it and could he lead us," Hans said.

They took off their aprons and rubber gloves; they were damp with sweat and they were tired. One of them looked at Captain von Prum.

"Either there is no wine or we have failed."

"And we have never failed."

"What is there for lunch?"

"And we have never missed our lunch."

"However, you are entitled to five and you will get five."

"I want my five," Captain von Prum said.

"You have an appetite for this," Otto said. "But five is the limit. We never go beyond it. This isn't the only work we do today. We go on to a place called Scarafaggio."

"I *know* the wine is here."

"All right," Otto said. "You're going to *get* your five."

The two young soldiers glanced at one another, and it was meant to be seen by the captain. It was a form of controlled contempt that was fitting for anyone who was not himself a member of the SS police.

It was during the time that they ate that Bombolini learned that the Red Flames, who had been held in the cellar with The Band, had gotten out and were on their way down from High Town into the Piazza of the People. There was Fabio and Cavalcanti the Goat and the young sons of Guido Pietrosanto and Tommaso Casamassima.

"There's no dessert, eh?" Hans said.

"All right," Otto said. He got up and washed his hands in a bowl of water. "This will be our dessert then."

Bombolini was unable to turn and look at them.

"I suppose you two are also members of the Fascist Party. Would you like to show me your cards and medals first?"

"I am a citizen of the Italian nation," Fabio said.

Bombolini felt his heart try to break with blood.

"Take off your clothes," Hans shouted.

"This is what I was talking about," Otto said to Captain von Prum. "Look at the eyes. Very defiant. Very brave. Filled with honor."

"And these are often the first to break," Hans said. "Because when they find they're not really *that* brave they give up entirely."

352

"They have no give to them," Otto said. "Like an earth dam and a big stone one. You can have a leak in the earth dam and still hold back most of the water, but those solid-rock ones, once they go, they collapse."

Bombolini, almost without his realizing it, had come between them. "I want to volunteer myself in place of the boy," he said.

They laughed at him.

"You said that they all break. Then break me. What difference does it make?"

"Because he defied us. We want to change the look in his eyes. We don't like him looking at us that way."

"Besides, why do you want to save him? What, are you sweet on him? Is that it?"

"An old fart like you," Hans said.

"I want to save his life. He once saved mine."

"All that you have to do to save his life, Bombolini," von Prum said. "Is to tell us where the wine is. Say the words and the boy is set free."

"Wait until we put Sparky on him, and then maybe you'll want to tell us something," Otto said.

Bombolini looked at Fabio, who had by then been put on the wet wood of the plank. The leather straps were limp from salt and sweat and urine. He had lost weight in the mountains and his ribs pressed against his skin, and because of the darkness of his hair he seemed whiter than ever before and thin and weak and breakable. There was no sign of fear on Fabio's face, and yet it is not wrong to write that Fabio was trembling so that even the straps could not control the twitching of his muscles. There was even, in truth, a look of resigned sadness on the boy's face, that men would have to do such things to other men.

Bombolini's problem was a very simple one. He believed now that under the pain of the torture all men would break. He had no faith at all now that the secret could be held. If he told and spared Fabio the pain and the brutality that were waiting for him, Fabio would not forgive him nor would the people of the town. If he allowed Fabio to endure the pain and then to tell, Fabio could never live with himself again. He wished that Cavalcanti, who was the other one in the room, was on the wooden plank. The

Goat, when faced with the wires, would be the one to tell. At least Fabio and himself could be spared, even though the wine would be lost.

"Before you begin," Fabio said, "I have something to say to you." They stared at Fabio in complete amazement. "You have no right to do this. This is a crime against people and you will some day pay for it."

They smiled then. They asked him his name.

"Fabio," Otto said. "Meet Hans. Hans, Fabio. I am Otto. I will help you tell the truth for once in your life."

"You have no right to do this to me," Fabio said.

Bombolini found that he could not stand there, that his heart felt as if it would break, that he was weeping for Fabio's courage and that he was trembling and his body was bathed in sweat.

"The little courageous acts some people feel they must play out," von Prum said.

They started Fabio much higher up on the magneto scale than they had the others, and it was as terrible as it is possible to imagine it was. Bombolini kept saying aloud, "I want to die. Please let me die before Fabio dies." But even through this he could see that von Prum was looking at Fabio as he had not looked at the others. Fabio, of all of them, had been able to keep from shouting at first, but then he began to scream, as loud as all of them. It was what Bombolini had feared and resigned himself to, and now was almost grateful to hear.

"I'll tell you, I'll tell, I'll tell, I'll tell," Fabio screamed. "Just stop it and I will tell you."

Perhaps he wanted to tell them then. He tried to speak, but he could not make a sound come from his throat when the electricity was stopped, and finally they were forced to undo the top leather strap and help Fabio sit up so that he could try to control his shocked tongue.

"You should have followed the advice of your people," von Prum said to Bombolini, "an old saying of yours—'When the situation calls for martyrs, make sure you send martyrs.'"

Fabio was trying to say something, and they gave him water. Von Prum was leaning forward toward Fabio then and he had the look of someone who is about to reach and obtain something he has wanted above all other things in his life. Perhaps it is true that Fabio wanted to tell them. And perhaps it was an error on the part of Otto and Hans that they had begun Fabio so high on the scale of pain that he was unable to talk until he had had the moment he needed to discover himself again, to find that he had taken the pain and that he was still alive, or that he would rather be dead than open his mouth to them.

"You have no right," Fabio said. "What are you doing to me? And you," Fabio said to von Prum. "You are the worst of them because you know better."

"Put him down," Hans shouted. "Put him back down."

When he was strapped to the table and the little metal teeth sunk into fresh parts of Fabio's body, this time to the penis and the throat, Otto turned to Captain von Prum.

"And do you want to do this by yourself now?"

Von Prum was stunned by the possibility that was offered him. It is the only word for it. He backed away from Fabio and then came toward him again; he was afraid to falter in front of these men. He found that his hand was filled with sweat, sweat cupped in the creases of his hand that was moving very slightly, opening and closing as it had done the time he had talked with Bombolini.

"Yes, I will do it now."

Now it was von Prum who trembled. He sat in Otto's seat, and his hand trembled on the brass arm of the magneto and in the end, when he finally pushed the metal lever, it was to the lowest of the buttons and he looked once at Fabio thrusting up against the leather straps and he looked away and down at the floor, until finally it was Otto who turned the arm up and up and Fabio began to scream so loudly that he drove von Prum away from his side, and all at once Otto turned the arm back.

"You can't keep it on low that way," Otto said.

"I did it," von Prum said. "I did what I had to do."

The difficulty with pain, for certain purposes, is that in the end it reaches a point at which it defeats itself, where even if it might be felt and understood by the person who is receiving it, the body can no longer respond to it, or the senses either. At one point Otto turned to the captain.

"You wanted to see about the pliers," he said.

"You might as well learn about the pliers," Hans said.

They took a fingernail, and Fabio barely moved. They took a toenail, and after that a tooth, and Fabio lay on the board and looked at them.

"You see, after the wires it is nothing," Otto said. "Only in the mind are the pliers meaningful."

There is no more sense and no more use in going on about Fabio. The SS men no longer believed in what they were doing.

"Must we treat him?" Otto said.

"I'm entitled to five," von Prum said.

They advanced then on Cavalcanti with a sense of duty about their work but they had no belief in their minds and it is possible to suppose that their hearts were no longer in their work. Nothing "creative," as Otto said, would be coming forth.

Had they only stopped then the secret would have been saved, but now there was Cavalcanti the Goat, the one who cared only about stealing a night with some woman who could not resist him. It could be said that because Cavalcanti saw what Fabio could endure, Cavalcanti would be able to do the same, but that would be stealing in turn from Cavalcanti. It was the Goat who more than all of them remained defiant and who suffered the worst for it.

Who is ever to pass judgment on the depth of a man's strength or the source of his courage until the moment has come? It is something we have learned. Who can afford to be disrespectful of people when they don't know what people contain within themselves?

There is no need to say what happened to Cavalcanti, but there is need to mention the meaning of it. It is something the people of this place should always remember.

The truth is this: If only one man among all of the rest will not break, as Fabio and then Cavalcanti did not break, then all of them, all those who so despise men that they believe all men can be broken and all men can be bought, *all* of them have failed and all of them are defeated, because one alone destroys them and one alone can give heart to all other men.

So, no matter whatever else happens here, we have this reason at least to be proud. Man is an animal, but he doesn't have to end as one. Perhaps this is the lesson the German never succeeded in learning.

Hans and Otto got up, and Cavalcanti was taken and thrown along the wall.

"That ends it. Five of them." They moved with their usual swiftness. They were extremely tidy people, and neat in what they did.

"You understand what it means," Hans said. "You have to accept it. There is no wine."

"No, there is no wine here," Otto said.

"You have to come to accept that, sir."

"We have never been wrong."

"We have never failed."

They had finished their packing and were putting a camouflaged tarpaulin over the equipment in the back of the truck when Caterina Malatesta came down into High Town to attend to the men in the room, and all along the edge of the piazza, from behind the doors and the windows, people groaned at the sight of her. It was she who would do it, the princess Malatesta, the goddess Malatesta, when the soldiers were two minutes away from leaving the piazza in their truck. They stopped when they saw her.

"Sometimes we make it six," Otto said. "In very special cases."

"We have Scarafaggio," Hans said but they watched her moving, unaware of them, unseeing even.

"It wouldn't take much time," Otto said. "The table is on top."

But von Prum had come across the piazza toward them. "Not this one," the captain told them, and they looked at him with some surprise and a little annoyance, because they had been deprived of a pleasure.

"Oh. Oh, I see," Otto said. He studied the Malatesta. "I don't blame you," he said. "You have nice taste."

They got into the truck and started up the engine.

"So, you are vindicated then," Hans said. "You were right all along. The SS will vouch that there is no wine."

"Yes, I am vindicated," von Prum said. He watched the truck turn into the Corso, then he started back toward the Piazza of the

People and there was no sense of triumph or even of belief in him. The smell of the room was very bad, and Caterina Malatesta was already at work, treating Fabio. Von Prum stood behind her for several minutes.

"I'm sorry about what happened here," he said. "These things occur on occasion. We are at war, and war has never been pretty to be in."

She said nothing and she gave no indication that she had heard him speak, and again he was silent.

"I saved you from something," he finally said to her. "I expect you to remember that. It wasn't an easy thing to do."

When she didn't answer he turned to leave; the smells were now too strong for him and he felt tired. Before he left, however, Cavalcanti motioned to him. It was a wild and thoughtless thing to do, but who can find it in his heart to condemn Cavalcanti for it? Perhaps, as Babbaluche said, his brains had been cooked in his head. His voice was low and the words came with difficulty, so Captain von Prum was forced to bend near Cavalcanti to hear him.

"I know where the wine is," Cavalcanti said. He smiled at the German through his distorted lips.

"You lie," von Prum said. Cavalcanti shook his head and continued to smile.

"You know I know where the wine is," he said.

"There is no wine," von Prum shouted, and because he couldn't stand the sight of the face that was smiling at him, he kicked Cavalcanti's face with his boot.

"You waited all morning to do that," Cavalcanti said.

"There is no wine," von Prum shouted. But he turned and ran.

"For that he dies," Copa said. "For that one thing, of all the rest, he dies."

"No, no, no," Fabio said. "You don't understand how we do things. For that he must live."

I T WILL BE difficult for someone who is not from here to understand that despite what had taken place the mood of the people was forgiving. The hand of death had rested on the city and then it had been taken away. But more than that, it was because the harvest was closing upon us and it was a good harvest, a rich harvest fat with promise, and the harvest, of course, is life here. There isn't the luxury of time to hate during harvest.

Something happens here then, and there is no power strong enough to hold it back. When the wind is right and coming up the terraces you can smell it. The first of the grapes, the fattest of them, will have fallen on the ground and the soil will be rich with the smell of their ripeness, and the ripeness, like messengers telling of things to come, fills the lanes and the piazzas of the city.

It becomes a time of demand here; there is no choice left about it if we wish to live. The grapes demand attention, and they demand to be picked; the wine demands to be made, and the people are helpless before it because their blood has been bred over the centuries to heed it. The donkeys know it and the oxen. If the vines could make a sound—and Old Vines says that they do and that he can hear them—we could hear them groaning under the weight of their pregnancy, demanding to give birth to the future wine they carry on their limbs. So it wasn't that the people forgave the Germans, because we have never done that, but that, because of the harvest, no one cared any longer. When the grapes call nothing else is heard. We cared only for that moment when Old Vines, listening to the vines, testing the grapes by mouth, looking at the sun and sky, talking with the gods of the grapes that he talked to, would announce that the hour had come, that the time was ripe, that Polenta should go down to the terraces and sprinkle cool holy water on the plump warm clusters and that God should keep His Good Eye on all of us while the harvest got underway.

It was for this reason that, when Captain von Prum went down the mountain with Sergeant Traub to Montefalcone, some of the people actually waved to them as they went.

"I don't understand them," Sergeant Traub said. "I swear to God, sir, I don't understand these people."

"It's very simple," Captain von Prum said. "They think they've won something. They think they can afford to be pleasant."

"They shouldn't act this way after what happened to them," Traub said.

"It is a matter of values," von Prum said. "They are deficient in values. I've come to despise them."

Things had been changing in Montefalcone. Many of the units stationed in the city had packed up and pulled back to the higher mountains in the north, where it was said the Germans would attempt to establish a winter line that would be easy to defend and expensive to take. Captain von Prum reported to Colonel Scheer, and the colonel was pleased to see him. He pointed to a report on the top of his desk.

"They clear you," Colonel Scheer said. "They vindicate you."

"But that's what I come to see you about," von Prum said. "I am still convinced the wine is in the city."

"Don't be a fool," Colonel Scheer said. "The SS says there is no wine, so there is no wine. The gods have spoken, the file is closed, von Prum is exonerated."

"But if it's there, I want to find it," von Prum said.

"Why?" The colonel was sarcastic then. "Your honor? Duty? A matter of principle, perhaps. In the name of God, we don't care about the wine just so we aren't held responsible for it."

"Because," Captain von Prum said, "if the wine is there they're laughing at me. Bombolini is laughing at me."

Colonel Scheer looked at his junior officer. Such fine points of behavior were beyond his personal experience.

"And so, as we say where I come from, you have a rat in your throat."

"If you wish to put it that way."

"And what would you do with the wine if you found it? It's too late for us to do anything with it, you know. We couldn't ship it now. We couldn't steal it if we wanted to."

Von Prum's voice was loud and for the moment he lost the poise which the colonel had admired in him.

"I'd smash it," the captain said. "If we couldn't take it from there I'd break it. I would break every bottle it was in my power to break."

Scheer smiled at him then. "Yes, you have a rat in your throat."

He got up from his seat and went to the window that looks down into the Piazza Frossimbone, where only a short time before the people of Santa Vittoria had dragged themselves along with their wine on their backs in public display. It was we who had the rats in our throats then.

"Then," the colonel said, "what you have to do—and never say that I suggested it—is to take a hostage." He turned back to the captain. "Have you thought of it?"

The captain shook his head.

"More important, can you carry it out?"

"Yes," von Prum said.

Once again Scheer smiled at him. "You've changed," he said. "Yes, you have the rat. Do you know something? I think you're becoming a proper German."

The thing of a hostage, Colonel Scheer told him, was that the people had time to think about what was taking place.

"You put his life on the conscience of the people. There's a very simple choice for them. If they tell you what you want to know, the hostage lives. If they don't, he dies and by their silence they have killed him."

There were other fine points to consider. The hostage, the colonel explained, must be put on view, in the public piazza, so that he is never out of their minds. When they go to work they see him and when they come back he is there. With good fortune, at night they can hear him moan or cry out in his sleep.

"And you would be surprised, Captain, even in Russia, how many little birds want to come and sing things in your ears. Mothers and daughters and lovers. And people he owes money to; they want him to live the most of all, especially in this country." The colonel was smiling once again. The captain was conscious that his heart was beating swiftly at the prospect of what was ahead.

"And don't forget the hostage himself. In Italy he's usually the first to hop up and get your ear, although he likes to pretend it was someone else all along."

Von Prum was openly excited by then, and he asked the colonel for written permission to choose a hostage in Santa Vittoria.

"My very dear von Knoblesdorf," Scheer said. "It's your honor you're trying to salvage, not mine. At this stage I have butter in my mouth, not a rat." He pointed about the office where the files were already being packed. "We're leaving, you know."

"Does it work?"

"Almost every time," Colonel Scheer said. "Of course it isn't as simple as it sounds. In case we lose the war, just in case, understand." He began to smile again. "You might have to justify what you have done."

"I understand that, sir. It's a risk I'm prepared to run."

And now Scheer was smiling as broadly as he had all of that morning. "And then there's always Him up there, eh? You don't want to forget Him."

"I already have."

He wished to go right then, but the colonel held him and they talked of the progress of the war although von Prum could barely hear him. That war was another war, which no longer belonged to him; his own was being waged within himself and with some people on a mountain.

At the door the colonel cautioned him again. "Try and get someone with a good family life," he said. "You will find that it is especially difficult for children to stand and watch their fathers die before them, all for the sake of a few words."

He held him again at the bottom of the steps. "You didn't say it, Captain."

Von Prum came to attention. "Heil Hitler," he said.

"Heil Hitler," Scheer said. "And von Prum?"

"Yes."

"God go with you."

The captain could hear the colonel laughing when he was at the motorcycle, and it ceased only when Sergeant Traub started up the engine.

There was never any doubt in the beginning who the hostage would be. When they reached Santa Vittoria it was dark and the captain found that he was tired, but as they passed the Fountain of the Pissing Turtle he felt revived again and the blood was rushing through his brain. He felt he could see him there, bound to the Pissing Turtle, his fat stomach showing through the front of his shirt, the eyes of the people staring at him, weeping for him and finally, sometime before the dawn, when no one else was about, asking for the captain and whispering to him: "Captain, I have something I want to tell you."

He went into his room and he wrote in his log and his journal, and the name of Italo Bombolini figures often in those pages. After he wrote he slept, and during that time something must have happened to his dream. Sometime before sunrise he woke and got up, and then he woke Sergeant Traub.

"Get up now and go and get me the one called Tufa," Captain von Prum said. "Get him out of his bed and bring him here."

YOU ALWAYS have wanted to be a martyr," the captain told Tufa. "I can see it in your eyes. And now I'm going to give you your chance. What do you say to that?"

"Thank you," Tufa said.

They tied him to the tail of the dolphin that swims down one side of the Fountain of the Pissing Turtle soon after the sun was up, to allow the people to see him there on their way to work. There was no need to announce the reason for his being there. As we say here, good is sometimes not noticed when it goes, but evil is always seen when it arrives. At first the people didn't want to leave the piazza, but it was Tufa who ordered them to go down to the grapes, and in a way the people were gratified, because the harvest was upon them and the pull of the grapes grows very strong.

"Don't you worry, Tufa," they told him. "We'll come and get you in the evening when it's dark. We'll cut you loose."

But those who knew Tufa knew he would never allow it. The cost for harming Germans had gone up along with all prices in a war. The fee was now twenty-five Italians for every German harmed. Near San Rocco, in a country village, when a farmer slapped the face of an officer his entire family and others in the village were put to death and the farmer was forced to live.

Bombolini did what could be done. He hid Tufa's mother so that no one could find her and so that she couldn't go to von Prum to save her son, and they put Babbaluche's daughter, who had the thunderbolt for Tufa, where no one would be able to find her. Then he went to see Caterina Malatesta.

"I don't believe that I have to worry about you," Bombolini said.

"I have only one question. Why was it Carlo? Why not someone else? Why not a Pietrosanto with fifty members in his family?"

"I don't believe I have to worry about you," Bombolini said.

She nodded.

"That's why Carlo Tufa."

The soldiers were decent about Tufa. They didn't believe there was wine, and they recognized Tufa as one of their own kind. They gave him cigarettes from Spain and oranges from Portugal. They set up a canvas roof from a stall in the daytime to shield him from the sun. There is something strange about looking at a young man in good health who you know will be dead the next day. You watch him because you watch yourself. But there was nothing to be seen in Tufa. He gave no sign of being worried or even of anything unusual taking place. One thing alone bothered him and it was Caterina.

"Where is she?" he asked Bombolini. "Why doesn't she come to see me?"

The mayor had no answer for him.

"Have you ever seen this done before?" Tufa asked Sergeant Traub.

"Oh yes, in Russia, in Poland. It's effective. They don't let you die, you know. There is always someone who wants to save you. It's very hard to become a martyr these days."

They fed him good soup and he ate it all, and one of the soldiers gave Tufa a chocolate bar that had been sent to him from home.

"I don't envy you," the soldier said.

"I don't envy the one who picked me," Tufa said.

"I mean to say, there's no wine, is there?"

"No, there's no wine."

"Then how can anyone save you?"

"It would be difficult to do."

"I don't envy you."

Toward evening, when the people were coming up from the terraces, all the soldiers were on duty, and they made a ring around Tufa and had their weapons at the ready. They allowed only Bombolini to come close to him. They talked about death and it didn't bother Tufa.

"We have a saying here," Bombolini told the soldiers. " 'Good wine and brave men don't last long.' "

"I don't know about your men," Heinsick said, "but your wine did all right."

Tufa laughed the loudest of them all. But behind the laughter, for those who could see it, was a worry about Caterina and a sadness. It was all that he asked and it was the one thing that was denied him. In late afternoon Padre Polenta came across the piazza, the cooling wind of the afternoon sending the skirt of his cassock flying up behind him, so that he seemed to be running even though he was moving very slowly.

"There is nothing in the book about such a situation," the priest said, "but if you will kneel and pray with me now something will come to me."

"We could always pray for the souls of those who are doing this to me," Tufa said. "We could forgive them."

"Oh no," Padre Polenta said. "That would be too much. There's a limit to mercy, you know."

After the prayers the soldiers stepped away from Tufa and the priest, to allow him to make his last confession, and in a few minutes they had finished.

"I don't know if I should give you Extreme Unction now or wait until the morning," Polenta said.

"You had better wait until the morning. There is no telling what hell I might raise tonight," Tufa said. The priest was reluctant to go and he finally came back to Tufa.

"It's a touchy matter, but in your confession you didn't repent for your life with the Malatesta woman," he said.

Tufa considered this for a moment. "I don't wish to repent for that," he said, and it became Polenta's turn to consider.

"It's not a *mortal* sin," he said finally. "Nothing mortal there. But I want you to understand this, it will mean a few hundred years' penance in Purgatory."

"Then that's a price I will have to pay," Tufa said. "You might tell her sometime that she was worth it," he said to Bombolini.

During the whole of that day it was possible at almost any time to see the figure of Captain von Prum through the windows of Constanzia's house. He would work over his letters and his logs for several minutes at a time, and then he would be drawn once more to the window with the same fascination that they say some men have when they watch a scaffold being erected for them. They even come to take pride in the work, it is said, pride that all this is being done for them.

"I am amazed at my ability to do this thing," he wrote in his log. "There is no other word that will describe it: I amaze myself."

Sometime in the early night one of the soldiers asked the captain if it might be possible for the hostage to spend his last night in bed and not on the stones of the piazza. The captain refused.

"It is in the night that the hearts crack," Colonel Scheer had said. "It's in the night that they begin to believe he really will die the next morning."

He had said one other thing which the captain was beginning to see was true. If once you begin with a hostage you must stay with the hostage or the people will know that you are not prepared to go to the end, to commit the ultimate act, and then your usefulness to your work and to yourself will have come to an end.

The thought both frightened and excited him.

At times he found comfort in a line that Nietzsche wrote and which he quoted in his notes and log several times that day, that in the long haul of history one life was worth nothing.

It was this line that Bombolini had once chosen to answer. "Then that's the difference between us," Bombolini had said. "To us nothing is worth one life."

"We shall see," von Prum had said.

Because he was a gracious man and was anxious to show that there was nothing beyond duty in this death, he allowed Bombolini at ten o'clock to pay a last visit to the hostage. Tufa was interested in only one thing.

"Where is she? Why hasn't she come?"

Bombolini could say nothing to him. He had gone to see her and she had refused to see him. So they stood in silence, and there was only the sound of the soldiers moving about in the darkness and of the water from the fountain.

"I never told her the story," Tufa suddenly said. He motioned with his head at the fountain above them. "Sometime when I'm gone I want you to tell her the story and tell her that I asked you to tell it to her."

"I'll tell her, Carlo." He wanted to go because he felt that he was about to cry and he didn't wish to embarrass Tufa with his tears. Before he went he kissed Tufa on one cheek and then the other.

"Goodbye, Tufa."

Tufa was smiling at him. "It's not goodbye," he said. "I have a whole half of a day ahead of me."

It is not easy even now for us to believe that the city slept that night. But Bombolini went home and slept, and they put a straw pallet down on the cobblestones and Tufa slept, and the people looking from the windows around the piazza began to go to sleep because the people had worked hard that day and they know that even when death is in the house life goes on and that beyond Tufa there were the grapes, brimming with life, to be considered as well the next day. The soldiers who were seated around Tufa had had their wine and they too were tired. The water pouring from the turtle was as steady and gentle as the wind that whispered in every part of the piazza, and it lulled them. Across the piazza the captain was awake and, although he had gotten ready to go to bed, he got up again and, for a reason he could not explain, dressed himself again. His intuition was good, because at the time that he was dressing, Caterina Malatesta was coming down from High Town.

She carried her shoes in her hand so she would make no noise, and she stayed in the shadows of the houses. There was a thin moon that night and there was light on one side of the piazza, but the far side was buried in shadow. The old women and old men who stay at the windows because for them to sleep is to die, must have seen her moving along in the darkness, but they said nothing. Whatever happens doesn't belong to them any more; they only watch and wait.

When Caterina was opposite the piazza from the fountain she stopped and attempted to see Tufa, but it was too dark for that. There was no movement of any kind then, only the water, and the usual night sounds, a child crying out for its mother, the heavy breathing of oxen up the side lanes and the deep-throated tunk of their bells as they shifted their positions.

The door to Constanzia's house was in shadow, so even the old people didn't see her then. At the door she put on her shoes—they were shoes from the city, with heels, and not made for here—and when she was ready she scratched on the wood of the door with her fingernails.

In the manner of such things, although the captain had not heard the sound before, he knew at once what it meant. He was pleased that Traub was not in the outer room, where he often slept, but was in the piazza guarding the hostage. Before he went to let her in, he straightened up the room and lit a second tallow candle which he put before a mirror so that it gave off a warm good light and then he went to the door.

He realized that ever since he had first heard the word "hostage" in Montefalcone, without ever admitting it he had been preparing for this moment. But even so, when he did open the door to her, he was unprepared for her beauty. In the books and stories it says that men are made breathless by the great beauty of a woman, and in this case it was as the books say. Her beauty was a force in the room that he felt; he was overpowered by it. She had spent that day in the classic way of great beauties, in warm baths, in oils, she had washed her hair and brushed it so often that the light reflected from it and she had dressed in the kind of dress no other woman has ever worn here because no other woman would know how to buy one or how to wear one, or would ever have the money to own one.

When he had dreamed of this moment he had dreamed that he would surrender, but that in surrendering, as it should be with any good soldier, the price would come high. He knew that what he was doing would in some way, perhaps a serious way, damage him; and yet he also knew that in the end he couldn't care about that, because this was what he had always wanted in his life. As it had been with Tufa all of that day, he found he could not take his eyes away from her, although he attempted to be casual and even careless with her.

"So you've come as I said you would come," von Prum said.

"Not in the way you said," Caterina said.

"No. Not from the snow or the rain or the cold. But you came. That's what is important. None of *them* came."

"None of them had anything to offer you."

"They could have brought me the answer to the secret."

"There is no answer."

He smiled at her. "You too, eh? No, that isn't the answer. It's because they know that after he dies, in a month or two they will have forgotten, because they know that in a month or two they themselves would be forgotten. They have souls of leather. I don't say that in disrespect."

"And we? We have souls of what?"

"I don't know that we have souls. Maybe that's why we put such an importance on living and dying."

The conversation was not going the way he had heard it in his mind before this night, and he didn't like it. He had wanted her to ask, to beg him just a little, to offer something that he could resist at first; and it was Caterina who was wise enough to change the way things were going.

"And what about the cognac you promised if I came?" Caterina said. "You seemed so certain I'd come you must have saved me some. I could use it now."

370

He looked at her with genuine pleasure. "What a good idea," he said.

He went to the other room to get the glasses and the brandy, but before he went into the room he turned and looked at her.

There was no need for either of them to speak then. They both understood what must take place. If someone was asked to buy something he must be allowed to examine what he was buying. She moved for him and he watched her. She crossed the room to the mirror and the tallow light, where she undid the scarf that held her hair and began to arrange it, with the knowledge that he was watching her.

To attempt to tell what lies behind a woman's beauty is a stupid effort. The very effort destroys the beauty one wishes to re-create. There was one thing about the Malatesta, however, that can be described. Von Prum, when he wrote about it, called it a "dark brightness," and then once he called it a "bright darkness." Maybe they are the same. But the thing of her beauty was the contradiction of herself. Her eyes were large and dark and the darkness of them served to emphasize the light of the eyes; the same was true of her dark hair which at the same moment was bright. She was lean and fine-boned, and yet she was voluptuous; but there is no way of describing her voluptuousness without destroying it. Because she was a capable woman the sadness that at the same time could be seen in her eyes in the end made her appear vulnerable. Everything about her was a contradiction of itself and the contradictions were so perfectly blended with one another that they created beauty. There was a maturity about the Malatesta which every beautiful woman owns, from the time she is very young, as if all beautiful women must have lived at least once before and known things that one life alone can't provide in order to arrive at the beauty they possess.

It is hopeless then to tell you. Every beautiful woman is beautiful in only her own way, otherwise there would be only one beautiful woman, and this is not so. As is said about the devil, they come in all disguises and in improbable places, and they appear in unexpected ways.

She was, as each of them is, a marvel. To von Prum there was about the Malatesta a quality beyond. That she would come to him as she did betrayed to him an instinct for destruction, a willingness to extend herself to the point of risking her own ruin. That was the thing which excited him beyond all other things; it was the thing beyond the glorious animal that he saw. Every man must have to see beauty in his own way as well.

He made an effort, as he had promised himself, to resist. He told her that he didn't like dark women, women with skin the color of olives, and that his dreams of women were of blond women with full white breasts who understood they were inferior to the men they adored, and who were happy that way.

"What do you have to offer?" he had said when he came back into the room with the glasses and the brandy.

"Myself," Caterina had said.

He allowed the brandy to work in him before he spoke again. There was no embarrassment between them.

"Do you really think that is enough for what I will have to do?" von Prum said.

"Yes, I will be enough for you," Caterina said. "I will be a good mistress for you. You'll see."

He looked away from her, because when he watched her the things he wanted to say were weakened by her.

"You won't regret it," Caterina said. It was said with the simple assurance of a woman who has known since she was very young that some part of her at least belongs in the dream of every man who has dreamed of possessing a beautiful woman.

"This thing could ruin me," von Prum said. "It could destroy me."

"You won't regret it," Caterina said.

"How do I know that?"

"Because I'll show you."

She had taken off her scarf and a dark outer coat which she had chosen to wear, and she came across the room toward him.

"Where do you stay?" Caterina asked. He motioned with his head in the direction of his room and she went past him and into the room, where she began to undress. He came to the door and stood by the entrance to the room.

"I want to watch you," he said.

"As you wish," Caterina said. She moved with the assurance of those who are beautiful in their bodies and as if he were not in the room. When she was halfway through undressing she asked for more brandy and she drank.

"As long as we're doing this," she said, "there is no reason why it should be unpleasant."

When he was beside her he began to tremble.

"That won't do," Caterina said. "Why are you trembling?"

"Because you're what I have wanted all my life," von Prum said, which was the moment of his surrender.

"Then we understand," the Malatesta said. "It is me for him."

"Yes."

"You won't regret it."

"No, I won't regret it."

"I'll make you a good mistress," Caterina said. "You'll see."

"But I will have to take someone else," von Prum said. "You understand that."

"That isn't what I came for," the Malatesta said.

They lay in the bed, and although the bed was small they didn't touch one another.

"Now what is it you want to do with me?"

"Nothing," the German said. "I want to lie here."

"That won't do either," Caterina said.

"Everything," von Prum said.

"Then come here."

* * *

Sometime during the night she said to him, "Have you realized now that you're only a man after all? A man like any other man."

She woke him before dawn because he had asked her to wake him then, before the people were up, and he got dressed and went out into the darkness of the Piazza of the People to the fountain and woke Sergeant Traub. Tufa was awake, lying on his back, looking up into the night.

"You can take the ropes off him," von Prum said. "He's going free."

373

It pleased Traub. "You heard him?"

"Yes," Tufa said. "I don't know whether to thank someone or despise someone."

It was still dark when Tufa crossed the piazza and started up to High Town. Once on the hill he could see the first light of the morning, and although he has never talked about that morning again it must be guessed that Tufa was happy then, because it *was* his life, and a day was beginning that he had not counted on seeing.

There was no Caterina Malatesta waiting for him, of course. When he reached the house some of the people were already up, and he asked them about her, but none of them would tell him. It was a long time, a day or two at least, before anyone in Santa Vittoria found enough heart to tell him.

WHEN DAWN came and it was found that Tufa had been freed, there was fear in Santa Vittoria. It could only mean that someone had told about the wine. But when it was found that the wine was safe, the fear became joy. They learned about the Malatesta and the contract she had made and the people approved of it. It was a very good bargain.

"She can always bring her body back when it's all over," Babbaluche said. "It's more than Tufa would have been able to do."

Some of the women were envious of the Malatesta.

But as the morning wore on, a new consideration occurred to some of the people and the joy died.

"Now it's someone else's turn," Pietrosanto said. "Someone else has to die in Tufa's place." And everyone knew it was true.

Everyone began to look at everyone else to see if they could see death in the eyes of their neighbor. There is a feeling here that death enters the body before the body actually dies.

"He wouldn't want someone like me," a man would say. "Why would he pick someone like me? You're more the kind he would want."

By afternoon, work on the terraces had almost come to a stop. Everyone was preparing for someone else's death and praying to God that it wouldn't end up being his own. By evening the city was in such a state that Bombolini was forced to go across the piazza and ask to speak to Captain von Prum. He was surprised to be invited inside Constanzia's house.

"I'm sorry to have to bother you on this day," Bombolini began, and he was embarrassed. He had almost said on your wedding day. He told the captain about the state of the city.

"If you must have a hostage, and it is a very bad idea," Bombolini said, "the people want you to pick one. Until you do the entire city is condemned. We have been tortured enough."

The words should have angered the German, but instead Bombolini found the German looking at him with a smile.

"There never really was any other choice from the start," von Prum said. "I had always thought of you, Bombolini."

During all of this time it had never once occurred to Bombolini that he would be the one to be the hostage.

"No," he said. "That wouldn't be a good idea." It caused the captain to laugh, but Bombolini was serious. "The city would lose a good leader. Without me here there could be serious trouble." It was a simple fact.

"And who would you suggest then?" von Prum asked. "Do you have some enemy you might enjoy seeing in front of a firing squad. Do you want the power of picking?"

He could hear Caterina moving in the other room and wondered if she was listening. He wondered if it had occurred to her that the next death would belong to her.

"I think the only way to do it is the way we did it before," Bombolini said. "Take it out of our hands and put it in God's hands. Let Him be the one to make the choice."

"The first one in the piazza?"

"No, no, they would never go into the piazza again," the mayor said. "I have in mind something different. A lottery."

He could see that the idea appealed to the captain.

"Put the names of all the people in a wine barrel and then let the priest draw out the name."

The idea of using the priest had an even stronger appeal to the German.

"You might call it a lottery of death," he said.

They said the words over in their minds, "A lottery of death." There is an excitement to the words.

"Would the priest involve himself in something like this?" von Prum said.

"Oh, yes," the mayor said. "This is God's work now. No matter who puts his hand into the barrel it will be God who chooses the winner."

"I would prefer the priest," the German said. "It's a strange word you use—*winner*. What if you are the winner?"

"No man ever believes he'll be the one to win a lottery."

"And if you are?"

Bombolini shrugged his shoulders.

"What could I say then?" he said. "God will have decided He doesn't need my kind of leadership."

The German called into the next room.

"And what if Tufa is picked by God this time?" he called into the room where Caterina must have been. "Wouldn't that be funny? What would you do then?"

"Then I'd threaten to leave you."

Von Prum smiled, and to his own surprise Bombolini found that he was smiling also.

Before Bombolini left they drew up the rules for the lottery of death. Women and children would be excluded. The honor of dying would belong to all men between the ages of sixteen and sixty, the same ages that the Italian government in the north of Italy had set for the conscription of soldiers.

"When?"

"The drawing must be held tomorrow morning so the people will be able to go to work," Bombolini said.

And so it was agreed.

When the mayor was at the door Caterina called to him and he went back inside and stood at the door of her room.

"Does he know yet?" she said to him. "How does he seem?"

Bombolini told her that he was tired and confused, but that he didn't know.

"Do you think he will understand?" Caterina asked him, and Bombolini was surprised by her question.

"You know Tufa. You know how he is made," Bombolini said.

"I couldn't let him die when I had a way to save him."

"It doesn't matter," the mayor said. "You put the horns on his head."

"But he's too old for that," Caterina said. "He's been other places."

"Yes, but he comes from *here*," Bombolini said. "To buy his life, you sold his honor."

"He knows I love him."

Bombolini was able to laugh at her for not knowing any better.

"It doesn't matter, don't you see?"

"And Tufa loves me."

"It doesn't matter," Bombolini said. "You broke the rules."

When Bombolini was gone von Prum took Bombolini's place at the door.

"Do you think he really believes that God picks the name from the barrel?" he asked her.

"Of course. It's the way they think here."

"It's very simple, isn't it? Very childish."

"Yes, they're very simple here and very childish," Caterina told him.

* * *

Before an hour had passed Bombolini had called a meeting of the Grand Council, and they met in Santa Maria of the Burning Oven, going in through the side doors one at a time so as not to attract any attention. They gathered to pick the winner of the lottery.

"I don't like to say this, because I admire you, Bombolini," one of the older men said, "but at a time like this, doesn't honor require that the leader make himself available to his people?"

Bombolini was gratified when the members of the Council voted the idea down before he had to answer. It is not easy to turn down the role of martyr when it is offered to you.

It was surprising, the number of people who the Grand Council felt were qualified to die for the city and the wine, and who they felt would not mind doing it.

"Take Enrico R——," one of them said. "He has no friends, he has no land, he doesn't owe anyone money. He's got no real reason to live. I'm sure if you ask Luigi he would be glad to do this for us."

"You forget," another member of the Council said. "Enrico happens to be married to my sister. She wouldn't let him do it."

They started down the list of names in Padre Polenta's record book, one at a time. When they came to the name of a member of the Grand Council they had the good manners not even to mention it but to go on to the next name. When a name that seemed to be a possible winner came up they would judge him, and some of the things that were said in Santa Maria that night, if they were to be repeated even at this time, would lead to vendettas and more bloodshed than was ever seen in those times. For a time they thought they had found the right man, the perfect winner of the lottery, in N.

No one liked N., and N., as far as anyone knew, liked no one in return. His own family despised him. If N. were selected his own family would hold a celebration. He owned a lot of land, a lot of vines, he had pieces of terrace spread all over the side of the mountain and a lot of the wine was his.

"The beauty of N.," Bombolini said, "is that, bad as he is, he is a man of courage."

"And a miser," Pietro Pietrosanto said. "He will die with a smile on his lips before he gives those bastards one bottle of his wine."

But it was pointed out that N. was also related by blood to fifty-six people in Santa Vittoria and some of them were a little bit crazy. It is revealing nothing to say that Fungo the idiot and Rana the frog, for example, shared blood with N., and it was impossible to tell when one of them might have some kind of religious vision or other symptom of madness and go to the Germans to save N.'s life if not his soul.

At the end of it all, one name came up again and again and would not leave the lists.

"But who has the courage to face him?" someone asked. "And what if he says No, as I know he will?"

"Emilio Vittorini, will you be one of us?"

Vittorini nodded that he would.

"Then go home and put on your uniform."

The delegation, when it was finally formed, consisted of Bombolini, Vittorini as a representative of tradition, Roberto Abruzzi as a representative of the outside world, Angelo Pietrosanto as a representative of the youth of Santa Vittoria, and Pietro Pietrosanto as a member of the military. For reasons that were obvious to everyone, it was decided to leave the priest at home.

Before midnight, since the curfew had ceased to be observed and the people, ever since the SS had come, no longer went down to the Roman shelter to hide from the planes, they met before Vittorini's house in the Corso Cavour and started down to Babbaluche's house to ask the cobbler if he would be good enough to agree to win the lottery of death and die the next day for the people of Santa Vittoria.

They stood outside his door for a long time before daring to knock on it.

"I think that Vittorini should knock," Pietro Pietrosanto said. "He is the most respectable of us and an occasion like this calls for respect."

Vittorini would not knock or be the first to go inside.

"Roberto is the only one who hasn't done something to make him be hated," Bombolini said. "Perhaps you would like to be the first?"

Roberto did not feel that a stranger should be the one to ask a man to surrender his life for a cause that wasn't his own. In the end, of course, it was the Captain of the People who had to knock and when the door opened had to be the first to go inside. Such is the price of leadership.

Babbaluche was smart. Some think he was wise, also, and some feel he was never wise. But all agree that Babbaluche was smart— as smart as some of the cocks here who always know when you are coming to get them and manage to die of old age on the roof tops before they see the inside of a pot. The moment the door opened he knew why they had come.

"You've come to tell me something," the cobbler said. "I only hope it's good news."

Bombolini made the error of looking down at his shoes at that moment, and as if the movement were a magnet drawing the others with it, every other head went down. When it came time to look up again—because it would be required to look at the cobbler when posing the final question—the mayor found that he could not bring his head up. So there was a long silence that roared in the dark, dirty little room.

"There is going to be a lottery tomorrow," the mayor managed to mumble.

"And you want me to serve on the committee."

"Even more than that," Pietro Pietrosanto said.

"That sounds flattering," Babbaluche said. And the silence was as deep as before. They could hear Babbaluche's wife breathing in the next room and the stomach of his ass, St. Joseph, whom he kept with him in the house, rumbling.

"It's a strange lottery, eh?" Babbaluche said. His voice was hard and cold and keen. "All the losers are winners and the winner is the loser."

The silence again.

"The big loser," the cobbler said.

"I know what you want," Babbaluche said after that. If the door to the house had opened then, Roberto says, every one of them would have backed out of the cobbler's house and into the Corso and not come back. "You want me to pick the name, because I'm the one who has no other reason to protect anyone, I hate them all."

"*Something* like that," Roberto said.

"Or is it the other way around?" Babbaluche said. "There's no reason to protect the cobbler, because they all hate him?"

No one could take his eyes away from the pieces of leather scattered all over the floor. They tried to make shapes and read things in the coils and scraps of leather on the stone floor. If for no other reason than for the words he said next, forgetting all the other things he did for them, the people of the city would have to honor Bombolini.

"Babba," he said, "we have chosen you because we think that you can do it best."

You must someday hear a peacock scream at the dawn to hear the sounds that came from the cobbler's throat. And the screams of defiance and wild joy and bitterness came, not once, but over and over again, until Roberto, for one, was fearful that he himself would begin to scream with the cobbler. It was the finest joke of all his life.

"It would be an act for all of Italy," Vittorini said, and the peacock screamed again. His wife and children were at the door of the room and he motioned them away.

"Where was all of Italy, where were all of you when they were doing this to me?" he shouted at them. He tapped his crippled legs.

He had been the first of all to be mutilated by the Fascists. A few Blackshirts from Montefalcone had come into the Piazza of the People and had seized him and in view of the people of the city they had broken his legs one after the other, and when he wouldn't salute the Duce they had made him eat a live toad. Since then Babbaluche had been a shame for Santa Vittoria to carry on its bent back.

"Let's go," Pietro Pietrosanto said.

"Let's go," Angelo Pietrosanto said. "We've made a mistake."

But the cobbler wouldn't let them go that easily. He was no longer able to eat anything, he lived on the acid in his stomach for breakfast and had the bile for lunch, he said, but this was too rich and fine a meal not to have taste for him.

"Tell me," Babbaluche said, "give me five good reasons why I should die for all of you?"

They tried to say things about love of country and of neighbor and brother, and the words were so much sawdust in their mouths. How is it possible to tell a man who has purged himself of love that in the end he should die for it? It was all food and sunrise for the peacock, and when he was silent they were silent.

"Let's go," Pietro Pietrosanto said. They began to back away and make the motions of leaving then.

"Sometimes the only decent thing a man can do is to die," Roberto said. He wanted to tell the cobbler that he knew, that he had tried it once. He knew that if he closed his eyes he would see the burning boy and the white ball bouncing. Perhaps there was something in the voice itself that made itself heard to the cobbler.

"Now you are saying something," Babbaluche said. "Aren't you ashamed of yourselves, leaving it to an outsider to say something? You may be smart, or you may have said it because you are a fool," he said to Roberto. "I don't know about you. But you have said something."

"We know that you are going to die soon, Signor Babbaluche," Roberto said. "We know that and you know it as well. That is why we came to you."

"But why didn't you say that when you came?" the cobbler said to the others. His wife had lit a lamp in the next room, and so there was light in the outer room where we stood. We could hear the woman and her two daughters moaning and crying.

"And that's just it," Babbaluche said to them. "I want to die on my own terms. I want to die my own way. I don't want to give them the satisfaction of killing me."

Roberto didn't know what to say because his mind doesn't work in the right ways for this place, but Bombolini knew what to say after that.

"But that *is* just it, Babba," he said. His voice was triumphant now. "When they kill you, you cheat them. You rob them of what they think they are getting. They demand a life and we give them a corpse."

And the cobbler began to smile, differently than before. Even though it hurt him, he began to laugh, from the stomach and not from the throat the way he had done before.

"You make fools of them," Bombolini said. "At the moment of your death you're laughing in their faces."

Now everyone was excited. It was the ancient thing here, something for nothing all over, this time turned inside out.

"You make them do what God would do next week, and they

must *pay* for it," Vittorini said. Babbaluche told them to keep God out of this.

"Will you tell them? Will you make sure, before they go, that they know?"

"No," Bombolini said. "Absolutely not. They must carry the shame and guilt of Babbaluche the cobbler around in their minds and in their hearts and rotting their souls until the day comes for them to die."

The cobbler actually tried a little leap in the air. "Italo," he shouted, "you are marvelous. You are so clever." He looked at Roberto. "You are honest, you see, but Italo is clever, and that is always better."

Then he was sad. As bright as he had been, the light had gone from him, and they could all read at once that death was indeed already sitting inside his body, waiting.

"But they'll know," he said. "They'll take one look at me and know."

But Bombolini had thought of that. "We're going to paint your face so you look fresh and healthy. We'll put walnuts in your cheeks to make them bulge. We'll stuff things under your shirt to make you look fat. Your voice is still good."

The cobbler was brightening again. It was amazing to see the way he could come back from the front door of death.

"Italo," he said. "We should have been friends. We could have done terrible things together."

Bombolini shrugged. "I was a clown and you didn't like clowns."

"But I should have seen through your mask."

"Yes, but I was a clever clown and so I wore a clever mask."

They made the plans for the morning, which was by then not too far away. As few as possible should know, so that when the name was picked from the wine barrel it would come as a surprise and a shock to the people. They decided at first that every name in the barrel should read "Babbaluche," but realized that would be a dangerous thing to do in case any German put his hand into the barrel. It was decided to put all the names into the barrel and to have Padre Polenta hold Babbaluche's name in the sleeve of his cassock.

"But would the priest do such a thing?" Roberto asked. They looked at him as if he were Fungo.

"Have you ever known a priest to lose at cards?" Babbaluche said.

They were going to take his wife and daughters away that night, but Babbaluche was against it.

"They should be in the piazza to faint and fall down and cry," he said. "No one can act the way they will act. Then take them away and have three other people take their place. The Germans will never notice."

The others left then, to start making a list of all the names and to set up the wine barrel in the Piazza of the People and to send someone down to paint the cobbler's face.

"Oh, I look forward to this," Babbaluche said. "My last trick on life, my death." The two men smiled at each other.

"Do you know what is even better?" Bombolini said. "Do you know what will happen over this? You will become a martyr. You will become a hero of Italy. The story will go all over Italy—the little cobbler who died for the secret of the wine."

It caused Babbaluche to laugh.

"Oh, if only I could be here to see it."

"You can't have it both ways, Babba," Bombolini said.

"It's the one problem of being a martyr. You never know for certain if they put you in the book."

"We'll put up a plaque to you, Babba: 'Santa Vittoria. The city where Babbaluche the Cobbler surrendered his life for his people.'"

The mayor was quite excited then. "Perhaps we won't have to make this a shrine for bakers after all. People might come here to see the home of the heroic cobbler."

"You might make it a shrine for cobblers. That would be better yet. Put a statue up with a halo on my head."

Bombolini shook his head, however. He had meant it seriously. "Cobblers don't make enough money," he said.

They sat for a time enjoying the wonderful joke. There were many things they might do with it. The cobbler couldn't take wine, but he could hold *grappa* down and he got a bottle and they shared it, drinking for a time in silence. Because they had both had nothing to eat for a long time they got a little drunk very easily.

"You know," Babbaluche said, "I *am* going to die tomorrow. In the joke I forget that sometimes. It's strange. I keep thinking of the trick and forgetting that I'm not going to see how it comes out. That I'm going to die." He looked around the room. "Think. This is the end of it. All of those years of work and pain and sickness, all the hopes I had as a young man, and this—this—this is the end. Nothing more. Can you imagine it? That I came all those miles and all those years for this? That my mother starved those years to bring me to this? Isn't that strange?"

After that, Babbaluche said something that was truly strange for him, and many people wonder if he really ever said it.

He said that he was afraid, not of death, but of not being remembered. And then he told about the thing that had impressed him most in his life. He had once been able to go to Venice, and when he was there he saw a bridge on which there hung a blue light. An innocent man had been hanged from the bridge and ever after that time the people who lived by the bridge, for hundreds of years, had kept the light lit in his memory and his honor and in payment for their mistake.

"I want you to put a light, a green light, in the Piazza of the People for the mistake of my life," Babbaluche said. "I want this under it:

> So That All Should Learn
> In memory of the cobbler Babbaluche
> He lived his life wrong but had the
> good fortune to die his death right.
> What a waste of a life!

Bombolini tried to argue with him, but he was not to be changed.

"Now get out of here," Babbaluche said. "I'm tired and sick and a little drunk, and I have a great deal of acting to do tomorrow. When will Angela come to make up my face?"

"Just before dawn. The lottery is at dawn."

"Two or three hours of sleep. It's a funny thing to need sleep in order to die. But, of course, I have to die right."

Bombolini went to kiss the cobbler on both cheeks, but Babbaluche pushed him away.

"None of that. Just because I'm going to die doesn't mean I have to put up with that."

"Well, anyway, Babbaluche, you're a brave man and, even if you don't know it, a good one."

"Bullshit," the cobbler said. "Those are my last words. Now, go. I have to be fresh for my death."

Bombolini couldn't bring himself to smile at a joke like that. At the doorway he held the handle for a moment and then turned back to Babbaluche. He was very serious.

"Babbaluche?"

"What is it?"

"Make me one promise," the mayor said. "Promise me not to die on us tonight."

The cobbler was shocked and his face showed it.

"What? And spoil a good joke?"

Bombolini could hear him laughing even when he reached the top of the Corso. Although it was still dark, he could see that the wine barrel was already standing there.

$\mathbb{A}$N HOUR BEFORE the sun came up Rosa Bombolini
went down to Babbaluche's house and woke him from his
drunken sleep.

"I thought Angela was coming," the cobbler complained. "At
least I could have that on my last day."

"You get me," Rosa said.

She rouged his sunken yellow cheeks and darkened his eyebrows and brushed his hair. She used wax from the top of wine
kegs to pad out his cheeks and old sweaters under his shirt to hide
the bones of his chest and back. When he looked at himself in the
mirror he was pleased. He looked something like what he must
have looked years before.

"You know, I wasn't a bad-looking son of a bitch," Babbaluche said. "It's fortunate for you you didn't know me then."

"I knew you," Rosa Bombolini said. "You weren't so much."

He looked at her with admiration.

"If it weren't for you, Rosa Bombolini, I would lose all faith in life," Babbaluche said.

"You still have one day to do it in," she said.

"Anyone else would have said, 'That's right, Babba, you were a pretty gay dog. How you used to strut. Why I can remember you strutting around the piazza on Sunday afternoon during the *passeggiata* like God's gift to women.' But not you. That would be asking too much with still a whole day to go." He shook his head. "I can still learn things."

"You're like the rest. You're like Bombolini. I don't care if you're going to die tomorrow or ten years from now. Why should I have to lie for you?"

"All right, put down the mirror," Babbaluche said. "I'm not so much. I begin to have an idea of what hell must be like, and it frightens me."

He had to lean on her in order to get up to the piazza, and when they arrived almost all of Santa Vittoria was already there, even though it still was dark. All eyes were on the wine barrel. Sergeant Traub was going through the names and he was satisfied that the names of most of the eligible men were in the barrel. He hadn't expected that Bombolini would put in his own, but they didn't want Bombolini dead either.

Padre Polenta came across the piazza and he made the sign of the cross over the people as he came. There was no man who could feel secure. His death was in the barrel. If the Germans found out what was taking place, a true lottery of death would take place. A young man began to stir the names with a long stick.

"It's out of our hands now," a woman said. "The angel of death is sorting out the names."

They watched the wine-dark barrel as if the man who was to die would come out of it, and not his name alone. They watched it and never took their eyes away from it, and as they watched it grew lighter and lighter, and the moment could not be delayed much longer. When the sun touched the highest tiles and began to slide down the dark wall and turn them bright yellow, Capoferro began to beat a slow march on his drum, a long roll followed by several short taps. Then finally Padre Polenta began a prayer and all the people knelt on the cobblestones and prayed for themselves and then for their brothers and fathers and husbands, and finally for the man who was about to die.

Captain von Prum had decided it would be wiser if he wasn't present, and at five o'clock in the morning Sergeant Traub came out of Constanzia's house and began to work his way through the kneeling crowd. The people leaped away from him as if his touch might be the one that signaled their doom.

"Let's get this over with," he said to the priest.

"This is a terrible thing to ask a priest to do," Polenta said.

"I didn't ask you to do it. I'm only a soldier. I carry out orders. I have nothing to do with this at all. My hands are clean." He turned to the priest. "Do you want me to leave it to someone else?"

"No, no," Padre Polenta said. "But it is a terrible thing to do. The choice might be God's, but the blood is yours."

"Pick the name," Traub said. "In the name of God, pick the name."

Capoferro knows what to do in times like these. He should have learned things in the one hundred years he claims to have lived. He rolled the drums again, louder this time, much louder, the old sticks thundering on the rim of the goatskin drum, and then Polenta's arm went up in the air and suddenly dipped down into the barrel like a kingfish going after a fingerling in the Mad River, and while the old man beat the drum the priest swirled his hand around inside the wood. The people strained forward. There was no proof that some mistake had not been made or some trick played. When death is at hand every possibility becomes possible. And then the arm came back out of the barrel—the bird had caught its fish—and the drumming stopped and the priest held up the paper. The silence was broken by a blast on wild old Capoferro's horn.

The priest looked at the paper as if he could not believe what he read on it or make himself say the words, and he passed it to Bombolini, who in turn passed it along to the sergeant. Sergeant Traub looked at it one way and then the other and he checked the pronunciation of the name with Bombolini and after that came to full attention.

Babbaluche.

It is strange how in a crowd, a mob even, the people always know where to look. The ones around the cobbler turned toward him first, and then all the others turned and then they began to back away from him as if by being close they might be included in his fate or that death might be catching.

"No," Babbaluche cried. "It can't be me. They don't want me. You have read it wrong."

The sergeant handed the paper to someone in the crowd, and it was passed along, from hand to hand, until the cobbler held it in his hand and read his own name. There was a scream—it was his wife—and then there were the cries of his two daughters, and they fell to the stones; they grabbed the sergeant and pleaded with him, they attacked Padre Polenta and demanded that he intercede with Captain von Prum and with God Himself. After that they were taken out of the piazza by force and put away so no one could find them and they could find no one.

"Yes. It's me," Babbaluche said. "What did I do to deserve this?"

"We have lost the finest cobbler in all of Santa Vittoria," Pietrosanto shouted at Sergeant Traub. "You've stolen our cobbler from us."

"God chose him, I didn't," Traub said, but he couldn't bring himself to look at the little man all alone now in the piazza, reading the scrap of paper on which his doom was written.

"Why me? I'm only a little man," he said.

Padre Polenta went and blessed him. "The ways of God are passing strange," he said.

"And so are those of priests," Babbaluche said.

They led him then to the Fountain of the Pissing Turtle and they tied him to the dolphin in the place where Tufa had been tied. From Constanzia's house the captain could see what was taking place in the piazza.

"Did you have to do it?" Caterina asked him.

"I had to do it."

"Thank God it's an older man," she said.

"He isn't dead yet. If he chooses to talk, he has life." He suddenly turned on her. "If you choose to talk he will live. He's there only because of you."

* * *

It was not a good night for the people of Santa Vittoria. Even though the cobbler was sick he still was going to die and in dying he was doing it for them, because if Babbaluche didn't go one of them would be called. And now that he was going, the people began to know that they were going to miss him. Babbaluche was the salt here.

He lived that night on *grappa*, since he could keep nothing else down.

"I wouldn't do that; you're going to have a terrible hangover," Traub said to him.

"Yes, but what a cure I have," Babbaluche told him. "A little drastic, but complete."

Padre Polenta came and asked him if he could bless him, that it couldn't hurt and might be a form of fire insurance, but the cobbler wouldn't allow it.

"If God personally shows me a miracle between tonight and tomorrow morning I'll let you sprinkle holy water on my head."

"But there are hundreds of millions of people. God can't show each one a miracle. He'd run out of ideas."

"Oh you of little faith," Babbaluche said.

"You don't go by the rules," Traub said. "Why can't you behave like the other, that Tufa?"

"Do you mean with honor and dignity?"

"Like a man of self-respect," Traub said.

"I think I'll try that," Babbaluche said and he made a stern and proud face and gave up the effort. "No, I think it's little late to learn."

All of those things went around the city and it was hard to feel in the proper way before an execution when the sun came up. The cocks began to crow on the roof tops (since von Prum had taken away all their dunghills) and on the doorsteps, shouting at the morning.

"I'll miss that," Babbaluche said. "I always liked the little bastards. I was envious of them. I used to lie in bed and ask myself why they were so happy to see the day come and I was so sad." It was the nearest he came to not being Babbaluche.

"Then I'd say, 'Well, the sons of bitches have no brains and I'm filled with them, so of course I'm sad—who wouldn't be?'" And everyone knew the cobbler was all right again.

They came and got him even before the sun had reached down into the piazza. They took the rope off and asked him if he would like to go down in a cart or on a donkey's back, but he told them he would rather limp along.

"I want to beat the drum for you," Capoferro said.

"Ask them," Babbaluche said. "They're in charge of all the killing here."

They allowed the old man to beat his drum.

The Germans were in their parade uniforms. Although it was already warm and soon would be hot, they wore their tunics and steel helmets. At a few minutes after five the procession marched out of the Piazza of the People, the soldiers going ahead, Babbaluche limping along behind them, followed by Bombolini, Vittorini in his uniform, and Capoferro behind them tapping on his goatskin drum.

The way to the rock quarry is down the Corso Cavour and through the Fat Gate and out above the terraces along a saddle of rocky land and cross the saddle to the quarry, where good marble used to be found.

No one planned what happened, but if there is ever another execution here we will do it this way. The people had lined themselves up all the way down the Corso, and as Babbaluche started down they reached out to touch him and say goodbye, to catch his eye or say something for a last time, and he smiled at them and waved back.

When they came through the Fat Gate and started across the saddle, they could see Rana and his deaf-mute father digging the grave that the cobbler would lie in that same day. That part we would do differently. Even for a Babbaluche it must be a strange feeling to see the earth come flying out of a hole and know that in a few hours the same earth will be lying on your face and in your mouth and you will be in there all alone, in the dark wet clay, while all of the rest will be out in the sun at work and making a living.

If one must be shot, the quarry is a good place for it. The stone is in the shape of a horseshoe and they were able to tie the cobbler to the stake they had put up for Tufa and step back from it, and there was room in the pit for all the people to watch and still be safe. Capoferro ceased his drumming and the only sound then was of the last people filing into the rock pit and the crunching of the Germans' hobnailed boots on the loose shale. Sergeant Traub asked if he wanted a blindfold.

"I'm entitled to all the sun I can get," the cobbler told him. "It warms me and I'm going to need it."

The sergeant stepped forward then and read something to him in German, some official form that turned Babbaluche into some kind of criminal and provided an excuse for the execution. When it had been read he took out a card and read from that in Italian.

"You are here provided one last chance to preserve your life. Answer one question only in return for it. Where is the wine?"

Some felt that they would hear the peacock's cry again, but Babbaluche made no sound. He began to smile at Traub and he could not stop the smile, and some of the people began to smile also, until the whole city was smiling.

"You have the right to say something," Traub said. He looked at his watch.

"It's all right," Babbaluche said. "You'll be back in time for your breakfast."

He looked out at us because he wanted to say something we might remember, but it must not be easy to think of words that might account for fifty years of life. The soldiers had come to attention in a practice run, and they had leveled their rifles at the cobbler and he began to smile once more.

"Why do you laugh?" Traub said. "This is a serious business."

"The rifles," Babbaluche said. "Those six little black eyes looking for my heart." He looked out at us. "They know," he said, "I don't have one."

Traub looked at his watch again.

"Take the cork clapper off the bell," Babbaluche said. "Give the poor bastards in Scarafaggio back their sound."

None of us recalls Traub giving any verbal order to fire, but the shots were fired and the sound was enormous in that quarry, and then the cobbler was leaning forward against the ropes of the stake. It was done. The smoke rose from the ends of the rifles and we were very silent. It was the silence of many and it was in its manner as enormous as the firing had been and so the sergeant ordered his men to reload at once and they formed a close rank and they turned and started out of the rock pit as fast as they could march without seeming to run from us.

"Long live Babbaluche," Bombolini shouted.

"Long live Babbaluche," the people of the city shouted. The sound shouted back at us from the high stone walls and that too was enormous.

We carried the body out of the rock pit and back up the goat path to the burying ground, the young men holding the body aloft and not bothering about the blood because there wasn't much and the cobbler weighed no more than a child. Capoferro beat the drum, *Pa pa boom. Pa pa boom,* and some goats ran alongside the body. An old woman who watched an ox for her living came over to the column.

"Killed somebody, eh?"

Someone answered her.

"It probably served him right," she said.

At the burying ground some young men got into the hole and they lowered Babbaluche down into it and put him down in the coat he had been wearing, still stuffed with old rags to make him look fat. There was no coffin, since Babbaluche himself was the coffinmaker; but he wouldn't have minded. "What a waste of good wood," he used to say. "Well, this idiotic nation is poorer by one box today."

Babbaluche's wife and children were there, but they had done their crying and now they were silent.

"How did he go?" the wife asked.

"Fine," Bombolini said. "He went just like Babbaluche."

One of the daughters put some grape leaves down into the

grave, and the other put the cobbler's eyeglasses in with him. "Just in case," she said.

They turned away then and went back out of the ground and through the piles of stones we have put there to make some kind of decent entrance, and when they turned there, Bombolini and the family and a few others, since most of the people had already gone down to the vineyards, Captain von Prum was there. His face was flushed and it was clear that he had been running, since his breathing was hard and his words came in gasps.

"I tried to stop it," the captain said. "I ran all the way."

They only looked at him, and some of them looked away.

"I wanted to stop it. I made up my mind it was wrong."

They started to walk past him then.

"I ran all the way. I ran as hard as I could go. I have a bad leg, too, you understand."

Bombolini alone of them stayed behind with von Prum. In the background he could hear the priest praying.

"*Asperges me, Domine, hyssopo. . . .*" He had sneaked back into the burying ground and was sprinkling holy water on the cobbler's face.

"Do you know Machiavelli?" Bombolini asked.

"Yes. We've talked about that."

"Do you know what he said? He said—and pay attention—'It is well that when the act accuses you, the result excuses you.'"

He began to go up toward the city again, and the German came along behind him. Bombolini wanted to tell him another one, that to an unjust government a martyr is more dangerous than a rebel, but then he decided the German would have to find that out for himself. When they came into the Corso the bell began to ring. They had not changed the clapper, but someone was beating the side of the bell with a metal hammer and it occurred to Bombolini how clear and pure the tone was, and he knew that Babbaluche was right, as Babbaluche had been all morning.

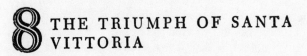

8 THE TRIUMPH OF SANTA VITTORIA

After that the whole spirit changed. We were the way that Babbaluche had been with Sergeant Traub the morning of his death; there was nothing left that they could do to us. Even if they found the wine, we knew and they understood that we would kill them. It was possible that if they found the wine they would say nothing about it at all.

We no longer saw them or heard them. They lived among us, but they were no longer a part of us. The soldiers spent all of their time in the wine cellar, playing cards among themselves and drinking wine. They were drunk most of the time. A few of the Good Time Boys went down to see them, but these were men who had lost a lot of money and needed to win it back again or face ruin, and so they were allowed to go. The Germans spent all of their time drinking and trying to apologize with their eyes.

It didn't matter. There was nothing they could apologize for. We might have hated them, but, for the time at least, Babbaluche had put an end to that. To hate the Germans would have ruined the joke of his death.

"Oh, it's all right," people would say to the soldiers, the few times people talked to them. "He was only the best cobbler we ever had here. But it doesn't matter. Believe us. It is just as he said. It doesn't matter."

We wouldn't allow them to apologize and that is a terrible thing to do to people.

Besides, there were the grapes, and the harvest was upon us.

We almost never saw von Prum after that, and we never saw Caterina at all. She alone of all the Santa Vittorians still suffered from the occupation. She was a prisoner in the house because he loved her, she was all that he had left and because he had vowed that if she left him the last thing that he would do was to see that Tufa died for it, and she knew that this was the one person he was still capable of killing.

We know a little of what he did. There are notes and letters that he wrote, even to his dead brother Klaus, which he never sent. He was attempting through himself and through writing and reading and through his love for Caterina to remake himself. He began to strip himself before her, layer by layer, which is a very dangerous thing for any man to do. He wrote this in his log:

I must look deeply into the chaos of my soul and plumb its depths so that the riddle of my existence will be revealed to me.

No one in Santa Vittoria could ever write a line like that. Fabio, perhaps, before he experienced his torture, but never after that. Caterina gave him some help by telling him one thing her husband, who had admired the Germans, had told her.

"The difference between the Italians and the Germans," he had said, "is that when the Italians do something bad they know they are doing something bad, but when the Germans do something bad they are able to convince themselves they have done something good. And that is why they are so much more effective than we are."

"I did some bad things," von Prum said. "See? I know that. But everything I did was for the country."

"What you forget," Caterina told him, "is that every place is someone's country."

"Someday, when this is all over, I'll come back here and I'll do something for the people here. I'll build them a new fountain, I'll help them build a school. Do you think they would like that?"

"Oh yes," Caterina said. "Come back and build them a school." And she was right about that. It's the way we are. We'll take a school from anyone just so they don't try to teach in it.

His plans for returning here some day and doing good works for us occupied his time. There are more notes on that as well. In the course of this he must have scoured his soul and bleached it a bit, because his sense of well-being began to return.

"I have looked into the chaos, I have plumbed the depths," he wrote later. "I have dropped a bucket into the inner well of myself and it begins to come up with clear water. The riddle of my existence is this: That although I have made errors and I admit to them, at the same time I am forced to conclude that, like it or not, in the end I am dedicated to the good life."

After that, he began to go out a bit, a few short walks in the piazza, and he smiled at the women at the fountain and was pleased to find that the smiles were sometimes returned.

"I think they understand," he told Caterina. "These are good people. They know that at the bottom of it all I am only a soldier and that sometimes a soldier is forced to do things that aren't nice but which duty demands be done."

He was happier with himself after that. He felt secure in himself once more. He had done his best, and he was content with most of it. If some people had been harmed, he hadn't wished it to go that way. He was at ease except for the one thing that always came back to haunt him. He was secure enough one afternoon, a day or perhaps two days before the harvest began, to ask Bombolini to come to see him.

"Don't go," everyone told the mayor. "It dishonors us." But he went.

He was surprised to see the Malatesta. Everyone had said that she was wasting away, it was what they wished to believe, but in truth she had never looked better to Bombolini. The hot tubs and the good food and the warm bed had not harmed her. He looked at her and when their eyes met he understood her at once. Why should she waste away because of him? Whose victory would that be? Babbaluche would have approved, Bombolini thought.

"I'm going to do something for you," von Prum said. "I am going to risk my entire professional future for you. We are not going to be the only Germans here, you understand. Sometime soon there will be a general withdrawal from the south and a stand will be made somewhere along a new line here. At that time there may be thousands of soldiers here. It is possible that a major battle could take place and it is possible that then the wine—oh, don't make that face, Bombolini; we aren't children—that the wine will be uncovered. The headquarters of my unit has already withdrawn. Records are in disorder. As commander of Santa Vittoria I am prepared to swear that the wine they find is legitimately your wine, that you have paid your share to the Reich, and the wine must not be touched."

Bombolini thought about the proposal, because there was in truth some merit in it.

"Then you would be the savior of the wine," he said.

"Yes, you can look at it that way. I have no interest in the wine. The wine is nothing to me. You know that. But now I would like to help your people. Give me the opportunity to save your wine for you."

Bombolini had gotten to his feet. He wanted to leave because he was afraid of doing something ridiculous or even dangerous.

"I cannot express how much I appreciate your generosity," he told the captain. "Only an extraordinary man could make such a proposal. It is with a sense of true sadness that I once again must tell you that there is no other wine."

There was nothing for them to say after that, and they looked for ways to leave one another.

"If you were a true host," Caterina said to Bombolini, "you would hide some wine so he could save it for you."

"Do you think a trick like that would work with Captain von Prum?" Bombolini said.

"Ask the captain," the Malatesta said, and Bombolini looked at him.

"No," Captain von Prum said.

Even the fear of the arrival of new Germans, possibly thousands of them, could not make itself felt here then. The only real fear left was Tufa. We were afraid of what he would do. If he killed Captain von Prum, even though the captain was dead to us already, the entire city could be made to pay the price for Tufa's honor. We were very thoughtless. We didn't think then that the one to pay the price would be someone else.

The German had called Bombolini for a second conversation, but it was never held. Before the mayor could cross the piazza he was stopped by the ringing of the bells and after that by Capoferro's drum and then by the people who came out of the houses into the piazza.

"The time has come," Capoferro shouted. "The time is now. Old Vines has made the test."

Von Prum came out of Constanzia's house and was forced to fight his way through the people who were running and shouting in the piazza then and getting the carts and animals ready.

"What's happening? What's wrong?" he asked Bombolini.

"Nothing's wrong," the mayor told him.

"I had wanted to see you about something important," von Prum said.

Bombolini gave him what we call the Fungo look, the eyes wide and staring and the mouth open.

"To hell with that," Bombolini said. "The harvest is on."

THERE IS *one* moment when it is right to begin to pick the grapes. One day too soon, and the grapes will have been deprived of all the richness that God intended them to receive; a day too late, and a touch of the devil's rot begins. On the right day the last of all the possible moisture has been taken from the air and the soil and the vines and the leaves and sent to the clusters of swollen fruit. The last bit of the sun has been absorbed by the leaves to warm the juice and cause the sugar to bulge against the skins. And when that balance is reached, which is known by men like Old Vines who have roots in the soil and their soul in the vines, the time has come to pick.

Nothing else exists for Santa Vittoria after that but the grapes.

404

There is no war, there is no other world. God doesn't exist, except as he lives in the grapes. The man who dies, for example, dies unnoticed and in silence. He goes unburied or, if the time is too long, the funeral is held and the mourners, usually only his immediate family, close the lid and run for the terraces. What tears are shed fall on the grapes and not on the grave. Children go unfed, but they understand they have no right to eat when the harvest is on. He who can move goes down to the terraces and cuts the fat grapes free from the vines and puts them in the baskets, which are carried to the carts and taken up the mountain to the wine presses where the grapes are pressed to death, only to be born in a new and beautiful form just as Christ was. The liquid runs clear and with no taste to it, into the great oak barrels which hold two thousand gallons each and are the pride of the city, since they hold the blood of the civic body. On the third day the liquid begins to storm (the word we use). The process of fermentation has begun and the grapes are struggling to be born again. The wine boils and hisses in the barrels like the waves at sea; the wine is storming. And when the storm is over, in a week or ten days, depending on the quality of the grapes, Old Vines will dip his glass into the barrel and hold it to the sun and at that moment we will know what the entire year has meant, whether we will go hungry in the winter ahead or eat when the rains and snow come.

On the morning of the day after the wine is tasted, the harvest festival begins. If the wine is good and plentiful, the harvest can be gay and even violent and wild; but if the wine is thin and the harvest is small, the festival can be sad and even bitter.

In the early days everyone works. Bombolini goes down to the terraces and sweats. Vittorini goes down. This year, for example, Roberto, although his leg pained him, worked with Rosa and Angela and the Casamassima family from dawn until dark and until he thought sometimes he would die. But he liked the work when it was not too painful. There was something satisfying about picking and holding the heavy clumps of ripe fruit, and he liked working by Angela's side, sweating together in the October sun, walking up the mountain together in the coolness of the evening. Once, next to her in the darkness of the leaves, without thinking about it, he put his hands on her hips and then around her waist and kissed her on the back of the neck, and she didn't turn or pull away or even move.

"You shouldn't do that," she said.

"Why not? I wanted to do it."

"We don't do that here. The boy who does that to the girl means he wants to marry her."

He had said nothing at the time, but later in the day he told her that maybe he would marry her.

"No." She pointed to her bare feet. "Americans don't marry girls with bare feet. Besides, what would I do there? I only know how to pick grapes."

"Do you know how to go to the movies?"

"Yes."

"You could go to the movies. You could sit in the movies all day and play the radio all night."

She thought about it. "No, I wouldn't like that. I like to pick the grapes."

"I was joking with you. They do more than that in America. You think about it."

"I like to pick the grapes. I like it here."

"You think."

To make up for the men who had been hurt by the SS, von Prum sent some of the soldiers down to work. Some of them had worked with grapes before and they were good at it. When Roberto saw Corporal Heinsick looking at Angela, watching her bend and straighten up and reach, he found that he wanted to shout at him. But then he went back to work.

There was excitement on the terraces. No one could remember heavier grapes and fatter grapes and bigger clusters. The baskets were the heaviest baskets ever and the presses were running behind, working finally by Longo's light far into the night, despite the threat of planes. All day the rich juice ran from the presses down the spillways into the barrels, a rush of wine filling the barrels more swiftly than they had ever been filled before. The wine was plentiful and if it was good too it could be the finest year in the memory of any person in Santa Vittoria.

There was excitement, but there was a humor too, since as the new wine began to run, thousands of gallons running from the presses and then a hundred thousand gallons washing down the wooden spillways, the answer to the first part of the secret, whether there was wine or not, was being spilled out in front of the Germans before their very eyes, and they were unable to see it, because they had no eyes for the wine.

When the harvest was almost over, when the vines were stripped so naked they looked indecent on the terraces, ravaged and even castrated, Bombolini decided on a daring thing. He went across the Piazza of the People and invited Captain von Prum and the soldiers to share in the harvest festival.

"I don't know. I understand it's like some kind of religious orgy. There's a great deal of drinking, and a kind of frenzy takes over. I don't think it would be a good idea," von Prum said.

"But it's a joyous frenzy," Bombolini told him. "There's no bitterness then. There are no enemies at the harvest festival. Not when the wine is rich."

"I'll give it thought," the German said.

"We've never had outsiders. It's in return for your offer about the wine. The people respected that."

Von Prum put a finger to his teeth and stared at the ceiling. "The people respected that," he said.

"They felt it was generous. We want you, in fact, to be honorary marshal of the festival."

"It's a very great honor," Caterina said.

"The greatest we have," the mayor said.

"What do you think?" the captain said to Caterina.

"I don't see how you can refuse," she said.

So Captain von Prum, in his soldiers' name, accepted the offer to come to the festival.

"I suppose you will want us in our dress uniforms," he said.

"It would honor the people," Bombolini said. "We're going to allow you to carry the statue of Santa Maria in the procession. And to press the last of the grapes. To tread on them in the old way, for tradition. The last of the wine."

"It's you who are generous," von Prum said. "You understand the art of forgiving. It is something I am only learning."

Bombolini prepared to go.

"Some of the traditions are a little strange and I hope you understand that," the mayor said. "It would dishonor the people if you didn't go along. We're very strong on our traditions."

Captain von Prum promised to obey.

HE WINE in the first of the barrels stopped boiling on the fifth day after the grapes had been pressed, and that meant that the harvest festival would be earlier than was usual. The nights were cool and heavy with fog, and the sediment in the barrels began to drift to the bottom and the wine to turn clear and cool.

All of the grapes except the ones that would be used for the traditional wine pressing had already been picked. The hanging grapes, the ones the women pick and save for the long winter when there is no fresh produce were hanging all over the city, from the stairs, over the door tops, bunches and clusters and mounds and bubbles of grapes hanging from every hook and nail on every wall in Santa Vittoria. On the night of the ninth day after the pressing had begun, Old Vines dipped his wine taster into one of the barrels, and the wine he drew out was almost clear.

"Get ready. Prepare yourselves," Old Vines ordered. "I taste the wine in the morning."

It is hard to put down what goes on here then. The line at the fountain was fifty women long because everyone wants to wash and even take a bath before the festival. Three men were sent off to get Lorenzo the Magnificent, Lorenzo the Wine Presser and bring him back with them. Three more were sent to San Marco della Rocca to get the band that always plays for us in return for a small barrel of new wine. Others went to get Marotta the Blaster, who would set off the fireworks with his son. It hurt us to have to hire someone from Scarafaggio although it was something to know that Marotta had not been born there and as such was not a true product of the place.

"Get to bed, go to sleep," all the mothers shouted; but it is almost a law here that no child sleeps the night before the festival. The old ladies, whose job it is, began to get out the straw hats for the oxen and the mules and to go pick flowers that they make into chains to hang around the beasts' necks. Some went down and got vines for a garland for the statue of Santa Maria and grape leaves to dress her in.

The young girls work on their hair and dresses, and the older ones try to make the traditional costumes respectable for one more time. The men do almost nothing. They scrape the mud and the manure from their boots and feet, and get out their black suits, those who own them, and they stand about and talk about the wine, over and over, endlessly, never tiring of it, saying the same things again and again as if they had just been invented.

They talk about whether it will be thin or fat, as black as night or as red as the eye of a pigeon, sharp or round, heavy or light, and whether it will have the true bouquet of the fruit, and most important, whether the wine this year will have the true *frizzantino*—the thing that makes the needles jump on the tongue and causes that stinging dance that all good wine makes in the mouth.

There is no drinking that night, so that the head will be clear, the hand steady, and the mouth purified for the new wine in the morning. Many of the men keep a watch around the fountain all night long in honor of the wine. They torture themselves then about how bad the wine will be in the morning, how rotten it will taste and how it will wound the taste buds on their tongues

"There's no reason for it to be good. Do you remember the cold rains two weeks ago? What else can you expect. It murdered the grapes."

It is as if one good word might cause the wine god to make it turn in the night. And it is protection: if you expect nothing at all, how can you be hurt? But also one must be humble before the wine, one must expect only the worst, one must present one's ass to the gods, as they say, and demand that it be kicked.

At two o'clock that morning, at the darkest time of the night, most of the women were up. Some of the animals, already draped in their flowers, decked in vines and wrapped in grape leaves, were wandering through the piazza not knowing what to do with themselves now that there were no more baskets to carry up the mountain. They were like the men.

"Even the krauts wouldn't want to steal this wine," someone said.

"Well, we can always sell it for vinegar."

All along the walls of the piazza children were sprawled out on the stones, curled in chilled balls, waiting for the dawn, because they were afraid of missing something in the morning. They knew what they were about, because had they been home warm in their beds they might have missed the first sounds that came roaring up the Corso Cavour.

It began, the day of the festival, in the darkness of the morning at a few minutes past four o'clock.

It didn't begin in the sense that a day usually begins, by degrees, a little at a time; it began all at once. It erupted; the day exploded on us.

A child ran into the Piazza of the People.

"Here they come," he shouted. "I saw them. They're at the Fat Gate now."

And right after that we heard them coming up the Corso Cavour as if they were trumpeting through a megaphone. The San Marco Penitentiary Thieves and Guards Brass Band. They must have walked the whole dark night through, good men, reliable men who have never let us down, down the mountain from San Marco della Rocca, out through the prison gates, across the valley and up our mountain until there they were, at the Fat Gate, blowing their lungs and hearts out in the last darkness of night, drowning out the children, overcoming the frightened bleating of the sheep and the tunking of ox bells, the sound of the guns we no longer noticed firing to the south, even outcrying the cocks, who had had their morning stolen from them.

"All Hail Garibaldi" at four o'clock in the morning, "Italy Forever" coming up out of the pipe of the street at ten minutes past four, "The March of the Alpini Brigade" near the top of the Corso, and by the time they got to the piazza and began to march into it, "Garibaldi" once more. There were a thousand people there to shout a welcome to them.

Eight men in all, eight in green-and-gold uniforms, eight good musicians, some of the finest thieves and bravest guards in all of Italy, five thieves and three guards, one piccolo, one trombone, one clarinet, two trumpets, cymbals, one bass drum, who would be supported by our own Capoferro, and the leader, the maestro Stompinetti, the Rock of San Marco, who had spent two years in Cleveland, Ohio, and knew all about it.

Bombolini welcomed them to the city of Santa Vittoria.

"I heard you were mayor and I never could believe it," Stompinetti said.

"The best we ever had," Pietro Pietrosanto said.

"Ah, well, I've heard crazier than that," the Rock said. "So you're the mayor. God bless the mayor, God bless the people, God bless the wine." He had a great voice, as big as the trombone he blew.

Polenta came out of the bell tower and with him were some of the older men of the town, dressed in their black suits and holding a canvas canopy over the priest's head to shield the silver chalice which was filled with the Eucharistic wafers. Everyone takes Communion on the festival morning, even if their souls are as spotted as their suits and as stained as the men who work the wine press. In a few minutes he would hold the Mass of the Grapes.

The people prepared to file into Santa Maria, when there was a command in German from Constanzia's house, and then a second, and finally the German soldiers began to file out into the piazza, lined up in rows of two. On a command from Captain von Prum they began to march in the direction of the church.

They were dressed in their parade uniforms, the only time they had worn them since the cobbler's execution. The leather on their wide black belts was polished as was the leather of their boots, and the silver buckles which say *"Gott mit Uns"* shone. They carried their rifles slung over the shoulder, carried bayonets and trench knives in scabbards and wore their metal helmets. Only Vittorini could outshine them. They marched, a parade march, a slow goose step in which they came to almost a complete halt before banging their hobnails down on the cobblestones again. Capoferro picked up their step—*brrrrrrm bang, brrrrrmmmm bang*—and the piccolo player played a sad lament for the dead. The Germans were impressive. At the church door Vittorini made a salute, and Bombolini welcomed them as guests of honor at the festival.

"As a representative of the German people and the German nation, we are honored to accept," Captain von Prum said.

"Wait until the Resistance gets their hands on this Bombolini," Stompinetti said. "What kind of an Italian is this. Why didn't he get down in the piazza and kiss his ass while he was about it?"

"Wait," the people around him said. "Just wait. He knows what he's doing."

The Mass was swift. Polenta had never been a believer in the long Mass. It was his belief that if God wanted to come down and bless the grapes and wine He would come down whether we spent an hour on our knees or ten minutes. The Mass was over in fifteen minutes.

On the way out of Santa Maria they could see the statue resting in the back of a large open cart, hung with clusters of red and white grapes, entwined with vines and dressed with thousands of grape leaves which fluttered in the early morning wind. And which soon, Padre Polenta hoped, would be further dressed with lire and even some dollar bills and bank checks from the Bank of America.

"The spirit of the harvest," Bombolini said to von Prum.

"We honor it," the German said.

At the foot of the church steps a large black wooden coffin was placed on two wine barrels.

"The first of our traditions," the mayor said. "It holds the corpse of the old year gone by. We destroy the old year and in that way give birth to the new that lies ahead."

"Very beautiful," von Prum said. "Very symbolic."

"Would you and your men care to act as honor guard?"

"We should be honored."

It is not an old tradition. The priest who had been here before Polenta had seen the tradition in another city and had borrowed it for ours. From the church door there is a wire and the wire runs from the church, down the steps and through an opening into the coffin. For reasons we no longer are sure of, a white dove is attached to the wire and then sent skidding down into the black box. When the bird goes through the opening it trips another wire, which sets off a bag of explosive powder, which in turn explodes the coffin. The Germans had stationed themselves alongside the box, three soldiers on each side, von Prum and his noncommissioned officers a little in front of it.

"The old is dead," Padre Polenta said from the top of the church steps.

"The new," the priest called out—and the dove began to skid down the wire, tied to it upside down by his pink feet—"is born."

The noise is raspy and sometimes the dove cries out, but it made no sound this year. The explosion, however, was as loud and complete as ever. Pieces of the coffin went straight up into the air and others flew out in all directions into the piazza. The smoke was so dense that from the center of the piazza it became impossible to see the front of Santa Maria. When it did clear we could see the Germans, all nine of them, face down on the piazza stones, mingling with ox turds, and several of them, better trained than the others perhaps, with their rifles already in their hands, kneeling and facing the people. There was a great cheer then, an enormous cheer from the people, because this officially opens the *festa*.

Some of the people ran to help the soldiers to their feet, and they tried to brush the manure and the axle grease off their uniforms, but without much success. Bombolini said something to the captain and he smiled and patted him on the back, but nobody was actually able to hear what he said because of the roaring in their ears.

In the center of the piazza, near the fountain, a platform had been built in the night and on it stood the first of the wine barrels, and by the barrel stood Old Vines. He looked then as he always did, as if he were about to be sentenced to his death and be dropped through the platform floor. Padre Polenta said a prayer and then a young girl, all white in her Communion dress, took a copper pitcher and turned the barrel tap and filled the pitcher with wine, and when it was full she handed it to Old Vines. There was no sound at all in Santa Vittoria then. Even the animals, who exist by the wine as much as we do, seem to know enough to be silent then. He held the pitcher in the air and then he began to pour the new wine into a large crystal wine glass which he then held over his head, the way the priest holds up the chalice before consecrating the sacred Host, and he turned in all four directions.

"It is *vino nero*," Old Vines called out. "Good and black." There was a roar from the crowd, but not a great one. It was a good sign, but not enough.

Now he lifts the glass to his lips and the people push forward, because they demand not only to see it but to hear the wine washing around in his mouth and being kissed by his tongue and lips, and then he spits it out and no one moves.

They knew it was good. He could not hide the look that began to spread out on his red face. The question now was, How good?

"*Frizzantino*," the old man shouted. And then there was the roar, the true roar, almost as great as the one that had greeted Bombolini so many months before.

"The wine is alive," he shouted. "It dances." He took more of the wine. This he swallowed.

"The needles on the tongue."

"Give us, give us," the people shouted. They reached up for the wine glass but he didn't give it to them then.

"It's as fresh as the air," he shouted. "It tastes like the sun in the sky." He had never spoken this way of the wine before. He told

415

them that the wine was fat but at the same time light, that it was fruity and yet not sweet, and that the bouquet was strong enough to drown the brain.

"It is a good wine," he said. The first of the desirable categories.

"It is a great wine." The cheering grew louder. They waited for the third category that is almost never awarded.

"It is a wine too good for men to drink," Old Vines told them. He was holding the glass up to the gods that only he recognized.

"We have grown a wine fit for the saints."

No one cheered then; it was a moment for reverence, it had gone beyond cheering.

As we do, the oldest of each family comes forward with a pitcher and the pitcher is filled at the barrel and the wine is taken back to the family and sipped and tasted and then drunk by all, from the oldest down to the youngest. When all the families had tried the wine the San Marco Brass Band broke into some gay song from the mountains to the south of here, and the time for reverence was past, and the uproar began in the piazza.

"Now comes a real treat," Bombolini shouted into von Prum's ear. "No outsiders have ever done this before. You are going to be allowed to help carry the statue of Santa Maria."

Teams of men carry the statue and it is considered an honor to be chosen. There are eight men to a team and each year three teams are chosen. With Polenta in the lead, the statue is carried around the Piazza of the People and then down the Corso Cavour through the Fat Gate and across the terraces. As he goes the priest blesses the doorways and the windows and on the terraces he blesses the last of the grapes of this harvest and the roots of the vines for the harvest to come.

It is not a heavy statue, but the distance is long, and when the day is hot it can prove to be work fit only for the strong. To many, carrying the statue is a kind of penance. It was as if they were saying to God, "I sweat for you, You sweat for me." It is also one of the ugliest statues in all of Italy and possibly the world. It was made of wax and cheap paint and plaster a hundred years ago in Montefalcone, and when a team of men left here to get it, on the way back they stopped in a roadside inn for some wine and left the statue out in the sun and the rain and it melted and turned black. When the people saw it they were horrified.

"No, no," the men who had carried it said. "It was a miracle. This must be the way Santa Maria really looked, all black and roasted. It was God's wish."

To this very day the city is divided between those who think Santa Maria's melting was a miracle and those who think the melting was a simple case of drunkenness, stupidity, lying and criminal neglect. The two groups are called the Miracles and the Melters.

It was also hollow, whether by design or by deceit has never been known.

The first team carried the statue all the way down the Corso Cavour, and the people came out and pinned lire to the statue, and those who had no money left food in her arms and put things in the cart that came along behind.

At the Fat Gate a second team took over the statue and it went down to the terraces. Most of the men were older men, some as old as sixty, but they held the statue high and went down the mountain and through the grapes at a good pace. Young girls were picking the last of the grapes and the German soldiers, getting into the spirit of things, helped them fill the baskets.

"You had better take it easy," Pietrosanto warned them. "You're going to be next with the statue."

"If those old men can carry it, we can carry it," Heinsick told him.

"They know how to do it. It's harder than it looks," Bombolini said. "They've done this for years."

"With one hand," one of the soldiers said. "One hand."

"I don't know," Pietrosanto said. Heinsick called Zopf over and told him to roll up his shirt sleeve. He had an arm the thickness of a man's leg. "One of your Bavarian oxes," the corporal said proudly. Heinsick himself was built like a bull.

In the center of the terraces the statue was set down on the cart to rest and the men and women and the soldiers walked across through the vineyards for the blessing of the vines. When the prayers were done and they came back, Bombolini asked Captain von Prum if his men were ready to accept the honor of carrying the statue.

"We have been looking forward to it," von Prum said, and the people applauded.

They lifted it up easily and put it on their shoulders and they started back up through the terraces at a good pace. It is traditional after the prayers for the people to sing their way back up to the town and the band plays, following along behind, because the sacred time is over and the wine waits in the piazza and the pressing of the last grapes will begin, and the greased-pole climb still lies ahead.

The Germans were good about it at first. The people here can't keep step, but the soldiers never lost a beat. Sergeant Traub counted the cadence even though he was one of the men under the statue.

"One two three four, one two three four"—in German, loud and clear and strong.

"You had better save your breath," Bombolini warned him, but the sergeant smiled and kept on shouting. It went very well then for at least a hundred steps, but after that Traub ceased to count and then the steps slowed a little and the band, to keep in time, had to play a little slower and the people had to sing a little slower, so after fifty more paces they ceased playing "Garibaldi" and began to play the "Lament for Sardinia," a sad slow song about some thieves who starved to death in the mountains there. Soon some of the people, even older men, impatient to get up to the piazza, began to go past the men carrying the statue and the men carrying it began to fall back.

"What's the matter with you?" von Prum called to them. "Keep it moving. Pick up the step."

For a short time after that, through a strong show of effort, they were able to pick up the step and Traub began to count again, in a small voice. But then it seemed to be too much for them once more and the step slowed and finally, still a long way from the Fat Gate, it ceased to be what could be called a step or a march at all but became a kind of clump, the way a tired man on a steep mountain puts down his feet, one after the other, with great deliberation.

418

"Close it up, pick it up," von Prum said. "You're disgracing yourselves."

It didn't work this time, however. The pace remained the same.

"I told you you shouldn't have picked the grapes," Pietrosanto said. "You were supposed to take it to the Fat Gate but I think that we should relieve you now."

The captain wouldn't consider it.

"It's these uniforms, sir," Corporal Heinsick said. "They're strangling us."

Heinsick's face was the color of our wine, *vino nero*, red, a deep, rich red, almost purple, almost black in the deepness of its redness. All their faces were red and sweat was streaming down them, salt in their eyes and on their lips and in their mouths, which was hard to get rid of because the men were gasping and sucking so hard for air.

"My heart is going to explode," Goettke suddenly shouted.

"Quiet," von Prum said.

"If the wops can do it, we can do it," Heinsick said. No one answered him.

"The first man to drop out receives a summary court martial," von Prum said, in a low voice that only his men were meant to hear.

It is a true thing that if the desire to live were enough, no man, for example, would ever drown. But there comes a time when the body can no longer do even what it deeply desires. The Germans' legs were quivering and it was only a matter of a few more steps before at least one of the sixteen legs would quiver too much and go under, which is what happened. The result was the same as missing a stroke with the oar of a boat. For one moment they stopped and teetered, they started to go back and held themselves and they ran forward a step or two, and there was a second at least when they came within a foot of the edge of the cart track and plunging down into the terraces with Santa Maria on their backs.

"The sacred statue," Bombolini shouted. "In the name of God, hold it."

The old women began to cry out. They shouted to the Mother of God to reach down and save Santa Maria, for Santa Maria to

419

save herself, and in the end the Germans held, although the veins were sticking out on their foreheads and their eyes were bulging.

"Who did it?" von Prum shouted.

"Me, sir," Goettke said. "I can't go on."

"Get out then," the captain said, and he pulled the soldier away and took his place beneath the statue.

"It's not so heavy," the captain said. "What's wrong with you men? I know what it is, too much wine drinking."

He was a tonic to them, for five steps. A man with a leg such as Captain von Prum possessed should never allow himself to get under a statue. Since his legs were not even, at every second step the statue would shift slightly and rest on his shoulder and it was as if an iron bar were pressing down on him, all the way from the shoulder to the bad leg, and trying to press him into the hard white clay.

"You are doing fine," Bombolini shouted in his ear. "Only four hundred more steps to go."

At those words Captain von Prum, for at least the second time in Santa Vittoria, looked into the face of failure. If they could cover one hundred more steps it would be something more than a triumph. But it would be a man who was not honest with himself, the kind of man who when someone spits in his face denies that he has been insulted, who would deny that the Germans did not go down without a great fight.

"All right," von Prum shouted at them. "We are going to go *up*. At three, we step off again. One, two, three, *step*," he called out. "*Step. . . . Step. . . . Step.*"

One of the soldiers, each time the captain called out Step, answered, "I die, I die, I die."

"Only three hundred and fifty more, Captain," Bombolini told him.

No one could say why they stopped. It is said that in a war no one can say why an attack stops. Each soldier has his own reason and his own limit, but all at once the attack stops. It was that way with the burden of Santa Vittoria.

"*Step*," the captain called out, and no one took a step. They stood where they were, and the statue shook with the effort simply to keep it from falling.

Six young men then—it was important to Bombolini that there were six and not eight—eased the poles off the Germans' shoulders and not one of them made a protest, not even Captain von Prum, and they slung the statue on their shoulders and started up toward the Fat Gate at a fast pace and even managed to break into a trot. Stompinetti saw them coming, and he broke into a Neapolitan quick step, and they went the rest of the way up to the Fat Gate as if they were going home for their soup.

The Germans fell where they had stood. They sprawled out in the white dust of the cart track and stared up at the sky, unable to move, or curled up in the dust to stop the shaking of their muscles. They were still that way when Lorenzo the Magnificent, the one who was to press our grapes in the old way, came up the mountain with the men who had gone to get him.

Lorenzo is mad, by his own admission he is mad, but he is also, as his name says, magnificent. There is no man in the world who does not recognize that Lorenzo is something very special and is not afraid of him or impressed by him. He is like a steel coil, all of him, his body and his mind drawn so fine and hard, pressed always so close to the breaking point, that if he ever breaks, pieces of himself will fly all over Italy.

"What's the matter with these bastards lying in the dust?" Lorenzo said.

"Quiet. They're Germans," one of the men with him said.

"I can see that. All I asked was why they were lying in the dust like pigs."

He went on, because he was late; but not one of them said anything in return or even looked at him when he talked.

"They look as if the Resistance got to them," one of the men with Lorenzo said.

"They look like Fabio and Cavalcanti after the SS got through with them," del Purgatorio said. "They look as if they have been tortured."

And this was true. When Lorenzo got up to the Piazza of the People, the statue of Santa Maria, which had been carried by nine or ten different groups by then, was being placed up on the platform on which Old Vines had first tasted the wine that morning. And when they were sure that none of the Germans had managed to recover and come back inside the Fat Gate, they took out the great boulder that had been put in the saint's belly and dropped it in a cart and took it away so that it would never be seen again. After that they carried Santa Maria back into the dimness of the church and put her back up on her dark dim pedestal, where Polenta began to strip her of the grapes and the vines and the lire that had honored her. She had served her people well.

FOR THE Germans the day seemed to have ended, but the festival was only beginning. There was the noon meal of cold cooked beans and raw onions spread on fresh bread and drowned in olive oil and then there was the new wine washing it down, buckets and glasses and pitchers and bottles and jugs of wine, and everyone went around shouting "*frizzantino* . . . yes, it is true, it is really truly *frizzantino*," as if the word had just been invented, until it became boring to hear, beautiful as the word is.

After lunch the people slept, except for those who still had business to do. Longo and a crew of men were converting the Fountain of the Pissing Turtle so that it would run with wine that evening. Marotta and his son were preparing the fireworks display, and Lorenzo, with some of our young men, was putting up the enormous barrel in which the last of the grapes would be pressed. The members of the San Marco Penitentiary Brass Band, having had at least five pitchers of wine each, slept in the piazza shadows with their instruments cradled in their arms.

At four o'clock the fountain began to run with wine and when the men cheered, the people began to wake up and come back into the piazza. The wine arched out above their heads, sparkling in the afternoon sunlight, and fell back into the barrel from which it had been pumped, foaming and bubbling and leaping with life. When the first of the Germans, Captain von Prum and Sergeant Traub, came back up into the Piazza of the People the fountain was already flowing with wine, the band was ready to play again and Lorenzo the Magnificent Wine Presser was standing knee deep in our grapes. It was a little after four o'clock when Marotta received the signal from Old Vines and fired a Roman candle out over the people's heads. As the little colored balls of flame began to hit the walls and drop among them, Stompinetti broke into the "Wine Presser's Song" and the festa was underway once more.

It is a strange song, a slow dance, since wine pressing is hard and heavy work. It seems very ancient and as if it had come from some other part of the world, because we have no other song like it. The trampling of the grapes must be done in a slow rhythm, in a swaying movement that goes back and forth and side to side more than up and down. There is a genius to everything in the world and Lorenzo was this way with the grapes. He knows how to make people use themselves to take from the grapes all that God put in them.

He began the dance as he always did, with his own woman, a Gypsy who looks as if she had spent one life already as a wolf, and when she was tired and he was through with her, he began to point at people in the crowd and they would come up and get into the barrel and begin to dance with Lorenzo. There is no turning away when you are summoned to the press. It would insult the wine and it would insult Lorenzo, neither of whom must be insulted. Anything is allowed to Lorenzo. The women hold up their skirts and show their legs and even their thighs, and Lorenzo holds them by the hands and by the arms and around their waists.

If the legs are good, strong and firm and brown and muscled, the men cheer the legs and the women shout suggestive things that any other time of the year would not be allowed.

He doesn't dress the way our men do. He wears very tight pants, like a bullfighter's. They stop at the knee and are very revealing, and it embarrasses the women and even some of the men, and then it is forgotten when the dancing begins. His chest is covered only by a vest that is decorated with silver and gold threads, and his arms and his chest are as hard as bone. But it is his face and his eyes that people watch. As the dance continues, Lorenzo becomes possessed by the motion of it, and finally he is mad and at the same moment under control. He seems to see everything at once and yet nothing at all. He doesn't seem like any of us then; he is superior to us then, and any man will admit it. He is a kind of god then, a god of the country towns, who looks like a faun and a goat and a man all in one. There is no end to his energy, he can dance on and on, because, as they say, he isn't human then, he is an animal and a god.

"You," he points, and the woman comes and he seizes her by the wrist, the strong brown hands with the stiff hair on the backs closing over the woman's hands, and they begin to move to the music, sometimes face to face or side by side, swaying to the music which is slow but not sad, sinking into the grapes and the juice that flows over their stained feet.

"Watch out for your women or you will lose them to me," Lorenzo suddenly shouts.

It is meaningless, because all women are lost to Lorenzo the minute the music begins. Every woman knows this and Lorenzo knows it and all of the men in Santa Vittoria know it. He dances with a woman until she yields to him, until she surrenders herself completely and he can move her to the left or right or in any way he wishes her to go, by a flicker of the eye, a breath, the touch of a finger. She belongs to Lorenzo then, and when she does he discards her.

The same goes for the men. It is a challenge with the men, and he never loses. He dances not until the man surrenders, but until the man can go on no longer. Then, when the moment is right,

Lorenzo flings the man aside and the people shout and jeer at the victim, and he goes on to the next. He had been dancing for almost an hour, which is a very long time to be in the wine press without resting, when he motioned for Angela Bombolini to come into the press. The men applauded her legs, and it surprised Bombolini. Why should they cheer the legs of a little girl, he thought. Angela is young and strong, she has her mother's arms and back, and it was a good battle. The others dancing at the far side of the barrel even stopped to watch, although it is supposed to be against the rules. Her eyes were very wide and bright, and at first she danced with Lorenzo but not for him. He looked into her eyes and she looked into his, and people could see that her eyes still belonged to her and not to him. But he has a way of reaching for what he wants to touch that cannot be resisted by a woman. It was not a fair contest. Angela's face was innocence at first, but there was the moment—and everyone knew exactly when it took place—when the face of innocence was replaced by something else and Angela began to dance for Lorenzo and the barrier that had been between them and held them apart was broken and down. She could not pull herself away from him or from his eyes or his hands. It is almost embarrassing to say that at that moment he could have done anything he wished with her, in full view of the town, and Angela would have accepted it. Her mouth began to open and he began to smile at her and she to smile at him, and there was no one else in the world then.

"She's no virgin now," a woman shouted. Bombolini turned to look at her.

"It's no use, Italo. He's making love to her with his eyes," a man said to the mayor, and he was forced to look away. In the door of the wineshop he could see his wife smiling. They were all alike in the end, he thought, every single one of them. He turned back again. The sweat was running down his daughter's face and it stained the embroidered linen blouse that was a girl's blouse and too small for her, and when he turned away once more because it was too much for a father to see—such things should take place in private—he saw Roberto at the side of the wine press, gripping the wooden staves and staring at Angela in amazement and anger.

He knew what Roberto was going to do, and he pushed through the people until he was behind him and he held him back.

"Don't get in there, Roberto," he whispered in his ear. "You can't get in until you are invited."

"But he's . . . he's . . ."

"I know that," Bombolini said. "It's what happens here. Do you think it's any easier for the father to watch?"

They both looked down, and as they did there was a shout from the crowd. He had released her, he had taken his fill of Angela, the surrender was total, the victory complete. She stood alone among the grapes as another woman came up into the press, and when the world began to come back to her she shook her head as if she had come back from a long sleep, or a dream even, and still unsteady she began to wade across the grapes to the side of the press.

"Angela," Roberto said. He cried the name. He held up his arms to help her over the side and out of the barrel, but she didn't see him. He said her name once more, and she didn't hear him say it. Instead, she climbed over the side of the barrel and down onto the cobblestones, her bare feet dripping with the juice of the grapes, and went past his arms and into those of Fabio della Romagna. No one except Roberto and Bombolini saw them, because there was something greater to watch. Captain von Prum had come out of the doorway of Constanzia's house. He had washed himself and changed into a fresh uniform, and he looked like the captain once more. Behind him in the doorway was Caterina Malatesta, and Lorenzo saw her and made a motion with his head.

"Stay where you are," von Prum said. "I don't want you to go."

"I have to go. He's seen me. It would insult the wine and insult the festival."

"I don't want you to go," the German said; but there was no way to stop her and he knew it. She started across the piazza and it grew quiet. The music played, but the others in the barrel stopped dancing and then they began to get out of the barrel. It would be a battle, because everyone could see at once what it was, the hawk against the goat, the hawk against the faun, the two of them alike, and unlike anyone else here, born a thousand years before any of us, these pagans, as alone and distant as the animals they reminded us of.

There is no way to describe the dancing of Lorenzo and the Malatesta. Her legs are long and very strong and her feet are narrow and long, and this is good for the grapes. There were times when she seemed to dance on top of them, to be free of them, and it was a help to her. He had clapped his hand around her wrist with a force that could be heard all over the piazza, and it was understood that he would never let the wrist go until he had won. And he did win, and we learned why.

The hawk is cold and aloof and dangerous, but there is something about a goat that must win, because the goat is better than the hawk and worse than the hawk, the goat will try anything; he will climb to the top of any mountain to get what he is after, and he will grovel in the manure pile, he will be bold and weak, stupid and wise, beautiful and ugly, mean and gentle, and in the end the goat will win because the goat always wants something more than a hawk wants it. Lorenzo wanted her more than the Malatesta wished to deny him.

"You are good," the Malatesta said. "You win."

"I am truly great," Lorenzo said.

He helped her to the side of the press and lifted her over it. It was the greatest honor he ever gave to anyone in Santa Vittoria. He was tired after that, because it had not been easy for him. There are years Lorenzo dances without a rest, but in some he has stopped and allowed the Gypsy to dance in his place. He wanted to rest then, but the German was in the wine press.

"Try me," von Prum said. "Dance with me."

"I'm tired now," Lorenzo said. "It wasn't easy."

"Try me," he ordered. Lorenzo shrugged his shoulders and went back across the barrel toward the captain.

"Take off your boots," he said. "You bruise the grapes."

He took off his boots and his woolen socks, and the women near the press said "Aaah" at the narrow whiteness of his feet.

"Take off your shirt. You're going to need to," Lorenzo said. They made the sound again when they saw the smooth whiteness of his arms and chest. He was not a weak man, but against Lorenzo's hard darkness he seemed like a child pitted against a man.

"You needn't hold my wrist," von Prum said.

"I need to," the goat said. "You won't know how to move in the grapes." His fingers closed on the German's wrist and he was locked to him.

They began to dance.

She didn't wish to see it, to watch him be humiliated in front of the people. There is something that is not amusing about the humiliation of a German. But it was something else, also, as if she knew that Tufa would be waiting for her in Constanzia's house when she went back to it. He was behind the door, in the darkness of the room, when she entered it. Even in the darkness she could see the wildness of his eyes. They were as wild as those of Lorenzo, but these were wild with loss and so were more dangerous.

"If you're going to do something to me I want you to do it at once, without talking," Caterina said to him. She could see that he held a knife in his hand.

"And so you gave yourself to him, too," Tufa said. "In front of the entire city."

"All women give themselves to Lorenzo. I'm no different."

"If he had asked you would have taken off your dress and lain with him in the grapes."

She said nothing.

"Admit it," he said. "Admit that."

"Yes, of course," Caterina said. "You know how I am."

He crossed the room and stood at the entrance to the small bedroom.

"And this is where you sleep with him," Tufa said. His voice held anger and disgust.

"What do you want to do with me?" Caterina asked. "What do you need from me?"

There was laughter coming from the piazza, and she knew they were laughing at the captain. Tufa had gone into the room and he was prodding the bed with the toe of his shoe.

"So this is where you curl up with the German? What do you say to him." He came back toward her. "Maybe sometimes you forget and call him Carlo, eh? Do you ever do that?"

She had turned away. She realized that she was bored, not by him, but by the necessity of going through with whatever it was Tufa would have to go through.

"Don't go away from me," Tufa said. He had meant it as an order, but it had come from his mouth as a plea.

"Do what you have to do, Carlo. If you have to use the knife, use the knife, but in the name of God, do it."

It angered him.

"You're so Goddamn brave. You're so above us," Tufa said. "Do you know what they do here when a woman dishonors her man? Do you know what they do with their knives?"

She turned back toward Tufa. "They cut them here," she said. "So they can't dishonor again."

"Yes, there," Tufa said. "It's very ugly and very effective."

She decided to try.

"I didn't dishonor you," Caterina said. "I came here because I honor your life."

It angered him. "You stole my honor from me," he shouted at her. "Who do you think you are, to take what is *mine?*"

She was bored with him at last, with the enraged eyes and the hurt voice and the words of honor. It is said that the most dangerous bulls are the bored bulls because they force the bullfighter to do something unwise and even dangerous. Tufa had come to cut her, but now he wished to kill her.

She told him, because she was bored and because she didn't care what became of herself any longer, that he was the same as the German, that they were the same man, that he didn't have the dignity of the fat mayor or the courage of the young boy Fabio.

"When all of this was over I wouldn't have come back," Caterina said.

"You would have come back," Tufa said. He was nodding his head, over and over again, and she knew he was dangerous, and although she didn't care she also experienced fear. "But I wouldn't have had you. I would have done this," Tufa shouted. The shout would have been heard in the piazza but for the music, which was loud and fast then, and the laughter of the people watching the German being dishonored in the wine press. The knife entered her stomach. The pain was not as bad as she had thought it would be, and the feeling she felt above all others was relief that it was over. She knew also that she would live.

All of Tufa's anger was gone. He pointed to the wound.

"Every man you give yourself to will know why that was done," Tufa said. "They'll hate you for it."

"No, some man will love me for it," the Malatesta said.

On the floor was a leather suitcase which had belonged to Caterina and in which Tufa had put some of his things. All of his rage was gone.

"I'm sorry I had to do that, but it was something that had to be done," Tufa said.

"I understand," Caterina said. "Don't apologize to me." There was a great deal of blood from the wound, but she was unwilling to tend to it until he was gone.

"I have my honor back," Tufa said. He had picked up the suitcase. The people were making a great deal of noise, and it would be a good time for him to go. "You were brave but I have my honor back."

"Go," she said. "For God's sake go." He stood in the doorway.

"I'm sorry," Tufa said. "But it had to be done."

It was necessary to stop the bleeding then, and she went back into the bedroom and took the bed sheet, and when she came back he was still there.

"What do you want of me?" she shouted at Tufa. "Do you want your knife back? Is that what you want?"

He said her name. It was an effort for him, and he couldn't say what he wanted, but at that moment she understood.

"I see," she said. "You want me to forgive you." She couldn't see in that light whether he nodded his head, but she knew.

"All right, I forgive you," Caterina said. "People who do such things shouldn't ask for forgiveness, but I forgive you, Tufa."

When he was gone she stopped the flow of blood, and she found her medicine bag. The cut was clean, and she was able to sew it with the good gut provided by the German army and to bandage it with the good bandages provided by them as well. All during that time she could hear the sound of the brass band playing in the piazza and the crazy old man beating on his drum, always a little behind the beat of the music, which for some reason comforted her. When she was through she changed her clothes, and when she went to the doorway to look into the piazza she was pleased to find that her legs trembled no more than when she had climbed out of the wine press a half hour before. It was beginning to grow dark in the piazza.

If Lorenzo had allowed the German to drop, he would have dropped down into the grapes and the must but Lorenzo held the German in his arms and he danced him. It was ugly to watch the way he did it, making a puppet of a human being and dancing him the way a child will dance a doll.

"All right, I want to sit now," the German said. "I want to rest." But Lorenzo didn't want him to sit or rest, he wanted him when he let him go to drop in the grapes and to lie in them and not be able to get up. It is hard to get up from the grapes. A short time after the Malatesta came to the door of Constanzia's house, Lorenzo let him drop and he fell face forward onto the grapes. The German tried to get up, but each time the grapes gave way and shifted beneath him and he fell again and again, until he could no longer make even the effort to rise. The barrel had held wine before and some of it blended with the fresh juice, the must of the grapes, and it stained him, the soft wool of his pants turned the color of wine, and his chest and face were as red as any of the wine in the cellar.

"Turn him over," Bombolini called to Lorenzo. "He'll drown in it."

"Let him drown," people shouted. "Let him drown."

Lorenzo reached down and took the German by his belt and turned him over, because even Lorenzo, who doesn't come from here, knew that we can't afford to have people drown in our wine. The fireworks began to go off then, and had von Prum been able to open his eyes from his bed of grapes he could have seen the first of the rockets soar up out of Santa Vittoria.

That should have been the end but the people here are vulgar about such things. They have no sense of the niceties of events. And then, a man of honor is condemned to die many times, just the same as a man without humor.

There still remained that night, besides the dancing, the climbing of the greased poles. Two tall, thin poles are put up in the piazza and at the top of each is tied a young pig. Two teams are chosen from the young men of the city, and the first to get their man to the top of the pole and steal the pig is named the King of the Festival and his teammates are his court, and they can do almost what they wish for the remainder of the night. It is not easy. Many years no team manages to reach the pig, and the festival is left without a king.

No one in Santa Vittoria thought that the Germans would accept another honor, this one to compete. But perhaps it was because they thought that by winning they might restore the honor they had lost, or perhaps it was that by competing for the pig they would make it plain that nothing had happened to them.

At eight o'clock, before supper and the dancing, the teams were chosen. We build a large fire then, before the two poles, and the poles are greased with the fat of freshly killed ox. There are many ways to get up the poles—to fly at them, to fling a young man up in the air against the pole and hope when he catches it, if he catches it, that he can hold onto it and then go up. There are all kinds of ways to fail. It is to the Germans' credit that when they agreed to compete they did not ask the people here for advice but went about the problem in their own way. They were systematic about it. At eight o'clock, when the contest began, four soldiers formed a square and two soldiers got on top of the four soldiers and then Captain von Prum, using the fountain as his pedestal, since he was the lightest of them, sat on the shoulders of the two soldiers on top. We were horrified when we saw that. They began to inch their way across the piazza from the fountain, past the fire, and it appeared that von Prum already was as high as the pig on top of the pole. But when he was next to the pole it could be seen that several feet, perhaps three or four, still separated him from the pig. Instead of throwing their top man to the pole in the manner we use to gain an extra foot or two, the Germans simply deposited the captain on the pole and, when he was secure on it, stepped out from beneath him. It hurt us, because it made us look like fools. For hundreds of years we have played this game, this sport here, and in minutes the Germans had bettered and mastered the difficult art.

"My boots," the captain called, and one after another they threw up his hobnailed boots. With the boots he could climb the rest of the way despite the ox grease on the pole.

There was still one chance for Santa Vittoria. Each team is supplied with one long bamboo pole with a sandbag on the end of it. It is called "the Ax," because it is used to "behead" kings. When a member of the opposite team nears the pig a member of the first team is allowed, if he can get high enough up on his own pole, to take one swing with the Ax to preserve the pig. It is an old custom here and a savage one, and we like it.

The pig was now screaming just above von Prum's head, as if he knew what fate was in store for him. How Rana the Frog got as high as he did on the second pole as soon as he did was not really known, because every eye, even those of the men who had flung Rana up and against the pole, was on the German who was inching his way upward. The pig was then only an arm's length away, so we were surprised to hear Rana shout for the Ax and to find him so far up the pole and then to hear him say, "Captain von Prum, sir. Would you turn this way, please, Captain? I have something for you, sir."

What was also surprising to all of the people, ourselves who had seen this many times before and the Germans who never had seen it, was how long it seemed to take the Ax to come around and to complete its full arc. It seemed to take forever for the bamboo to swing around and begin on its way, slowly and massively, as if it were a cathedral door closing. And what is surprising was that von Prum did nothing at all about it. Perhaps he never saw it, or perhaps he was the way they say people are before a snake springs to strike them. But he looked at the padded head of the Ax swinging toward him, picking up speed all the while as it came, the way a fly looks at a lizard before it licks him with its tongue, right up to the moment when the sandbag met his protruding head and flipped him off the greased pole, backward, in one such clean movement that it looked rehearsed at first until it was remembered that there were no nets below and until we heard the captain meet the cobblestone of the piazza and even Rosa Bombolini turned away.

It was the Italians who went to him first; not one of the Germans moved from where they stood. Pietrosanto picked up the captain's head and held it in his lap.

"You almost had the pig," he said. They allowed Rana to go to him.

"It was a fair blow," Rana said. "You took it like a man."

He was not unconscious then, but when they attempted to pick him up and carry him across the piazza to Constanzia's house he lost consciousness and they put him down by the fountain.

"He needs water," Heinsick said. "Put some water on his head."

Someone pointed to the fountain.

"There is no water now. There is only wine."

"Put some wine on his head," Bombolini said.

They filled a small copper jug with wine from the fountain, foaming and fit for a saint, as Old Vines had said. They propped the captain up by the fountain and began to pour the wine over his head. It ran down through his hair and over his face, and it lay in his grease-stained clothes in puddles.

"In the name of the Father and the Son and the Holy Ghost," a woman said while the wine ran.

"In the name of Santa Vittoria," Bombolini said, "in the name of the people," as the cascade of wine-dark liquid continued, "in the name of the holy wine."

They took him across the piazza when the wine did him no good and put him on the bed in his room and folded his hands in the same way we do for the dead. When all of them had gone except for the Malatesta and Sergeant Traub in the next room, Bombolini found a card belonging to the captain and wrote these words on it and put it in the captain's hand:

A proverb of the country:
He who steals for others ends up being hanged for himself.

He went out and closed the door behind him and when he got into the piazza the dancing had already begun. It was some of the wildest dancing we have ever done, but even over the sound of the band and the voices and the leather against the stones Bombolini could hear the guns sounding in the south. Something very big was underway.

435

THE DANCING ENDED at two o'clock in the morning and the Germans came at five. These were, as Pietrosanto said, the real Germans, hard, bearded men who were fighting and running for their lives. The soldiers were men from the Hermann Goering Parachute Division and they came through the Fat Gate and up the Corso Cavour in little half-tracks whose treads crushed the tops of our cobblestones into powder. They never looked at us. They moved through us with the assurance of men who knew that if so much as one shot was fired at them by some Resistance fighter, they would burn the town to the ground. They ran along the top of the Fat Wall and they looked through the windows of the houses that faced the valley and the River Road beyond, and they ran up into the bell tower and studied the countryside from there and on a map, and finally three or four of the highest officers gathered in the Piazza of the People and compared what they had found. We could have told them that this town was no good to fight a war in. It is placed wrong for everything except growing grapes.

"It's no good," one of the officers said, and the others seemed to agree.

"What's the name of that place?" one of the Germans asked Vittorini. He pointed down toward Scarafaggio.

"Scarafaggio," Vittorini said. "It has a good command of the Montefalcone highway."

"Yes, Scarafaggio is the place you want to fight in," Bombolini said to them.

"If you're going to fight," Pietrosanto said, "Scarafaggio is the place to fight in."

All three of them nodded, and the German looked at them as if they were an animal act that sometimes comes to the towns and the cities here. Talking dogs and counting mules and dancing bears.

"Shut your *mouths*," he said. "Who is in command here?" He spoke very good Italian.

"Do you mean the Italian in command or the German?" Bombolini said.

"Italian?" the officer said. "Italian?" His rage was so swift and so genuine that Pietrosanto for a moment was certain that he would kill Bombolini on the spot.

They led the officer across the piazza and they pointed to Constanzia's house. What happened after that was unfair to Captain von Prum. They found him in bed with Caterina Malatesta, since she had felt too weak to go to her own home and she was also afraid of what childish act he might commit if she left him then. They pulled him out of the bed, his hair mottled with wine and blood, his body dyed in it. He was too stunned and too sick from the fall he had taken the night before to protect himself.

"This is the shit we leave behind to run things while we fight," the parachute officer said. We could hear it in the piazza. He slapped Captain von Prum in the face and there was nothing the captain could do but stand in the room and look at the floor. It must have been very painful.

"Where are the rest of your men?"

"I don't know," von Prum said.

The officer looked at the other officers with him.

"He doesn't know."

He seized von Prum by the nose and he pulled his head to the left and right. "He doesn't know," he said. "He doesn't know." He stepped away and he kicked von Prum in the testicles, and the captain went down to the floor.

"You make me sick. You disgust me," he said. "Consider yourself under arrest."

He told the captain that when they stabilized the line at San Pierno he was to report to him there for disposition of his case after he had withdrawn his men and equipment from Santa Vittoria. The captain tried to get up from the floor.

"Stay down," the officer shouted at him. "Don't rise. You aren't permitted to stand with men. What is your name?"

"I've had a serious accident," von Prum said.

"What is your name?"

"Mollendorf," von Prum said. "Captain Hans Mollendorf." One of the younger officers wrote down the name. The senior parachute officer pointed at von Prum stretched on the stone floor. He was naked.

"This is the kind of scum who is destroying us," he said. They left then, and within ten minutes all of them were in the Corso Cavour and going back down the mountain.

We were helpful to the ones that were left. We were glad to help them. The women gave them cups of hot tea made from field herbs and grass, and the men gave them *grappa* to get the blood going again. The small truck was already in one corner of the piazza and some of the men wheeled the motorcycle and the sidecar from the shed out into the piazza. The women tried to make the soldiers' clothes as presentable as possible although it was not an easy job and they were not very successful. All of the uniforms were stained with wine and grease and sweat and manure and blood. We collected their helmets, which had been left all along

438

the cart track up from the vineyards, and their tunics. We found the field packs they wore on their backs and in an old wine basket we piled all of their personal things, a few books in German and razors and old towels. All of them had drunk far too much wine the night before and they were still a little drunk. The sound of firing from the River Road and the valley, although there was nothing to be seen down there, was very loud.

"It wasn't bad here," Heinsick said.

"It was good here," Private Zopf said, "considering it was a war."

One of them took some lire and put them on the top of a wine keg in a corner of the Cooperative Wine Cellar office.

"This is for the wine we drank."

Traub took money and put it on the barrel.

"This is for the wine we stole."

It wasn't much money, it was nothing, and yet it was something. They left the office, and the people began to help them carry their things up the Corso Cavour to the Piazza of the People. Captain von Prum was already in the piazza putting things in the back of the truck and in the sidecar of the motorcycle. He moved very slowly; he was in pain and he was confused. He ordered the gray file cabinet taken out of the house, but when they found it difficult to get it into the back of the truck they put it in the piazza again and forgot about it.

"What about this?" Bombolini asked. It was the air-raid siren.

"You can keep that," Sergeant Traub said.

"Once each year we'll sound it and think back on these days," Bombolini said.

The captain stood in the piazza and looked across it at the bell tower and at Santa Maria of the Burning Oven, at the People's Palace and at the Fountain of the Pissing Turtle. He seemed to be seeing things as if storing up a last memory of this place and yet not seeing things at all. He walked across to the fountain. It was silent then; the wine was not flowing and the water had not begun.

"Would you like me to start it up?" Bombolini said.

"Do what you want with it," the captain said. Someone began to pump the bicycle, and the generator began to turn and finally to drive the pump, and the wine began to spout again from the turtle.

"I never asked why it did that," von Prum said. "Why the turtle does that."

"I can't tell you that," Bombolini said. "It's a secret that only the people in Santa Vittoria know."

"I don't want to know it then," the captain said.

Some of the soldiers were already in the back of the small truck, crowded among their packs, hunched on the hard wooden seats. Vittorini came up into the piazza then, dressed in the uniform with the sword drawn and the Italian flag suspended from its blade.

It was very quiet in the piazza. We had always dreamed that the day they left would be a day of great celebration. We were happy to see them prepare to go, but the day after the festival is always a sad day. The long summer is over, the harvest is in, all the promises of the year past have been met or have failed and what we call the dead time, the season of the dead, was upon us. Captain von Prum came back from the motorcycle. For a moment we had thought he was getting in it and that it was the time to go, but he had stopped and come back toward Bombolini. The men of the San Marco Brass Band, who had been afraid to go home because of the firing along the roads, put down their instruments.

"You did this to me," Captain von Prum said to Bombolini.

"Whatever was done was done inside of you," Bombolini said. "We did nothing here."

"I came here to treat you with decency and respect and honor, and it's come to this. I made a mistake."

It was more than Bombolini was willing to hear.

"We have a saying here," the mayor said, "and you should listen to it. 'If the dove chooses to fly with the hawk his feathers stay white but his heart turns black.' It was in you all along."

"I treated you with honor, and you returned it with humiliation."

"It was in you all along. You struck me with your fist in my face."

"That was nothing. That was an order."

"And you turned the handle on the electricity for Fabio. You couldn't keep your hand away from it finally."

Von Prum was silent then. He looked as if he wasn't hearing what was being said, but he must have heard.

"And you put our cobbler to death. You forget that. What your kind do is to forget."

The Malatesta was in the doorway and he saw her. There was a moment when we thought that he was going to go to her, but he stayed where he was.

"What you people have to remember, your kind, is that there is no cure for birth."

Von Prum turned away from him and started toward the motorcycle.

"And there is no cure for death," Bombolini said, "if you think about it."

The German had stopped, and perhaps the mayor had touched something in him. He was angry and confused at the same time. Pietrosanto wanted to stop the mayor because men can become dangerous when they are this way. They were looking at one another.

"If you think about that," Bombolini said once more, "you might think about becoming human beings for a change. Now get out of our city."

The engines of the truck and the motorcycle had already been started up, and the captain got into the sidecar. We had always thought we would cheer that moment and we made no cheer. The people were in the doorways and all along the Piazza of the People, and just as they had that first day, they stood in their doorways all down the Corso Cavour as if to watch a hearse go by. The truck had already reached the Corso and then dipped over the steep lip and started down. The band began to play then, a song that they play here when the wedding is over and the guests are supposed to drink their last glass of wine and go home. The motorcycle started and just as on the day that it had come it didn't go directly to the Corso but began a tour of the piazza. But von Prum didn't see us this time. His eyes were so set and so cold and so distant from us that it was hard at the time to believe that they would ever close again, even on his death. Vittorini was saluting, but von Prum didn't see it, nor did he hear the band playing for him. Some of the people waved and he didn't see them either. As before, the motorcycle came toward Bombolini and halted.

"If I came back here some day after the war is over, what would your people do to me?" Sergeant Traub said.

"Nothing. They would do nothing to you," Bombolini said. The sergeant smiled the smile that deformed his face so badly.

"So they could forgive us then?"

"They could forgive you," the mayor said.

"Just so you pay for your own wine," Pietrosanto said.

"Like other people," Bombolini said.

It startled them when von Prum spoke. His lips barely moved. There was no expression of any kind in his voice or in his face. The eyes had not changed.

"Is there more wine or not?"

Bombolini smiled at him.

"Is there more wine or not?"

They all were smiling at the captain then, but we don't know whether he saw the smiles.

"Is there?"

Traub started the engine again and very slowly this time he moved past Italo Bombolini and Vittorini, who still stood with his salute unanswered. Traub touched the edge of his helmet, but it wasn't what Vittorini wanted. We could see the captain's lips moving. He must have been asking the question again, but it was not possible to hear the words over the sound of the engine.

They started down the Corso Cavour, and the people were smiling at the Germans, the women and even the children. In the piazza they could only see the Germans' backs, and then they were gone.

At the Fat Gate one of the things that are fated to take place here happened. It was done by the younger men, whose warm blood leads them into errors of taste. They lack the proper sense of things that a man like Bombolini, whose blood has cooled, has learned. They stopped the motorcycle at the gate, and before Traub could start it up again they handed the captain a wicker basket in which was packed twelve bottles of Santa Vittoria's best wine. On top of the fresh straw around the bottles was a card written in Fabio's finest hand:

Take this wine as well.
Don't thank us for it.
We won't miss it.
There are one million—
1,000,000—
one million more bottles where these came from.

The people of Santa Vittoria

"Where?" Traub said.

"That we can't tell you," Fabio said.

"We don't want it. We don't even want to see it. We just want to know *where*." Fabio shook his head at them. He was very gentle about it.

"No, no. That will be your torture. Don't you see?"

Traub nodded.

"That will be the hot wires in your brain," Cavalcanti said, and Traub continued to nod. Fabio turned directly to von Prum then.

"Ten years from now, if you are alive, you will wake up in the night and you will start going over the city again, house by house and street by street, trying to pick up the church and look under it, and it will begin to drive you mad. Where did you fail? you will ask yourself. How did they fool you? And you will know only one thing for certain."

Fabio paused to be sure that von Prum was hearing him.

"What?" Traub said. "Certain of what?"

"That we are laughing at you. That we were laughing at you when you came and we always laughed at you and that we will always laugh at you."

When they heard the engine begin again, the people ran to the Fat Wall from the Piazza of the People because they wanted to see every movement of the leaving. When the motorcycle went through the gate and could be seen again there was a little cheer from the people on the wall. It was the first noise they had allowed themselves. There was the beginning of a feeling of joy, but as long as the Germans were still on the mountain no one would allow himself to go beyond that.

443

"Something can still happen," they told each other. "You watch. Something will still go wrong."

They tortured themselves with it and they tortured each other, because there is a sweetness in torture when you feel that it can't harm you.

Of all the people on the wall only Bombolini wasn't happy. People saw it and it puzzled them.

"What's the matter, Italo? Why are you sad? Why are you looking that way?" they asked him, but he couldn't tell them, and they turned away to watch the progress of the motorcycle winding its way down the cart track through the terraces. He left the wall and went back up the lane past the church into the Piazza of the People where he was alone, pleased that he was all alone, until Fabio came up from the Fat Gate into the piazza.

"So you told them of the wine," Bombolini said. He shook his head.

"But not where it was," Fabio said. "That's the true torture."

Bombolini continued to shake his head. "It lacks perfection, Fabio. But it doesn't matter, Fabio. Nothing matters now." He began to walk across the piazza to the Palace of the People.

"Where are you going?" Fabio said. "The people want you on the wall. Your place is on the wall."

They could hear a louder cheer than before, and Fabio guessed that the motorcycle had reached The Rest and was halfway down the mountain. Soon it would dip under the mountain's shadow and be lost to the people on the wall.

"I'm going away, Fabio. I'm leaving."

Fabio was astonished.

"This was my great moment. It's all over for me now." The mayor held up his hand. " 'In time of trouble men of talent are called for, but in times of ease the rich and those with powerful relations are desired.' You see? There's no place for me here."

Fabio didn't know what to say to him.

"You'll miss my wedding," he finally said.

Bombolini shrugged. "I don't want an ending that lacks perfection," the mayor said. "The curtain is down, and it's time for the actors to get off the stage."

They had passed the fountain when Roberto, who had been

with Fabio at the Fat Gate, came into the piazza and started as they had for the Peoples' Palace. The people on the wall were silent and the Germans had either stopped or were in the shadow.

"This is a great day for you, Roberto," Bombolini said.

"Yes," Roberto said, but his face was as long as Bombolini's.

"You'll be leaving us, Roberto."

"I suppose so."

"The sooner the better, Roberto."

"I guess so."

"Never stay in a place where you don't belong."

Roberto nodded.

"To live in a place where you don't belong is to live in hell," the mayor said. He started up the palace steps, but he stopped when they heard a very loud cheer from the top of the wall. The motorcycle, Fabio figured, must have come back into view again near the bottom of the mountain. The mayor turned to Fabio.

"One rule, Fabio. One law that must be respected. Never grow old where you once have been great."

There was a second cheer, and this one was very loud. Bombolini turned around on the steps and came back down into the piazza.

"I had better take a look," he told Fabio. He began to walk toward the lane that leads to the wall. "Just a peek," he said. "A last look and then I'll be gone." He was moving very fast and almost broke into a run. "Remember what I said, Roberto." He was running by then. "I'll be leaving myself."

Fabio and Roberto watched him go.

"He'll never leave," Fabio said. "You'll be gone, but Bombolini will be here." The two of them began to walk toward the wall. "You're the lucky one, Roberto. You'll be gone, and he'll grow old."

The next time they saw him he was on top of the wall, and the people were silent. The motorcycle had reached the foot of the mountain and it had come to a stop forty or fifty yards from the entrance to the Roman cellar. There had always been a belief here that the Germans knew, that the last great joke would be the Germans' joke, and that their last act, while we cheered their departure from the wall, would be to destroy the cellar with the wine.

445

It is the belief now that Captain von Prum stopped at the foot of the mountain to choose whether to turn left and go south toward the advancing armies or to go north toward his Fatherland and the punishment that awaited him there. He turned north and he went toward the dark open mouth of the cave and then passed it and turned onto the goat trail that crosses that part of the valley.

Still no one cheered then, because he still could be seen. Partings to be correct must be perfect. There can be no speck of the departed left in any least part of the eye. All must be gone.

When they crossed the valley they turned up into the higher mountains beyond Santa Vittoria. We could still see them, not the men or the motorcycle itself, but the high white plume of chalk that rose up behind them, a towering flag above the vineyards that marked the movement of the enemy through the grapes on the other mountain as surely as the wake of a ship in the sea. And then even that was gone.

* * *

We heard the soldiers coming before we saw them. They were hidden by the low hills that mask the River Road. They took the turn that leads down onto the cart track, where the splinters of Bombolini's cart were still scattered on the sand, and came into our view, a long column of soldiers in battle dress led by two bagpipers wearing kilts. We watched them cross the valley and start up the mountain and when they came into the piazza they paid no attention to our cheers. They were hot and tired and thirsty.

"Royal Sutherland Highlanders," their leader said. Even Roberto found it hard to understand what he said. The soldiers had crowded around the Fountain of the Pissing Turtle and they looked at it but it was dry. There was no wine and there was no water.

"Have you anything to drink?" the officer asked.

"He wants to know if we have anything to drink," Roberto told Bombolini. The mayor turned to the people in the piazza.

"Do we have anything to drink?" he shouted to them. The people began to smile at each other and then to laugh. "He wants to know if we have anything to drink," Bombolini shouted to them. "Do we have anything to drink?"

There was such an outburst then, of shouts and laughter, that the soldiers became worried about us. They didn't know what to do about us. They had never seen anything like this before. Bombolini turned to Roberto and although they were only a few feet apart he shouted to them.

"Tell them this, Roberto," the mayor shouted. "Tell them God yes, we have something to drink."